W9-AHG-740

Acclaim for
KATHLEEN EAGLE'S
THE NIGHT REMEMBERS

"A magical story of feeling and hope, the courage
to reach for redemption, and the incredible,
simple power of love. A tale to cherish
and lessons to hold close to the heart."
Tami Hoag

"A compelling story . . . This rich tale
shows how love can unite very different
people in deeply satisfying relationships."
Sunday Chicago Tribune

"A powerful story of a new family coming
together out of abandonment and despair."
Detroit Free Press

"The plot is complex and filled with the kind of
magic I associate with mainstream authors like
Anne Tyler, Amy Tan and Alice Hoffman."
Milwaukee Journal Sentinel

Other Avon Books by
Kathleen Eagle

FIRE AND RAIN
THE NIGHT REMEMBERS
REASON TO BELIEVE
SUNRISE SONG
THIS TIME FOREVER

Avon Books are available at special quantity discounts for bulk purchases for sales promotions, premiums, fund raising or educational use. Special books, or book excerpts, can also be created to fit specific needs.

For details write or telephone the office of the Director of Special Markets, Avon Books, Inc., Dept. FP, 1350 Avenue of the Americas, New York, New York 10019, 1-800-238-0658.

KATHLEEN EAGLE

The Last True Cowboy

AVON BOOKS ◆ NEW YORK

This is a work of fiction. Names, characters, places, and incidents either are the product of the author's imagination or are used fictitiously. Any resemblance to actual events, locales, organizations, or persons, living or dead, is entirely coincidental and beyond the intent of either the author or the publisher.

AVON BOOKS, INC.
1350 Avenue of the Americas
New York, New York 10019

Copyright © 1998 by Kathleen Eagle
Excerpt from *The Last True Cowboy* copyright © 1998 by Kathleen Eagle
Excerpt from *The Runaway Princess* copyright © 1999 by Christina Dodd
Excerpt from *The Sweetest Thing* copyright © 1999 by Barbara Freethy
Excerpt from *A Rogue in Texas* copyright © 1999 by Jan Nowasky
Excerpt from *Someone to Watch Over Me* copyright © 1999 by Lisa Kleypas
Inside cover author photo by Lorrie Bettenga
Visit our website at **http://www.AvonBooks.com**
Library of Congress Catalog Card Number: 97-44255
ISBN: 0-380-78492-0

All rights reserved, which includes the right to reproduce this book or portions thereof in any form whatsoever except as provided by the U.S. Copyright Law. For information address Avon Books, Inc.

First Avon Books Paperback Printing: February 1999
First Avon Books Hardcover Printing: June 1998

AVON TRADEMARK REG. U.S. PAT. OFF. AND IN OTHER COUNTRIES, MARCA REGISTRADA, HECHO EN U.S.A.

Printed in the U.S.A.

WCD   10 9 8 7 6 5 4 3 2 1

If you purchased this book without a cover, you should be aware that this book is stolen property. It was reported as ''unsold and destroyed'' to the publisher, and neither the author nor the publisher has received any payment for this ''stripped book.''

To honor the memory of
Delano Spencer Eagle
1957–1997

In wildness is the preservation of the world.

Henry David Thoreau, "Walking"

The Last True Cowboy

1

From the beginning, it was the woman.

The rest of the High Horse setup wasn't anything K.C. Houston hadn't seen along the monochromatic trail of ranches he'd worked for from Montana to Texas. "Prettiest ranch in Wyoming," the owner had told him. Maybe it was, but meadows were meadows and mountains were mountains. It was the woman standing next to the rail fence that drew his fancy directly. Women often did, but this one hit him hard, right from the beginning.

He turned the radio off and rolled the window down as he slowed his pickup. A chilly spring breeze slid into his shirt. He'd been headed for the house, but the woman was closer and far more compelling. He thought about calling out to her, asking for directions he didn't need just to get her to turn his way, but he didn't. He just watched. She stood motionless, while the wind made a fluttering flag of her burnished brown hair and a loosely pegged tent of her white shirt. Her intensity captured him completely.

His pickup purred as he let it crawl over the gravel road. He felt like a crude tourist walking in on a pilgrim saying her prayers. *Let me distract you,* he thought. *Turn this way and let me pull you down to earth.* But she simply stared, as if something on one of the snowcapped mountain peaks were calling to her, claiming every receptor in her body. Whatever it was, she was lonesome for it. She was yearning for it, leaning toward it like a flower in a window. Whatever

1

it was, there was some rash and equally lonesome part of him that envied it.

He dismissed the thought of speaking to her. Had she turned, had she even moved, he would have taken it as a cue, and he would have stepped up to the plate. But she didn't. She remained inaccessible, like a painting he'd seen once and filed in the unfailing scrapbook of his memory. A mystifying feature in an otherwise familiar landscape, she was out of this world, beyond his reach. That fact alone made his palms itch.

Her image lingered in his mind as he drove on, once again heading for the house. He knew she wasn't his prospective boss's wife. He remembered something about a sister, but he'd funneled the family talk in one ear and out the other. What K.C. knew for sure about the man he had come to Wyoming to work for was that he, too, loved horses. Women, no, at least not the way K.C. loved women. Horses, definitely. It was K.C.'s business to recognize the symptoms. He earned his living off other people's horse fever, and Ross Weslin had the fever about as bad as it could get. But a wife was doubtful. If he had one, she was an unhappy woman.

In fact, if the woman at the fence was Mrs. Weslin, K.C. knew right then and there that he was bound to get himself fired before the summer was over. He could overlook a lot of things, but not an unhappy woman. Not for a whole damn summer. Women and horses were K.C.'s favorite kind of folks. He had superb instincts about both. Give him five minutes with a sullen woman or a skittish filly and he'd know exactly what she needed. He also had good instincts about fulfilling those needs, and he had turned his instincts into an art form. It wasn't the kind of art a person could hang on the wall, but K.C. liked to think that making a gentle-hearted creature happy, even temporarily, required an artist's touch.

But he had come to Wyoming for Weslin's horses, not his women. He got paid only for working his fine magic with horses, and his pockets, like his gas tank, were flirting with *E*. He was beginning to wonder where the Weslins kept their horses. Empty acres of spring-green pasture flanked the road, which followed the course of Quicksilver Creek. K.C. spotted a coal-black Angus bull using the trunk of a scrawny poplar tree as a scratching post, but he wasn't seeing much activity around the outbuildings and split-rail corrals. And he'd yet to see a horse, except on the sign above the gatepost. He was still looking as he drove across the narrow bridge that spanned the swollen creek and headed toward a copse of crabapples and old cottonwoods.

It was a man's house, a massive structure that stood amid the trees like a bird with its wings outstretched, too heavy to fly. Two single-story annexes, faced with a layer of gray river rock topped with one of tan fieldstone, flanked its main portion, where a second story of pine logs rose above the stone. Red bluffs faced the creek on the east, and the mountains rose to the west. K.C. liked the way the house fit right into its surroundings like craggy leavings from some prehistoric geological upheaval. Someday he'd have himself a house. Maybe not as big, but it would have that natural look.

A rock path, already tufted with spring grass, led him to the steps of the huge stone-pillared front porch. The front door creaked, and a slim, blond, sleepy-eyed woman poked her head out. Her scowl melted when K.C. pushed his hat back with a forefinger and smiled.

"Afternoon, ma'am. I'm looking for Ross Weslin."

"Ross is . . ." She gave him a quick, skeptical once-over. "Why?"

"He asked me to come to work for him. The name's K.C. Houston."

None of this appeared to be ringing any bells with her, but her interest in his message was clearly secondary. She liked his looks. Most women did.

"I train horses."

The bemused look in her eyes didn't change. She stepped onto the slate porch, her shapely legs and small feet bared under the trim black-and-white Sunday dress she'd obviously been napping in. He figured she must have been curled up somewhere when he'd come knocking on the door, and he pictured her smooth, pale legs folded up to her breast, her dress just covering her bottom.

He raised his brow as he glanced over his shoulder at the gravel driveway. "The sign about four miles up the road says 'High Horse Ranch.' Did I take the wrong fork somewhere?"

"No, this is the Weslin place. Ross's . . ."

Something about the way she tipped her head quizzically struck a familiar chord, and K.C. realized that it was her resemblance to Weslin. Younger sister, he figured. He'd spent little time with the man, but Ross Weslin was curiously memorable. Quiet to start with, but once they'd got to talking, K.C. had found him to be sociable enough, agreeable, pretty high-minded in the way he looked at things. Even passionate, although that was a word K.C. would have been happier tagging on this *female* Weslin.

She was blinking up at him and putting her question to him cautiously. "When was it he hired you?"

"Well, you know, he's inquired a couple of times about when I might be available, but I've been pretty busy. We met up at a cuttin' competition last summer. He said he was still interested, and I said I'd try to get to him in the spring. I called about a month back, maybe two. Guess I wasn't too specific about a date."

"But he told you to come?"

"Yes, ma'am, he surely did."

She shook her head. "I can't imagine why."

Didn't surprise him too much. The way K.C. remembered it, Weslin liked to keep people guessing. He'd offered a deal, then sweetened it a little, then hinted that there might be a few added benefits if a guy liked the setup once he got started and felt like staying on. K.C. generally preferred a simple, straightforward, cash-on-the-barrelhead arrangement, for which he willingly guaranteed results. He'd had one too many "sweet deals" fall through on him. He had a knack for dealing with horses. Dealing *in* horses was another matter.

Dealing in horses meant dealing with guys who were out to make a buck, which meant business, which meant there was bound to be a hitch somewhere. K.C. had run into too many hitches lately. He could see them coming, too, but he kept telling himself, *This one's different. I can make this one work out.*

Not today, though. Today he needed a job. *Forget the women, Houston; you're here to see a man about some horses.* And he wasn't looking for any "deal of a lifetime." His usual fee would do him just fine.

Weslin had been eager to get him here, as though his horses were on some kind of a timetable. Special horses, he'd said. Remarkable horses, a page out of history. K.C. had felt a stirring of real interest in the horses, but at the time, he'd been a little uncomfortable with the man's bright-eyed eagerness. His own circumstances were more than uncomfortable just now, though. He needed a job. He was on the fly, and he needed a place to light.

"Mustangs, he said, and he swore up and down they were worth my time." He flashed a lazy smile. "Which don't come cheap."

"No, I'm sure it doesn't." The blonde folded her arms and eyed him steadily, winding up for her comeback. "Ross died three days ago. We buried him this morning."

Died? "The hell."

"Ross was my brother."

"I'm real sorry, ma'am. He couldn'ta been more than . . ." Rather than guess, K.C. shook his head. The news put a crimp in his plans, but his own inconvenience didn't compare to the considerable bother of being dead. "Accident?"

"Carelessness," the pretty woman said with a sigh. "But everybody's careless sometimes, in one way or another."

"That's a fact."

She had a sweet smile, but it was a bit too coy. "I'm sorry you wasted a trip. How far have you come?"

"A ways." The miles were easily shrugged off. "There's always another job. A brother's something else. I'm sorry for your loss, ma'am."

"Thank you."

He stepped back, courteously touching his hat brim. "Sorry for the intrusion, too."

"Maybe . . . I don't know exactly what we're going to

do now, but maybe we could find something for you to do, at least for a few weeks.''

"I'm not a hired hand, ma'am. I'm a horse trainer."

"Oh. I guess we don't need you, then. I have no idea what Ross could have been thinking." She arched a delicate eyebrow, her tone cooling. "But it probably had very little to do with mustangs."

Whatever she was getting at was family business, not his, but he felt honor-bound to offer what testimonial he could.

"I didn't know him very well, but he seemed like a good hand. He didn't hog the floor, had an easy laugh, ready to buy a round when his turn came, keen eye for good horseflesh. We'da gotten along just fine." He ended on a nod, started for the porch steps, then stopped, thinking, *Well, what the hell.* "You mind my askin', you got a sister?"

She offered that coy smile again. "Why? Do *I* look like I'm already taken?"

"No." Which was why he figured she probably was. "Ross mentioned sisters." He gave a perfunctory shrug. "I just wondered about his family, is all. He was a nice guy. My condolences to . . . everybody."

"Thank you. I'll tell my sister."

He would have told her himself when he drove past the fence, if she'd been there. But she was gone.

She persisted in his thoughts, which was probably why he did the impossible in a place where there weren't many ways to go astray. He took the wrong road. Didn't even notice right away. He was looking at the green countryside and thinking how choice those sawbuck rail fences looked running alongside the gravel road, about how the woman had looked and what she might have been looking for and thinking about.

Then he noticed the horses in the side-view mirror. The big buckskin in the lead seemed to be chasing him down, like a guy trying to catch up to give him something he'd left behind. He pulled over, kicked the parking break on and hopped out to get a good look.

They were wild. There was nothing driving them, nothing hindering them. They ran just to run. They'd never been bridled, and no man had dampened their spirits. They had that thing most cherished, most coveted, most feared and most abused by most men. Real freedom. And they were utterly beautiful.

Their pure, faultless motion stirred him, drew him in, just as he'd been drawn to the intense stillness of the woman by the fence. With the woman, it was weighty and heartfelt, wanting and wishing. With the horses, there was never any waiting, never any need to want. They ran in his blood. The pounding of their hooves penetrated the pounding of his pulse. They were six moving as one, muscles rippling, manes flowing like ribbons, tails waving like flags unfurled, like freedom. They saw him there, of course, and it struck him that they were putting on a show for him, mustangs on parade. As they passed him, they angled away from the fence, toward the green hills.

Scarcely a quarter of a mile away, the buckskin suddenly called out to his brothers and skidded to a halt. K.C. couldn't see what it was—a rattler, maybe a badger or just the unexpected flash of an aluminum can. Whatever it was, they were suddenly talking up a storm, kicking up a cloud of dust. Beginning with the buckskin, they reversed their direction and galloped straight for the fence. One by one, they sailed over the rails and darted across the gravel road, all but the last two. A big sorrel and a small black-and-white paint refused the jump. Instead they followed the fence line again, retracing their steps, and for an instant K.C. was flanked by wild horses, four across the road, two inside the fence, whinnying on both sides.

He was mesmerized. For a time he simply watched, amazed that they permitted him this proximity. Then he came to his senses, turned his pickup around and followed them, allowing them to set the pace. He wanted to see what they would do, wanted to warn off any oncoming vehicle, wanted to . . . just wanted to stay with them for a little while. They were wild, but they hung together, looked out for each other. And they had come to him.

They led him back to the T, where he'd turned south. There the two inside the fence called to the other four. The buckskin led the way, back across the road in front of the pickup. Now they followed the fence line—two on one side, four on the other—heading west, toward the ranch and the mountains beyond.

Damn, if Weslin's wild horses hadn't turned K.C. around. Had he been a superstitious man, he might have thought they were trying to tell him something.

Hell of a long way to drive for nothing, cowboy. Maybe that was the message. He laughed out loud. Didn't take too much horse sense to figure that one out.

But when he reached the blacktop, he turned north. He decided to spend the night in the little hole-in-the-hills town of Quicksilver rather than head south. He owed himself a night on the town.

2

It wasn't much of a town, and K.C. should have been looking for another job rather than checking out the local nightlife. He wasn't desperate enough to take a job as a ranch hand, but he had to find a place to stay, and he had to be working soon. He'd never been much good at putting money away, and he had his expenses, customary and otherwise.

Regular meals was one. He had himself a tasty T-bone at the Cut Proud Café, then made two calls, but neither panned out. Marlys Dillard was sure sorry her husband had already hired someone else to start their touchy Thoroughbred colts. If they'd known K.C. was available, he would have been their first choice. Hers for sure, she said, which meant he wasn't missing anything but more trouble. The second call was to Phil Terpin, who wanted to hire him but didn't want to pay his price.

It had been a long time since K.C. had worked for cowboy wages. He had to believe there would always be work for a trainer with his reputation, but the way the livestock market had been lately, people were letting their horses go. This wasn't the first time he'd gotten himself into a deal that didn't pan out, and there was really nobody to blame for this one. Certainly not Weslin. Being put to bed early was no reflection on a man's character, especially if he'd been put down with a shovel.

The thought that a young guy like Ross Weslin could be

9

kicking around his colt-starting plans one minute and kicking the bucket the next was just a little too sobering. It led K.C. to questions like, if he died tomorrow, who would bury him, and where would they dig the hole, and would they have to sell his pickup to buy a box to put him in?

Rather than project any answers, he paid for his supper, grabbed a couple of toothpicks and headed out to the plank porch that fronted the entire block. He leaned against the awning post and breathed deeply, craving a smoke worse than he had in months. A beer would do him. He stuck a toothpick in the corner of his mouth and rolled it over his tongue as he counted the saloons on Main Street.

He decided to try the Watering Hole, a little place that looked pretty lonesome sitting way down at the end of the street. Lonesome suited his mood. He noticed the eerie light that glowed behind a red curtain in the window above the sagging porch roof, started to imagine what might be going on up there, then shut those thoughts down. He wasn't *that* damn lonesome.

Downstairs, the place was pretty dead. Two old-timers, both half shot, sat at the end of the bar recounting elk-hunting stories. A frizzy-haired woman waited for one of them, her glazed eyes fixed on the demolition derby on the TV above the bar. K.C. felt a little sorry for her and for the squat, shuffling bartender, whom he tipped generously before he tuned out the whole sorry gathering.

He stayed long enough for one beer, his second-choice brand, only because the painting of the long-legged, porcelain-skinned nude over the bar drove thoughts of death from his mind, leaving just the woman. Not the nude, and not the woman he'd spoken with at the High Horse, but the other one. The one he was *wishing* he'd spoken with.

When he'd had his fill of lonesome, he moved on to the Lowdown Saloon. He could hear Garth Brooks wailing on the jukebox, and he thought, *Hell, yes, I've got friends here.* He hit the bat-wing door with one shoulder and found what he was looking for—a lively party where they served up his brand in a bottle. The first taste made him feel right at home.

He planted an elbow on the bar and turned to take account of what the place had to offer besides low lights, down-home music and the right thirst quencher. He saw plenty of Western atmosphere. The walls were all decked out with stuffed animals—the real fur and fin variety. The doors in the back corner were labeled "Pointers" and "Setters." In the opposite corner a few couples were taking advantage of the dance floor. That was promising. K.C. felt some toe-tapping coming on as he tipped the bottle up for a second draught.

Then he spotted the woman, the one he'd dubbed *the woman at the fence*. Would have made a fine painting, but she was real, and she was there in the flesh, and she was something else.

What exactly it was he still couldn't quite figure, but he was damn sure going to find out. She was sitting at a corner table, looking just as solitary as K.C. had been feeling. He wondered why people kept sashaying by her table without saying a word. She'd just buried her brother. In a town the size of Quicksilver, that had to be common knowledge. There ought to be some neighborly laments delivered, at least in passing.

He watched the waitress set an old-fashioned down and pick up an empty wineglass. The woman was drinking for serious, not for social. K.C. was about to change that.

But all he could come up with for openers was the obvious. "I'm sorry about your brother."

She looked up slowly, her dark eyes empty and distant.

He pretended to see a question in them. "I stopped by his place today, talked to your sister. I saw you, too, but you were . . ." *Empty and distant*. He shrugged and gave a tight-lipped, sympathetic smile. "You didn't see me."

She took a closer look at him now, sorting through her mental file of faces, frowning a little as she tried to place him. "You were there this morning?"

"No, I didn't know anything about the, uh . . . him being . . ." He shrugged, sympathy mixing with frustration. He'd come all the way to Wyoming for nothing. "I ain't from around here, didn't know about the funeral. I just stopped by to . . . to see him."

"Ross was your friend?" she asked gently, as though he might be hurting, too.

"No, not . . ." She wanted him to be. He could see it in her eyes, the way she flinched a little at his denial. She wanted all the help she could get in keeping the memory alive.

He dropped his gaze to the bottle in his hand.

"I didn't know him real well. I'd see him at a stock show now and again. Met up with him in Denver last summer, had a beer with him. Said he wanted me to come to work for him. He seemed like a hell of a nice guy. I just wanted to tell you . . ."

"Sit down and have a drink with me." She patted the spot beside her on the brown vinyl seat. "I promise not to be morose. In fact, I insist that we both refrain from being morose, and if you'll agree to that condition, I'll buy the drinks."

"I'll agree to the first condition, but not the second." He slid into the booth, serving up his usual just-for-you-honey smile. "A man's got his pride."

"A woman's money threatens a man's pride?"

"Only on the first date."

"Date?" She bucked up some as she offered him a sad excuse for a smile and looked him straight in the eye. "Are you a pickup, or am I?"

She was reaching for nonchalance, but he had a hunch she was venturing into unfamiliar territory.

"I don't know about you, but I'm not ready to analyze our relationship quite yet." Gesturing with his beer bottle, he figured he'd show her what real nonchalance looked like. "These things seem to work out better if you just let them sort of unfold."

"I'm sure you're right. No matter how many questions you come up with, they never turn out to be the right ones. There must be a better way." She tasted her drink, winced, then sipped again. "So you came looking for a job?" He chuckled, and she lifted one slight shoulder. "Humor me during the unfolding. Some habits are hard to break, and asking stock questions is one of mine."

"Jobs generally come looking for me." She questioned

him with her eyes this time, and he smiled. In some circles his name would have been the only answer anyone needed, but it would mean nothing to her. It was a thought that somehow bothered him. "I train horses."

She drew a quick frown. "Ross always broke and trained his own horses. He loved horses, even though he was allergic to everything that goes with them. Grass, hay, dust, you name it. But as long as he had his allergy shots, he was . . ." She drew back, drew her memories back in. "He *offered* you a job? When was this?"

"Talked to him a month ago, maybe two. He told me to come up as soon as I could."

"Really?" She wasn't doubtful, just surprised. Her brother was still surprising her, which was just what she needed. It meant he hadn't slipped away completely.

K.C. understood that her questions were really for Weslin. It had been a while since he'd been in her shoes, walking around with his gut clenched around that kind of sorrow, but he knew all about being cut loose and drifting, the way she was now.

"I can't believe he did this." She shook her head. He knew she wasn't doubting him. She was doubting death. "I mean, sure, he's been talking about the horses a lot, about all his plans. It was easier for both of us that way. But he knew . . . *we* knew. We just never said." She looked to K.C. to anchor her with living, breathing reassurance. "If you say it, it's like you're giving up. Isn't it? I mean, you shouldn't give up."

He couldn't answer that one, didn't even want to try. Instead he laid his hand over her forearm, withdrawing only when she glanced away.

"I'm just surprised he didn't get hold of you to call it off," she said just before she buried her nose in her drink.

"It's not always easy to track me down. It's no big deal."

"You didn't know he was sick?"

He shook his head and waited to see whether she wanted to fill in the details. She was thinking about it, taking his measure. Her doleful brown eyes betrayed her need for an ally, and K.C. was struck by the way her defensiveness only underscored her fragility. He had half a mind to go over to the jukebox and plug in a few quarters. George Strait was singing "All My Exes Live in Texas," and the lyrics weren't exactly what K.C. wanted the woman to hear while she was looking at him that way.

"He *was* a hell of a nice guy," she said finally. She fortified herself with another dose from her glass, then smiled. "He was shy, basically. Very, very shy, but he did have friends. Not very many people came this morning because, well, he was a very private man. But you know what I saw?" He shook his head. "The wild horses came. I saw them. They came to say good-bye."

He nodded and smiled, picturing a scene straight out of *My Friend Flicka*. A few more drinks and she'd damn sure have him crying in his beer if she kept this up. "I saw them as I was leaving."

"The wild ones?"

"Six of them, led by a big buckskin. Same bunch?"

"I counted six. So it wasn't my imagination."

"Not unless you're making me up, too."

She laughed, then shook her plush hair back and challenged him with a look. "If I am, what have I devised? Are you a nice guy?"

"I guess that's something you'll have to decide for yourself."

The waitress was headed in their direction. He signaled for another round. The first few bars of "Any Man of Mine" had him smiling, then singing along. It was a woman's song, and he invited her to look at him and share in the notion that a man ought to do right for a woman. She smiled a little and shook her head, not knowing quite what to make of him, which was good.

"Tell you one thing. I'm one hell of a good dancer." There wasn't much to be made of him, but he was willing to put what there was at her disposal.

She raised her glass again. "Sadly, I'm not."

"I'm a good teacher, too." He took her glass and set it down as he took her hand. "Come on, darlin', we agreed to shove Mr. Sadly off in the corner. This is just what you need."

She was stiff at first, distrusting her body, but he eased her into it, using the music as a lubricant, leading her body with his. People were noticing her now, and their stares were hardly discreet. Here in Quicksilver, tyin' one on after a funeral was one thing, but dancing was plainly something else.

He drew her in close, sheltering her from the stormy scowl he glimpsed beneath the brim of one sweat-stained hat. "Are these people your neighbors, or just cowboys passin' through?"

"Like you?"

"Like me." He glanced past her. A woman with tomato-red hair was giving them an unabashed once-over.

"These people are wondering whether *I'm* just passing through." She looked up at him, her face inches from his. "It's funny. I haven't really lived here since I was a kid, but I always tell people that I'm from Wyoming."

"But you're from . . ."

"I live in Minnesota, but I'm still from Wyoming. And these people were my brother's neighbors, some of them friendly, some not. Ross was very friendly if you gave him a chance—well, you know that—but he was . . . a maverick." She smiled wistfully, her gaze drifting as she remembered, her body relaxing as she gave the direction of its movement over to him. "My brother had some dreams, some ideas that didn't please some people. Too liberal."

"Mmm, that's a cuss word."

"Not that he cared much for politics. Just horses."

"This is horse country." He smiled. The music stopped, and he kept right on talking as he guided her back to the table. "Maverick country, too, I expect."

"There are all kinds of horses and all kinds of mavericks, wouldn't you say?"

He slid into the booth beside her. "I'd say this is a fragile land. Grazing land for some. Wild country for others."

"People have been fighting over how the land should be used ever since the first white men laid claim to it." She reclaimed her drink, gesturing with the glass. "Just south of here there's a memorial to some sheep ranchers who were murdered by cattlemen, back around the turn of the century. They disagreed over how the land should be grazed."

"Horses don't threaten the grass," he said absently. He was looking for the girl with the tray. "Not like cattle and sheep."

"But some people consider them a threat," she said as she contemplated the remains of her drink. "Some horses."

"You're talkin' mustangs again."

She nodded. "My brother loved them dearly. Some of his neighbors think they ought to be ground up and packed in cans."

"They can be a nuisance," he allowed, then smiled when she looked up. "Neighbors."

"Yes, they can. I'm sure they can."

"You have good neighbors?" She questioned him with a look, and he shrugged. "Where you live now, I mean. Somewhere in Minnesota."

"Where I live now," she mused, as if she'd lost touch with that, too. "I don't even know most of my neighbors. How about you?"

"I've got friends, but no neighbors."

"Family?"

"What's family? Hell, I'm a cowboy. Easy to love, but hard to hold. Gotta go where the wind takes me." He shrugged again. "Or the job, but *wind* sounds better."

She acknowledged his claim with a charitable smile. He thought about asking her who she had besides a dead brother and a flirty sister. She wasn't wearing a ring, but his experience had proved that sign to be unreliable. Then one of her neighbors stopped at their table and told him all he wanted to know by greeting her as "Miz Weslin." She made no offer to introduce the stocky, graying rancher, who asked her if they needed any help out to the High Horse. She said things were okay and thanked him for his concern.

"You'll let me know before you put any land on the market?" The man shifted, cleared his throat, uncomfortable with asking. "I'd like to have first crack at it. Them developers, they been nosin' around, wantin' to turn God's country into a suburb for Hollywood or some damn thing. We ain't gonna let that happen."

She slid both hands around her glass, locking her fingers as if she were jealously guarding the last ounce of her drink. "Nothing's been decided, Chuck. We just buried Ross this morning."

"Damn shame, young fella like him." He wagged his head, then leaned over the table, looming closer. "You let me know if you need any help."

"Thank you." She was barely audible.

He nodded, shifted again, then stood there, creating a lump of silence surrounded by barroom chatter. Finally, Chuck got to the point. "You know, them mustangs, they're nothing but . . ."

She warned him off the subject with a look.

"Well, we'll talk about them later. You just let me know what you women over there need. I'll send somebody over. Hell, I'll go over there myself whenever you say, you need anything rounded up. You got enough feed?"

She said they had. K.C. could feel her edginess. He looked the man in the eye and with a subtle nod warned him to back off.

He did, but not without a parting bid. "You just let me know what you need."

She offered curt thanks as she reached for K.C.'s hand and glanced in the direction of the dance floor. He was glad to oblige. The tempo had picked up with the flying fiddles of an Alan Jackson tune. It took some doing, but he got her to look into his eyes, feel the music and dance. Pretty soon he had her putting more heart into it, letting him swing her, smiling at him over her shoulder when he twirled her.

She was a beautiful woman, bone-deep beautiful. Like a fine-tuned horse with collected gaits, she was easy to guide. She had a silkiness about her, a rich, natural luster that made him feel raw and coarse, yet powerful, too, and he liked the feeling. She was unsure of the steps, but he was right there to lead, the country rhythm thrumming in his blood. She was getting the hang of spinning under his arm, making him do it again and then again, like a little girl cajoling her daddy. When he caught her at the waist he could feel his rough skin pricking her soft blouse, and he knew it would do the same to her skin. He'd have to sand down some calluses to please a woman like her.

The music slowed, and she stepped in close and slipped her arms around his neck, as though they'd been dancing together for years. He held her and rocked her, side to side, letting her take refuge with him in the music and the motion. She turned her face to his neck, and he could feel the warmth of her breath when she whispered, "Where are you staying tonight?"

"Haven't thought that far ahead."

"Where are you going from here?"

"South, maybe west." He slid his hand slowly from the small of her back up to the center, pressing her close so that he could feel the rise and fall of her chest against his. "But that's beyond tonight. Way beyond where I am right now."

She tipped her head back and looked up at him. Her face was dewy, and her eyes glistened. "What are you thinking about now?"

He smiled. "Don't have to think when I'm dancin'. Comes natural."

"Lucky you."

"You've stopped thinkin' about it, too. You were workin' pretty hard there for a while, countin' every step, but now you're just movin' along with me."

She hesitated, stiffened a little.

He splayed his fingers over her back. "Don't."

"Don't what?"

"Don't start thinkin' again."

Her smile came slowly. "How can you tell?"

"I can feel it."

"You can feel me thinking?"

He chuckled. "Oh, yes, ma'am."

"Maybe you'd like what I'm thinking."

"Maybe you'd like what you're feeling if you'd just . . ." He taught her with his hips. She laughed, and her hips improved on his move. "There, that's it. Just dance with me."

"It's easier than I thought." She gave her head a sassy toss. "Past tense. I'm not thinking anymore."

"Attagirl."

He danced her over to the jukebox, pumped it full of quarters and invited her to pick some songs. She told him to choose. "Fast or slow?" he asked, and her answer was so soft, so demure, it made him wish the crowd away as he drew her into his arms on the first strains of a country ballad. By the time they'd danced through his selections, he was high on the sweet scent of her hair and the sweet feel of her body moving with his. It seemed pretty foolish to order another drink.

But when he asked, she said she wanted one, and he was ready to fly to the moon for her if she told him it would cheer her up. She asked about his work, and he told her that starting colts was his specialty, but he could train a horse for almost anything the owner had in mind. He let her lead him up and down the garden path of conversation.

In the middle of it all she looked at him suddenly, studied him hard, then smiled. "I think you *would* be easy to love."

"You do, huh?" He smiled, too, but he was wondering what he'd said to bring her to that conclusion.

"Yes, I do." She gave up studying him in favor of contemplating her nearly empty glass. "And I'm right on schedule. I'm at half past giddy, which means maudlin is about a drink away." She slipped her arm around his neck and gave him a peck on the cheek. "And that you can do without. Good night, sweet cowboy."

He felt a little stung by her abrupt departure, by the motherly kiss that was about as welcome as a pat on the head, but when he saw how unsteadily she made her way toward the door, he followed her. He caught up with her just as she was stepping off the boardwalk. She turned the corner, and he wheeled around her, shoving his hands as far as they would go into the front pockets of his jeans as he matched her pace.

"Nobody's ever loved me and left me quite so fast before."

She laughed and linked her arm with his as though they'd been friends forever, and they strolled together. He figured she was headed for the little parking lot behind the bar, which was where he'd left his pickup. He decided that if she was heading home, he'd be doing the driving.

"You haven't told me your name."

"I assumed we had a tacit agreement to keep our names a mystery, since you're just passing through." She tipped her head back. "It's a pretty night, isn't it? Peaceful and still. No wind to blow you anywhere."

"It'll pick up tomorrow. Always does."

"And then you just go? South or west or wherever the road takes you?" She glanced askance, measuring him up for something. "Maybe I should hitch a ride. Would you take me with you?"

"Sure." He nodded toward the parking lot. "South or west? You choose."

"Right now? Choosing would take some thinking."

"True. We don't want that."

"So just take me with you." She tightened her grip on his arm. "Anywhere. This is a one-time-only offer, cowboy. I'll go with you anywhere."

"How about if I take you home?" He'd already adjusted their course in the direction of his pickup.

"I don't think I really have a home. Home is wherever I hang my hat."

"Did you hang it in the bar?" He didn't know what to call her, but he sure wanted to kiss her, just for the way she was looking up at him with her eyes full of girlish innocence. "Your hat."

"What hat? I'm footloose and fancy-free, just like you. Drifting along with the tumbling tumbleweeds." A faltering step made her laugh. "Okay, stumbling, but I'm usually very steady. Very, very steady."

"Lean on me."

She did, as she sang, "Lean on meeee." She laughed again. "You know that one? It's not country."

"I know all kinds of songs."

"Do you sing a lot, just sing your heart out without feeling the least bit self-conscious? All cowboys sing, don't they? How about driiiftin' along with the tum-bul-ling tumbleweeeds . . ."

He sang along, until she stopped suddenly. "I don't know why I'm trying to sing. I'm flat as a board."

"I wouldn't say that." He smiled as he pulled to a halt next to the passenger's side of his blue Chevy pickup, which was, for the moment, his home. He had a few things in storage, but all the gear he needed or cared about was stowed in the back of his pickup, under the custom topper.

"Why not? It's true. My mother says it's true. She pointed it out to me when I was about four or five." She stuck out her hand and cut an imaginary swath through the air. "Absolutely flat."

"I expect it *was* true when you were four or five."

"Ah, but there's flat, and then there's *flat*. 'You can't carry a tune in a tin bucket,' was what she actually said. And I can't."

"A bucket's no place to carry a tune. You carry it close to your heart, it won't be flat."

"You are one smooth-talkin' cowboy." She started fingering one of his shirt buttons as she sang softly. He joined in, because the truth was, she did need the help. "Driiiftin' along with the tumbling..." She stopped abruptly. "Would you like to tumble me, cowboy?"

He didn't miss a beat. "Yes, ma'am, I sure would."

"But you're not going to, are you?"

"You're not gonna let me, darlin'. I ain't *that* damn smooth." He put his hands on her shoulders and returned that frank stare of hers. He wasn't about to "tumble" a woman who was half lit and all confused, but he didn't have to walk away completely unsatisfied. "I'm thinkin' about kissing you, though. Can you feel me thinkin' about it?"

"I sure can."

"Some things a guy likes to think about first."

She smiled. Her face shone, all sweet and pearly in the moonlight. "For how long?"

"I've been thinkin' about it off and on since I first saw you."

"Even when you weren't thinking about dancing?"

"Off and on," he repeated. "It's one of those thoughts that comes on stronger each time. Right about now, the thought of kissing you is burnin' a hole in my brain."

Still smiling, she grabbed a handful of his shirtfront and tugged a little. "You're smooth, but slow."

"That's right." He leaned closer.

"Agonizingly slow."

"It's better that way."

He moved his thumbs up the sides of her neck, then drew them back along her jaw, thinking he would hold her face and this moment in his hands, keep it simple and soft. But as his mouth covered hers and his tongue tasted hers and his lips danced with hers, *soft and simple* flew away. When he lifted his head he found that they were holding each other close, breathing each other, each searching the other's eyes for confirmation.

Was that what I thought it was? Did you feel what I felt?

He had to step back, just to get his bearings.

She frowned a little. "You're going to take me home now?"

He cleared his throat, hoping it would clear the rest of his head.

"Yes, ma'am. Right to your door."

Julia said little as she watched the desolate, moon-washed low country slide past the window. The road turned from pavement to gravel, and the rocky bluffs loomed like dark ships on either side of an inky channel. The pickup was a little tugboat, then, gliding easily among them. Julia was being tugged home by a skipper in a cowboy hat. She stole a peek at him and turned away, smiling.

She felt surprisingly relaxed, deliciously mellow. She didn't think she was quite drunk, but she believed she was closer than she'd ever been. Anesthetized. Nothing seemed quite real. She'd just tried to seduce a cowboy, and he'd politely turned her down. How real could that be? Stranger still, it didn't bother her. Maybe it would tomorrow, but for now, she was blessedly numb.

She was even humming along with the fiddle music playing softly on the radio. She didn't know the song, couldn't sing, never tried, certainly not in front of anybody. But she was doing it tonight, and with a cowboy. He'd been helping her out with about every other verse. He could've done better, she thought, since he was the only one who knew the words, but he couldn't be expected to appreciate the rarity of the occasion. He barely knew her.

Knew her, but barely.

Might have known her better, might have known her bare, but he'd declined. Declined to recline.

"How about letting me in on the joke?"

He'd read her mind. Or had she laughed aloud? She laughed now. "Oh, just crazy things, running through my head. Strange night, strange man, strange thoughts. You know how it goes."

He just smiled.

"Go ahead and say it. Strange woman."

"I've got thoughts runnin' through my head, too, darlin', and that ain't one of them."

"You've got your mind on the road ahead. Good man. Good driver. Good cowboy." *Good cowboy? Foolish girl*, said the mother of her mind. *No such animal.*

"My dad was a cowboy." She glanced at him. "Did I ever tell you that my dad was a cowboy?"

"You never did."

"He's dead, too. We buried Ross right next to him, up on Boot Hill. We've got our own Boot Hill out at the High Horse. That's where we put them. Boot Hill." He flicked his gaze at her, looking for cues. "That's not what I was laughing about. Boot Hill is no laughing matter."

"Not for a cowboy."

"Not for all the young cowboys who know they've done wrong. Because that's where they end up. Boot Hill. My dad died young, too." But she was okay with it now. She was okay with Ross, too. They'd stuck with the High Horse regardless, lived their own lives, finished them out early, and that was that. Like the man said, easy to love and hard to hold.

"You're a reckless breed, you know that?"

"That's what makes us cowboys."

"But you had a chance tonight, and you didn't take it. You declined to do me wrong." She laughed, feeling especially pleased with her wit tonight. "You could go to Boot Hill tomorrow with a clean slate."

"With your blessing?" He laughed, too. "I've run into some hard-hearted women in my time, but none that wanted to consign me to Boot Hill quite so—"

Horror flashed in his eyes as he hit the brake.

"Jesus . . ."

Julia flopped like a rag doll, pinned to the seat by her shoulder belt as the cowboy grappled with a vehicle gone wild. The quiet night suddenly became raucous. The shrieking wasn't Julia's. The puttering engine didn't belong to the pickup. The steel guitars weren't calliope music, and it wasn't the carousel that was moving, but the horses, springing out of the darkness, careening across the narrow path of light, vaulting over the hood.

They'd gone off the road, but they were still upright. She heard the release of a seat belt, the sliding of a body across the seat, but she saw only the light and dark. In the light there were disjointed pieces—a fence post, a sorrel flank, the flash of a tail, the flicker of a moth's wing. The rest was dark.

"You okay?"

She moved—head, arms, hands, hips—slowly pushed herself away from the door, a piece at a time. "I think so."

Hands hovered over her, afraid to touch. "You hurt anywhere?"

"I don't . . . what hap—"

"Goddamn ATV. I think that's what it was." He touched her shoulder now, slid an unsteady hand down her arm and released her seat belt. That his hand trembled startled her. "You . . . you sure you're okay?"

"The horses . . ."

"I'll see about them. You stay put." He seemed torn between duty to her and duty to the horses. She saw this in his eyes as he touched her hair, as though he were lifting a curtain to take a peek at something dear. "Okay?"

"Are you?" She touched his face because she was glad he was there with her, because the living, breathing wholeness of him was such a welcome sight.

"Yeah. I don't think I hit them."

He was a tall, lean silhouette in the headlights. She sat

up when he gestured, becoming a semaphore in his bright white shirt.

"Look in the box behind the seat. Should be a wire cutter."

Somewhere in the darkness a horse squealed.

"What's wrong?"

"Hurry! They broke through a wire gate."

She got herself moving. Draped over the back of the seat in the extended cab, she found the box and the tool he'd called for, then flung the door open and stumbled into the ditch grass. "I found it!"

The horse was crying frantically. He had to be tangled in the wire. Like a relay racer, Julia poured her focus on the essential tool and homed in on her teammate's extended hand. "Be careful. Is he—" She could see legs flailing, hear the animal struggling, trying to get up. Pain and terror reverberated in the huge cavern of night. "What can I do?"

"You can maybe aim the headlights a little better, but do it easy, okay? He's scared real bad. And stay back."

He spoke quietly to the horse, but he moved quickly, smoothly, no motion wasted. The buckskin rocked on his side with his front legs shackled, kicking, throwing his head and heaving his body. His shrieks said *Don't touch me*, but the man ignored them. Julia couldn't hear his words, but his tone was a soothing counterpoint to his quick, decisive advance. He dodged a flailing leg as he planted his knee on the animal's neck. He managed to control the buckskin's head with one hand on the nose while he drew the wire cutter out of his back pocket, snipped the wire and flung it aside.

He backed away, leaving both the horse and Julia momentarily spellbound. He spoke again. The horse lunged to his feet and fled across the flat, into the dark shelter of the bluffs.

"Will he be all right?"

"Couldn't see the damage real well. Didn't have enough light."

He turned, gave a wry smile. She'd failed to do her part. But when he laid his hand on her shoulder, she felt like a teammate again, her lapse forgiven. She noticed that his hand was steady now. It would have to be for the job he'd just done.

"You could send somebody out to check tomorrow, but they probably won't find him," he told her. "Somebody was runnin' them around with an ATV. Is this your land?"

"I'm not even sure. I'm not that . . ." She glanced over her shoulder as he walked her back to the pickup. "It *was* a wild horse, wasn't it?"

"Oh, yeah, he's wild. Nice horse, too. That's the bunch I saw earlier." He looked back at the broken gate. "Is that somebody's idea of a sport? Chasing them around at night like that?"

"They live in the mountains. Ross . . . they were Ross's, um . . ." They were the part of her brother that his family hadn't buried.

And she was losing it. All the mellowness, all the cleverness, were fading. The anesthesia was wearing off. He could see it, too. They stood next to the pickup now, and he was rubbing her arms, shoulders to elbows, making her skin tingle.

"The ones who came to say good-bye," he recalled.

"Does that sound crazy?"

"Not to me."

"No crazier than what you just did, nor any more impossible."

"I know what I'm doing when it comes to horses. That might be the only time I'm *not* crazy." He opened the door for her, adding in an aside, "The only fancy of mine that's not impossible."

"Horse fever can ruin a good cowman," she told him when he slid behind the wheel. "That's what my grandmother says."

"I wouldn't know about that." He shifted into reverse and backed out of the ditch.

"You're strictly a horseman."

"Yes, ma'am."

They were back on the road. He hadn't even checked for damage to his pickup. Pretty easygoing, she thought. "A cowboy, but not a cow*man*."

He smiled. "Exactly the kind your mama warned you about."

"Exactly the kind she married." The headlights illuminated the High Horse sign above the road. There were no lights on in the cabin that housed Vernon and Shep, the two hands who had been with Gramma forever. "Would you like to stay? There's an extra room at the house."

"I'd like to stay, and not in the extra room. But sooner or later I'd be headin' down the road, wouldn't I?"

She nodded tightly. He'd had his fill of the High Horse and its empty invitations, its promises not kept. Tomorrow he'd congratulate himself for escaping a close call with a besotted woman and a bunch of wild horses.

And well he should.

He parked in the driveway. Julia looked up at the house they'd soon have to sell. Its dark windows stared back like sad, hollow eyes. Oddly, she remembered her father's face. In the end, it wouldn't have bothered him much to sell the place. Her mind's eye ought to be filled with Ross's face tonight, and her grandfather's face, and all the faces in the photographs behind those old walls, and the horses that belonged in the mountains. Not the father who had never quite reached adulthood because he was too busy being a boy. A cowboy. Why wouldn't a grown man feel silly calling himself a *cowboy*?

Her throat burned. This was it; the end of a long day and a hard road. Her mother was inside, along with her sister and her grandmother, all asleep. She had to go in and occupy her space among them now, even though she wouldn't have to face them again until morning. But there were faces crowding in on her tonight, trapped horses screaming in her head, and where was Ross, who had loved them and looked after them? Where was her brother, who had always been her best friend, even though she'd failed to be his?

"It was good of you to help him," she told the man who called himself a cowboy. "He'll be okay, won't he?"

"He'll be okay. How about you?"

Julia stared at the house that never changed. It was always there, right there in the same place. No matter how long she'd stayed away, she could come back and there it would be. Minus another Weslin man, but otherwise still the same. It belonged to the women now, and they'd surely have to sell it, sooner or later. She and her sister had given up this life a long time ago.

Her eyes stung. Her lips trembled. She hung on as long as she could, putting off her next breath. When she finally drew it, her whole body quaked with the grief she could no longer disallow.

She heard him move, felt him reach for her. He spoke to her softly, the same way he'd spoken to the terrified horse. She turned to him, and she soaked his shirt with her tears.

3

Sally Weslin had business with the judge at the Parker County courthouse, but she didn't mind waiting. Henry Moscow, county judge for going on ten years now, was reading Sheriff Don Jurgensen's report, while a tall, broad-shouldered cowboy stood before the bench, hat in hand, waiting for the ax to fall. Don's chicken scratch was a bear to figure out. Henry had already shoved the paper under his nose twice for clarification, which the sheriff haltingly provided. The cowboy waited quietly, patience personified. That and his keyhole stance were the marks of his breed.

The courthouse still felt like part of Sally's territory, maybe even more than the High Horse. She'd had it in her mind for some time now that the ranch belonged to her grandchildren, whichever of them could make a go of it, and she'd liked the way that notion played out for her when she tried to imagine her corner of the world without her in it.

The ranch had become her legacy to them. It had always been a family proposition—first the Harrises, then the Weslins—and she'd been counting on her grandchildren to carry on. But the courthouse was personal territory for Sally. Years ago her term on the bench had been her own doing, an endeavor nobody expected her to take on, stick with for very long or make good in, but she had. And she kept that piece of her life banked in her own account, hers and hers alone.

With its beige walls, oak tables, black chairs, tall windows, and with the short walk from the back door to the front, the courtroom was stark and spare except for the blaze of red, white and blue behind the bench, the stars and stripes for country, the buffalo for state. It felt like a place of balance. Two sides to every story, two verdicts to choose from, two ways to go, but, finally, only one judge. Sally had gotten used to having the final say, or acting as though she did. It was an illusion, of course, the idea that any "say" was ever final. But in this room it felt real if the judge played the part right, and Henry Moscow was learning. He was at his best when he was putting attorneys in their place.

Sally remembered him at his worst. When she had been sitting on that bench he'd appeared before her, pleading no contest to everything from smashing windows to setting fire to Wayne Eckroth's haystacks. Over at Parson's Trading Post, Orin Sandler, who would bet on anything, had offered heavy odds on Henry celebrating his twenty-first birthday behind bars.

She couldn't remember right off exactly when Henry had started cleaning up his act. She remembered when he'd stopped by the ranch to see her, told her he was headed for law school and that she was his inspiration. She wasn't sure just what she'd inspired in him. Now he was about as self-righteous as a former smoker, sitting up there on the bench, clutching that gavel like he was apt to hit somebody over the head with it any time.

Sally hadn't gone to law school. She'd been elected simply because she was a Harris, and because, at the time, the choices had been pretty slim. Over the years she'd had her share of jobs, which was the way of things in a sparsely populated county. People pitched in. City people could afford to specialize, but in Parker County there weren't enough players to cover all the bases, which, to Sally's way of thinking, only made life more interesting. She'd driven a school bus for a while, which had brought in a little spending cash. She'd been a volunteer firefighter before they'd made it a formal organization, bought everybody jackets and caps emblazoned with the new "Fire Hawks" logo, then put in some fool age limit so she could be only an "honorary" member. She'd been county superintendent of schools years back, even served a term as county coroner.

Her favorite sideline had been wielding that gavel, but like everything else, it was only a sideline to ranching. And as with everything else, there had come a time to retire. She had a whole list of "honoraries." Now it was time to sit back and enjoy the notion that she'd participated in the shaping of the young people who had taken over. Another illusion, she realized. At her age it should have been a safe bet that she would not outlive those she'd shaped, but her son had frittered his short life away without ever making shape or sense of it. Sally took comfort where she could find it, and seeing how Henry was still coming along lifted some of the heaviness she was feeling. She knew no bet worth taking was ever safe.

Henry finally raised his head. "Are you represented by counsel, Mr. Houston?"

"No, sir." The cowboy shrugged. "What's the point? I failed the balloon test. I was over the limit. What's the fine?"

"Have you been living under a rock, Mr. Houston? Driving under the influence is a serious charge, with serious consequences for a conviction."

"It ain't like I hit anybody, or any *thing*. I wasn't even hardly speeding." Houston lowered his head, fingered his hat brim and finally muttered into his shirtfront, "What kind of consequences am I looking at?"

"Jail time, Mr. Houston. A considerable fine. Probably both." Henry checked his watch, then glanced up at the clock, which was behind Sally. He nodded and sat up a little straighter when he saw her. "We're going to break for lunch. You be back here in exactly one hour. Did you get a good breakfast in the hoosegow this morning?"

Sally smiled. She'd always liked the word "hoosegow."

"It was tolerable, I guess."

"Then I suggest you use the next hour to find yourself qualified legal representation."

"I don't know anybody around here. I'd just as soon

represent myself. Throw myself on the mercy of the court.''

'' 'The man who represents himself has a fool for a lawyer,' '' Henry recited, then looked to Sally. ''Or was that 'a fool for a client'? I can never remember. He's a fool either way.'' Sally nodded. Henry pushed his chair back. ''The extent of my mercy is giving you this time to get to know somebody here. Time was, you'd have to go lookin' in Cody or down to Casper for an attorney, but that's all changed. Everybody's getting out of the city nowadays, moving into the burbs.'' He wagged a forefinger. ''We've got everything you need right here in Parker County, Mr. Houston. Don't go too far. We're in recess until one-fifteen.''

Sally was back on the road before one o'clock. Her brief visit with Henry Moscow had left him with plenty of time to eat his lunch. She'd also checked on the legal status of the leases and grazing permits, just to make sure the buzzards that were sure to start circling any time now couldn't rip off a piece of High Horse meat while she was busy tending to the fresh wounds.

It had been a strange funeral. People paying respects to the Weslin family, mostly. Sorry for their troubles. Ross had been a private man, kept to himself, didn't have many close friends. There was nobody except for the family to claim they were going to miss the departed in a personal way. The four Weslin women walking into that most final of all farewells like four prize cats, emerging from their separate boxes, arching their backs and their tails and circling, searching for footing in a peculiarly female way.

Fay, the children's mother, wasn't staying any longer than she had to. She would be saying her good-byes to the girls right about now and heading out in the car she'd rented at the Cheyenne airport. Fay didn't fancy being out in the middle of nowhere without a vehicle at her disposal, even for a day or two. She was fond of saying that she'd done her country period, and she knew better. ''Never again will I be marooned on an atoll of log piles in a sea of grass.''

Sally had always enjoyed Fay's theatrical talk. It was strange to watch her spirited daughter-in-law suffer through the funeral in stiff-necked silence. Fay generally spoke her mind, which must have been buzzing inside that head she carried so regally as she stood by Ross's casket. It wasn't just a matter of losing her son. She'd severed a lot of emotional ties along with the apron strings a long time ago. But burying him beneath the very sea of grass she'd cursed, right next to the ex-husband she'd also cursed—that must have been the kicker.

And then there were the girls. Dawn had never had much interest in the ranch, but Ross had predicted that Julia would take up the slack. She would pick up where he left off. She had dreamed the dream with him when they were kids, and they could still make it happen. He could draw up the plans for her, show her how. Oh, he had all kinds of ideas about how she could put her experience as a social worker to use there at the High Horse in some kind of summer program for troubled kids. He had it all figured out, he'd said. As soon as you get better, Julia had said.

Fever dreams, Sally thought now. Ross had been sicker than any of them had realized. Once he'd taken to his bed, he'd deteriorated quickly, but he'd picked his time, somehow dressing himself and heading out into the night when no one was looking. He'd left no widow and no offspring behind him. Just four women who hardly knew each other anymore, so worn and frayed were the ties that bound them. But death had a way of drawing in on the ties. So did age, and Sally was feeling the pinch.

She had to laugh when she passed the new sign on the billboard in Don Jurgensen's pasture: HELP MANAGE WILDLIFE; WEAR FUR. The sign would probably get him reelected a whole lot faster than DON JURGENSEN FOR SHERIFF would. She was still having herself a chuckle when she topped a rise in the roller-coaster highway and saw the cowboy hoofing it along the right-of-way adjacent to the pasture that belonged to the sheriff who'd arrested him. Life sure had a way of supplying the chuckles when a person needed them the most.

Sally slowed down when the cowboy turned and stuck

his thumb out for a ride. He stood tall and proud in a way that said he could use a ride, but he could also get where he was going without it. A day-old beard accented the contours of his square jaw and the shallow cleft in his chin, which he elevated triumphantly as she pulled up beside him. Sixty years fell away, just for a moment, and Sally's old heart revved up like a twenty-year-old's. Those crystalline blue eyes, so full of masculine vitality, could have been Max's.

She reached across the bench seat and cranked the window down. "Where're you headed?"

"Texas." Young Mr. Houston smiled, and the spell was broken. It had taken Max a week or more to work up a smile. "How close can you get me?"

Sally gestured for him to climb aboard. "Closer than you will be if you take this road. Hop in, and I'll help you out."

"All I need is a ride, ma'am."

She wagged her head, the sage elder, and pointed down the rolling highway as she crimped the steering wheel for a U-turn. "That way lies calamity, Mr. Houston."

He was sputtering some, his hand on the door handle, and for a second she thought he might try to bail out. But her turn was too quick for him. She flashed him a triumphant grin of her own. "Indulge an old woman's impulse, Mr. Houston. I don't get impulsive that often anymore, so I got a feeling this was meant to be." The pickup kicked into a higher gear, matching her own sudden power surge. "Maybe I'm your new fairy godmother."

"Just my luck. My old one knew the way to Texas."

"Guess that's why she's been replaced. A couple of miles down the road, you were gonna realize the mistake you were making on your own, and you were gonna turn around and go back. The trouble is, you'd've been doubling back right in front of the sheriff's place, and sometimes he goes home for lunch." She indicated a log house nestled in a copse of ponderosa pines.

"Did they send you out after me?"

"Is there any doubt that I'd be the right person for the job?"

He laughed easily. "No, ma'am."

"Nobody sent me. I was listening in on the proceedings. What you need is someone to get you off the hook with Henry Moscow, and I'm just the woman who can do that."

"You a lawyer?"

"I'll go you one better. I used to be the judge." She slowed down to the posted limit and waved to the folks heading out of town, first a Suburban, then a pickup pulling a stock trailer. "It'll go a lot harder if you try to walk away."

"Hell, they impounded my pickup, then gave me an hour to find myself a lawyer. They've got me cold. I said I'd pay the fine. What do I need a lawyer for?"

"A DUI is a serious charge."

"So I've been told." He watched a power line disappear overhead as they turned a corner and drove under it. "How much can it cost me? I figure the pickup oughta cover it, split two ways between the sheriff and the judge. But you throw in a lawyer . . ." He thought about it, then shook his head. "I've been down this road before."

"How far did you think you'd get?"

"A few miles on foot, a little more if I caught a ride. Walking felt better than waiting."

"Would working be better than sitting in jail?"

"I won't sit in jail. One night and I'm ready to sell my soul for a hacksaw." He slid his hands over his knees, rubbing them as though they ached, as he stared at the two-story red brick building looming at the end of the block. "What kind of work?"

"It's honest work."

He snickered. "That's what I came here for, but the guy up and died on me."

"Ross Weslin?" she asked, and with a look he asked her how she'd guessed. "My grandson. I'm Sally Weslin."

The expression in his eyes went soft. "Oh, jeez, I'm sorry."

"Are you K.C. Houston, the trainer?"

"Yes, ma'am."

K.C. touched his hat brim reflexively. It felt good to be recognized as a person with a whole name again. Whenever anyone called him "Mr. Houston," he was tempted to

glance over his shoulder. No names had been formally exchanged last night, as he recalled, but Wyoming seemed to
be chock full of Weslin women. The family resemblance
was unmistakable, now that he was looking at her as a
woman with a name rather than as somebody with a vehicle.

Her face was worn soft and puckery, like a shirt he'd
thrown in the wash and ruined. She didn't mess with the
color of her hair. It was gray going white, pure and simple,
but she had a full head of it, and it was kind of cute the
way she had it cut, short and square. She was a small, trim
woman, a little stoop-shouldered, like she'd carried some
heavy loads.

"Sorry about his passin', ma'am. I only met him a couple of times, but you could tell he was a good hand. Had
a good eye for horses."

"Where the horses were concerned, he had a soft heart
and a softer head, but he was a good hand. None better."

She was offering him a job, replacing a grandson whose
death had apparently left three women, one ranch and mis-
cellaneous horses without a man to tend to them. Hardly
the kind of work he was looking for right now. All he
needed was a well-heeled horse fancier with a good string
of colts wanting the K.C. Houston handle. No sad, lonely
women, no high-handed husbands or jealous boyfriends, no
human strings. Just a good string of green colts and a paycheck when the job was done. Simple as . . .

"What do you need done?"

"The list's about as long as your arm." She eyed him
speculatively. "So Ross was gonna hire a horse trainer."

"Far as I was concerned, I was hired." Like most West-
erners, he did business on a handshake. He was beginning
to realize that Weslin's offer was probably all blueberry pie
in the Wyoming sky from the start. But that didn't matter
now. "You sure can't blame a guy for dyin'."

"You can, but it doesn't change anything." She draped
her arm over the steering wheel and turned to him. "He
was a dreamer to the end, my grandson. What I need is a
ranch hand."

"I'm a horse trainer."

"And you've built yourself a fine reputation. I'll bet you're used to getting paid pretty well." She glanced past the windshield at the big double doors of the courthouse. "But you've got yourself into some serious hot water here in Parker County. Like I said, I can help you out, but then you'll have to return the favor. And what I need is a good, all-around cowboy."

"I came here for a job, ma'am. I don't mind working, but I'm kinda specialized."

"We've got plenty of horses. We've also got calves to be branded and cattle that have to be moved up to summer pasture."

"Who's 'we'?"

"For right now, you'd be working for me. Do you mind working for a woman?"

"I get along just fine with women." And if he went to work for Sally Weslin, he had a feeling he'd have his hands full. "I don't mind payin' a fine or workin' one off, but I ain't going to jail."

"That's right." She nodded. "If you're willing to let me handle Henry, you're going home with me."

Much to his surprise, that was exactly what happened. He turned the business over to her because this was her town, and he was nobody here. He was well acquainted with the consequence of being nobody.

The woman was a marvel. The years had probably shaved a couple of inches off her height, but it was no great loss, because they'd done nothing to diminish her stature. She knew her own mind, and she had no trouble reading everyone else's. K.C. ended up representing himself with Sally calling the shots. When the judge started trying to play hardball, she backed him down with answers to every challenge. To K.C.'s displeasure, paying his fine and getting out of town by sundown wasn't even an option. At least, not while they were looking. Judge Moscow agreed to a continuance, which Sally said was as good as a second chance. If he followed Sally's strategy, he would be able to exonerate himself. He would work for her for a few months, go in for a few safety classes and a little counseling about his drinking, build some credibility, and when they went back to court, everything would work out fine.

K.C. knew damn well he was being bulldozed straight into Sally's bunkhouse, but as he had no choice, he decided to enjoy the ride. He had to admire the way Sally worked. It wasn't the deal he'd driven all the way up here for, but he was willing to go along with her for a while—as long as she had a place for him to stay and a job for him to do, and would keep him out of jail. She was an interesting woman. She made the first two Weslin women he'd met all the more interesting. They were both easy to look at, and if they had half their grandma's spunk, K.C. might just be in for a memorable summer.

Beginning, as did anything memorable, with a woman.

4

Julia sprawled in a corner chair with one leg hooked over the arm, feeling queasy and willfully wallowing in her entitled mood. She wanted her mother to notice and toss out a remark about the way her posture made her look, but so far Fay had been too busy packing. When in doubt, Fay made herself busy, and the doubt rarely showed. Julia admired that. It was only in recent years that she'd begun consciously sorting out the things she admired about her mother. Her posture, for one. Fay practiced what she'd always preached to her daughters about posture. It was the outward sign of her confidence, which Julia also admired. There were times when she'd depended on her mother's confidence. Someday she would tell her, but this, once again, would not be the day. This was a packing-and-moving-on day for Fay, the kind of a day that tormented Julia, although she could not think why.

Julia's younger sister looked cute the way she was perched on the bed, surrounded by small pillows. Dawn always looked cute. It was a kind of cuteness that called for cuddling, and Dawn had always gotten her share. Julia had done it freely herself when they were younger. *Much* younger.

So there they were, the three of them together in the same old room after years of polite evasion. It felt like old times, which was to say, Julia felt like a child in her mother's presence and a homely stepchild in her sister's. It was foolish to feed into such textbook twaddle at her age, but there it was. A pounding headache made it so easy to be sulky this morning.

Eager-to-please puppy that she was, Dawn watched Fay's every move as if she were waiting for some new curiosity to fly out of the flowered makeup case before her mother zipped it shut. "What are we going to do, Mama?" she finally asked.

Julia bit back a retort.

"Well, girls, I guess that's up to you. I have no part in it." Fay reached for her tiny black dress. "Sally *says* she'll go along with whatever you decide. Whether she actually means it remains to be seen."

A single fold was all it took to make the dress fit neatly beside the tiny black shoes. Doll clothes, Julia thought. Dawn and Fay still wore the same size, wore their clothes the same way. Neatly tailored, perfectly coordinated, like the ivory slacks, blouse, shoes and belt Fay wore now, with a few elegant bits of gold.

Fay looked up, smiling. "Ross may have found a way to get you two to agree on something for the first time in . . . how many years?"

"Gramma could still keep the house, right?" Dawn asked rhetorically. "Stay here as long as she wants."

It went without saying that Dawn wanted to sell the High Horse. Promises and concessions would come first, then the bottom line. She placed a ruffled pillow squarely on her knees. The pink and white pillows were left over from the days when Julia and Dawn had shared the room. Fay had said it was the only room in the house she could bear to sleep in now, her little girls' room, so Julia had vacated her bed when her mother arrived. There were no more little girls in the house. They were women, and women knew how to be accommodating.

"I think she'd be better off in town now," Dawn continued. "But there's no hurry. Sooner or later—"

"Sooner or later comes to all of us," Julia said. "Sooner than later."

"That's really deep, Julia." Dawn flashed her a sly

smile. "You look like hell this morning. Where were you last night?"

"Raising hell, obviously."

Dawn snickered. "From deep to rich. Tell us all you know about raising hell, hon. We've got a minute."

"It's not worth the effort." Julia spared a tight smile. "Neither is raising hell. That's what I know."

"It is when it's done right. Right, Mama?"

"I'm glad I don't have to worry about what you mean by that, sweetie. You're on your own."

Fay's flippant tone didn't quite fit with the care she was taking with the last of her belongings. No one else had thought to wear a black veil at the funeral. No one else owned one. It was just like Fay to call attention to herself that way, Julia had thought. Never pass up an opportunity to show the country folk a little class. But as she watched her mother's hands slowly fold the silk as if it were part of some ceremony, Julia remembered that she'd seen the veil not once but twice before. Fay had worn it for two other Weslin men, both times looking regally beautiful and tragic, like a president's widow.

She looked at Julia, as though acknowledging the memory. "It's certainly not worth the effort out here in the desert. I wouldn't waste my time if I were you."

"Raising hell?"

They stared at each other for a moment, each challenging the other.

Say what you mean for once, Mother.

I don't have to. You know.

Finally, Fay smiled. "If everything is relative, as you used to be so fond of saying, surely there's no percentage in raising hell in Wyoming. One's barely a step up from the other, and I'm sure I couldn't tell you which is which." In one smooth sweep she ran the small suitcase's zipper around its track. "Which is why I don't want to miss my plane."

"I wish you'd stay a few days, Mama."

"I can't, baby." Fay had a different smile for her younger daughter.

Gentler, Julia thought, and it surprised her to hear herself saying, "Why not?"

"Because I'm already all dried up." With a strangely sheepish laugh she grabbed a tube off the dresser and squeezed a dollop of hand lotion into her palm. "This place has a way of just sucking you dry. Have you noticed? It takes every bit of—"

"Of what?" Julia insisted. Her voice had gone softer as she watched, transfixed by the small hands that moved in a way that defined elegance, always had, with an act as simple as putting on lotion. Still, she pushed, because she knew the answer, and she wanted to make her mother say it. "What does it take?"

"Everything." Fay gave her a piercing look, then filled the hole between them with an empty smile and an airy shake of her head. "Every drop of life-giving moisture in your body, so keep the lotion handy as long as you insist on staying around."

"I've got vacation time coming, but I can't stay forever," Dawn said. "Unlike *professional* people, I just can't take a leave of absence from my job."

"I was needed here," Julia said.

Needed. Another relative term. The truth was, she'd had three jobs in the past twelve years, and she wasn't sure what her profession really was anymore. She'd started out as a counselor, then a school social worker, then a case worker with the child protection agency in Minneapolis. She'd filled out enough forms to wallpaper every room in every house in Quicksilver. She'd determined who qualified for services and who wasn't needy enough. She'd taken charge of destitute and broken lives because people needed her professional advice, her understanding, her care. Her signature.

"I would have come sooner if somebody had called me," Dawn said for the tenth time.

"It wasn't a death watch. We didn't—"

"I know. We haven't exactly been close." Dawn pulled her feet up and folded her legs akimbo, plopping the pillow in the well they made. "And then there's Roger, which is, you know, not working out at the moment."

"You haven't given him much of a chance, have you?"
Julia regretted the question even before it was out. She'd
told herself from the beginning of this odd reunion that
Dawn's marriage, her relationships, even men in general,
were topics to be avoided.

Dawn was literally bristling, with her short, usually chic
hair sticking out at all angles. "Maybe he hasn't given *me*
much of a chance. Did you ever think of that?"

"Nope." Julia chuckled. Dawn's whining amused her,
but so did her own nagging impulse to scoot up to Dawn,
appease her with a piece of candy, then brush her pretty
blond hair for her and fix it with a satin ribbon. Silly impulse. It had to be the room.

Fay intervened. "If I were you, I'd just hire somebody."

"To do what?" Julia asked absently.

"Whatever has to be done."

It sounded like the instructions Fay had once given to
the veterinarian charged with putting Julia's aging cat out
of its supposed misery. Julia sat up, taking her turn at bristling. "Do you actually think we have the right to take
matters into our own hands as though Gramma weren't
even around anymore?"

Fay shrugged. "She'd basically turned the place over to
Ross. The controlling interest was in his name."

"This place was his life, Mother. It made perfect sense
to put his name on it."

Fay was not about to go soft on the issue. "The only
thing that makes sense now is to get somebody *in* here to
advise you on how to get the most *out* of it."

Julia felt her boot heels automatically digging into the
carpet in the face of her mother's imperious stance. "We
both have to agree, you know. If one of us refuses to sell,
we can't sell."

"That was their way of offering the same kind of carrot
Sally held out to Ross. Stick around and become the next
head honcho."

"*Their* way?"

"You don't think that will was all Ross's idea, do you?"

"It leaves Gramma at our mercy."

"Right." Fay turned to Dawn, who was still sitting on

the bed, hanging on every word. "You might think about setting some deadlines for yourself. It looks complicated, what with all the different kinds of property—the livestock, the equipment, the land. But you get Sally to help you set up a timetable, then hire the help you need. Those two old fools she keeps on just out of pity—"

"In the last few months Vern and Shep have kept things going," Julia said.

"Well, now it's time to draw it to a close. Sally knows that. She's run out of *menfolk*." Fay put a bitter spin on the quaint term. "And you'll need help."

"Vern and Shep are 'menfolk.' What we need is a *man*, right?" Dawn smiled. "A cowboy type."

"Stay away from cowboy types. Your father was a cowboy type. They're worthless." Fay regarded her daughters. "You're grown women now. I can say it. They're worthless."

"Oh, Mother, you didn't exactly wait till we were grown to say it," Julia reminded her with a wistful smile that was not really for her mother, but for her own secret. She was thinking of her night out. There were parts of it she wanted to tell them both about, just to prove to them she had it in her. But she wouldn't, because their skepticism would take some piece of it away. He was gone anyway. She would keep it for herself.

"Well . . ." Fay glanced out the window, where cottonwood leaves rattled in the morning breeze. A touch of tenderness seeped into her stage whisper. "Surely you knew."

"Surely we did. Divorce was a dead giveaway."

"But he was still our father," Dawn put in, much to her sister's surprise.

"And now he art in heaven." Fay glanced back and forth between them, her smile odd-looking and feeble. She turned around suddenly, toward the dresser, and in the mirror Julia saw the smile slip away. "I'm sorry. That was crude. Life's too short for . . ." Her fingers trembled as she smoothed the linen dresser scarf. "Life's much too short. Damn that brother of yours for squandering his."

"Oh, Mama . . ."

Dawn hopped off the bed and rushed to her mother's

side. They embraced and consoled each other so easily. Julia envied them that ease, the ready solace. There had to be something wrong with a woman who would turn to a stranger for comfort, but guarded herself like a hermit crab in the presence of her mother and sister. She knew all she had to do was get out of the chair, just make a move, and they would include her.

But she held back. She stared at the tube of hand lotion on the dresser, listened to the sniffling and closed herself off. *Your brother*, Julia thought. Not, *my son*.

Fine, then, Ross was Julia's. Her brother, her friend. That meant he was her loss. *Crude* was a bit of an understatement. Whatever Daddy was or was not was history, and now Ross . . . Fay had damned Ross time and time again. She'd berated him for everything that made him Ross: for wearing cowboy boots to school after they'd moved back East, for not having friends—*refusing* to make friends— for quitting college, for coming back to the ranch. She'd damned him as a boy and damned him as a man; damned him for living and now damned him for dying.

But then, what were mothers for?

"You'll have to drive like a bat out of hell to make that plane now, Mother." Finding herself up, out of the chair, moving precariously close to the tender mother-daughter display, Julia reached around them and grabbed the suitcase off the bed. When in doubt, be helpful, she told herself. "I'll take this out for you."

"I'm coming." Fay gave Dawn one last squeeze and a peck on the cheek before she drew away, launching the final string of hollow proposals. "We should spend some time together soon. This summer sometime. We could rent a cottage at the beach. Wouldn't that be fun? Just us girls. I do it all the time with Karen and Paula. Two dear friends. You haven't met them, Julia, but Dawn has, and they'd love to join us."

"Just you, me and Julia would be better, Mama. I mean, not that I don't like your friends, but they didn't know Ross, either. It would just be hard." Dawn hung her head and shoved her hands up the wide, cuffed sleeves of her pink bathrobe. "I don't know. It's like we need some time for just us."

"That would be nice," Fay said mechanically. She gave her daughters' old room one last look. "Better get myself on the road, huh?"

Julia was moving down the hall with the luggage ahead of the last of the vacuous plans and glib good-byes. It felt good to burst through the door and feel the warm spring sun. She stowed her mother's suitcase, closed the trunk and turned toward the sound of the mincing footsteps on the slate path.

Fay took another look at the hulking house, homing in on her old bedroom window. "He knew how I felt about this place. I think it destroyed us. I really do." She blinked hard. Her artistry with makeup didn't stand up as well in the sunlight as it did in the shadows, but she was still a stunning woman. "I know that's why he moved back. And I guess, in the end, he found a way to get me to come back, too."

"Ross didn't live his life to spite you, Mother. You never really knew him. You never—"

Fay folded her arms and leaned back against the car, giving Julia the look she hated, the Mother-knows-all look. "How well did you know him, Julia?"

She wasn't going to get her with that one. "Better than you ever did."

"Really?" Fay chuckled and shook her head. "I know my limitations. I know I'm not the world's best mother. I had children because . . ." She shrugged. "Because I got pregnant. I did the best I could. Maybe I owe you all a whole litany of apologies, but what good would that do?"

"None."

"I'd enjoy seeing you more often. If we could just be friends . . ."

Julia laughed, the easiest response. "How can we 'just be friends'? You're my mother. The only one I've got."

"Better than nothing?" With a smile Julia could only regard as charitable, Fay laid her hand on Julia's arm. "I do love you, Julia."

It sounded like a formal notification. Julia stared at the

low branch on the cottonwood tree in the side yard, where
her father had hung her first swing. He'd made it from an
old tire, and Fay had told him it looked tacky. Julia swallowed convulsively against any more burning in her throat.

"I know this isn't going to be easy for you and Dawn.
Handling all this." She gave Julia's arm a parting pat. "It's
up to you, you know. That's the way he left it. He was
trying to be fair to Dawn and to give Sally her due, but it's
really going to be up to you."

"It always is."

"Responsibility was always something you assumed. I
never forced it on you. You just took it."

Julia sighed. She didn't remember it that way, but she
was running out of comeback steam. "I'm not up to it right
now."

"Get some help. Do it quickly. Sometimes you just have
to . . ." The advice gave way to some new interest at the
far end of the porch. Fay straightened suddenly, peering.
"Are those our . . ." She moved closer, and Julia followed,
curious. When had her mother's hair gotten so red?

"Look at that," Fay marveled, one hand on her daughter's arm, the other pointing out a trail of shoots just burst-
ing through the stubborn ground next to the stone-faced
foundation. "The lilies we planted are still there. See?
They're coming up." She set her small leather purse in the
new spring grass as she squatted beside the flower bed without straining her slacks, without dirtying her knees. So ef-
fortless, Julia thought, as though her elegance served as a
buffer. "Remember when we put these in?"

"I remember."

She watched her mother spread her hands out and brush
them over the pointy sprouts. She remembered, too, that
she had learned her love of flower gardening from this
woman. Fay had a remarkable way of getting down and
getting things in, getting them to grow without really getting dirty.

But when had her hands become so creased? Where had
the small, pale brown spots come from?

"These should be divided, Julia. They'll go on forever,
but they need to be tended a little bit, you know? They

need a little TLC." Fay looked up. Her redder-than-ever hair caught fire in the sun. "Maybe if you have some time while you're here . . ."

"Or maybe if you wanted to stay a few more days."

"I don't belong here." She came to her feet slowly, soundlessly, hands braced on her knees. "I tried, Julia. I really tried, but I always felt unsettled. I couldn't find a way to be part of this life." She glanced wistfully toward the red bluffs beyond the blue-black creek. "Just having his children wasn't enough."

"Enough to keep you—"

"Enough, enough." She waved her hands as though warding off a second helping. "But that's not something you'll ever have to worry about. Not if you keep your wits about you, and you've always been able to do that quite nicely." They shared a look, an acknowledgment of Julia's good sense. "We've always counted on you for that."

"Who's 'we'?" Julia asked as she leaned down to pick up her mother's purse. She felt sick and sterile inside, and she wondered if there was anything she could take for it.

"All of us. But not all at the same time." Fay spared Julia an air kiss in return for her purse. "I've *got* to fly. Look after your sister. Keep her away from cowboys and other hazards. You know Dawn."

"Do I?"

What a stupid question, Julia told herself as she followed her mother back to her car. She wanted to keep the conversation going. She wanted to ask about dividing the lilies. The crazy thought of some desperate person grabbing her mother's arm or the car keys or the car door flashed through her mind.

"Of course, you do," Fay was saying. "You know she's full of surprises, which is what makes her so infuriating and so lovable." She turned and smiled and touched Julia's shoulder. "Be good."

Julia smiled, too. "Does that mean no cowboys for me, either?"

"I don't have to worry about you." Fay ducked into the car, laughing merrily. "Cowboy charm only works on the young and foolish."

*   *   *

She'd surely felt foolish enough. It was one of the few times in her life that Julia had awakened in the morning, remembered the night before, and thought about crawling under the bed. But then she'd reminded herself that she would never see him again. He was on his way back to wherever he'd come from, and she would be, too, once the estate was settled. She'd almost succeeded in tucking him away safely as a private memory until her mother had made her smug comment.

When had Julia stopped being young, and what was wrong with being a little foolish on rare occasions?

After Fay left, Julia spent several hours mucking out the barn. Mindless dirty work. She went back to the house with a hot shower in mind, stopped at the kitchen sink for a glass of water, glanced out the window, and there he was. Last night's cowboy was back, strolling through the backyard with Gramma, who was walking with her arms folded, which meant she was talking business. Julia was afraid to guess what kind of business it might be. Fairy-dust business, probably.

They'd stopped discussing real business at the High Horse months ago. It was too bad Ross had allowed this man to drive all the way up here for nothing. Too bad, but there it was. A waste of the man's time. She had all but dismissed the concept of wasting time or of thinking of it as a measurable thing, a limited commodity. The three of them had been coasting on fairy dust, she and Ross mixing her nostalgia for times past with his dreams for tomorrows that would never come, their Gramma Sally standing by, just the way she always had.

Ross had had plans for the coming summer. They all knew he was dying, but no one wanted to put the process on a timetable by suggesting that summer might not come for him. They knew, but they didn't say it, for saying it would have made it so. It was left up to Ross to say it when he was ready. He never was. Instead, he talked about rounding up the wild horses this summer. It had to be done this summer in order to save the herd. He never said why they needed saving, but he said he had a plan. As soon as he could ride, he and Julia would take a couple of horses and head for the mountains, the way they used to when they were kids, and he'd tell her about his latest plan.

Ross had always been full of plans. He'd never let anyone else dictate his life for him, and Julia had always admired him for that. But some plans were real, and some weren't. The difference was understood, never specified. If you got too specific, you could get bogged down in details, so planning and dreaming were always done in general terms, right up to the end, when death turned out to be one of those heavy, bog-you-down details a person simply couldn't avoid.

This cowboy appeared to be another sticky detail Ross had left behind, one she'd hardly avoided. She'd kissed him, in fact. She'd cried on his shoulder, and she didn't even know his name. He wasn't real. He'd figured into one of Ross's endless horse dreams somehow, but the dreams had gone the way of the dreamer. Nothing left but details and loose ends. She thought this one had made it pretty clear that he wasn't about to get tied up.

The voices sounded pretty jovial, coming in the back door. Gramma was asking him about somebody who raised Quarter Horses who was apparently a mutual acquaintance. He was yes-ma'aming her in that seductive, soft-toned drawl Julia had become fixated with the night before. She backed up against the sink. She could hear them carefully scuffing on the sisal mats in the mud room, and she thought about her own boots sitting out there, caked with manure. Her jeans didn't look too bad, just a few smears.

Beaming as though she'd bagged a trophy buck, Gramma led him into the kitchen. The cowboy was beaming, too, looking straight at Julia over the top of her grandmother's mostly white head, and she wondered what he thought *he'd* bagged.

"And this is my granddaughter Julia." Sally cast her guest a quick, over-the-shoulder glance. "*Weslin*. Julia Weslin. Julia, this good-lookin' young cowboy is K.C. Houston."

"We've met, Gramma." She nodded, gave a tight smile, but when he took his hat off, she was struck anew by the winning way he had with those laughing blue eyes. They'd surely been her downfall the night before. Not *downfall*, really. She'd stumbled, but she hadn't exactly *fallen*. She squared her shoulders and pumped some sauce into her smile. "He is young, isn't he? How did I miss that little detail?"

"You were blindsided by the good-lookin' part."

"Quite possibly."

"Ain't that young," he claimed as he raked his thick, nearly black hair back with splayed fingers. "Clean livin' keeps me well preserved."

"Well, I'm glad you've made friends with each other, then, because K.C.'s coming to work for us."

"Gramma?" Julia questioned the wisdom of Sally's call with a look, which her grandmother answered in kind. She turned back to K.C. "I hope she told you what you're getting into. We don't need a horse trainer. We need . . ." She gestured, frustrated. "We probably need a cattle broker. An auctioneer. We need—"

"We need a damn good cowboy, and that's what we've got," Sally informed her. "It's been a while since we've had anybody staying in the bunkhouse, so I'll have to give it a going-over, get some of that junk out of there."

"I'll do that, Gramma."

"No, you'll take K.C. out and show him the High Horse. I'll rustle up something for—"

"Actually, I was just about to—"

"Well, well. Back again?" Dawn was all of a sudden standing in the doorway. No sound, no warning. She was just there, looking bright and fresh in her summer slacks, undoubtedly smelling clean.

"Yes, ma'am. Looks like I'll be workin' here after all."

"How nice. I'm not a ma'am. She's a ma'am. She's a ma'am." Dawn gave each of the other women a deferential nod, then tilted her head and slipped him a dazzling smile. "I'm Dawn. Doing what?" He was lost in the smile. "Working here doing what?"

"Whatever Sally's got in mind for me, I guess. She's holdin' my marker."

"That's right, I am. Did you get enough to eat?"

"Yes, ma'am."

Sally already had the refrigerator door open. "They must have a new cook over there at the Cut Proud. Some granola head from Jackson Hole, most like. I don't care what that girl said, I know there was some soy stuff in my hamburger. You need something to drink?" She bumped the door shut and set a plastic pitcher on the table.

"I'm fine, ma'am."

Sally already had four glasses out. "We need a man around the place, girls. I know that sounds old-fashioned, but it's the God's truth. We need a strong, healthy, able-bodied man, so I went and got us one." She was pouring pink lemonade. She glanced at Julia. "Actually, Ross got us one."

"A horse trainer," Julia said, taking the glass her grandmother handed her. "Ross wasn't thinking straight."

"That makes two of you. This is not a good time to sell out, if that's what you've decided to do. And K.C.'s a cowboy. He knows horses, he knows cattle." She slapped a glass of lemonade in his hand. "Don't you?"

"Funny you should ask."

"If you don't, you can learn. Hell, my Max didn't know which end of a cow quits the ground first before he met me. I coaxed him out of a boxcar, brought him on home and made a cowman out of him quick enough."

"It's her favorite hobby," Dawn said.

"Hobby, hell. We were married for more than thirty years." She handed Dawn a glass. "Did I ask you if you were married, K.C.?"

He was sipping and grinning. "Ma'am, your questions just keep gettin' funnier all the time."

"Just wondered whether we'd be putting anybody else up in the bunkhouse."

"Not on my account."

"Good." She raised her glass, toasting her new man. "That's the way I like 'em. Good-lookin' and single. Bottoms up."

"Now, hold on, Sally. When I said whatever you've got in mind for me, maybe I should have mentioned a couple of exceptions."

She laughed. "Don't worry, cowboy, I don't have the time or the patience to break you in right."

"I'll let that one go till we get to know each other better. You got yourself a hired man." He studied his glass. The convivial tone had slipped from his voice. The role clearly wasn't his favorite. "And I've worked my share of cows. How many are we talkin' about?"

"We had to sell a few more heifers off last fall than I would have liked, but there's still a good-size herd here. Julia's gonna show you around."

"Do I have any help?" he asked.

"You've got me and two other old-timers, Vernon and Shep. They share that little log house down by the main gate, both been with me for years. We were all three sort of semiretired, you might say, but the boys managed most of the calving this year. They'll do what you tell 'em if it's in their power. They may move a little slow, but eventually they'll get 'er done." She raised her glass again, this time in Julia's direction. "These girls, they're both good help when they wanna be. Now that Ross is gone, they've got some decisions to make. But the work won't wait, so you and me, we'll just keep the place running while they consider their options."

Dawn claimed the empty pitcher and took it to the sink. "There's only one option, Gramma. You know that." She ran some water, then sloshed it around in the pitcher as she spoke. "Ross tried to make it complicated, but it's really very simple. One option, given the circumstances. The sooner we get on with it, the better."

"You can't move but so fast on disposing of something that took several lifetimes to build, young lady."

"The High Horse is rightfully yours, Gramma," Julia said, "no matter what the lawyers say."

"No matter what anyone says, honey, the work won't wait, and we've got a new man on the payroll now. I want you to show him around."

Dawn upended the pitcher in the sink. "I wouldn't mind going along."

"On horseback?" Julia challenged her sister with a look.

Horses were the trump card, the one her sister couldn't play.

Dawn glared back. "You can cover more ground in a shorter time in the pickup."

"Not necessarily the ground our new man needs to cover his first day on the job. Do you want to ride with us, Dawn?"

"Not this time." She turned to K.C. "I'm not comfortable on a horse. I don't know how to ride. I haven't had much practice." With a glance she pinned the blame on her older sister.

"You hate horses," Julia reported.

"I don't hate them. I'm afraid of them." She softened her tone for K.C. "I honestly wish I *could* ride, but I just can't seem to get past my fear of the size and the power of the animal. Julia doesn't understand. She and Ross took to it naturally. But I'm the baby."

"They left you out, huh? Like Sally says, it's never too late to learn."

"I'm just so uncoordinated."

"That can be fixed." He slid Julia another one of his confederate winks. "By the right teacher. Should we maybe take the pickup this time out?"

He'd just taken himself out of any *we* she was willing to participate in. "Maybe you should."

"That all depends on where you want to start," Sally said.

"Well, let's see, which way's the wind blowing? South?" Julia gave the man a disaffected glance. "Dawn can probably find her way to the south pasture, which would be as good a place as any for you to start."

"Don't be like that." Dawn looked genuinely affronted.

"Be like what?"

"Like you're the only one left, the only one who cared. You ran off last night when we all needed to talk."

"Now it's your turn to run off." Julia reached behind Dawn and poured half a glass of lemonade down the drain. "I'm not ready to talk."

"This isn't like you, Julia. You're always the sensible one. Let's just all—"

"There's no need to make a big production of this." She set the glass down carefully, spoke with measured restraint. "You go ahead and take the hired man for a ride."

"Did we walk in on the middle of something?" K.C. asked Sally.

"The end of something, more like, which is why it ain't a pretty sight." Sally patted his arm. "This place is, though. You go take a look at it and see what you think."

"You're interested in what I think?"

"You come highly recommended, son. My grandson sent for you. That's good enough for me."

All right, Julia thought. Sally had said the magic words. The peacemaker's name had been invoked. "I was just about to take a shower, anyway," she said, offering Dawn a token of truce. "If you wouldn't mind giving K.C. a little tour, I think Ross had some stuff stored in the bunkhouse. I'll get it out of the way."

Sally handed Dawn the keys to her pickup. "South pasture," she said.

"Where the cows are?"

"Cows and calves. You'll know them when you see them."

"I know what you're up to, Gramma," Julia said when she heard the pickup start. "What kind of 'marker' are you holding?"

"What kind of a time did you have last night?" Sally folded her arms and braced her backside against the sink, and Julia wondered when Gramma had hatched that mother look. Sally must have read her mind. "I'm not asking for details, just a general rating. What's he got besides charm?"

"What are you looking for, Gramma? You hired him."

"Ross hired him. A horse trainer, God love him. Maybe he forgot how many saddle horses we got rid of last fall. Still got a few, you know, but I guess the boy's dreams were galloping wild and free in those mountains right up until the end." She drew a quick frown, wrinkling her wrinkles. "Where'd you leave the car?"

"In town. He brought me home. Charm and good man-

ners, Gramma, that's all I can vouch for. I was feeling . . .''
She sighed, looked out the window and watched her sister
drive away with the man she was vouching for. Men adored
Dawn, always had. Deep down, Julia couldn't really blame
them. Dawn was adorable. ''Or *not* feeling, I guess. Like I
was beside myself, or outside myself, maybe, just looking
on. I should be hurting.''

Sally surprised her with a hard pinch on her arm.

''Ouch!''

''There you go, Queenie, you're hurting.''

Julia stood there rubbing her arm, smarting, scowling. It
took her a moment to find the will to laugh. She put her
arm around Sally. ''You're a mean old woman, Gramma,
but you're all I've got left.''

''How did it go with your mother?''

''Same as always. We just slip into the same old pool
and tread water for a while.''

They stood there for a moment, each with an arm around
the other. Finally Sally gave her one of her signal pats.
''Let's straighten out that bunkhouse so the man won't be
too sorry he picked us over the alternative.''

''Which was?''

Sally laughed. ''Probably not as bad as I made out.''

5

The bunkhouse had housed a dozen men at a time during the High Horse's heyday. It had since served as occasional guest quarters, but finally it had become Ross's personal museum. He had been a tireless collector. Julia wasn't ready to sort through his personal belongings and wonder about the little oddities he'd stowed away, so she pushed the boxes into the back room with the extra furniture, leaving one good bed, a small dresser, some shelves and a lot of empty space that needed cleaning.

There were several old saddles on free-standing racks that she thought she'd move later. Ross's first saddle was among them. Their father had traded in Julia's first saddle when she'd outgrown it, but Ross had refused to part with his. He was going to keep it for his own son, he'd said. Just a few weeks ago he'd told Julia that he'd saved it for her children. "It goes with the High Horse," he'd said. "Along with me and Gramma. And the horses up on Painted Mountain. The High Horse horses."

She lined the saddles up along the empty wall, beneath the windows, heaving and shoving and thinking, *Ross, oh, Ross, how could you let this happen?* He'd gone without leaving a son. He might have left some small, sweet version of himself behind instead of all this stuff, just stuff.

Her throat prickled again as she remembered the way they had so often sneaked into the bunkhouse when they were kids. It was a good place to hide out during the dreaded "look after your little sister" routine. After Daddy had put a padlock on the door, they'd climbed through the window. The lock had made the hideout even better because Daddy would assume they couldn't get in, and Fay wouldn't come looking for them with "the brat" in tow.

Julia started airing out the place. When she reached the window on the east side, the one that was shaded and sheltered by the crabapple tree, she closed her eyes and pressed her forehead against the glass, cooling her face. Finally she flung open the window and looked down. The cinder blocks they'd stacked up so they could get inside were scattered in the reedy grass. Her face heated up again. She could almost see Ross's stubby brown fingers with their chewed nails gripping the windowsill. She imagined reaching for him and hauling his scrawny body inside.

They'd found stuff the ranch hands had left behind, like beer that tasted awful warm and a can of snuff that had made them both sick. They'd hidden some of their own things in the back room, like cheese pops, magazines and the stories they'd written together in a spiral notebook. They would discover that Daddy had a few things hidden there, too, but that would be later, toward the end of their time living together. The time she cherished most.

"I know what I'm going to choose for my reward for my good report card," Ross announced.

"What?"

They were sitting side by side on the floor, backs to the wall between two of the bunkhouse beds so that no one could see them through the windows. Ross smiled, creating a little suspense while he helped himself to another handful of cheese pops from the bag Julia had talked Shep into buying for her when he last went into town. They weren't supposed to eat junk food. If they pleaded "just this once," Fay would read off the list of unrecognizable ingredients to them as proof that the package contained poison. Bad for Ross's allergies. Everything in the world was bad for Ross's allergies.

"I want Duchess's colt."

Julia gave him a no-way look. Horses, Fay said, were

the worst thing for Ross's allergies. It was one of an ever-growing list of topics for disagreement between their parents.

Julia tossed a cheese pop into her mouth. "I was thinking of something like, you know those chemistry sets with all the little bottles? I could be a mad scientist." She'd been thinking a lot about what she wanted to be. Not who, but what, because that was what people always asked whenever they found out how well she did in school. *What* do you want to be? Becoming a worthwhile somebody seemed to have a lot to do with becoming a worthwhile some*thing*, and whenever she was asked to choose, given the chance to choose, she regarded the choosing itself as a test. There was a correct and worthy choice every time. This time it was a chemistry set. "And it wouldn't be too expensive."

"Duchess's colt is gonna be a long-distance runner. You can tell by his chest. A little bit by his legs, but more by his chest." He was repeating his grandfather's projections, to which he added a theory of his own. "Duchess was bred by Lightning."

"You don't know that for sure."

Julia believed in what she saw. Ross believed in what he dreamed. But the white stallion from Painted Mountain was more than a dream. They'd both seen him. Ross had named him. In the stories they'd been spinning together, Lightning had become a wonder horse. Julia put the details of color and shape and definition into their stories, but it was Ross who made the adventure.

"I told you, I saw him. He was racing up and down, right along the fence. All he had to do was jump over it."

"Which you didn't see him do."

"Yeah, but I know he did. He was just sizing up the situation that night. I know he came back. Lightning wouldn't give up until he got the job done."

It was something their grandfather might say. But Duchess was their father's mare. They both knew Daddy would have been furious if he'd thought the white stud had covered the mare before some fancy "papered" stud had had a chance, so Ross hadn't told anyone but Julia what he'd seen through his bedroom window.

"I wish I could've seen him jump that fence. I bet he just sailed over like a glider plane." With a powdered cheese-tipped finger Ross demonstrated the kind of jump he envisioned. "He's the boss, Queenie."

"Daddy would have shot him."

"You think so?"

"I know so." She plunged her hand into the bag. "It's too much to ask for the colt. Daddy just meant a small reward. You always ask for too much, and then Daddy feels bad when he has to say no."

"It's what I want. He told me to think about what I wanted, and that's what I want." That and more cheese pops. Ross had so few doubts about what he wanted. "Do you really want a chemistry set?"

"I could do reports for school. I might even discover something. Mix up some new formula for, I don't know, cough medicine or something. None of the ones you buy ever work very well." She had watched Ross use a lot of it. "I know Daddy would think it was a good choice and kind of unusual for a kid my age."

"Maybe he would." Ross shrugged and glanced away. "For about a minute before he started thinking about something else. Go for something you really want."

"I don't want to choose something stupid. Like in the stories where they get three wishes and they waste two? I want to make sure I make a good choice so I won't look like an idiot at the end. Maybe it won't be a chemistry set, but it'll be something important. It won't be anything childish."

"You'll never decide on anything. If you ever got three wishes, you'd try to put them in a bank or something."

"And you'll ask for that colt, and he'll say no, and then you'll both just be mad at each other."

"I'll get my colt." He bounced a few orange curls in his palm, then popped them into his mouth at once, puffing up his cheeks with what he wasn't supposed to have. "He'll be mine, but he'll have that wild blood in him, so he won't really belong to me, but he'll let me ride him. He'll be the fastest horse in the state."

Julia lifted her gaze to the window. All she could see

was blue sky, but the house was over there, with her bedroom, hers and Dawn's, right next to their parents'. "They
were fighting again last night."

Ross ignored her. "I'll name him Thunder, and we'll go
up to Painted Mountain, and the wild horses will just come
to us, because he's one of them."

"Did you hear them? They were yelling about . . . something about things she found in his pickup."

"I might move up to Painted Mountain. Up to the cabin,
at least for the summer. You want to?"

They both knew it was impossible, but he would never
admit it.

"She says she's going to leave him, leave here. She says
she's taking us with her."

He reached for the bag. "She always says that."

They took turns reaching into the bag, saying nothing for
a while, just eating their fill of forbidden food.

"Why do you always come up with the cheesiest
names?" she challenged him finally. " 'Thunder' and
'Lightning' are just so cheesy."

"How about 'Fay' and 'Mike'?" He aped his parents as
a thunderstorm, his slender fingers slicing through the air,
his smooth cheeks puffing up with explosive sound effects.
He laughed, and he got her to laugh, too.

But within a year, Fay Weslin took her three children
and returned to Connecticut, which was her home and always had been.

Julia had just flung a white top sheet into the air when
the door opened behind her. She turned, startled, jerking
the sheet back, so that it missed the mark and trailed to the
floor.

K.C. Houston grinned and dropped a large green duffel
bag next to the door. "Dawn tells me this is where I should
stow my gear."

The mention of her sister pricked her like a mosquito
bite. She wanted to smack it away, but instead she fought
the sting with a cool smile. "If you think you'll be comfortable here. Otherwise, we certainly have room at the
house."

She reeled in the sheet. While he'd been off with her sister, she'd cleaned up, both the room and herself. A shower and clean jeans had boosted her confidence, which had been flagging lately, she knew that. But she also knew how to get it back. She'd learned from her mother, the master. Start with clean face and hands, the proper tone and the right words.

"Rather Spartan accommodations, but my grandmother thought you'd appreciate the space."

"What does that mean? Plain? Plain and simple suits me fine." He pushed his hat back, tucked his thumbs in his belt and surveyed the long, narrow, dormitory-style room with its whitewashed log walls and natural brown beams overhead. "This place is big enough to hold a dance in."

"And you'll have it all to yourself. Closet. Storage room. There's a bathroom through there. It's just your basic, utilitarian bathroom."

She was clutching the sheet in one hand, pointing out the doors to all the amenities with the other. His bemused smile said he was only half listening. What he was thinking about did not interest her. He'd said he was leaving, and he was supposed to be gone.

"*Plain* bathroom," she amended cordially, "but functional. Everything works. I don't know how long you plan to stay. Ross generally hired some extra help when it came time to put up hay. If we do that . . ."

He was watching her, waiting. She turned away, snapped the sheet up in the air and let it float over the bed. "One thing the High Horse doesn't lack for is buildings, so if we do that . . ."

He stood opposite her, the sheet adrift between them. "You didn't think you'd ever see me again, did you?"

"Ever?" She laughed, her gaze boldly meeting his. "I wasn't thinking that far ahead."

"Turns out it wasn't that far. And I didn't get very far."

"With me, or from me?"

Still that bemused smile in his eyes. "Down the road."

"I was in a strange mood last night," she said lightly as she went back to her bed-making. The proper tone, the right words.

"We had a blue moon last night." She glanced at him briefly, questioning his point. "Second full moon in a month," he explained. "Is that how often the mood strikes you? Once in a blue moon?"

She jerked the sheet under the bottom corner of the mattress. "That's exactly how often I'll be doing this service for you. You'll have to bring your laundry up to the house, but we'll take care of—"

"I know how to run a washing machine." He pulled the sheet taut and folded a quick, crisp hospital corner on the opposite side of the bed. Much neater than hers. "I'm what you might call a liberated cowboy."

Chastened by his gentle tone, she sighed and tried to come up with a warmer smile. "I really do appreciate your help last night. My getting behind the wheel would have been hazardous to the county's health."

"You think the county might owe me one?"

"I think I do." She took a folded Hudson Bay blanket off the top of the dresser. "If you ever need a designated driver, please give me a call."

"What if we both need one?"

"How often do we get a blue moon?" She shook out the blanket. He caught the opposite edge, and they set about putting it on the bed together. "Did my sister give you the grand tour?"

"I don't know. Drove along the creek, saw some cows and calves, a jackrabbit, couple of antelope. Is that as grand as it gets?"

"The High Horse is one of the oldest ranches in the state. One of the few still in the hands of descendants of the people who homesteaded it. It has a grand history."

"I guess the history wasn't part of the tour." He was looking at her as though he wasn't sure who she was, whether she was the same woman he'd met last night, whether she remembered what he remembered.

She shrugged. "Dawn isn't interested in that part of it, but it's not her fault. She was still pretty young when our parents split up. She's a city girl."

"She says she's interested in learning how to ride."

"Well, good. That'll give her something to do. A reason

to stick around while we sort things out.'' It was an opening, but he didn't ask what things.

She plopped two pillows beneath the iron headboard. ''I don't know how Gramma managed to talk you into working for her, but I hope you realize it won't be whatever Ross had in mind.''

''And what do you figure that was?'' He folded his arms, eyeing her as though she'd threatened him with latrine duty.

''My brother was a romantic. And I'm afraid he was quite incurable.'' She turned away from him, feeling diminished by her own remark. She knew Ross would have laughed and told her to lighten up. ''We can move those saddles out of here if they're in your way.''

''I like the way they look there,'' he said.

''Would you know anything about them? They're antiques, probably. Some of them, anyway.'' She ran her hand over the leather seat of the nearest one, from the cantle to the unusually large saddle horn. ''Ross was a collector.''

He moved closer, but he kept some space between them as he turned his interest to the saddles. ''That one looks like an old Mexican saddle. It's got a platter horn cap. Nice set of tapaderos,'' he said, pointing to the ornate stirrups. He stepped over to the next free-standing rack and gripped the hornless swells of a smaller model as though he was thinking of trying it out, then traced the edge of the open channel in the middle of the seat toward the cantle. ''This is a McClellan cavalry saddle, the old 'butt buster.' Probably close to a hundred years old.''

''Really?''

He nodded. ''Bet I could pass a horse test, too.''

''You already did, last night.''

''No sign of those mavericks on Dawn's tour. Did you send anyone out looking for them? Or maybe you went out and checked yourself?''

''I was going to tell Vern about it. They're probably back up in the mountains by now, our summer pasture. We've leased the land since way back when, so we think of them as our mountains, but it's really federal land.'' She glanced out the window, but she could only see the red bluffs that banked the creek. No mountains. No horses. "You said we wouldn't be able to find them."

"That don't mean you don't go out and take a look."

"We will," she said, wondering why she'd thought his observation the previous night had discharged her duty.

"And the reason I'm still here is because I hung around just a little bit too long. Ran into Sally this morning, and she made me an offer I couldn't pass up." He was still testing the feel of the old saddle under his hands. "And I'm still waiting for the romantic part about your brother."

She shrugged. "What could be more romantic than a herd of wild horses, running free up in the high country? Catch a few to thin the herd, hire a trainer to turn them into terrific trail horses, cutting horses, whatever he was interested in lately. But there's still that wild bunch up there, the descendants of horses that have always been there. It's a wonderful bit of romance."

Just like the idea of a ranch held together by the same family from one generation to the next. Romantic if the devotion held up, too.

He looked at her as though he thought there had to be a catch and he was waiting for her to say that he would be asked to perform some epic feat, some miracle. Or be accused of something.

"Ross is dead," she said. "He took the romantic part and left us with the practical part. Like cutting the dream loose."

"Whatever you say." He rapped his knuckles on the hard seat of the cavalry saddle. "That guy, Chuck, who came over to the table last night? Sounded like he wanted to help you with that. Does he ride an ATV?"

She laughed. "I can't see Chuck barreling around at night on an ATV. I'm sure it was some kid."

"Pretty dangerous prank," he said. "Is this a private herd, or does the BLM figure in somehow?"

"My grandfather always said they were just part of the High Horse. He died not long before the protected areas were established back in the early seventies, and Gramma didn't want the Painted Mountain horses moved, so she just claimed them. We've always leased the land, and the horses have always been there." She liked the way that sounded. *Always* and always. And then she added, "Before the Bureau of Land Management even existed." And she realized she liked that even more.

"So nobody's messed with them much."

"Ross used to hire people to round some of them up periodically, but recently that hadn't been happening much. He had a lot of plans, though." She had walked around the Mexican saddle and parked herself next to the first one in the row, the pony saddle. "Mainly, he believed, as our grandfather did, that the horses belonged here."

"And the neighbors disagree."

"The politics of the environment." She liked the sound of the term. It was one she'd heard Ross use. "So many things are changing. The West is changing."

"It's been changing for a hundred years. The deer and the antelope still play around pretty good, but the buffalo don't roam too far, and there's considerable disagreement about where the wild horses fit in."

"They have to be managed," she said. Even Ross had admitted to that necessity. "Some of them have to be culled, but no matter what the law says, some of the culled horses go for slaughter if they're not broke to ride."

"Sometimes even if they are. I've seen it happen plenty when the price is right." He shrugged. It occurred to her that he was wearing the same white shirt he'd had on last night. She remembered how bright it had looked in the moonlight, how unafraid he'd seemed, how quickly he'd moved once he'd seen the horse's plight. She wondered where he'd slept last night after he'd refused the bed she'd offered him. In his pickup? "But I ain't a horse trader," he was saying. "All I do is train 'em."

"Have you worked with mustangs? As a trainer, I mean."

"Yes, ma'am, I have."

"Many of them make wonderful saddle horses."

"Some of them do."

"And I'm sure that's what Ross had in mind for you."

"He talked about . . ." He looked up at the ceiling, chuckled a little and shook his head, as though he'd spied a gremlin in the rafters. "Well, it doesn't matter much now. Cut the dream loose. That's a good way to put it." He shoved away from the saddle and walked toward the door.

"By the way, I ain't no *ma'am*," she drawled, following with, "no matter what my sister says."

"There you go." He turned, approving her parody with a grin. "Did I tell you, I spotted that break in the fence on my grand tour? I ought to take a ride out that way and have a closer look."

"I guess fixing fences will be part of your job."

"Mainly, I want to make sure that buckskin wasn't worse off than I thought."

"I was going to tell . . ." So she'd said, but she should have done it sooner. Then she reminded herself that he was the one working for her. Or for her grandmother, which was now—and this really took some reminding—the same as working for her. "This is a cattle ranch. You do understand that the cattle are the main concern."

"When you hire on as a ranch hand, you understand that you'll do what needs to be done." He bent to pick up his duffel bag, came up with a little frown. "You don't run sheep, do you?"

"We used to, but when Ross took over, he said no way was he raising sheep."

"That's good news." He tossed the bag into the closet. "Going back to punchin' cows is one thing, but a man's got his pride."

"So you've said. Aren't you going to unpack?"

"What's 'unpack'? The gear's now stowed." He peeked into the bathroom, gave a nod as though some small requirement had been satisfied. The towels she'd left on the shelf, maybe, or the shower itself. "How long was your brother sick?" he asked.

"Not very long, really. Well, I don't think he'd been sick long. He always worked so hard, even though he was always . . ." She thought about the week she'd spent at the ranch during the past summer. Ross had looked a little thinner, but he hadn't said anything about being sick. He was always taking medication for his asthma, so she hadn't thought anything of a few pills. "The truth is, I don't know.

I should, but I don't. He didn't talk about it.''

"If he didn't want you to worry about it, I expect you'd be doing him a favor by leaving it at that, remembering him as a guy who worked hard and didn't complain. That's the kind of guy you don't mind ridin' for.

"Now me, I'm an easy keeper, especially if I'm ridin' for a woman. Ridin' for three women, I'm triple easy. Just give me three squares a day, a roof over my head at night, and put a good saddle horse under me.''

"I'm afraid ours aren't going to be up to your standards.''

"I ain't one for checkin' pedigrees. I value a horse by how much try she shows me. How much heart.'' He walked over to her, and she realized she'd been standing there next to the door like a dolt, glued to the floor, just watching the way he moved. "You wanna show me what you've got?''

She saw the teasing in his eyes, and it made her feel a giddiness she hoped didn't show. "I've got a few years on you, cowboy, so put a sock in it.''

"I assure you, ma'am, that isn't necessary.''

She gave him what one of the kids she'd worked with recently had called her Mother Superior look.

"Would you just relax?'' He laid a hand on her shoulder, let it slip down her arm. When he smiled, she realized the look in her eyes had probably softened, maybe even gone shy. "I ain't lookin' to check your teeth, either.''

"If you did, you'd get bitten.''

"Wouldn't be the first time.'' He tucked his hands into his back pockets. "This roof is just fine. You show me a horse, call me when it's time for chow, and I'll start lookin' after whatever you've got. Whatever needs lookin' after.''

6

He followed her along the path above the creek that led to the horse barn. A meadowlark called to them from the rail fence that bordered the little pasture where a chestnut mare grazed near her fawn-colored foal. Julia was telling him how Ross had sold several saddle horses and broodmares last winter, cut way back, and they were down to just a handful, as though apologizing in advance for what he'd have to ride.

K.C. listened politely, frankly hoping for a green mount with a few rough edges that needed his particular attention anyway. Give him something worth doing during the day while he checked the lady's cows and mended her fences. He slid the bar on the big red doors and swung them open. She showed him the tack room first, well supplied with Western saddles arranged on their wall pegs and racks, a variety of bridles and halters hanging in neat rows. She told him she had straightened up in here weeks ago, and he allowed that he appreciated an orderly tack room, and he'd be sure and keep it that way.

She reached for a blue nylon headstall as she pointed to a blue saddle blanket and a black saddle. "Grab those if you want to feel useful, and I'll just show you what we've got."

She marched down the plank floor between the rows of mostly empty stalls with new purpose. He watched her glide though a dusty shaft of sunlight admitted by the window in the gambrel peak, then into the shadows, straight to the last box stall. The horse's name was emblazoned on the door, blue on white. A mottled white face greeted the woman with ears pricked and cocked forward. She stepped into the stall, baby-talking the mare in a voice that began to quiver around the edges. She took a deep breath. For a moment he thought she was going to let go again, but she didn't. Instead she comforted the horse, stroking her neck and pulling bits of straw from her mane. The mare was all the while looking at him from her stall, sizing him up.

"Ross talked about breeding her this spring. He'd even picked out a mate for her." She led the frost-faced black mare from the stall and cross-tied her. "Now I guess I'm just as glad she's not bred. Would you like to try her out?"

Her smile was so sad it made his chest ache. She looked like the little girl who was offering him her last puppy. But he said he sure would, and he helped her dust the sleek Arabian mare off with a brush and saddle her. She'd obviously enjoyed some pampering but not a lot of riding in recent months. She balked at taking the bit, but he talked her into it, and when he led her outside, the sunshine showed off her flashy coloring.

She had a little winter hair yet to shed from her mostly black coat. Her frosty roan face blended into black cheeks and throatlatch, and she had plenty of white chrome setting off her black hooves and blended into her silky two-toned mane and tail. K.C. had always favored Quarter Horses for versatility, but this Arab, if she turned out to be a lady, just might change his tune.

He took the time to rub her chest and neck, let her snuffle around his hands and check him out a little before he swung into the saddle and pranced her around the corral. She had a nice feel and plenty of spirit, but she was slow to respond to his signals. "She's a fine horse," he announced, "but she does need some work."

"She does not," Julia protested, shading her eyes with her hand as she squinted up at him from the ground. "That's Ross's favorite horse. He rode her all the time, until just lately."

"Like I said, she needs work." He adjusted his hat, indicating his final word on the matter. "Which is why people hire me, Julia. I'm a contract rider. I don't get sentimental over horses, don't even own one myself. But I get along with them pretty good, and I can put a nice handle on them."

"Well, I'm sure he had other horses in mind when he asked you to come to work here." She hovered close to his knee as she rubbed the mare's neck, again consoling her. "This was Ross's horse. A one-man horse, really."

"You mean like in the movies?" He leaned to the side to speak to the horse. "You gonna try to buck me off, Silver Girl?" The jaunty ears dismissed the idea, beneath her dignity. "Guess not. Fickle female."

"Her name is Columbine."

He laughed. "What kind of a name is that for a horse?"

"It's perfect for her. It's a wildflower with kind of a light face." She held up curved hands like blinders next to her flashy brown eyes. Suddenly she was all sunshine, like a black-eyed Susan. "And then they have blue bodies. Up in the mountains they get really blue. I thought of the name myself."

"Don't Arabs usually have Arabian-sounding—"

"I'm giving you the prettiest horse here, and her name is Columbine."

"And it's a beauty of a name, too," he said, sliding his hand within a fraction of an inch of where hers lay on the mare's neck. "It's your turn, Julia. Take a ride with me. I want the grand tour this time."

She tipped her head up to him. A breeze obliged her by sweeping her hair back from her face. "If you think I'm taking any kind of turns with my sister, you're sadly mistaken."

"The oldest is used to going first. The youngest gets left behind."

"Ah, you've commiserated with her already," she said airily. "Which one are you?"

"I'm a well-adjusted orphan child, darlin'. First, last and only." He leaned back with a cocky smile. "Show and tell, Julia. Show me the real High Horse, and tell me whatever history you think I oughta know while I satisfy myself that

that buckskin was able to hightail it back to the mountains.''

She checked her watch. "We'll start by introducing you to Vernon and Shep." And before he could say something smart, she explained, "Your crew."

They saddled a bay gelding she called Sky, which K.C. allowed was a nice, simple name. "Sky Pilot," she informed him, "is another mountain wildflower."

"I take it you named him, too."

"I did. I was always in charge of names."

"And a fine job you've done, right, Columbine?" He rode up to a basket-handle gate latch, flipped it open, gave the gate a push and finished with an "after-you" gesture.

"Except for the mustangs, but I'm sure Ross had a name for every one."

The mare wouldn't let him close the gate from her back on the first try, but he circled her around twice and talked her into cooperating. They crossed the bridge and trotted into the sun for half a mile or more.

He watched the way the late-afternoon sun caused a riot of deep reds and golds to flash in Julia's dark brown hair. He hung back half a length just so he could watch the flow of her movement, but when he spotted the dust wake of a vehicle, he moved to her side.

Chuck Pollak, Julia told him without enthusiasm. From the hill above the road, Pollak's silver pickup looked like a missile bearing down on the High Horse. They converged, pickup and riders, at the side of the gravel road. Pollak braced an arm over the steering wheel as though he was still lining up a shot, stuck his rubicund face out the window and gave a taciturn nod.

"Hello, Chuck," Julia said. "What brings you out this way?"

"Well, I've come to have a talk with Sally about what to do with these damned horses that are trying to take over the whole goddamn country. They're like women, I guess." He gave a dry laugh. "Can't live with 'em, can't shoot 'em."

Julia lifted her hair off her forehead, then let the wind

take it from her hand. "I'm glad to see you're not armed, Chuck."

"Nope." He raised his palms toward the windshield. "Just came over for a peaceful parley. I got some horses penned up over at my place that I think belong to you folks. They were raisin' hell with my mares. They're wilder'n hell. Some of your Painted Mountain breed. Don't know what good they'll ever be or what you'd ever do with them."

"Well, obviously Ross's plans for them have been suspended."

The palms went up again. "Like I said, I'm just trying to help out, any way I can."

"I appreciate that."

"I'd load 'em up and bring 'em over, but like I said, they'd bust the trailer apart. One's wire-cut pretty bad. I'm thinking you'll probably be gettin' rid of them soon . . ."

"A big buckskin?" K.C. asked. He remembered the man from the bar. Pollak was trying to size him up and chat with Julia at the same time. His squinty sidelong appraisal came off as contemptuous, but K.C. realized he had all the advantages of a man sitting tall in the saddle with his back to the sun.

"Seen you last night, but I don't believe I've had the pleasure."

Julia started in with an introduction, but K.C. swung down from his mount and took care of the matter himself with a handshake. "K.C.'s working for us," she put in from above.

"Is that a fact?" Pollak rubbed a thumb over his bristly chin. "K.C. Houston. Seems like I've heard that name."

"K.C.'s a horse trainer."

"That's what I was thinking." Pollak's scowl deepened. "What would you be wantin' with a horse—"

"So how many horses are we talking about, Chuck?"

"Six. Yeah, there's a buckskin got himself hung up in some wire, looks like. You ask me, they're about as useless as a pack of coyotes, but you might find a buyer for two or three of them. I could call up a guy I know . . ."

"I'll get the horses moved," K.C. said with a nod to Julia. "If that's okay with you."

"How soon?" Chuck clearly figured he had a man's ear now.

K.C. adjusted his hat. "Well, I'll tell you what, Chuck. I just now hired on. And you just offered to help the Weslins out any way you can. How soon does that offer expire?"

"It doesn't expire. That's exactly what I'm trying to do here. We've been neighbors, good neighbors, and, what the hell, I'm always willing to—" Pollak finally cut the stammering and looked at Julia. "Whenever you say."

"That's kind of you, Chuck," she said. "I appreciate that. As you know, Ross was devoted to those horses, and right now all I can think about is . . ."

"I understand, Miz Weslin. You've got a lot to deal with right now. I'll be glad to keep the horses penned up until you can move 'em. I don't mind throwin' 'em some hay. But that one that's cut up?" He wagged his head slowly. "Nobody's gonna get close enough to do anything for him, I can tell you that."

"We'll see to him." K.C. remounted, then turned to Julia. "All you gotta do is say when and show me where."

"Sounds like you got yourself a real cowboy, Miz Weslin. Tell you what, they're hard to find these days."

The rustic cabin stood, like the gatehouse for a great manor, within a quarter mile of the entry to the ranch. Two black-and-white Border collies came running over, barking only to greet them and to announce their approach. Two wiry, leather-faced men ambled out to the front yard to investigate. The smaller man with the slight limp, Shep Simonson, came through the front door smiling, while Vernon Clay, who'd been chopping firewood in the backyard, rounded the corner of the house looking pretty perturbed until he saw that it was Julia who'd come calling. He set his ax on the cable spool serving as a workbench, dusted his hands on the seat of his jeans and waited his turn to shake hands with the newcomer.

"The boy mentioned you," Shep was saying as he vigorously pumped K.C.'s hand. "More than once, he said he had a line on a real specialist. Guy who can put the spur to them colts and show 'em who's boss from the start, but, hell, I didn't think there was much chance in him gettin' a guy like that to come."

"I'm not much of a bronc rider. Don't own a pair of spurs."

Shep shoved his hands in the back pockets of his oil-stained jeans, tipped his head way back and grinned. "I got some I can let you have dirt cheap."

"You ain't gonna sell him none of that damn rusted-up, bent-up, broken-up old junk you got hangin' in there on the wall." Vernon tapped Shep as he reached past his shoulder for K.C.'s handshake.

"How's he gonna buck them mustangs out without a good pair of spurs?" Shep looked wounded. "Ain't rusted up, neither. There's collectors who'd pay top dollar for some of them spurs I got in there. They say there's people out East who'll buy anything Western."

"Does K.C. look like he comes from out East?"

"You're treading on some thin ice now, Vernon." Julia was busy giving the dogs their required head-scratchings.

"Hell, Queenie, I remember the day you was born. Don't matter where you've been nor how many sheepskins you got tucked away, you and your brother, you've always been Weslins. 'Course, that little sister of yours, she's her mama's girl. Not that your mama ain't a fine woman, mind you, but—"

"She gets your drift, Vern." Shep returned the warning tap, but he had to settle for the tall man's arm. "You still hiring on to work them wild colts?"

"I've hired on," K.C. said, glancing at Julia. "The boss hasn't told me exactly what she's got in mind for me."

"Vernon and Shep know this place as well as Sally does."

"Not quite," Vernon said quietly, smoothing his voluminous gray mustache with his knuckle.

Shep rocked back on his boot heels. "Nope, nope, nope, not quite, not quite as good as the judge."

"But pretty darn good, and we'll be counting on you to

help us break Mr. Houston in as . . ." Julia glanced at K.C. "Foreman."

They'd exchanged more of these looks than concrete details, and this one took him by surprise. "Foreman?"

"Well, now, that will be an honor, ma'am. And just let me say . . ."

"I don't know what we're going to do about the place, Shep. I have to be honest with you. But the operation can't just come to a screeching halt now, can it?" She glanced from the short old codger back to the tall one as she ruffled one of the dogs' silky ears. "Right, Vernon?"

"No, ma'am, it surely can't."

"So however Gramma managed to coax, cajole or just plain . . ."

"Charm," K.C. supplied. "She charmed the socks off me."

"Yep, yep, yep." Shep cackled. "She'll do that, won't she?"

"Yep, yep, yep," Vernon mocked. "You sound like a hoarse coyote."

"What in tarnation is a *horse coyote*?"

"An old dog that couldn't get—"

K.C. folded his arms across his chest and grinned. He'd worked with a lot of Sheps and Verns over the years. They were the backbone of the working ranch, and they were a dying breed. "You boys must know something about the colts Ross had in mind when he asked me to come to work for him."

"Well, yes, I expect we do," Shep allowed, drilling his sidekick with a sideways scowl. "I expect we do."

"Uh-huh. Well, I expect you'll point 'em out to me, just out of curiosity."

"I think branding will be first up on the agenda." Julia straightened. One of the collies had wandered away, but the other was planted at her feet in a ready sit, hoping for more attention. "After we collect the horses Chuck Pollak has penned up over at his place."

Both men came to attention, both craggy faces compressed in disgust.

"I told you that was his pickup," Vernon muttered.

"He come over here lookin' for trouble? He thinks he's gonna take him a bite off the High Horse, well . . ."

"Well, the High Horse ain't carrion for the likes of that old buzzard," Vernon finished.

"Carryin' . . ." Shep puzzled over the word. "Where would we be carryin' Pollak?"

"*Carrion*," Vernon shouted. "Dead meat. Buzzard bait." He turned to K.C., checking his tone. "You gotta be patient with him, Mr. Houston. Limited vocabulary. Long on useless old junk, short on brains."

"The name's K.C. And you can probably give me some vocabulary lessons, too, Vern. Words make an interesting hobby."

"Well, he's got plenty of them," Shep grumbled. "Thinks he's Jesse Jackson Shakespeare, or some damn . . ."

"Just like perfectly good old stuff that nobody appreciates anymore," K.C. said with a nod to Shep.

Shep's face lit up like Christmas. "Hell, you go to that little museum they got over in Ten Sleep. I got one of them mangles, like they used to use for doin' laundry. It's just like the one they got over there." He turned to Julia. "And that museum in Meteesee? I give them some stuff I had, just straight out."

"Hardly made a dent in his hoard," Vernon grumbled.

"Well, I had a few duplicates." Shep was rocking back and forth now, energized, full of himself and his treasures. "You wanna come on in and take a look? You see somethin' you like, it's yours." His gnarled hand sliced through the air. "Straight out, it's yours."

"We got time to take a look, boss lady?" K.C. would gladly have given the old cowboy what was left of the day.

"We have time for a quick peek. Shep's collection requires a whole afternoon to fully appreciate. Preferably a rainy one."

"It requires a whole damn fortnight," Vernon muttered, bringing up the rear as they all trooped into the cabin.

"He always talks like that." Shep backed out of the way to let his guests into the cabin. It was like diving into a cave, so dark and rustic was the interior. Shep, the doorman, went after Vernon as the tall man ducked inside. "Take your nose out of them books once in a while, you might know something about how real people talk. Nobody knows what a—"

Eyes afire, Vernon speared a finger at K.C. "You know what a fortnight is?" One nod down, he wheeled on Julia. "You know what a fortnight is?" Another nod, and he completed the circle, his finger inches from Shep's nose. "See there?"

Shep jacked his jaw up and down a couple of times, glaring at Vernon's back, finally muttering something about two-dollar words. Vernon was on his way to what was clearly his half of the cabin's multipurpose main room, where the bed beneath the window was neatly made, the chair next to the lamp table devoid of cast-off clothing, the shelves carefully arranged with books. The space was as orderly as a lifer's niche in an army barracks.

The other side of the cabin looked like the back room of a pawn shop. There was stuff everywhere—in boxes, on rickety old tables, hanging from the ceiling, the walls— there were kitchen gadgets, toys, ice skates, crocks, baskets, boots, snowshoes, appliances, horse gear, even an old hospital bedpan. And in the middle of it all, a rumpled bed.

K.C. looked at Julia. She shrugged, smiled, her eyes alight with the affection she felt for these two old men. His throat went dry as he watched her turn her attention to a tangle of tin egg beaters.

"Let's have a look at those spurs, Shep."

Shep shoved an old pop crate under K.C.'s nose, and they picked through the collection together. Some of the spurs were singles, he conceded, and some had belonged to cowboys he'd worked with, so even if they were broken, he admitted to harboring some sentimental attachment to a few of them.

At the bottom of the box K.C. found a small pair of silver spurs, bound together with a leather thong. "I've seen some just like this," he told Shep as he spun one of the little rowels. He'd had a pair, in fact, kept them rolled up in a sock in the back of his locker in one of the dorms he'd been consigned to when he was a kid. But a matron had found them during an inspection. She'd taken them away, declared them sharp objects. The boys at Texas Youth Correctional weren't permitted to keep sharp objects. He never saw his mother's spurs again.

"That there's a lady's spur," Shep was saying, poking at the shank with an oil-encrusted finger. "See the little flowers engraved here?"

"Hers didn't have any engraving," K.C. said absently.

"You like those? You're sure welcome to them."

K.C. drew himself back from where he'd gone drifting and immediately sensed Julia's notice. He put the spurs back into the box. "No, thanks, Shep. I wouldn't have any use for them. Tell you what I could use, though." He took a quick survey. "You got an extra radio that works?"

"Have I got a radio!"

"Has he got a radio," echoed from Vernon's section.

"Lemme see, now, I got a dandy over here I fixed up myself." Shep plunged directly into a select pile and soon backed out, carefully wrapping the cord around an avocado-green model. "Works fine. She'll pull in two, three stations out here without an antenna. No static or nothin'." K.C. started to reach for his billfold. "No, no, now, I want you to have it, Mr. Houston. This is just my way of saying . . ." Shep placed the radio in K.C.'s hands with great ceremony. "Welcome to the High Horse."

"I'll put it to good use, too, if you're sure you wanna part with it. Hell, this has gotta be worth . . ." K.C. knew how important it was to offer some appraisal, to admire the plastic box from all angles. "A pretty penny, I'd say."

"Don't you worry about that. She's all yours." Shep did the flat-hand gesture. "Straight out. Next time maybe we'll swap."

K.C. nodded. "You like doin' a little horse tradin' once in a while?"

Vernon groaned.

"Well, maybe once in a while."

Redoubled groaning issued from the corner.

Shep's eyes sparkled as he jerked a thumb over his shoulder. "He don't generally make a sound without words attached. Must be somethin' he et."

K.C. wandered over to Vernon's side, drawn to the bookshelves. He tucked his new radio in the crook of his elbow while he read the titles. Vernon was rich with K.C.'s kind of reading material. He pulled out a hardcover copy of Zane Grey's *Riders of the Purple Sage*.

"You wanna read that?" Vernon asked. "You can sure borrow it."

K.C. opened the book and smiled when he saw the familiar names. "I've probably read it twenty times or more. It's one of my favorites."

"So you've got your own copy."

"Oh, yeah." He slid the book back into its slot and scanned down the shelf. "I see some I don't have, though."

Vernon's bony knees cracked as he stood up from the bed. His shadow fell over the spines of the books. "Take anything you like."

K.C. pulled out a copy of an Oakley Hall novel he didn't think he'd read. "You mind? I'll get it back to you in two, three days."

"Take your time. Take two." He reached over K.C.'s head and pulled out a newer paperback. "This one's a real ripsnorter, if you like a little bit of a mystery on the side."

Shep came up with a paper bag, which K.C. tied to his saddle as he described the broken wire gate and the equipment he'd be needing first thing in the morning to transport the horses Pollak was holding. It was decided that Vernon would repair the gate. Shep would help with the horses.

"You just made yourself two friends for life, and it took you less than thirty minutes," Julia said as they rode away. "Pretty impressive."

He flashed her a smile. She looked pleased, and he felt good about that because he wanted to please her. They were riding side by side at an easy trot.

"A word to the wise. Don't break the spine on Vernon's books."

"Gotcha."

"Do you really intend to read them?" she asked. His smile dimmed. He reined in his horse with a subtle signal, cutting her off and forcing them both to a halt. She met his gaze, then shrugged. "Just curious."

The mare pivoted, and he urged her close to the gelding, so that he and the lady were knee to knee. "Without even using my finger." But he lifted a finger, leaned closer, laid it on her lips and said quietly, "Without *even* moving my lips."

He wanted to turn and ride away, as far as he could get, before he started turning himself inside out for this woman. Worse than that, he wanted to grab her face and kiss her hard. But he did neither. He simply looked, then, slowly, smiled. And she didn't laugh at his joke until he did.

7

*T*he High Horse and the Lazy P had been muscling
up against each other for nearly thirty years. They were like
two stone rams standing head to head, each challenging the
other to be the one to try to cross the river first. Julia particularly liked the ram image because it reminded her of
the picture of her great-grandfather that hung over the buffet in the dining room. Edward Harris—"old goat's
beard," she'd once called him—had owned the entire valley at the turn of the century, but the boundaries had
changed considerably over the years. Each chapter in the
family history was marked by a changing of boundaries.

Vivid mental pictures of the whole sequence lived in
Julia's mind, complete with maps, for she was the designated keeper of Gramma's stories. Edward's sons had split
their holdings into several ranches, all part of one family
company, which had prospered until beef prices dropped
after the First World War. Then Henry Harris, Sally's father, had overextended himself by trying to buy his brothers
out. In the years that followed, Sally had watched her father
break his heart over each piece of the High Horse that he
had to cut loose.

The northernmost section, which Edward had dubbed
The 86, had changed hands four times before Chuck Pollak
had finally made a go of it. Pollak's Lazy P had grown
over the years, spilling across Quicksilver Highway to the
east, gobbling up chunks of the basin between the Bighorn

and the Absaroka mountains. But the High Horse, which bounded the Lazy P to the south, also slipped a long arm around Pollak's back to the west, hooking over his head with its leases and its grazing permits in the mountains. Pollak's summer pasture was some forty miles north of his place. Painted Mountain would have been so much closer, so much more convenient for the Lazy P.

The mountain loomed pale blue and white, like a reflection of the bright blue morning sky. It dominated the range, the hulking mother of the surrounding cluster of lesser peaks. Julia felt it hovering over her as she drove the big white High Horse pickup and gooseneck stock trailer through the wire gate K.C. had just stretched aside. All that grazing land, she thought, so full of her family's roots and so close to the Lazy P. Pollak's silver pickup was parked next to the corral, and she wondered whether he was sitting there looking up at the mountain and grinding his teeth. Or maybe he was salivating.

Over the years he'd made a few offers to buy land, trade permits, swap, share, wheel and deal. Ross would have none of it, and Sally had supported his stand even when she knew that Ross wasn't always thinking about productivity. His heart was full of horses. Meanwhile, Pollak had filed one petition after another, complaining about the wild horse herd, but he continued to tip his hat and go through all the motions of being neighborly. Can't blame a guy for trying, Sally always said. On the contrary, you ought to expect it of him.

Julia offered K.C. a smile, and he nodded as she drove through the gate, leaving him to hop in with Shep, who was following behind with a second trailer containing the portable panels they would use to work the horses into the stock trailer. K.C. had said little on the short drive over. She'd offered to let him drive, but instead he'd turned the radio on, slid down in the passenger's seat and pulled his hat down until the brim nearly rested on his nose, and let some Patsy Cline wannabe yodel him to sleep. Shep had still been talking the poor man's ear off when they'd left the house after supper last night.

Julia turned the radio off now as she approached the

weathered six-foot-high corral. The six horses huddled together in a tight pack in the far corner looked scared
enough. She rolled her window down and said hello to
Chuck and his squinty, pooch-bellied son, Cal, but she
wasn't eager to get out of the pickup. Not until she heard
the doors of Shep's pickup whap shut and saw her own two
men amble over to parley with the host.

The four men bellied up to the corral rail. The horses
packed together tighter, nostrils flaring. The men backed
away, four hat brims taking turns bobbing as they cooked
up a plan Julia wasn't ready to get in on yet. It wasn't just
her being a woman that made her feel marginal. It was
being a visitor in her own home. It was owning a ranch
and not being a rancher.

She climbed up on the bottom rail of the old corral and
hooked her elbows over the top one. The windmill above
the stock tank creaked. Water dribbled from the spigot into
the brimming tank, creating ripples that sparkled in the
morning sun. A magpie swooped down, helped itself to a
drink, then sailed away.

The horses would have gone that way, too, or any way.
Every sense was alert, every muscle ready. All they needed
was an opening. There were two sorrels, one mostly white
roan, a blue roan, the big buckskin with the wire cuts on
his front legs, and a small black-and-white paint who
seemed determined to wedge himself under the larger sorrel's nose.

"I like that buckskin," K.C. said as he climbed up the
rails beside her. "But those wire cuts are sure to get us off
to a bad start, him and me."

"Are you planning a relationship?"

"I just made a bet with your neighbors. Said I'd ride that
one by Independence Day." Cal Pollak was helping Shep
unload the corral panels while Chuck offered a random
hand and plenty of advice. "Chances are we'll be able to
run them right into the trailer, no problem. But I want you
to stay put right here, if you wouldn't mind."

She was inclined to put up an argument, just on principle,
except that he made his request sound so heartfelt. The look
in his eyes actually said, Please. "I'd like to help," she

said. "They're trapped. What could they do?"

"Every once in a while you get one that would sooner go off a cliff than give up his freedom." Arms resting on the top rail, they both watched the horses, who, in turn, watched them. "Now, these guys have been penned up a little while, and ol' Chuck's supplied room service. He says he thinks one or two sampled the hay he left for them, which is a surprise. But you never know."

"They're not dangerous. They're just scared."

"They're wild." He turned to her, a canny smile in his eyes. "They're not flowers, Julia. They're not like your sweet Columbine and Sky Pilot."

"More like Thunder and Lightning?"

"We'll see." He adjusted his hat against the sun. "They're all fairly young studs. I think what we've got here is a little bachelor band. Stallions that have been chased off by the dominant stallion often form their own band. They'll kinda tag along after the herd. It's unusual for them to stray too far."

"I told you why they were here."

He nodded. He wasn't going to dispute her theory about the horses paying their respects, and she appreciated that, probably more than he knew. She cherished few illusions, and this one gave her particular comfort, like a memorial she'd erected herself.

"Cal said he got lucky trapping them in a washout this morning and running them in," K.C. said.

She heard the skepticism in his voice. "They must have been exhausted."

"I'd say so. Cal don't know nothin' about no midnight ATV rider." He nodded in Cal's direction. "His words. Asked him if there wasn't some kinda law around here about harassing wild animals with motorized vehicles, but he didn't know about that, either. Must have been kids, he said. If that's true, seems like the sheriff has a job to do or somebody's sure to be burying a kid real soon."

"But you don't think it was kids."

He shrugged, his eyes, blue and clear as lake water, intent on the horses.

"They're beautiful, aren't they?"

"I like the two sorrels and the blue roan all right." He smiled wistfully, some vision dancing in his eyes. "But that buckskin, I bet he'd carry you to the top of that mountain without breaking a sweat." He glanced at her. "Once he got to know you pretty good."

He gave her a deliciously brash smile, full of wild promises. He could tame lightning and thunder, and he might be willing to do it just for her once he got to know her. She had both a weakness and a loathing for grand promises made by men who smiled at her that way. She took a deep breath and warned her heart to take it easy, stay put, stay the steady course. But damn, if she didn't have to drag it back from following after him as she watched him walk away.

K.C. backed the stock trailer into the smaller of the two corral gates and assigned Shep to be the doorman. Then he and the Pollaks used the portable metal panels to build an alley along one side of the pen, leading to the open gate and the stock trailer. Cal and Chuck were then given hazing stations.

K.C. approached the horses, talking to them quietly. They started shuffling around, sizing him up, looking for a way out. The injured buckskin made the first move, skittering down the makeshift alley. K.C. closed in, convincing the smaller sorrel and the two roans to follow the buckskin. With a little coaxing, all four clamored aboard the trailer.

But the paint had turned the other way, slipping behind K.C., who was intent on the majority. He glanced back, realized that he wasn't going to get the other two on this try and signaled for Shep to close the door on their catch. Meanwhile, the little black horse snorted, squealed, abruptly darted across the corral, heading straight for Julia.

She watched, fully anticipating a reversal, an instant change of direction at the barrier. She stared, stunned, as the paint careened headlong into the rails. She jumped back just before the impact, the vibration shimmying through her from the ground up. Two wooden rails cracked, but the fence held.

The horse shrieked. The Pollaks began shouting and

waving their arms like a couple of mechanical toys gone berserk.

But the tone of K.C.'s voice did not change, nor did he retreat from his position between the big sorrel and the paint. "Whoa, now," he said, and added in the same calm voice, "You guys—Chuck, Cal—just back off now, and keep your heads."

The paint was dazed, whinnying pathetically, and then the sorrel got into the act, whinnying and pacing along the fence. The paint wheeled, reared and pawed the air, crying like a child begging to be lifted from a playpen.

"That one's crazy," Cal shouted as he grabbed at his father's shoulder. "That one's a goddamn man-killer."

The sorrel squealed and bolted from the corner. Cal hit the corral rails and scrabbled up to the top. The senior Pollak turned, tripped, crashed to his knees, lost his hat, then his dignity. He raised his arms over his head and howled like a whipped dog as the big sorrel sideswiped him. K.C. stepped between the stallion and the crumpled man. Without taking his eyes off the sorrel, he quietly warned Pollak to calm down and get the hell out of the way.

The paint came down staggering like a boxer who'd taken a blow to the gut, but he plunged a second time, straight for the fence. Julia saw the hurt coming again, saw the terror in those cloudy blue eyes, started to wave him back, and then it hit her. The paint couldn't see.

Before she could say anything, a pickup door slammed. Cal Pollak was headed back into the fray, brandishing a rifle.

"That sonuvabitch is crazy. Look out, hey! I'm shootin' the crazy sonuvabitch."

"Jesus," K.C. breathed. "Put the gun down, Pollak. Open that . . ." He glanced at Shep, then at Julia, then back to Cal, who was bobbing and weaving, trying to decide whether to shoot from the shoulder or the hip. K.C. waved him back. "Get out of the way, for crissake. We're letting this one go."

"The hell you say!"

The poor little paint was battering himself, bouncing off the rails while the sorrel paced nearby, screaming like an outraged parent. In the middle of it all, K.C. sidled up to Cal and jerked the rifle away, leaving him confounded by his suddenly empty hands.

"Make yourself useful and open the drive-through gate," K.C. told Cal. He nodded toward the ten-foot panel. "This one goes free."

"Let him go in my pasture? He's a man-killer!"

"Oh, for God's sake, what kind of cheap horror flicks have you been watching?" He signaled to Julia to scale the fence. Shep was trying to draw the sorrel's attention, but his bum leg put a hitch in his stride. As soon as Julia was within reach, K.C. handed her the rifle with one hand while he shoved Cal in the direction of the gate with the other. "Let this animal go free. The only thing he's gonna kill is himself if you don't turn him loose."

"K.C., this horse can't see," Julia reported gently from her perch on the fence, but Cal was already complying with the order. Easing in close, talking to him quietly, K.C. touched the horse's flank. The paint jumped away and found his freedom through the open gate.

The pacing sorrel kept up with his panicky whinnying. "Shut the gate," K.C. ordered, "unless you want to lose this one."

"K.C., I think that horse is blind."

"Blind?" He pushed Cal out of his way and followed the paint through the gate, watching it closely as he latched it shut. Ears swiveling like radar antennae, the paint stumbled around in a circle, whimpering like a lost child. The sorrel whinnied. The paint whinnied back. "Damn, you might be right. I just thought he was glass-eyed," he said, referring to the horse's blue eyes.

"Close up, they look a little cloudy," Julia said. "But he couldn't see where he was going. I could see it in his eyes when he came toward me."

The sorrel whinnied. The paint whinnied back.

"You're not leaving no blind stud loose in my pasture," Chuck protested from his perch on the other side of the corral.

Head held high, nostrils quivering, the paint pranced in a tight circle like a circus horse. K.C. signaled for surcease of commotion. He stayed close to the fence, talking to the horse, who was all ears, attuned to every sound.

"I don't think this horse is going anywhere by himself, Pollak. Shep?"

"Yo," from the gateman.

"Can you take that load back and bring me an empty trailer?" K.C. was still intent on the paint.

"I can turn them loose in the horse pasture."

Cal found his voice. "You're not leaving that blind horse."

"I wouldn't leave him out here alone, Pollak. He depends on the herd. He'd die here." The whinnying continued, sorrel to paint, paint to sorrel. K.C. smiled. "He'll stay close as long as the sorrel keeps talking to him."

"What good is a blind horse? Best thing you could do is shoot him. Hell, you'd shoot him if he busted a leg."

"Damn, you sure are hung up on those old Westerns, aren't you, Cal?" K.C. chuckled, sparing a glance toward the black cowboy hat on the other side of the fence. "If he busted a leg, I'd call a vet."

"You can't just shoot a wild horse, Cal." Julia cradled the rifle, feeling a little like Annie Oakley sitting up there on top of the fence. Her side was in charge. "Your dad can tell you that."

"You're damn straight about that," Chuck allowed. "They've got more protection than the First Lady's jewels."

Shep started in with a quiet laugh. K.C. chuckled, too, then Cal, nodding, displacing a little gravel with the toe of his boot. A long moment passed. Tension subsided. Nobody moved too much. The two horses riveted their attention on each other, calling out persistently. The paint became more agitated when K.C. made the first move to withdraw, moving cautiously, signaling the others to follow suit. They gathered near the Pollaks' pickup. Julia returned Cal's rifle. Cal said nothing, just nodded as though he'd been the one to give it to her.

"Listen, Cal." K.C. stood between the two men. He was taller than both, so it was easy to lay a hand on each man's shoulder. "Chuck, we appreciate your help getting these horses loaded up. We couldn't have done it without you. Right, Julia?''

She nodded, eyeing him, a little dumbstruck by the *we*. But she liked being part of it.

''Now, what we're left with is a situation best handled without a lot of fuss, you know what I mean?'' He extricated himself from the Pollak bookends, looking over at the corral, making sure the paint was still there as he moved to stand next to Julia. ''You leave them to me. I'll have these last two out of your hair before the day's over.''

Chuck folded his arms over his stout belly. ''How do I know you won't just let them go? I don't want no blind stud in my pasture.''

''He'll be going home to the High Horse.'' The paint whinnied. K.C. smiled. ''Him and me, we've got some talking to do, and that'll take some time. You don't wanna wait around.''

The Pollaks were finally convinced to head on home. Julia wasn't sure whether it was K.C.'s politic persuasion or the warm sun almost directly overhead.

''You don't have to wait around, either,'' K.C. told Julia. ''Why don't you hop in with Shep?''

''And miss Dr. Doolittle at work?'' She gave him a saucy smile. ''I'll be very quiet, I promise.''

He glanced away, adjusted his hat in that nonplussed cowboy way of his, looked down at the toes of his boots, finally looked up and grinned. ''If you don't run along, there won't be any presents under the tree.''

She smiled back. ''What are you going to do?''

''Nothing much. Just talk.'' Shep was already pulling out slowly, stock trailer in tow. K.C. gave him a high sign.

''About what?''

''Nothing that would interest you, just—'' He stuck his thumbs in his belt and shrugged, grinning. ''You know, stud talk.''

She groaned as the pickup rolled up beside her. He opened the door for her and she climbed in, but she leaned out the window and smiled as the pickup started rolling away. ''What makes you think I wouldn't be interested?''

He returned her direct look with one of his own, topped

off with a knowing smile. She watched him in the side mirror, standing there, getting smaller. She felt like a schoolgirl. The only place she wanted to be right now was back there on that sage-and-greasewood flat, suspended from the corral rails, watching that cowboy work his magic on a scared, sightless mustang.

Releasing the four wild horses in the little pasture adjacent to the horse barn was easier than loading them up. Ross had built this pasture, with its six-foot fences, to accommodate his wild horses. Shep thought he'd get Vern to ride along with him, back out to collect their new man. On an impulse, Julia reclaimed the passenger's seat.

Shep gave her a curious look. "You wanna play pretty-bird-on-the-wire some more, Queenie?"

"Let's stop by the house," she said. "I thought I'd bring him some lunch."

"He's comin' right back."

"What if it takes a while? Like all afternoon."

"You gonna watch him?" Shep's glance skittered past her as he downshifted to swing around the metal pipe that formed the cattle guard. "All afternoon?"

"Maybe," she allowed, and Shep chuckled. "I just want to make sure he gets something to eat." It was hard to keep a straight face with Shep cackling, but because he was having so much fun, she managed. "Well, that is my responsibility, as the . . ."

"Boss lady?"

"The boss lady's granddaughter." A white curtain moved in the window of the big house, and a face appeared. "One of her granddaughters," she amended.

It was Dawn who made the lunch. She never ate much, but mention of preparing food always stirred her imagination. She was a magician in the kitchen. When she found out why Julia was rummaging through the refrigerator, she knew exactly what would make a lovely tailgate picnic, and she put it together in a flash. Leftovers from last night's fajitas were the foundation for pita sandwiches. Within moments lunch was ready to go, and so was Dawn.

They found K.C. in the corral with both of the horses.

He had removed a couple of panels from the alley and maneuvered the pair into a smaller crowding pen, where they stood quietly. He said they'd been "chatting some."

"And here these girls thought we might be at this all day, so they brung us some chow," Shep said. He pulled the cooler out from behind the pickup seat and set it down in a patch of bristly bunchgrass and stubby new sage.

K.C. thought lunch was a fine idea, and he allowed himself to be served on the shady side of the stock trailer. Dawn had made sandwiches with and without sprouts. He said he'd try the latter. The bread looked funny but tasted fine, he said, and Dawn popped a soft drink open for him while she asked a host of questions Julia knew he couldn't possibly have the answers to, like how the horse went blind and why it wasn't dead. He entertained her with fairy tales—the paint was probably cursed or protected by an enchantment of some kind—and she made a big production of lapping them up.

Julia sat on the trailer's running board, pocketed her dark glasses and felt the cool breeze bathe her face while she sipped on a can of pop. She let Dawn handle the chitchat, said maybe five words all totaled. When K.C. praised the lunch they'd made, she took the high road. She credited her sister.

"I have a few little talents. Simple ones, like cooking," Dawn said as she lay a hand on Julia's shoulder. Julia looked up at her, surprised by the gesture, even more surprised by the warmth in Dawn's crystalline eyes. "My big sister was always the brain in the family," Dawn was saying. "She has a master's degree, but she doesn't know how to make her bed. Which I did for you this morning, Julia, you're quite welcome." She measured an inch of air between her flawlessly manicured thumb and forefinger. "Julia's about this close to having her Ph.D. in—what, Julia? Sociology?"

"I'm not quite that close."

"She's a social worker," Dawn said.

It was a subject Julia didn't particularly want to think about right now, so it was without thinking that she reported, "I may be an unemployed social worker soon."

"Well, maybe you should think about getting back to work soon."

Julia shot her sister a warning glance.

"Julia has a very good job. An important job, working with needy families." Dawn's smile was for Julia. It shone in her eyes and seemed utterly genuine. "I've always been very, very proud of my big sister."

At once touched and discomfited, Julia stared at the hole in her pop can. She rarely discussed her academic achievements or her career with Dawn. Dawn had always been impressed by titles and salaries, and she'd once said she didn't see much difference between graduating and graduating with honors unless it meant more money, or a fancy title at the very least. So Julia rarely discussed anything other than family with her sister. She lifted her shoulder, just slightly, but it was enough to drive her sister's hand away. They shared a brief look, an unspoken question, an apologetic smile. The rare moment had passed.

"Frankly, I think I've gotten kind of burned out. Maybe I'll just go back to school full-time and finish that last little bit." Julia measured it the way Dawn had, between thumb and forefinger, sans manicure. "The dreaded dissertation."

"I dropped out of as many programs as Julia's completed, which is a lot. She's just so smart."

"I'm not *that* smart," Julia said, and then she laughed at her own defensiveness. "Okay, maybe I am. I like school." She glanced at K.C., inviting him to share with her. "I especially like books."

"Do you know, I think you caught that bug from Vern." Shep was busy sorting through the cans in the cooler for a second root beer. He'd already devoured his fill of sandwiches. "Ol' Vern, he's one for the books, all right. I remember him readin' to you. Ross wouldn't sit still for all that readin', but you'd crawl up in ol' Vern's lap whenever you caught him with a book. I guess you'd be about the only woman, alive or dead, can claim she's been allowed to sit in the lap of ol' Vernon Clay."

Julia smiled, remembering. "He sort of took over after Grampa died."

"Hell, you know why, don't you?" Shep grinned, surprised when Julia shook her head. "You don't know why?"

Again she shook her head, inviting the old cowboy to wax sentimental over his memories of her childhood.

He clucked his tongue, his gaze drifting to the striated red bluffs that bolstered the cloudless sky. "Well, it was just his way, is all. Fillin' in for Max whatever way he could. I told him, I said, 'There's other ways, Vern.' " He shook his head, chuckling. The sound of K.C. crumpling his pop can reeled the old man back, and he glanced at Julia as though to recover his bearings. " 'And anyhow,' I said to him, 'little kids don't read Westerns. You gotta read her them kids' books.' But you'd come down to the bunkhouse, and you'd start in. 'Whatcha readin', Vern?' And he'd just read you any ol' thing."

"*Riders of the Purple Sage*?" K.C. asked her.

"Oh, yes." She nodded, smiling. "Much better than the funny papers Grampa used to read to me."

"Which I wouldn't know, because I was too young to get in on any of this." Pouting, Dawn poured the last of her pop into the grass. "Which is probably why I became a dropout. Vernon never read to me."

"He never read to me, neither." Shep closed the cooler, muttering into his shirtfront as he fastened the latch. "Didn't stop me from listening, though."

The two horses clambered aboard the trailer without incident, the paint sticking close to the sorrel this time. K.C.'s easygoing manner allayed their fears, and his strategy left them only one direction, so in they went. The portable panels were reloaded into the smaller trailer. Shep started to hand K.C. the keys to the pickup with the stock trailer, but K.C. deflected the gesture Julia's way. "I'll ride shotgun with the ladies in case they blow a tire," he said.

Dawn sat in the middle, but, of course, she had to cozy up to K.C. because of the floor shift. And he had to put his arm around her. Julia kept her eyes glued to the two-lane blacktop, paying almost no attention to the conversation about Dawn's recipe for Texas barbecue and about her friend who had moved from Connecticut to Galveston and what did she encounter in her backyard the first week but some awful stinging ants. Fire ants, K.C. supposed, and he said he'd run into them himself now and again.

They unloaded the horses first, then Dawn. The silence, in the absence of her cheerful chatter, was deafening. K.C. got out to uncouple the gooseneck from the hitch in the pickup bed. Julia watched him in the side mirror as he hopped over the side of the pickup, jacked up the trailer and signaled for her to pull away. She didn't move.

"Whenever you're ready," he told her as he approached the pickup again. She watched him in the mirror. "Anything wrong?" he asked.

She peered up at him through her sunglasses. "I would still like to know how you got that paint into the corral."

"You would, huh?" He braced his arm on the roof of the pickup, cocked his shoulders and leaned in close. "If I tell all my secrets, I might be out of a job."

She adjusted her sunglasses. "Whatever the secret is, it probably requires the hands of a master."

"That's true." With his free hand he took her sunglasses off, smiling when he could see her eyes. "Patience and masterful hands."

"And the right words," she allowed, reaching for her glasses.

"It also helps to be able to see their eyes, so you know what they're really thinking." He held her gaze with his while he played with her, let her touch the glasses, grinned, withdrew them again. "A little common sense never hurt, either."

"That goes without saying."

"Too often it does. You really wanna know what I did?"

She nodded. Yes, she wanted to know, and she wanted him to favor her with the answer. *Favor her*. His smile was so damn slow in coming, it made her fidget. It was so damn knowing, it made her furious. It was so damn beautiful, it made her shiver.

"I just opened the gate."

8

The radio Shep had given K.C. pulled in country music, both the current stuff and his favorite classics, and an oldies rock station for variety. He liked to flip some music on first thing in the morning, especially if he'd slept alone the night before. If he was alone at the end of the day, he didn't mind spending the evening with a book, a little music and a beer.

There was a time when he couldn't go to sleep unless he had the radio playing. Back then he'd sometimes bunked with older guys who'd given him hell about the music, even though he'd kept it down so quiet he knew damn well it wasn't really bothering them. The way some of those guys snored, a freight train couldn't compete. Eventually K.C. had found other ways to help himself fall asleep. Gentle ways were the best, ways that made him feel quiet inside. Getting close to a woman generally did the trick for him.

K.C. loved women, not girls, and it wasn't age that determined the difference. It was *woman kindness*. It was heart. He had learned how to love a woman from one who had lifted him out of a terrible loneliness, tucked him under her wing and treated him kindly. Billie Tuttle was her name. He remembered that summer as though he'd watched it unfold through a diaphanous curtain. Whenever he thought about it, he could still feel her practical, down-to-earth woman's hands touching him gently. He could smell the drugstore lotion she'd always used on them, taste the farm's salty artesian water on her skin.

He was fifteen that summer, but nobody had talked about age in specific terms when he'd hired on at the Tuttle place. Billie was twice his age, and her husband's age was twice hers. A gaunt-faced, lanky boy with a strong back who was willing to work for practically nothing but a place to stay and three squares a day was a godsend for the Oklahoma farmer. He wasn't about to ask what K.C. was running from, why he had no identification, no relations, nothing but a small duffel bag containing a few clothes. In fact, the old man hadn't said much the whole summer. Every morning at breakfast he would lay out K.C.'s chores. At supper he'd tell him what needed to be done over. If he had no complaints, he said nothing at all.

K.C. had standing permission to turn his dirty clothes over to "the missus" and to use the shower after supper. Then he went to his own room in a little shack that was used mostly for storage. It had once been the Tuttle home. There was no running water, but he had a privy out back, and inside he had electricity and screens on the windows. The Tuttles had supplied him with a firm bed, a radio that worked and a lamp. Food, shelter and sanctuary. He was fixed up just fine.

He found some old paperback books stored in what was once a kitchen. A few were mildewed and mouse-eaten, but they were mostly readable, and they became his friends, his only friends until the night Billie came walking in unexpectedly. He'd been reading about a guy walking in on a woman taking a bath, and here he was getting walked in on himself, and he had one hell of a bulge in his shorts. Billie waved a package and announced that she had brought him three pairs of new socks.

"I mended your shirts, but there's not a thing I can do with a sock that's worn through in the sole," she explained as she shut the door behind her and came right on in, bright-eyed and a little flushed. He figured she must have gone into town after supper, and maybe she'd just gotten back. The pale yellow hair she normally pulled back into a weedy clump was loose around her shoulders, fixed with a barrette, and she was wearing lipstick.

Chagrin set his face ablaze. His heart hammered, first from scrambling to pull on his jeans when she knocked and now from standing there in the shadows in front of his bed with her so close. He hung his head and mumbled his thanks. She reached up to brush his hair off his forehead. Her hand felt cool and comforting and made him stiffen up all over.

"Don't be embarrassed, K.C. Hard as you work, you more than earned them. I'll slip some Fruit of the Looms into the grocery cart next week."

Oh, jeez. "I appreciate the offer, ma'am, but I don't—"

She laid a finger over his lips. "It's no trouble. I've got nobody, I mean, no kids to buy for. It's a small thing, socks and underwear." Her hand had ended up on his bare, blazing-hot shoulder. She squeezed a little, as if she were testing a fresh peach. "You've filled out some since you come here. You were pretty ganted up."

He swallowed hard, still hanging his head. He knew his face had gone all red. "You're a fine cook, ma'am."

"Billie," she chided. "When Tuttle isn't around, I'd like to hear you call me Billie. I hardly ever hear it anymore."

He looked up. "Ain't that a boy's name?"

"I don't think it has to be." She stepped back, smiling a little. "Do I look like a boy to you?"

"No, ma'am."

Before he could restrain his gaze, it fell to her tank top and the red and white stripes straining across her full bosom. Two small bumps made him wonder what kind of a bra she was wearing, made him think about the woman in the bathtub, made him turn away abruptly and toss the package of socks on the bed, right next to the book with the gunslinger on the cover. "I mean, not at all. I just never heard of a gir—woman with the name of Billy."

"It's spelled with an *i-e* instead of a *y*." She touched his arm. "Are you sure you're nineteen?"

He gave her a sheepish smile and shook his head. "I'm only seventeen. I'll be eighteen in a couple months." He figured she'd buy that one, especially since it was couched in a confession. He was damn near sixteen, so it wasn't much of a lie. "I said nineteen 'cause I don't think of myself as a juvenile. I can do a man's work, so I can take care of myself. Eighteen's just a number." He shrugged. "But you tell people you're eighteen, they think you're lyin', kinda like twenty-one."

"Or twenty-nine."

"You're not that old, are you?" He had her figured for at least that. "You sure don't look it."

"I'm in the neighborhood." She thrust her hands behind her back, as though they might try to make a liar of her; then she gave him a little smile. "You're very wise to leave it at that."

"Age is about the last thing I wanna discuss, ma'am." He took one of the paperbacks off the neat stack he'd made of them on the floor in the corner. "Are these your books?"

"I think they belonged to my husband's first wife. She died." Billie dismissed the book and the first Mrs. Tuttle with a shrug. "We've been married almost ten years. He was a lot more, well, cheerful when I first met him."

"He seems like a . . . *fair* man."

"Fair?" She gave him an expectant look, as though she didn't think he was serious. He was. She shrugged again. "Fair enough, I suppose. Do you have enough blankets? Tuttle thought you'd enjoy kind of having your own little place out here, but if you're not comfortable . . ."

"This is fine. I like the privacy."

"If you ever feel like watching TV . . ." She eyed the stack of books. "We don't get but two channels, and Tuttle always wants it off by ten."

"You always call your husband 'Tuttle'?"

"It's one of those funny little habits married people get into, I guess. He's Tuttle, and I'm the missus." She moved to the window, absently claiming, "Could be worse," as she peered toward the house.

"He goes to bed early?"

"His day starts at sunup, ends at sundown. He's always asleep by full dark. I can't get to sleep that early." She rested her head on the window frame, still peering into the dark. "I love summer nights."

"Yeah, me too."

"My sisters and I used to sneak out on nights like this. We'd talk real big about doing something wild and evil, but all we ever did was smoke on the sneak or go skinny-dipping in the reservoir." She turned, pressed her back to the wall as if she were dodging bullets coming at them from outside. "Do you smoke, K.C.?"

"No, ma'am." She looked disappointed, so he said, "Well, sometimes." It was a lie at the time, but he was willing to make it true if it meant being with somebody for a little while.

"Would you wanna go somewhere and sneak a cigarette with me? I only seem to enjoy smoking when I do it on the sly."

"Sure."

He put on the shirt she'd mended for him and followed her down to the creek, where they smoked and slapped mosquitoes and whispered about silly things like bullfrog language and the color of Betelgeuse. He was glad it was dark, because he didn't inhale much that night. She didn't touch him much that night, either, not physically, but a few nights later she admired his chest, and that took some touching. She noted the lack of hair, wondered whether his father had a hairy chest. He said no, he didn't, figuring there was maybe a fifty percent chance he wasn't lying. It thrilled and embarrassed him when she made his nipple pucker up with the feathering of a fingertip. She assured him that, with the same kind of stimulation, hers would respond the same way. The next night she let him discover the wonder of that truth for himself.

Since his mother's death he'd had little time for girls. His concerns for freeing himself from the restraints of a system that took away his choices had occupied him until he'd finally managed to duck it completely. After that, he'd had all he could do to stay free of the placements and the case workers and the state schools and keep himself alive. Now, suddenly, he'd been touched by a woman in a whole new way. He could hardly think about anything else but the next lesson she would teach him, the next marvel she might introduce him to late at night.

The only problem was Tuttle. Cold and surly as the man was, he was still Billie's husband and K.C.'s employer. K.C. was finding it difficult to look him in the eye. He pitted his urge to confess and be done with it against his instinct to protect a secret that he decided was Billie's to disclose or conceal, as she saw fit. Better judgment won out over guilt. A showdown would surely have brought the sheriff down on his head.

He was half relieved when Tuttle told him he couldn't use him anymore, and he thought maybe Billie was, too. She slipped him a pack of cigarettes and some extra cash in the sack lunch she made for him. She managed to whisper that she'd be lonesome for him, but she didn't offer to go with him. He was glad of that, too. He'd imagined her making a big scene, quitting her husband for him, and the idea of it choked him up a little, the way it played out in his head. But he knew it didn't make any sense. No matter what he'd made her believe about his age, no matter what he believed about his new level of maturity, he was in no position to take care of anybody but himself. And that farm was her home.

K.C. had been with a lot of women since Billie, but she occupied a special place in his heart. He looked back now and remembered how awkward he'd been, how green, how raw were his needs, but she'd taught him patience. She'd tutored him tenderly. She'd never betrayed his trust. He'd been too young for her, too young to be on his own, too young for a lot of things, but looking back, he realized that his life simply was what it was. He wasn't going to bewail it, didn't want to analyze it. Billie Tuttle had taught him how to love a woman, and he figured she'd done a fair job of it. He'd had no complaints.

After he'd read for a while, he shut his light off, stripped off his jeans and his briefs and stuffed them in the laundry bag Sally had given him with instructions to "fill 'er up." An owl called to him, telling him he had company. Moonlight filled the tall windows. Julia had mentioned putting curtains up, but he'd told her that curtains didn't belong in a bunkhouse. He could see the house beyond the trees, standing against the night sky like a dark fortress. A light in a second-story window drew his focus, then his fanciful attention. He decided that it was Julia's room because he wanted it to be.

He wanted her up there where he could watch out for her, where she might watch over him. He'd perfected the art of being on the outside looking in. He could even enjoy the melancholy moments like this one as long as he didn't wallow in them too long. He'd give her the summer, he decided. His best time. He was prone to the blues in the winter months, when he felt like the lone sparrow left behind, when his joints ached from the cold and his memories leaned toward regrets.

He'd give her a whole summer, he thought. It was the best of what he had to offer.

Julia sat at her grandfather's desk in the room her parents had shared and poured over the books no Weslin man had ever been known to manage successfully. Sally had provided a quick overview, then left them in her granddaughter's lap, saying it was bedtime for her. She'd given Julia one of those long, heavy looks, patted her hand and risen effortlessly from the sofa as though, wherever she was going, she was already halfway there. She wasn't fooling Julia, who knew exactly what charge her grandmother thought to give her. Her son, Julia's father, had lost the heart for ranching. Her grandson had had plenty of heart but came up short in the stamina department. Julia had the heart. She had the stamina. She lacked the balls.

The thought made her laugh aloud. Gramma would surely get a kick out of it, too, and Julia filed it away to be used in the conversation they would have on the subject sooner or later. She loved the High Horse. She did not want to preside over its demise. If they sold out now, the house wouldn't have to be part of the bargain. If they tried to keep the place going, everything would soon be mortgaged. They would quite literally have to bet the farm on the possibility of turning a shopworn social worker into a rancher. And Julia was no gambler.

From the looks of things, Ross hadn't been much of a manager. He'd cut back on the cow-calf operation and tried running steers. He'd bought high and sold low. Running cattle appeared to be just an excuse to have horses. Dear stars-in-his-eyes Ross had loved his horses.

Julia loved horses, too, and she loved the idea of ranching. But she couldn't see herself as a rancher. She never allowed herself to dream about doing anything unless doing it reasonably well fit into her own very pragmatic picture. She could handle a horse, yet that would be only a footnote on a rancher's résumé these days. Sally Weslin was a rancher, but Julia believed that her grandmother was the last of her kind. Not that there weren't other female ranchers; there simply weren't any more Weslin ranchers.

Julia had been a teacher, a counselor and a social worker. She'd never been more than "pretty good" at any of those jobs. She was the best there was at being a student, though nobody wanted to pay her for that. Professionally, she'd always been able to manage research and paperwork, but she hadn't worked any miracles with people. She'd tried. She'd had wonderful visions. She'd always wanted to make a difference with her students and her clients. A big difference. She wanted someone to say, "You've changed my life." Nobody ever did, but she kept plugging along.

Then one day she'd made a difference. An awful, sickening difference, one that no one would thank her for. She'd removed three young children from their mother's custody. Standard operating procedure. A neighbor had called the police when the children were discovered locked out of their apartment building in below-zero weather. The mother had gone to another apartment, and the six-year-old had decided to take her brother and sister and go look for her. Once the children had been picked up by the police, Child Protection Services took over, and the incident became the focus of a community debate, with Julia caught between the rule book and common sense.

Officially, she'd given simple agency answers to complicated human questions, and she'd started feeling like a theme-park robot. Unofficially, she'd called the one person she could talk to about anything and told him what she couldn't tell anyone else. The system had gone awry, and she with it.

"Tell them what they can do with their regulations in triplicate and come on home," Ross had said. She couldn't, she'd told him. She was responsible. Finally he'd asked her to come home because he needed to see her, and to do it quickly. He was, he admitted, very sick. No, not just the usual. This was something else. This was not something he could live with. Julia had taken a leave of absence. She had come home to the one person she could talk to about anything. She had come home to a terrible sorrow and a terrible truth. The road she'd always taken for granted had never truly run both ways.

But Ross was gone now. The High Horse was not, not yet. Every time the word "sell" came to mind, Julia pushed it back. Not now, she thought. She couldn't get into that, not tonight, not tomorrow, not just yet. Decisions were impossible to come up with at the moment. She knew Dawn was ready, but Dawn was *always* ready. Act now, consider the consequences later; that was Dawn.

Julia wasn't ready. She didn't feel like thinking or discussing or studying or doing anything that might lead to a decision. Not now. She couldn't face any more finalities right now. She closed the ledger and turned out the light. Moonlight drifted over the room, turning the heavy furniture into colorless dark curves and pale surfaces. She could barely make out the faces of three children in the photo portrait above the desk. She remembered the day it was taken.

She remembered Mother trying to fit everything into one hot, dry August afternoon, Ross sullen as always after visiting the allergy specialist, Dawn whiny as always after a long drive and a bout with car sickness, and Julia just being Julia. Somebody had to get the others organized. There she was, tipping her head to one side, trying to look picture-pretty. There was Ross, trying to look strong and hardy. And there was Dawn, who never even had to try. She could be whining and kicking one minute, a little doll the next. Oh, yes, Julia remembered that day. She couldn't remember where Daddy had been—he'd avoided trips to town, especially for kid appointments—but she knew they'd still been together then.

She was drawn to the window, filled with pearly moonlight. Across the lawn, beyond the little gazebo Mother had ordered in a kit from the lumber yard, beyond the crabapple trees and the vegetable garden plot, beyond the point where the yard ended and the prairie sod took over, the old log bunkhouse stood in solitary silence. The windows were dark. Gramma's new hired man was sleeping there.

Julia's cowboy. As long as she didn't say such a foolish thing out loud, surely it was all right to fantasize. Her heroes had always been cowboys. Fine and dandy, Mother would say, as long as you don't have to live with them. K.C. wasn't just any cowboy, either. He was a specialist who made a living gentling horses, the big, beautiful creatures whose one-step-away-from-wildness appeal had certainly rubbed off on him. He was more like Dawn's type, more like Dawn's age, probably more like Dawn. He won people over without trying. Like Dawn, he surely had to be taken at face value.

And, like Dawn's, what a sweet face it was.

A knock on the door startled her.

"Queenie?"

"Come on in, Gramma. I'm awake." The door squeaked on its hinges. "Just don't turn the light on. The moonlight makes everything seem so milky soft."

"I could hear you still stirring up here. Floors are about as creaky as my old bones." The bed added its squeaks to the mix as Sally sat down beside Julia, nightgown to nightgown, knee to knee. "I'm feeling a little guilty about saddling you with those books. I tried to get your brother to keep them up, but he wasn't much good at it, and I'm not as sharp on the details as I used to be."

"We've got a cash-flow problem, Gramma."

Sally patted Julia's knee. "It's not as bad as you might think. The leases are paid up. We don't owe on anything until fall."

"It's going to be hard to give it up completely, isn't it?"

The response was slow in coming. "Is that what you've decided to do?"

"We should be planning for fall," Julia acknowledged with a deep sigh. "We should let our lawyer know that we're open to offers, don't you think?"

"I don't like to let them handle too much of my business. Lawyers and other vultures. They'll strut around, pace back and forth trying to work up a head of steam to impress you with. All they got going for them is that head full of steam." Sally rubbed her own knees now. "Pressure. They've got everybody convinced that pressure makes the sun rise and set."

"Not out here," Julia pleaded. "Surely not in Wyoming."

"Life isn't any easier here. I never said it was. It takes a special breed to survive here. I told your grandfather that the day I proposed to him."

Julia smiled in the dark. She loved this story, never tired of digging for new details. "Did he accept immediately?"

" 'Course he did. I came with one hell of a dowry. The man warn't no fool." Sally's stiff hands went still on her knobby knees. "Spent the rest of his days workin' his skinny arse off, too, making this place every bit as much his as it was mine."

"That devotedness kinda skipped a generation, though, didn't it?" Julia reflected quietly.

"You mean, your dad?"

"My *parents*. They must not have had what you and Grampa had. Not even to start with."

"I want to say that they started with a legacy, but maybe it was a curse for them." She wagged her head. "Maybe it was."

"My mother knew exactly what she was getting into."

"Oh, honey, if you believe that, you've been watching too much Disney. When you sign up for married life all head over heels and blind with passion, how can you possibly know exactly what's in store for you?"

Julia let the silence speak for her.

"She did love your dad, you know. She truly did."

It truly didn't matter anymore. Gramma's story was the one Julia wanted to hear tonight. "Were you head over heels and full of passion?"

"I needed a man." Sally wrapped her arms around her middle and laughed. "I did. I needed a man, pure and simple. Back in those days you could just say it straight out."

"Why didn't you pick one you knew a little better? I'm sure you could have had your pick."

"What makes you so sure of a thing like that?"

"I know you." Julia grinned and bumped shoulders with her grandmother. "You're Sally Weslin."

"I was Sally Harris. Sally Harris was different. She had some spunk, all right. She had the Harris mettle. She got to be a Weslin, and she became an alloy." Sally rose and padded across the bare wood floor on bare feet to her husband's old desk. "It was a good mix," she said as she laid her hands on the back of the padded chair as if she envisioned him sitting there. "He made me stronger. I made him stronger. It was a damn good mix."

Her hands stroked the leather. Julia imagined a young Max in that chair, a young Sally standing behind him and rubbing his shoulders. Thirty-two years was a long time. Thirty-two years of sleeping in the same bed, sharing every other thought, rubbing each other's sore places. More time than Mother had had with Daddy, but from the way Gramma spoke of him, from the way she touched the chair he'd occupied so many years ago, Julia could see and feel and understand that thirty-two years had not been nearly long enough.

Sally turned to her in the near dark. The moonlight dressed her softly now, and the years melted away.

"I picked Max Weslin—it was me who did the picking, and that's just plain history, that is—but I picked him because I liked the way he was put together, the way he carried himself. I put him to work, and I liked the way he went about doing a job. I liked the way he treated me. Different from the way other men treated me."

"Different how?"

"Like he was my equal and I was his. Not that we were alike, because we weren't. But we could balance each other because we were equal."

"Even though the High Horse was yours."

"Didn't matter. I inherited it, but Max made it his the

honest way. He gave it his life. Now, there was no way I could have known from the start that it was gonna work out like that. I had it in my head that I was latching onto a piece of clay, and I was gonna mold that clay into the kind of man I wanted him to be, make a Harris out of him.''

"But he made you a Weslin?"

"You know, there might be some real sense to those hyphenated last names.'' She leaned down close to the back of the chair. "Don't worry, cowboy. Weslin it's been, and Weslin it stays.'' She paused, then laughed and slapped the back of the chair. "Did you hear what he said, Queenie?"

"No,'' Julia whispered, sitting there wide-eyed in the dark, believing. "What did he say, Gramma?''

" 'You change it now, old girl, and you won't be sleepin' up here on Cloud Nine with me.' ''

The laugh they shared faded to quiet. Julia drew her knees up to her chin, wrapped her arms around her legs, feet on the edge of the bed. It was a night for sweet fantasy. "Do you think Ross has found his cloud yet?"

"I expect so. It was always hard for him to be anywhere but up in those mountains. He tried, though. He tried real hard.''

"He couldn't breathe. That's what killed him.''

"That's not what killed him, Queenie. That's what released him when he was ready to go. And yes,'' she said, walking the floor again for her grandchild, returning to sit beside her on the bed. "In answer to your question a while ago, yes, it would be hard to see the place go to someone else, but not *that* hard. Not as hard as it was seeing them go. All of them. Michael was the second son I buried, you know.''

"I know.''

"We've got too much staying power for our own good, Queenie. We Weslin women, we just don't wear out.'' She folded a cool hand over Julia's toes. "So you find a nice young one. By the time you get to be eighty and he's maybe sixty, he might be catchin' up to you, agewise.''

Julia smiled, tickled. "So I should be looking for a sixteen-year-old?''

"Nice hunk of hard clay. Shape it up the way you want

it." Sally cranked Julia's toes as though she was trying to get a light to come on. "Just make sure his mama's weaned him first. That was Fay's mistake."

"What do you mean? Daddy wasn't a mama's boy."

"I spoiled your daddy. You know that, don't you? Spoiled him real bad."

"He wasn't bad, Gramma."

"There were times . . ." Sally drew back, leaned back, her voice drifting on a sigh. "Well, there were times when I was glad I wasn't married to him. I can say that to you, Queenie, without feeling like a traitor, because we both loved him. Now, here's the deal . . ." She reached for Julia's toes again. It felt like a hug, the way she closed her hand around them. "I'm gonna let you get some rest, but the deal is this: cash flow is just like any other flow. One source dries up, you find another one. A Weslin woman is never afraid of her naturally resourceful . . . nature. That's what we've got goin' for us. A resourceful nature. 'Course, your mother injected a few other assets into the bloodline. If I had legs like yours, I'd use those, too."

"Gramma!"

"All I had was twenty-five thousand acres of land, leases, permits and assorted livestock. Did I mention debt?"

"Should *I*?"

"Not right away. Assets first, then debt. Remember that when you're studying those books. I've got a habit of approaching it kinda backwards."

"I noticed." The columns were backward in the ledgers.

"But it's the only way it makes sense to me. Credit comes first in my books. Then debit. Did you know the High Horse has been on the verge of bankruptcy twice?"

"No." It was a story she might want to hear, but some other time. Right now she was concerned about the present. "How close are we now?"

"Ochh." Sally levered herself up from the bed with a dismissive gesture. "We've got credit to spare. We just don't have a lot of cash."

"Guess that makes us fairly all-American." Julia thought about their cowboy, and it occurred to her that she didn't want to lose him for insufficient funds. "How are we going to pay the help?"

"I was planning on leaving that little problem up to you. Now, over the years I've found a variety of ways to skin the cat, depending on the, uh . . . well, the breed of cat you're dealing with. Take Vernon and Shep. They've got their own little piece of the High Horse, deeds are in their names and they don't care about money. Shep's a horse trader. He'd rather swap for what he wants than do business in cash. And I expect Vernon's got enough money stashed away someplace to put himself up at the Plaza Hotel for all eternity if it ever struck his fancy."

"But there's the question of hay, and whether we want to go ahead and put in the oats. That'll take some cash." Sally planted her hands on her hips. "And then there's our cowboy."

"*Your* cowboy."

"Cowboys generally look forward to payday."

"Guess that makes *them* fairly all-American."

"Especially young cowboys, so you might wanna start looking at some of the other options I mentioned."

"Not really, but you were getting to that."

"Well, you know, in the past I've taken on a job or two, worked outside the home, as they say." Sally folded her arms beneath her droopy breasts. Now she was talking business. "Or once or twice I've put something up for sale. Or you figure out some other way to put our assets to work. The High Horse has assets up the as-sets," she quipped, and Julia giggled. "And, of course, you can always make promises."

"Pay him with promises?"

"Oh, cowboys love promises. Living on promises keeps them slim. Gives them a reason to go out and get drunk once in a while. Gives them something to write songs about."

Julia let her feet slide to the floor. "Maybe we should put Dawn in charge of payroll."

"Like I said, I'm leaving that up to you." Sally moved to the window. Her contemplative face was bathed again in moonlight. "There's plenty of interest out there in acquiring the High Horse, but it's not the kind I like to see. It's money. Just money. Not a decent promise anywhere, just cold cash.''

"Chuck Pollak—''

"Chuck Pollak.'' She clicked those *k*'s like a speech coach as she turned from the window, her face taking refuge in the shadows. The moon made a halo of her white hair. "Chuck would carve the place up. Have you seen what's happened to Jackson Hole? Well, it's spilling over with Californians. They'll turn the High Horse into a golf course community.''

"Gramma, I'm not . . .'' Julia's chin dropped to her chest, and she mumbled into her flannel nightgown. "I'm not Ross.''

"I know who you are, Queenie.'' Sally took a step from the window, one cautious step. "I talked to the lawyer just yesterday. He'll do whatever we want, whenever we're ready.'' Another step, a softer tone. "I'm asking you to give me the summer. If you can spare it.''

Sally Weslin rarely asked for anything. That she had to ask, so humbly, in such a timorous voice, her own granddaughter . . . Julia swallowed hard and tried to clear her thistly throat. *If you can spare it.* She nodded.

"Is that a *yes*, Queenie?''

Julia tried to laugh, but it came out more like a warble. "If you'll stop calling me that.''

"One more summer, then,'' Sally said, ignoring the request. "Jack Trueblood wants to talk to you about this deal him and Ross had worked out for bringing some kids over on some kind of work detail. I told him you'd call him tomorrow.''

"The summer program for the correctional school?'' How had they gone from lawyers and giving Gramma one more summer to some harebrained scheme of Ross and Jack Trueblood's? And her grandmother was already moseying along, headed for her own bed. "I thought that was all just sort of—''

"You call him. It might be more variety, you know? Some kinda cat-skinnin' option that might turn out to be right up your alley. You just never know.'' Sally opened the door, turned, her voice all full of smiles. ''Doesn't hurt to keep an open mind, especially when it comes to cats and cowboys.''

9

It was a brisk, bright, forget-the-coffee kind of morn-
ing. K.C. saddled up and headed out early with Vernon to
start moving the cows and calves in for branding. The sky
was pristine blue, not a cloud in sight, and the purple and
yellow blossoms dotting the rolling grassland put on as
pretty a show as K.C. had ever seen in Texas or anywhere
else in the spring. He had to admit he was falling fast for
Wyoming. Off to the west, the snowcapped mountains were
looking especially majestic this morning, with the lush
folds of their pine-tree-dappled blue-green skirts draping
the perimeter of the grassy basin. He wanted to ride up
there and wander for a while, find an alpine meadow, strip
down in the sun and get high on the scent of the pines. But
today he had work to do.

He braced one hand on the saddle swells and stood in
his stirrups for the trot, scanning the draw below for calves
tucked into the sheltering brush by their mothers and left
in the watchful care of one cow, the calf-sitter. It occurred
to him that if this was God's country, then God was a
woman, at least in Wyoming. Those mountains were surely
female. He remembered Ross Weslin describing this place
as "heaven's foyer" when he'd predicted that if K.C. came
to work at the High Horse, he'd never want to leave. "I've
got a sister for you, too," Weslin had said, the kind of joke
you could tell a guy was half serious about. *For him to
what?*

The wildflowers made him think of her, and he asked
the mare whether she could spot the one she was named
for. "You see any columbines, you tell me, and we'll take
her some," he told the mare. "The only one I know for
sure is prickly pear. That yellow flower there, see?" He
pointed to the low, spreading cactus, abloom with pink buds
and buttery, tissue-paper blossoms. "Don't think we wanna
be picking any of that stuff."

I've got a sister for you. Pick her.

Pretty damned direct for a doting brother. Pretty strange
suggestion, too, fixing his well-educated sister up with a
saddle tramp. Was that why he was really here? Why would
a dying man want to hire a horse trainer? He remembered
the night Weslin had insisted on buying him a drink to
celebrate, after a horse that K.C. had started as a two-year-
old had won the cutting horse competition at the Denver
Stock Show.

K.C. had felt a little funny around Weslin. He tried to
ignore the talk about Weslin being gay, but he couldn't help
thinking about it when they sat down at the table together
and Weslin gave him a wistful sort of smile and said,
"Women seem to like you."

"I like women," K.C. said, thinking about the one who
had just greeted him with a sassy slap on the ass. Pretty
little redhead, couldn't remember her name. "I like them
very much."

Weslin nodded, smiling like he got the message, loud
and clear. "She left her mark on your face." K.C. laughed
and went after the lipstick with a cocktail napkin. "What
do you like about them?" Weslin asked, and when K.C.
gave him an incredulous glance, he shrugged it off. "No,
I'm serious."

"Hell, I like their spirit, their heart."

Weslin looked at him as though he found the answer to
be intriguing. K.C. decided to take the reaction at face
value; he'd said something interesting. If Weslin had been
a woman, K.C. would have known better. Women weren't
interested in what he said so much. It was more the way it
was said. That and the way he listened.

K.C. glanced at the dance floor. Watching people dance

always made him tap his toe, itching to get out there and enjoy the music with some sweet partner. He leaned across the table. "A woman's heart is different from a man's. It's not a matter of soft, even though there is that softness about some women. It's more like extra room, maybe a secret chamber. They always seem to have a little hope in reserve."

"Heart." Weslin seemed to be turning the word over in his mind, like a questionable coin. Finally he smiled. "That's not the part most men would name."

K.C. shrugged as he sipped his whiskey. "I generally just say I'm a leg man and let it go at that, but you did say *seriously*."

"And I don't threaten you."

"Threaten me?"

"Seriously." Weslin chuckled, sat back sipping on his bourbon and water. He was a good-looking cowboy, a little on the thin side with slender, elegant hands, but the kind of a guy a woman would surely notice.

"My life is full of women, too," he said, as if he'd read K.C.'s mind. "Women I love. Women I hate. Women I hate to love. I know just what you mean by a woman's heart. There's a gentleness about them that scares some men, I think. You've got it just right, though: gentleness and stamina. Unbelievable combination, but there it is."

K.C. raised his glass in fraternal agreement. "If we were talking about horses, we'd call it *try*. Some guys don't appreciate that, either. They say they do, but the first thing they wanna do is *break* her, break her in, which means break her spirit."

"And when that doesn't work out, they come to you."

"We talking about women or horses now?"

Weslin smiled. "We're talking about soft hearts and gentle creatures. Do you ever get tired of trying to make amends for other men's mistakes?"

"It's probably fifty percent of my business," K.C. said. As for women, he figured it wasn't possible for one man to make amends for the mistakes of another. He'd gotten himself in trouble over it a time or two and given up trying. Thought he had, anyway. He sure as hell meant to.

"You're the kind of man a guy wants to introduce to his sister." Weslin planted his elbows on the table, cradling his drink in both graceful hands. "Come to work for me. You play your cards right, it could be the last time you work for somebody else."

"I'm working for myself," K.C. told him. "I get more calls than I can handle. Got nothing tying me down, so I'm free to take the offers that appeal to me."

"You don't have a place of your own?"

"I don't even own a horse right now. But I will one day. I've got time."

"Lucky you," Weslin muttered into his glass. He came up smiling. "Trade me some of your time."

"What have you got to trade, besides a herd of wild horses?"

Weslin thought about that for a moment before he decided on "A place of my own."

K.C. had teased him about throwing in the sister, and then they'd talked horses. *Nice guy*, K.C. had come away thinking, but he'd be spending the winter in West Texas, thanks.

But by late winter he was ready to move on. In fact, he was more than ready to get as far away from West Texas as he could. There were a few lessons he seemed to have trouble getting through his thick head, and most of them had to do with betting on the wrong horse or the wrong woman.

Lucky you, Weslin had said. Trouble was, K.C. had a way of pushing his luck.

Vern appeared suddenly at the top of a ridge, waving his battered black hat. K.C. eased the mare into a lope. Gray-green sage swished against her lunging legs, and gravel rattled behind her as she carried him up the sunny hillside. The old cowboy pointed to the rocky gulch below the ridge. A gray flannel-looking foal had somehow gotten a back leg hung up in a rock heap. A black mare paced nervously, one eye on the intruders, the other attending to her hapless baby, whose frantic whimpering made K.C.'s skin prickle.

"Wild mama," Vernon reported. "Baby's worn himself out trying to get loose. Look up there." He nodded toward the next ridge. A coyote trotted along the top at a distance that was safe enough for the moment. "He ain't alone," Vernon said. "He's got friends on the other side."

K.C. scanned the draw, then the ridge. "Well, she's got us."

The granite was covered with blood. It was a small outcropping with a fissure as treacherous as any trapper's device. The foal's flesh was torn away all the way down to the cannon bone. While Vernon held the horses, K.C. took off his shirt and began tearing it apart, using his pocket knife to start each strip. He glanced at the older man, who looked amused. The hard-twist ropes they both had tied to their saddles would be too stiff, too hard. When he was working with horses he always carried soft cotton rope, but today he'd planned to work cattle. The horse expert had been caught unprepared.

Bare-chested now, he shrugged back into his denim jacket and approached the wild pair carefully on foot, speaking softly, assuring the mare that he was there to help her baby. He hunkered down close to the foal and soothed it with his best tools—patient hands and a deep, quiet voice. The mare talked to him, too, and kept up her pacing. Terrified as she was of the men, she would not abandon her baby.

K.C. used the strips of cotton to hobble the foal's free legs so that he couldn't hurt himself. They lashed the hard twist to the rock, and Vernon enlisted some horsepower to liberate the baby. After some hasty bandaging, the foal rode home with K.C., draped across his lap, and the black mare followed at a safe distance.

Julia was sitting on the porch with Ross's friend Jack Trueblood when she saw the riders. They were too far away to identify, but Julia knew exactly who they were. She'd been watching unwittingly, one ear, one eye looking out for some sign, and now that she'd spotted him she was losing track of her side of the conversation with Jack altogether.

Trying to rein herself in was useless. She was like a rookie fireman who kept thinking she smelled smoke. All morning she'd been popping her head up, swiveling it, sniffing, looking ridiculous and grateful there weren't too many witnesses. There wasn't any smoke. It was just that cowboy, the one who was too young and too charming and too physical. Everything about him was purely physical. Hardly her type.

Type? She probably shouldn't think about a person as a type, but it was only a word, and K.C., the ramblin' cowboy, was indeed a certain type of man. The kind taken at face value, which was seriously attractive, but hardly serious. Which was why she felt more than a little silly every time she caught herself wondering where he was and what he was doing. She'd started out the morning wondering whether he'd slept comfortably, then why he hadn't come to breakfast.

Then it had occurred to her that maybe he didn't see much use in helping three women and two old men pick up the pieces of a once-grand ranching operation just so they could put it on the market. Maybe he had better things to do, less complicated things, the kind that would be more appealing for an uncomplicated man, and maybe he'd hopped into his pickup at the crack of dawn and headed south.

But Julia had checked. The pickup that had been added to the High Horse fleet was still sitting in the Quonset building Sally called "the garage."

She'd chided herself roundly for checking.

"How about it, Julia?" Jack was saying. "Can we give it a try?"

Oh, the summer program. Ross's final brainstorm. Dear, sweet, impractical Ross. When he'd suggested it, she'd thought it was a pipe dream. "Your own program, Queenie," he'd said. "Run it your way on your own home ground. No hassles from the bureaucrats." She couldn't believe he'd actually gone this far with the idea, sick as he'd been.

"How many weeks would it last?"

"The grant calls for an eight-week program." Jack tipped back the green wicker chair, its hind legs grinding against the slate porch. "Ross was excited about this program. I thought he'd hang in there through the summer just to see us get the thing off the ground. I really did."

"You planned on using our facilities while Ross stood at the window and watched?"

"He said one of you would be involved, either him or you. I thought he'd talked with you about it. You were part of the proposal."

"He mentioned it, but didn't tell me about the grant. I thought . . . Did Gramma know?"

"I knew about the idea," Sally announced through the screen door. She gave it a push, and it whined as she stepped outside. "I didn't know too much about the details. Couldn't worry about dreams and schemes this year. Not that they don't add spice to the mix, but there's been salt aplenty lately. I've just been trying to keep things going here, Queenie."

"I know you have."

"It's a good idea, though," Sally said. "You could make it work. You've got the right kind of background to set something up for those boys at the reform school."

"They don't call it that anymore, Gramma," Julia said absently. She'd been watching the riders, thinking how they both rode like natural appendages on the horses; how, at this distance, they looked ageless and timeless and wholly uncommon.

She stood, drawn to the porch railing. "Is he carrying a calf?"

All three left the porch and walked out to meet the riders, who crossed the bridge at an easy, clip-clop trot. The foal was draped over K.C.'s thighs, a wide-eyed, trembling, unwilling captive bleeding on his jeans.

"We're gonna need a vet," K.C. said. Jack stepped up to help Vernon lift the foal down as K.C. explained the foal's predicament. He nodded over his shoulder. A horse was barely visible on the ridge overlooking the creek that flowed down from the mountains and wound behind the house. "That's his mama. Quite a courageous lady. Never let us out of her sight. I expect she'll come closer yet, and I'll be able to run her in. If we're gonna save him, we'll need her help."

Vernon and Jack laid the hobbled foal on the grass in the shade of a big, rustling cottonwood while Julia took charge of Vernon's horse, looping the reins over a low branch of the tree. She didn't know whether to call veterinarian Mark Wylie for instructions or load the poor, frightened foal into a truck and take it directly to the clinic. She hated emergencies. She wanted time to think things through, a tendency Ross had teased her about not long ago. *Just pick a course and go for it.* She'd call.

"Damn broomtails." Arms akimbo, Sally was scowling over the proceedings. "Now, look, you boys have been messing around with this all morning. Am I gonna have to get those cows rounded up myself?"

K.C. swung down from the saddle. "We couldn't hardly leave him out there for the coyotes."

"Survival of the fittest," Sally said. "They're wild."

"Yes, ma'am, but the poor little guy was stuck between a rock and a hard place, staring into the jaws of—"

"Don't recite me any tearjerkers, cowboy. I've heard them all."

K.C. looked at Sally, surprised.

She leveled him with a deadpan stare. "They sound better at night, either under the stars or between the sheets. Remember that."

"Yes, ma'am."

K.C. looked to a fellow cowboy for some hint as to how he was supposed to interpret "between the sheets," coming from their boss. Vernon was busy mopping inside the crown of his hat with a red bandanna as though he'd worked up a powerful sweat on the ride back. The old cowboy was so mortified by Sally's comment that he had to let it sail right over his head. It was the cowboy way.

"We got a good count this morning, Judge. They're all bunched together pretty good, too. All we gotta do is drive 'em home." Vernon put his hat back on, adjusting it as though he was trying it on for size. "Don't you worry, now; we'll be ready to brand."

"I'll take the foal to the vet," Julia decided. Maybe this wasn't such an emergency. Nobody seemed too panicky.

"We can put him in the back of my Jeep." Jack was

searching his pockets for his keys as he headed for the vehicle, which was parked on the gravel driveway. "I've got plenty of room. Took the backseat out and fixed it up to haul my dogs."

K.C. responded skeptically, glancing first at the Jeep, then at its owner. Julia interjected a quick introduction, and the two men shook hands.

Jack opened the Jeep's rear hatch. "Mark Wylie's clinic is right on the way to the school, and I'd like to take Julia in for a quick tour. This is big enough, huh?" His glance skittered past K.C. It was Julia's approval he was interested in. "I can bring over some boys to help with your branding. Give them a taste of the work, kinda let you check them out."

Sally cleared her throat.

"Okay, okay, so we had an incident a few months back with the Community Action Squad," Jack admitted, one hand thrust in his jeans pocket, the other hooked above his graying head on the handle of the open hatch. His explanation was for Julia. "We assign them to different public programs to help out with chores and whatnot. One of the kids did steal some stuff from the museum, but everything was recovered, hardly any damage done." He shrugged. "And, well, there was that knife fight during the church supper, but nobody really got hurt."

"Spare me the details, Jack. I know these kids."

"They'd be well supervised," he promised. "You and I will plan a program that keeps them so busy, they'll . . ." He glanced past her. K.C. had hauled the foal into his arms, and he was headed for the garage. "Uh, K.C., the Jeep's over here."

"Two weeks, ten days," K.C. muttered, his boot heels scuffling in the gravel. "I'll take him myself."

Julia hurried after him. He let her stop him and turn him around. He said that the foal needed attention now, but the look in his eyes said something else, something she doubted he even intended. He glanced at Jack, then looked at Julia. Finally he let her persuade him to load the foal into the Jeep.

He ducked the hatch, backing out just as Dawn walked

up behind the group, rubber slides flapping at her heels. "What's all the fuss?"

Julia noticed her first. The men were busy with the foal. It was amusing to watch them turn, one by one, their eyes widening, two by two. Naked, she would have been less of a spectacle. The black thong bikini was just enough fabric to create the illusion of perfection. K.C. was the last to get an eyeful when he backed right into her. His eyes lit up like Las Vegas. He caught her arm, mumbled an apology, wondered if he'd stepped on her.

Stepped on her *what*? Julia wondered. Nobody was looking at anyone's toes.

"No, no . . . Ohh," Dawn crooned, spotting the foal. "Poor little thing. What happened?"

The men were thunderstruck. They took turns tossing odd pieces of information out of dry throats.

"He, uh, got his leg—"

"—caught in, uh, uh, crack between—"

Even Jack had a detail to supply. "Two, uh, two big rocks."

"On the beach," Julia said. She couldn't help smiling, feeling a touch of pride. It was no wonder these three were reeling; her baby sister was a knockout. She reached for the big white cotton shirt trailing from Dawn's fingers. "Down in Cheyenne. You must have walked right past him, Dawn."

"Beach? There's no beach in Wyoming." She looked at her sister, blinked innocently, then smiled. "Oh, you. I fell asleep in the sun. I'm probably going to be very sorry tonight, but it's such a nice warm day, and I'm so sickly pale."

"Here." Julia slipped the shirt over Dawn's shoulders. "Have mercy on your sickly pale skin and these guys' doggy-lollin' tongues. The sun's busy making all kinds of leather even as we speak." She turned to K.C. and gave him a canny little smile as she tapped the back of her hand under his chin. He closed his mouth and returned her smile. "I'm going into town. I'll pick up something with aloe. Anything else?"

"You owe me a shirt."

She glanced through his open jacket at a chest that was anything but sickly pale.

"Seventeen long, use your judgment about color and try not to keep the foal away from his mama too long," he said with a pointed glance at Jack, who was climbing into the driver's seat.

"You'll get her in?"

"Damn straight I'll get her in."

"She's bound to be a handful." Julia looked up at the ridge, but the mare wasn't really the handful she had in mind. "It won't take me long to consider Jack's proposition."

Jack had stayed for supper after they brought the foal back, all tranquilized, stitched up and x-rayed. K.C. had brought the mare in, and he and Vernon had gone back to work and missed the meal. It was well after ten when Julia heard them in the kitchen, helping themselves to the leftovers. She started down the hall to join them, but then she heard Dawn's voice, then Gramma's, and something made her back away. Too many people, maybe. A full kitchen. K.C. was laughing. Dawn "ouched," and Gramma scolded her for something. Julia had put some lotion on her sister's back earlier, scolded a little herself. Probably time for a bit more of each, the dressing-down and the lotion.

But someone else would see to it. There were enough people in the kitchen.

"Little girl, little girl, don't you lie to-oo me . . . Where diiid you sleeeep last niiiight . . ."

The black mare's ears rotated like the eye of a periscope, attending to K.C.'s movements as much as to his voice, both of which were silky and smooth. He had her haltered and tied to a corral post with her baby close by where she could see him. The little charcoal-gray foal, whom K.C. had dubbed "Mischief," followed his every move like a curious pup, jealous now over the attention his mother was getting. He liked it when K.C. rubbed his face and neck just the way he was doing the mare.

"In the pines, in the piiines, where the sun do-on't shine . . ."

He used a firm touch and worked her all over, from her neck to her shoulder to her back, while he sang to her. When he got to her ears, she balked at first, and he went back to the last thing she'd accepted and worked his way up to the more sensitive parts.

"And you shiv-er when the cold winds bloooow . . ."

Julia had been standing near the fence for some time, quietly watching, but he'd taken no notice. He'd put in several long days getting ready for branding, but after supper he never seemed to be too tired to work with the horses. They had to get to know each other, he said, he and the mustangs. He had to show them that his hands weren't weapons, that he could get close without hurting them.

"What do you think, boss lady?" he asked finally without turning to her, without even varying his tone or his pitch, so that the mare must have thought she had a name now, too.

"I think it's remarkable that she'll let you touch her like that. How much time have you spent with her?"

He ran his hand down the leg carefully, reaching for the fetlock. The mare let him pick her foot up, just a few inches, just for a moment. He spared Julia a brief but triumphant smile. "Less than I've spent with you."

"You'd hardly know what a wild thing she was only yesterday. What's your secret?"

"You just caught me at it. She makes my heart sing." He started rubbing her shoulder again. "Don't you, Wild Thing? Hmm?"

"Does she have the makings of a saddle horse, do you think?"

"Yes, ma'am, she sure does."

"She's beautiful, isn't she?"

He didn't have to answer. Julia stepped up on the bottom corral rail and stacked her chin on top of her hands on the top rail. She could almost feel his hands as she watched him painstakingly making his way over the horse's hip. Whenever the mare's muscles bunched under his hands, he kept rubbing until she relaxed them.

"Will you do it, then?"

"Will you?" The mare resisted his attempt to pick up her back foot, but she didn't kick. She merely jerked her foot away. *Uh-uh, mister, not that one.* He moved to her other side, glancing over her rump at Julia. "If I saddle her for you, will you dare to take a ride on the wind?"

She smiled. "You remind me so much of my brother sometimes. But if he'd had his way, they'd stay wild and free."

"She can stay free-spirited. We don't have to take anything from her. If we earn her trust, she'll take us places. Won't you, girl? You'll show us all your secret places up there in those mountains, places where we can touch the clouds and tickle the angels." He rubbed the mare's back. "Was your brother ticklish?"

"Only on his feet."

"Perfect." He was working his way toward another back fetlock. "How 'bout you, Miss Wild Thing? Are you ticklish?" Muscles bunched, then relaxed, and K.C. took the foot in hand. "Easy, girl. I don't know when I've ever seen a prettier foot. Perfectly round, nice smooth bevel to the hoof wall. Never been touched by a file. You've got feet to make all the girls jealous."

"I can't believe she's letting you do that."

"I'm talkin' nice to her." The mare took her foot back. K.C. chuckled. "She liked my singing better, though."

"She likes the sound of your voice."

"You got your branding crew all lined up?"

"Some kids from the juvenile correctional facility. It's sort of like a reform school, you know, for boys who've gotten into trouble. Sometimes there's a history of truancy, maybe repeat offenses of some kind, maybe their parents just can't handle them."

"I get the picture." She could have sworn his back muscles had just bunched up under his new blue shirt, the way the horse's did. "Kind of a holding pen for wild kids?"

"I've worked with a lot of troubled kids, and they're not always wild. A lot of them are scared. Just like the horses."

She got no concurrence on her wonderful analogy. He

had worked his way back to the front of the mare, rubbing her neck now, moving toward her head.

"Anyway, the guy you met the other day, Jack True-blood? He pitched me this idea he and Ross had cooked up for a summer program. Bringing kids out during the day to work on the ranch. He said they had a program all worked out, and they actually got approved for a grant. There'd be kids who really wanted to participate, to work with the stock, willing to behave themselves and cooperate completely, or they'd be cut from the program."

He released the slipknot and slid the lead rope away from the post with exaggerated care.

"What do you think?"

He looked at her, bewildered. "What do *I* think?"

"Do you think we could do something like that here? I said I'd look at the proposal."

No response. The mare didn't seem to realize she'd been untied yet. He was talking to her so quietly, Julia suddenly felt like she'd walked in on a private conversation. He finessed the halter off the mare's head seemingly without lifting a finger. The mare trotted over to her foal, who quickly claimed her teat.

"Have you ever worked with kids, K.C.?"

"I train horses." He draped the lead rope and halter over the top rail, scaled the corral and dropped to the ground right next to her. "You're already stretchin' it with the cows, boss lady."

"How long will it take you with this horse?" She turned to him, resting her shoulder on the fence. Now the evening sun was in her eyes, and she had to block it with her hand in order to look into his shaded face. "Before you try to ride her."

"As long as it takes."

"How long is that, usually? For the average horse."

"What's an average horse? Average is a mathematical term." He smiled, flirting with her now. "I'd teach her to count, but I don't have much of a head for numbers myself." He took his hat off, set it on her head, adjusted the brim so it shaded her eyes, and grinned. "You look great in a hat, you know that?"

She laughed. "You're impossible, you know that?"

"You've got me all wrong, ma'am. I'm easy. I'm not only possible, I'm probable." He tucked a wisp of her hair behind her ear. "But don't ask me how probable, because that would take messin' with some numbers. And I don't do numbers."

"You train horses."

He nodded. "I train horses."

"I just want to know how long—"

"That's the other secret. It takes me just as long as it takes her." He mirrored her pose, folding his arms, propping his shoulder against the corral, the look in his eyes softening for her. "And I'll sing to her until her heart is content."

His hat had left his thick dark hair a little crimped, and he smelled of horse sweat, and he looked tired, but he was quite possibly the most beautiful man she'd ever laid eyes on. She couldn't resist touching the hair that fell across his forehead, brushing it back only to watch it tumble down again. "Are you for real?"

"Damn straight." He smiled again. A blue sparkle danced in his eyes like a bouncing ball punctuating the lyrics he sang softly. "Little girl, little girl, don'tcha lie to me . . ."

10

Branding was a social event as well as an annual chore in the valley around Quicksilver Creek, and the High Horse branding traditionally kicked off the season. Being first had long been Sally Weslin's prerogative, but the ranks of the residents who remembered why were dwindling. As far back as the 1940s, Sally had set the standard, inviting all the neighbors out to the High Horse for a long day of old-fashioned hard work, followed by an elaborate spread and a fiddle music fest.

The party had become smaller over the years. Many of the old-timers had sold out, retired, moved away, passed away. But for those who were left, branding was still a time to get together and slap each other on the back for making it through another Wyoming winter and getting the calves on the ground in the spring.

Sally's grandson had not made it through the snow season, but spring had come anyway, with its promise of renewal, and there were calves on the ground. She was willing to forgo the live music but not the food, and not the old-fashioned hot-iron branding. Not yet. Not while her granddaughters were still there and she still had cowboys on her payroll.

The day before the event was spent moving the cows and preparing the meal. Sally worked alongside her granddaughters in the kitchen, but just before sundown the voices of her other girls came drifting through the kitchen window.

She wasn't going to miss that glorious sight, not this year. This year she was going to take it all in, every last detail. Out the door she went, fired up her pickup and beat the boys to the gate when they drove the last of the herd into the small pasture next to the corrals.

It was a beautiful sight. The confluence of cattle fairly flowed into the valley, following the creek like a wide run of molasses, horses pushing them along, dogs yapping at their heels. The men whistled and waved coils of hard-twist rope to keep them moving. Sally's heart thumped in her breast as she pushed one iron gate open and shooed her girls through. It must have been the cold breeze that made her eyes tear. It must have been the dust the girls were kicking up that made her throat burn.

Not far away K.C. rode drag, pushing the tail end of the herd. It was a role that yielded his customary view from the saddle and the kind of moment that put him in his place—detached, marginal, wanting. Shep called out to the dogs, directing them to shag would-be strays back to the bunch while K.C. and Vernon pushed them through the gate. When the task was complete, Vernon approached Sally with a tip of his hat, dismounted, and together they closed the gates.

Just closed the gates. But when the two came together, it was like a ceremony. K.C. watched them standing there side by side, surveying the pasture's holdings. Each time Sally spoke to Vernon, he nodded solemnly. Finally she touched his arm, and he dipped his head to one side, leaning closer to hear her as the cows bellowed all around them. The old man attended to that hand on his arm as closely as to the words in his ear. Vernon was devoted to Sally. More than devoted.

K.C. wondered whether the woman returned the old cowboy's affection. From where he sat in the saddle, he couldn't tell, but Vernon was an open book. And Shep knew—you could tell by the way he kept to his business and gave them this couple's moment, uninterrupted.

You could also tell that Vernon saw more than an old woman when he looked at Sally. He was lovesick, plain as day. K.C. had seen that look before, maybe even worn it on his own face a time or two, but not for some years. And not for as many years as he'd be willing to bet ol' Vern had. That long-suffering lovelorn look reminded him of another old cowboy, a good hand who had taught him the heart of what he knew about gentling horses.

Tully Mack had trained some of the best trick horses on the rodeo circuit, including Karla Houston's Amazing Houdini, but K.C.'s mother had never known how Tully felt about her. Or if she did, she never said. K.C. remembered asking her if she was going to marry Tully, and she'd laughed and said that it wasn't like that between her and Tully, that he was almost old enough to be her father. But that hadn't stopped Tully from loving her something fierce or from treating her son like his own kid, at least for a few brief years. Tully drank too much, his mother had said, as if that explained why his feelings for her didn't count. The guys she had feelings for always drank their share, too, and most of them treated her like shit to boot.

K.C. had missed the old cowboy after the Tully Mack Show went bust. Missed the Amazing Houdini, too, but the bank had a lien on the flashy trick horse. But he'd missed his mother the most.

He'd missed the old Karla Houston, the one who had been the star attraction of the Tully Mack Show. She was billed as "The Comanche Princess," capitalizing on the heritage of the grandmother K.C. had never known. He was supposed to look like her, though. Whenever he had asked about her, his mother would say, "Look in the mirror." And Tully had always said he had Comanche horse sense, like his mother.

A gymnast on horseback, Karla could do it all—Roman riding, fire ring, suicide drag—but she was never the same after the show folded. She'd never found another horse, couldn't stick with any other job, and the men had gone from bad to worse. None of that had stopped Tully from loving her. For that, surely, was why he'd offered to take care of her twelve-year-old son after her sudden death. But the case worker had turned the offer down, saying Tully Mack didn't have a proper home.

A proper home. Someday K.C. hoped to find out just

what that meant. He hoped it might have something to do
with the way ol' Vern was looking at Sally.

When the old cowboy finally glanced his way, K.C. dismounted. It was time to get a feel for the stock-working
setup. The Weslins had never used a mechanical calf table,
Vernon told K.C. as he walked him through the pens and
chutes, proudly showing him what was clearly Vernon's
personal setup, the rail fence and steel panels and gates he'd
arranged and rearranged over the years until he'd had the
system working just right.

"No calf table?" K.C. grinned at Sally, who was perched
on a stack of square bales on the other side of the fence,
looking regal and proud. She was sitting up high enough
so she could watch the evening shadows fall over the cows
already feeding on new grass. He figured she was probably
ten or fifteen years older than she looked, and this herd of
fine stock cows was her life's work. This was her moment.

She had a little teasing coming.

"You're afraid of making the job too easy for us?"

"She don't like putting cowboys out of work," Shep
shouted out. He was busy topping off the stock tank with
fresh water, and his limp was more pronounced than usual.
K.C. figured the ride had been hard on him.

"I'm just too cheap to buy one of those contraptions,"
Sally said. "Some change is good, but sometimes it pays
to stick with the tried and true, just so you don't lose sight
of what the words 'tried' and 'true' mean. Rope the calves
and let the young folks flop 'em," she told him. "It's nice,
having young folks around. Don't you think so, Vernon?"

"If they mind their manners."

"I expect you boys to see that they do," she said. "We
might just go ahead with this program Ross wanted to try
out here. Queenie's thinking about it, and I'm thinking it
would be good for her."

"*If* those boys can mind their manners," Vernon repeated. He'd found a loose hinge on one of the gates. With
a gesture he got K.C. to lift the gate so he could take a
wrench to the hinge bolt.

Sally stood up, bracing her hands and pushing off on her
knees. "They say that it helps some of these wild kids to

be around animals. Learning how to handle animals maybe gentles the kid a little bit. What would you say, K.C.?"

"I'd say you're putting together quite a collection of strays this spring, ma'am." Holding the weight of the gate off the hinge, he cast her a teasing smile. "Is this your hobby or something? Takin' in bad boys?"

"Never thought of it as a hobby. Maybe it's my destiny." She laughed. "Hell, maybe I'm *your* destiny."

Jack Trueblood arrived at daybreak, as he had promised, with a crew of six yawning, scratching, stretching teenage boys. Julia recognized a few of them from the day Jack had given her a tour of the school. They all wore boots and jeans, but two were without jackets despite the morning chill. Julia found a couple of Ross's denim jackets for them. The bigger boy accepted with a simple thanks and headed back outside, but the small, dark-haired boy examined the jacket as if he were considering a purchase.

"So he's dead, huh? The one who was gonna start a summer program for us?"

Julia assented with a "Mm-hmm."

The boy checked the label on the jacket. "So I'd be wearin' a dead guy's jacket."

"He hadn't worn it for quite a while. It's been hanging in the hall closet."

He took the plunge, thrusting an arm into a sleeve. He spared her a glance, as if to say okay, he was going to take her word that the jacket wasn't haunted. "So do we get to ride any horses today?"

"You get to wrestle calves today, Paco. Have you ever done any calf-wrestling?"

"Nope." He bobbed his shoulders, assessing the fit of the jacket. "Is this like a rodeo thing? Do I get to rope the calf?"

"Have you ever done any calf-roping?"

"Nope. Hog-tied my brother once," he confessed as they stepped outside to join the rest of the group, which had spilled from the porch into the yard. Two of the boys were making friends with Shep's dogs. "Hey, Chad, you ever roped anything?"

"You mean, like . . ." The tall boy with a mop of sandy blond hair swung an imaginary loop over his head, which, with the sun coming up behind it, took on the blaze of morning. "Not exactly. I rounded up some bikes once and herded them into my cousin's garage. Cops took 'em back, though. Do we get to ride horses today?"

They got to take turns, those who could prove they knew something about riding, but mostly they got to work on the ground. Separating the calves from the cows was the first order of the day, running the calves into the pens and sorting them. The series of chutes, holding pens and sorting gates adjacent to the corrals made the job less complicated than it looked. A sea of animals, sorted with the help of the two dogs, filled the fences. The cows stretched their necks and bellowed in protest of being parted from their babies, who had good reason to bawl. Once the branding got started, the acrid smoke that billowed above them carried the unmistakable smell of seared hide and scorched hair. Their mothers kept calling out to them. Each offspring knew its own mother's voice and would run to her call as soon as it was able.

Vernon wielded the branding iron. Shep had a deft hand with the castrating knife. Sally turned the vaccinating gun over to Julia, who was glad she didn't have to do ear tags. Stapling the numbered tags on the calves' ears had been her assignment for the past two years, she said, and she was ready for something new. Next year she could brand, Vernon said. She and Sally exchanged a glance, and then she looked elsewhere, toward the pens, then to the cows milling and lowing outside the pens. Next year was another country.

Chuck and Cal Pollak and a few other neighbors arrived by midmorning to help out. Chuck took charge of the chutes and gates, while his son rode around swinging a loop as though he expected something that needed to be roped to be jumping out in front of him at any time. Jack True-blood was like a sheepdog, yapping at the heels of the six boys, who were willing to give any chore a try, but getting them to stick with it was another matter. That left K.C. to direct the whole show. He took to the job pretty well, he figured, for a guy who generally preferred to work alone.

But he had to keep an eye on the kids. Jack was doing okay shagging them around, keeping them from slacking off, but Jack didn't know jack about handling livestock. The boys needed the same kind of attention K.C. always paid to a skittish colt. You had to stay calm, take your time showing the way and let them know when they were doing right.

"Careful, there, partner." He hunkered down next to Paco Morales, the littlest guy on the team, the one who kept trying to get in there even though he was scared, maybe a little head-shy. He had the calf in a death grip. "This one's not cooked, so there's no point in tearing his leg off."

"You said stretch him out. I don't want him to kick me."

"He's just a baby," K.C. explained as he showed the boy a firm but flexible hold. "You're a man."

Paco relaxed a little under K.C.'s tutoring hand, but not without complaint. "Hell, that last one just about kicked me in the . . ."

"Just about put an end to his manhood," scrawny, freckle-faced Merle piped up from a few feet away. He and the beefy kid with the chipped front teeth looked pretty smug about the way they had their calf immobilized.

"Which hasn't hardly gotten started yet," Paco's partner, Barney, added, bumping his glasses up with the back of a grimy hand. "That hair on his upper lip is just what escaped from his nose."

Paco released the calf's leg long enough to give Barney the finger and get himself kicked in the thigh. "Ow! That ain't no baby."

"There's only one big baby around here, Paco, and that happens to be you."

"Go fuck yourself."

"Vern!" K.C. signaled for the branding iron.

"You two hold still," Vernon warned as Julia came up behind him. "My aim ain't quite what it used to be."

The boys grumbled, turning their faces away from the smoke.

"Hey, you got any of that foul-mouth serum handy,

Queenie?" Vernon said as he stepped aside to let Julia do her job. "We've got a couple of hands here who seem to be sorely in need of inoculation."

"You guys can't behave, it'll be next January before you see the outside again," Trueblood shouted. He was perched on the rails twenty feet away. He'd just lit a cigarette, and he was looking at K.C. "Gotta keep 'em busy, is all."

K.C. waved, nodded, then dropped a hand on Paco's shoulder. "Catch me another one, partner. You go easy on the babies, watch your mouth around the ladies and you'll do fine."

That was all it took. The boy decided he had a job to do, and he was willing to go after it without being told. K.C. caught himself wondering what Paco had done to get himself into a reform school, *correctional facility*, whatever the hell they were calling it these days. Caught himself, looked at the boy again and turned away. It was none of his damn business what these kids were doing locked up, or what they were doing at the High Horse, for that matter. Sally could have her little hobby. Getting the job done was his business.

"Hey! Leighton! Is that your name? Leighton?" The chipped-tooth boy nodded eagerly. K.C. pointed to an ice-cream pail planted in the dirt next to Shep, who was down on one knee beside what was about to become a steer calf. "You take that bucket and you follow Shep around with it. You're his assistant. Don't make him call you twice. Got that?"

A couple of the boys hooted. One made a remark about Leighton being the "ball boy."

Leighton scowled.

"It's a man's job, collecting the balls," K.C. said, dead serious as he handed Leighton a can of antiseptic spray. "You got the stomach for it?" Leighton looked at the can, stammered a little. K.C. laid a hand on his shoulder and leaned in close. "It's one of those things you feel shitty about but you know it's gotta be done, so you cowboy up and you just do the job."

Leighton grimaced. "How bad does it hurt?"

"The spray helps." He assured the boy with a nod, a

subtle wink. "Kinda makes you thank God for small favors."

"What *small* favors?"

"*All* favors. Can you handle it for me?"

The boy flipped him a thumbs-up sign and went to work with Shep.

Dawn brought drinks and snacks for a tailgate break at noon, but at the end of the day when the work was done, it was time for serious chow. The men stripped down to the waist and gathered around the stock tank to wash up. They were covered with grit, soot and calf slime, so they weren't going near the house. Not that they wanted to. Branding was a day spent outdoors. The chow line would form in the front yard beneath the trees, and nobody would worry about how he smelled or what he had on his boots. It was time to sprawl in the grass and enjoy feeling good and tired.

Trueblood's boys clustered around the buffet table that had been set up on the porch, near the front door, while the men hung back in a cool male cluster of their own, waiting to be the second wave.

"What do you think of our plan?" Jack asked. K.C. gave him the look he wanted, inviting elaboration. "Summer program out here for the boys. I think Ross wanted to get it going for Julia as much as anything."

K.C. nodded. He wasn't in a mood to ask why.

"She's got a hell of an education, but I gotta tell you, it's a tough profession these days. You know, working with this kind of kid. I mean, I can understand her getting burned out, especially some of the places she's worked."

Jack offered K.C. a cigarette, which he declined, even though a cigarette would have tasted pretty good right then, and he'd been doing well, cut way back. But the phrase "kind of kid" put him off, made him downright tense in the gut. Jack popped a cigarette in his mouth, lit it and went right on talking.

"Ross had this idea about bringing Julia in on it, you know, get her out of the city. So we wrote this proposal. Damn, you just never know, do you? I mean, you plant a tree in the fall, you wonder whether it'll make it through the winter. You never think maybe *you* won't be here to see it leaf out.''

"So we'd have to give them stuff to do, huh?'' Shep lifted his hat and rubbed his bald spot as he eyed the boys on the deck. '' 'Course, Queenie's a real pro. She knows her onions as far as that goes, being a social worker. But Vern and me, we're gettin' too old to put up with any shenanigans. You think this can work out, K.C.?''

"I'm just a hired hand, Shep. I don't get paid to think.''

"You ain't no hired hand.'' Cal Pollak whacked K.C. on the shoulder with the back of his hand. "After the other day, I was thinkin' you looked familiar, so I dug out my *Western Horseman* magazines—I save 'em all—and I looked and looked until I found what I was lookin' for. Hell, you're K.C. Houston.''

K.C. gave a tight smile. That was exactly the way he remembered it, too.

Another whack on the arm. "Hell, man, I've read plenty of stuff about you and the way you train horses. Your picture was even on the cover of that other horse magazine. You know the one.''

He did indeed. "It's been a while.''

"Shee-it, you're a celebrity, almost. I was tellin' Dad . . .'' He turned to his father, who was studying the ground, arms folded over his paunch, but he was listening. K.C. figured not too much got past Chuck Pollak. "Well, we always break our colts ourselves, you know, never brought in no trainer or nothin'. But, hell, I like to read up on what other guys are doing.''

"Ross Weslin was a good one for coming up with fancy ideas,'' Chuck allowed quietly, still studying the patch of grass below his belly.

"Nothing fancy about me,'' K.C. said. "I just do what comes natural.''

"That's what you said in that one article I read. You said sensitivity was as natural for a man as for a horse. You sure about that?''

"They put it into print.'' K.C. shrugged. "Guess that makes me pretty damn sure of it.''

Cal laughed. "I guess so, you being the expert. I don't have time for a real touchy horse myself."

"Well, that's generally how I earn my living. I get paid to take the time."

"What's a guy like you doing here, you don't mind my askin'?"

"Working." K.C. laid a hand on Shep's bony shoulder. "Just another High Horse hand."

"Friend of Ross's?" Cal asked, his tone suggestive. K.C. looked through him. Cal grinned. "Friend of one of the girls."

"Friend of the judge's." K.C. smiled when one of the boys opened the screen door and Julia came out with a chocolate layer cake. "Right now I'm a friend of whoever wants to feed me."

"How long you figure on staying?" Chuck asked.

"Well, now, Chuck, I'm a contract rider. I take on a job, I like to see it through. My reputation is for guaranteed satisfaction. I don't move on until the job is done and the boss is satisfied."

Chuck nodded, thought it over for a moment, then took a more direct approach. "You think they'll be looking for offers soon? I don't want to push. The one thing I don't want to do is push."

"You go right to the head of the line, Chuck," K.C. said with an "after-you" gesture in the direction of the porch. "You won't have to push. You're a guest."

Julia helped Dawn and Sally set out the casserole dishes, roasters and kettles of food on the picnic tables. Dawn had done most of the cooking, and the hearty spread surprised Julia. Not the quality, but the down-home dishes and the generous quantity. Dawn had always been a good cook, but she favored gourmet fare. The potato salads, baked beans, fried chicken and barbecued beef brisket on the buffet table didn't seem like Dawn. Especially since it tasted like traditional High Horse.

"It's Gramma's recipe," Dawn was telling the Pollaks, who were singing praises for the brisket. "I love to cook. Just point me toward the kitchen, and I'll do the rest. I used to own a restaurant." She slid Julia a cagey you-know-me smile. "It was one of my best failed businesses. Glorious place, fabulous food. My downfall was that I spared no expense."

"That's the Weslin in you," Sally said. "Your dad was a spend-it-while-you-got-it kind of a guy, too."

"Was he?" Dawn turned to Chuck. "Did you know my dad? I'll bet you two went to school together."

"Played basketball together in high school."

"Did you? Was he good? I hardly remember him." She gave Julia a strange look, as though she thought her sister had kept something from her, hoarded all the memories for herself. But then she smiled, and Pollak started in recollecting the year the Quicksilver Cowboys had been championship contenders.

Their dad, the contender. Dawn seemed to be sucking up every detail, truly interested, and Julia was a little taken aback. Maybe she really hadn't heard these stories before. Their dad at his best. Dawn at her best. Her "best failed business" remark hadn't sounded like sour grapes, and Julia thought she'd seen a kind of solicitation in her sister's smile. *Know me, Julia. This is part of me.*

Their mother was fond of saying that when Dawn was good, she was very, very good. Yeah, *but*, Julia always wanted to say. But what? This was Dawn at her best. She was irresistible, and men, in particular, adored her. No one would have guessed that she had spent the past two days cooking. She looked fresh and smelled like lilacs. She was wearing a pale lavender blouse with denim pants that were too well tailored to be called jeans. Julia smelled like fried hair and cow manure, like everyone else, which didn't bother her as long as she wasn't standing next to her immaculate sister. But she was not about to let the foolish bothering part show.

She caught herself searching for K.C. whenever she surveyed the group, officially on the lookout for needs and requests. He'd catch her at it every time, and he would send her that soft, knowing smile of his above the heads of those who milled around in the space between them. The visitors from the boys' school had taken to K.C. as a fellow out-

sider. Like a little swarm of drones, they hung close to him,
saying little as they shoveled chicken and beans into their
mouths, cheeks billowing, eyes darting while they chewed.
He appeared to be at ease with this role, like a pair of old
boots he'd slipped into without thought. He nodded occa-
sionally, commented quietly, laughed the same way. He
was one of those rare people whose confident, unruffled
presence attracted kids.

Julia made up her mind about the summer program then
and there. It was actually more of an instinctive determination than a rational one. She would deal with reasoning
and logistics later. The basic elements were already in
place, and she'd promised Gramma the summer. She had a
feeling about K.C. and the horses and the kids. Something
told her Ross was tuned in to that feeling somehow, and
that he was plum tickled about it.

By nightfall the cows had been moved to the small pasture north of the house. They were still calling out to each
other in the dark, the calves still mothering up. The party,
such as it was, had broken up, everyone heading for a hot
shower and cool sheets somewhere.

Julia enjoyed the shower but resisted the sheets. The
night held a certain attraction for her that sleep did not. The
bright quarter moon and its attendant stars shed their milky
light over the rocky ridge beyond the creek and the rail
fences and rolling grass. She followed the voices of the
herd. No longer the indignant clamor that had filled the
afternoon, the voices in the dark were comforting, full of
"mother's-here" solace.

Julia pulled an old crocheted shawl close around her
shoulders and followed the path along the fence. The creek
trickled and splashed and hurried on past her in the dark.
Up ahead, where the fence turned a corner, she saw the
glow of a cigarette, then the silhouette of a man waiting
there in the dark. She knew who he was. She could tell by
the way her skin tingled beneath the shawl and her insides
fluttered. Her response to him was unwilled, probably un-
warranted, but she was immersed in it the moment she re-

alized that he was the attraction the night held for her. The
cowboy at the fence.

"I haven't seen you smoke," she said as she joined him
there. No need to explain or comment about the night or
the moonlight. It felt as though he'd been waiting, expecting her.

"I don't, usually." He sent a trail of smoke into the night
air above his head. "Used to a lot. Bad habit. One of several I've been trying to break." He hooked his boot heel
on the fence rail and listened for a moment. The cows were
indistinct, shifting shadows. "You can almost hear the
scolding, can't you? Like they told their kids to stick close
and stay clear of those weird two-legged critters. They
didn't listen, and look what it got them."

She eased forward on the balls of her feet until the fence
rail caught her at the waist. "Maybe it's us they're scolding. Or warning. *Don't mess with my baby anymore.*"

"Maybe they're just making their joyful noises over getting their kids back. When it's bad is after the calves get
shipped. The cows sing a different tune then, don't they?
You can tell they're hurtin' then."

Oh, yes, she remembered. "I always wanted to hide
somewhere after the calves were shipped, but Ross used to
go out and talk to the cows."

"He did, huh?" She heard the smile in his voice. "What
did he tell them?"

"That he was sorry." She gripped the shawl and folded
her arms tight, hugging herself, holding herself in. "I'm
seeing him everywhere I look. You must get tired of hearing me talk about him."

"I like hearing you talk. Whatever you want to talk about
is fine by me."

"Let's talk about you," she said, and he groaned. "You
were really good with those boys, K.C." She watched him
drag deeply on his cigarette. "Better than Jack, and they're
his job."

"All I did was treat them like I would anyone else.
Maybe they're hard cases, I don't know, but put 'em in a
holding pen like that, they might as well go ahead and
stamp a label on the back of their shirts."

"Wouldn't a summer program here be good for them? There's so much here, such a variety of activity, and good people. You, Vernon, Gramma . . ." He laughed, shaking his head. "Yes, *you*, K.C. They really responded to you. They could come over during the week, just during the day, part of the day."

"They could take off."

"We'd keep a close eye on them. Where would they go?"

"Anywhere." He made the word sound like a wish remembered. He let it drift for a moment, then reeled it in. "Someplace where nobody knows anything about them, where they can be free to make a new start."

She turned to him, still resting her hip on the fence. "They're just kids. Most of them will be able to do that when they turn eighteen."

"Some guys can't wait that long."

It was the most he'd told her about himself. "A man who understands what that's like might be just the right person to—"

"I'm not the right person." He sucked one last, deep drag, then ground his cigarette out on the top of the fence post. "You're the one who could make a thing like that work if you wanted to."

"How would you know that?"

"You said you were a social worker. I've known a few social workers in my time. I can spot a kindhearted one a mile off." He cast her a sidelong glance, teased her with a smile. "Those are the ones a guy can get his way with if he works it right."

"Oh, really?" She laughed. She was efficient, she thought, and fair, and she knew all the whys and wherefores, but she'd left kindhearted behind with her twenties. "So much for that idea. All I need is to have some kid get his way with me."

"Part of my job as your foreman is heading them off at the pass. Any male whose intentions are the least bit crafty, I'll haze him over in the corner and set him straight." He demonstrated the sinuous motion with his hand. "Young and old alike."

"Dawn's the temptation around here. I'm the older, wiser sister."

"Why do you keep bringing up age? Are you trying to impress me, or scare me away?" Even in the dark she could see that sparkle in his eyes. "Either way, it ain't workin'."

He'd led her away from her purpose again, but she was going to get something out of him yet. Case history. She was a professional, after all.

She smiled. "How did you get to know your share of social workers?"

He adjusted his hat and peered at her through the dark. "Most agreeable breed of woman there is, next to teachers."

"It's not a 'breed.' It's a vocation, and I used to be pretty good at it, but I don't know. It's gotten so bound up with red tape, so . . ." She sighed. "All right, so *intrusive* sometimes. You end up manipulating people's lives in a way that I'm not sure we have a right to do. Not that we shouldn't be protecting the children, because, of course, we must. But sometimes we presume some people to be poor parents simply because they're, well, poor. Or black, or unmarried, or, you know, different somehow." He was nodding, and she realized he'd done it again. "How did you get me started on this? We were talking about—"

"You're thinkin' about quitting it altogether."

His voice was part of the night, the forgiving night that knows without seeing and makes it easy to say more.

"I just don't think I'm right for it anymore. Or it's right for me, or whatever." She dipped her chin, tucked it into her shawl. "I'm simply tired."

"Have you thought about becoming a rancher? You've sure got a nice place here."

She wasn't cold, but she shivered. "I've thought about it, and what I think is, I don't know the first thing about ranching."

"Yeah, you do." He turned his back to the fence and boosted himself up, seating himself on the top rail. "You're at home here. I think that's the first thing."

Home had nothing to do with it. It wasn't the being or the living that mattered; it was the *doing*, and doing well.

"Ross wasn't doing very well at it, either, from the looks of the books. Spending more than he was taking in."

K.C. shrugged. "I know how that goes."

"Do you? But, hell, you're a *celebrity*," she said, mimicking Cal Pollak.

"You caught that, huh?" He chuckled as he reached for her and drew her between his knees to stand facing him. "Does it buy me any points?"

She tipped her head back and thought, *A point for every star*, but she wouldn't say that. Too foolish, even though the move felt smooth and easy, as natural as dancing with him. She wouldn't tell him that this was exactly where she wanted to be, close in, making a circle of two, with a center place for confidences. But neither would she move away.

Her smile was tentative. "Telling me more about who you are would buy you lots of points."

"I doubt that. Either you get to know me or you don't." He ran his hands over her tightly wound arms the way she'd seen him do to the wild mare, petting her, coaxing her to loosen up and let go of herself. "I'm getting to know you. You don't have to tell me a thing." His hands were courteous and attentive, not intrusive at all. "But you can if you want. What do you want me to call you?"

She laughed nervously. "*Not* 'Queenie.' "

"People who love you call you Queenie."

"I know. It's because . . ." He was putting her arms around his waist, pulling her closer. The shawl hung between them, brushing his knees. He smelled of spicy soap and leather and cigarette smoke. She tried to keep breathing steadily, keep talking. He was nuzzling her hair, brushing the side of her face with his chin, which felt like fine sandpaper and gave her goose bumps. "I was a bossy kid," she reported stubbornly. "I guess I used to be kind of a royal . . ."

"Give me a royal command," he whispered into her hair. She swallowed convulsively, and he chuckled. "Come on, lady, boss me."

"You're off duty."

"A cowboy's always on call." He rubbed her back, fingering her vertebrae like the keys of a flute. "All you gotta do is say when and show me where."

"This might be a good time for a kiss." She drew back a little. "But I don't want to be charged with anything."

"I never had a cradle." He feathered his lips across her forehead, tickling her with whispered words. "People generally don't rob the cabbage patch."

"I was thinking of sexual harassment."

"What's that?" He lifted his hand to her face, stroked her cheek, then her hair. His eyes glittered, pale and soft as moonlight. "I'm just a simple cowboy, honey. With me, a kiss is just a kiss."

"Your hat's in the way."

"Take it off."

Her shawl slipped a little when she reached up, lifted the hat and laid her arm around his shoulder as his mouth descended to cover hers. Every aspect of her was suddenly focused and funneled into their kiss. His mouth was wet and warm and overwhelming, his tongue titillating, and the small, gratified sound he made was utterly endearing. All that surrounded them stood silent and still while they kissed, first hungrily, then shyly, then hungrily again.

And when he finally lifted his head and she caught her breath, and the night flooded back with its riotous stars and shimmering moonlight, she whispered, "Oh," and he whispered her name.

They looked at each other, feeling what they felt and searching for some explanation for it, each searching for a matching feeling in the other's eyes.

"Answer me straight out, K.C. You're not . . ." *Not what? Not going to hurt me? Not serious?* "You're not just any hired hand. Why are you here?"

"It's where I ended up." He shrugged, smiling diffidently. "So I'm here for you."

"Go *on*!" She laughed and gave him a little shove, tipping him backward. "*I'm here for you.*"

"Watch it, darlin'." He slipped back, caught himself at the crook of his knees, but he was still holding onto her. "If I go down, you're goin' with me." From a position less precarious than it looked, given his rider's legs, he grinned at her. "Where do you want to end up?"

"With both feet on the ground." She tugged on him, laughing, and he sat up, laughing, but the laughter died as they righted themselves. "I depend on that, you know." She was still smiling, but the teasing was gone from his eyes, and the quiet need was back. "The ground," she whispered. "Under my feet. I depend on it."

"I know you do," he said, and he kissed her again.

11

*D*awn woke up freezing in the narrow bed from her childhood, her whole body wound into a tight coil. Her first thought was that Roger was gone again. But as the noise outside registered as cow din, the yapping dogs nipping at the retreating edges of her sleep, she remembered that it was she, not her unpredictable husband, who was gone this time. Gone West, for God's sake. Gone crazy, sleeping with the window open because she'd panicked when she'd dreamed she was trapped in the barn again. She could still smell the dust and the horse shit.

The luminous numbers on the nightstand said it was much too early to get up. She heaved herself off the bed anyway and went to close the window, squinting, defending what was left of her drowsiness in the hope of going back to bed and picking up where she'd left off after she'd gotten out of the damn barn. But she made the mistake of noticing the light swelling on the horizon, tinting the mountains purple and gold. And she saw the movement beyond the trees below the window, the cattle crowding through the far gate, like pepper carefully poured from a box.

She remembered. They were taking the cattle to the summer pasture today. She couldn't see faces, but she knew the riders. Vernon, Shep, K.C., Julia, a couple of those juvenile delinquents. Big trail drive, big event, big fun— they'd been all abuzz about it last night at supper, laughing about how sore Julia was going to be after a long day in the saddle. She slammed the window shut and snapped the blinds. God, she hated horses!

Damn, she wanted to ride along with them.

How hard could it be? All you had to do was get up in that saddle and sit there. She wasn't five years old anymore. Nobody was trying to put her back on the same evil Shetland pony that had already stepped on her foot, nipped her arm and made her fall off and get hung up and almost die. Nobody was going to tell her to stop being a baby and kick him, just kick him and make him go. That advice was about the extent of her natural memory of Michael Weslin.

If you don't make him go, you're gonna get left behind.

But she might fall off.

Stay here with Mom, then.

Stay behind and watch TV. Play in Mama's makeup. Talk to the cat. Be a good girl and stay out of our way.

She really ought to be able to ride a horse. It wasn't something that required a college degree, for God's sake. She *was going to* learn. K.C. Houston was going to teach her, very soon. And she was going to enjoy the lessons. Very much.

The jangling phone spoiled the hush in the house. On the third ring, Dawn conceded that there was no one else around, so she answered. It was Roger, calling her all the way from Connecticut.

"I didn't get you up, did I?" He knew damn well he had. "I just thought I'd give you a call before I head for work. I talked to Merrick yesterday. He says we probably won't see any money from your share for a while, no matter what, but the way it's set up, your grandmother still has a lot of say in the matter. The ranch is incorporated as a family business, but with anything agricultural like that, the overhead is so high that the shareholders—that's you, now—probably don't stand to get anything out of it unless there's a liquidation. And it sounds like the way it's set up, you can't just liquidate your share. Which means—"

"I know what it means, Roger." Roger's attorney friend had never impressed her, but his free advice was priced right.

"There has to be an appraisal done, right? But Merrick

says that unless there's a big mortgage or something, the place has to be worth millions. *Millions*, honey.'' She could hear him slurping at the other end. Coffee, probably. ''How old did you say your grandmother is?''

''I don't know. Eighty-something. Do you know how old *your* grandmother is?''

''I haven't seen my grandmother since they put her in a nursing home. I'm not even sure she's alive, never mind how old she is.'' Pause. Dawn could almost hear him thinking. ''I suppose I would have heard something if she died. Somebody would have called me, right?''

''With your family, Roger, who knows?''

''Yeah, like the Weslins are all that close. Big difference is, my grandmother's not sitting on a million-dollar property.''

''Keep that in mind.'' She could smell coffee. Somebody had made some downstairs, and she really wanted a cup of it. Much more than she wanted this conversation.

''Yeah. Like I'm thinking, if we can get them moving toward liquidating the thing, we could probably borrow against your share.''

At least he wasn't saying *our* share. ''Gramma wants to wait until fall.''

''For what?''

''Julia promised her the summer, I guess.''

''What did she do that for? This is the time to sell. Anybody who knows anything about real estate knows spring is the time to put it on the market. You think I should come out there?''

''You could have come for the funeral.''

''I wasn't invited.''

''We didn't send out invitations.''

Stalemate.

A moment passed before he reported, ''They keep calling from the store, asking when you're going back to work.''

''Just stall them off. Julia took a leave of absence.''

''Yeah, well, I don't think that's an option for you.''

''What, I can't find another job selling women's underwear? I can always get another job. With any luck, I won't have to.''

She pictured Roger sitting on the stool at the kitchen counter, holding the receiver from the wall phone next to his freshly shaven cheek. The imagined scent of his cologne displaced the smell of coffee. She smiled. No matter what his shortcomings in the caring and sharing department, her husband was the sexiest man alive, bar none.

"Our ship is coming in here, Roger. Once it's safely tied up in the harbor and the auctioneer is taking bids on the cargo, I'll head home, but I really have to stick around and do what I can to hurry it along."

"How's your sister?"

The question pricked Dawn's bubble, but a replacement filled in immediately. Roger was now smiling at someone sitting across the counter from him. Someone with long dark hair and nice legs, also freshly shaven. Probably wearing Dawn's new bathrobe.

"Julia's fine." He might have known that firsthand, had he chosen differently a few years back. He might have been with Julia, might have had and held Julia. He'd settled for Dawn.

"So, what, you just sit around all summer watching cows eat grass?"

"That's basically it." She gave a joyless laugh. "You wouldn't believe how dead this place is. The hired men do most of the work while we Weslin women sit on the porch, sip our margaritas and let the wind fill our hair with sand."

"What men?" Roger wasn't big on margaritas. "What hired men?"

"Gramma's still got those two old ranch hands around, plus now she's hired this cowboy." Have a little soap, she thought with a smile. All it took was a suggestion. Roger was a bubble maker, too.

"What cowboy?"

"Just some ranch hand."

He was quiet for a moment. The woman sitting across from him evaporated. "So what's the difference between a ranch hand and a cowboy?"

"In this case, probably about forty years. The guy's really quite a horse trainer, I guess, came looking to work for Ross, and Gramma talked him into staying around for a while.''

''Goddamn. You shouldn't be hiring people now; you should be letting people go. What does he look like, this cowboy?''

''What difference does it make what he looks like? He dresses like Joe Texas and smells like a horse.'' *Translation, Roger, he's a hunk.* She was laughing easily now that she had the upper hand in the game they had been playing with each other since day one, a game in which the undeclared rules had been changing since day two. ''He gets along fine with the little doggies, which is all that counts, right?''

''Right.'' Roger chuckled, warming to the challenge. He truly believed that in a war of good looks, he would ultimately be the last hunk standing. ''Get them doggies rollin', is all I've got to say. Your grandmother's willing to sell if that's what you and Julia want, right?''

''That's what she says.''

''And that's what Julia wants, too, isn't it?''

''Julia and I don't talk much; you know that. But what else could she want? There's no one left. She's a social worker, and I'm . . . I'm *whatever*. But together we make up the end of the Harris-Weslin, up-on-their-High-Horse line.''

''It could change everything for us, Dawn.''

''Could it?'' They had been talking divorce lately. Maybe not actually *talking*; it was more like they'd hurled the word at each other, along with a few choice epithets and accusations. Instruments of the game.

''Of course it could. We've always gotten along better when we had money.'' Then, quietly, as though he really thought he could make her believe he was still her champion: ''I just want to see you get treated right. You know, fair.''

''That makes two of us, Roger.''

The drive to the high-country pasture was another tradition as old as the High Horse. The calves had been given a couple of days to recover from the stress of branding,

time for Vernon to "educate" K.C. about the route High
Horse cattle had been driven over every spring since Vernon had first signed on with Max Weslin. It was the same
trail the Harrises had used, back in the days when Sally's
daddy, Henry, ramrodded the drive.

Vernon seemed to think K.C. needed to know more than
just the lay of the land, so he'd taken him out in the pickup
the day before the drive. They couldn't follow the route in
the pickup, but they were able to hit some of the high spots.
Vern told him the history behind every fork in the trail and
every watering hole. He produced a yellowed map, drawn
in black ink, delineating the trail. Creek, washout, timber,
a flat called "Sheep Bucher" and a place called "Hony-
com" were all labeled in a small, neat hand. The mountains
and trees marched across the page in orderly rows, and the
tiny horses on Painted Mountain were beautifully rendered,
but the spelling was worse than K.C.'s own. This was
clearly a valued keepsake, and K.C. was sure his pocket
wasn't the place for it. He tried to give it back.

"You're ramroddin' this one, K.C.," Vern said, waving
the paper away like the last piece of meat on the table. "I
remember when Max gave me that map, he said the same
thing. 'You're the ramrod now, Vern.' First year Max come
here, ol' Henry drew this up for him, and he kept it all
those years until he give it to me. But those little drawings
and the notes?" He reached across the pickup cab to touch
the paper in K.C.'s hand once more, grazing the sketches
lightly with a yellowed fingernail. "Max added those himself. He could draw real good. The judge had some of his
drawings framed. They're up on the walls, up to the
house."

K.C. hadn't seen much of the house, other than the
kitchen, dining room. He'd declined Dawn's invitation to
come in and watch TV one night, saying he was tired. Truth
was, he'd been saving his evenings for the mustangs. Besides, the main house wasn't his territory. He didn't belong
there.

He nodded, making a second attempt to return the map.
"I've spent my life moving from place to place, so I've
got a pretty good sense of direction."

"Oh, I can believe that." Vernon gripped the steering wheel in both hands. "You keep that with you. Take it out and look at it from time to time. Kinda helps you to get your bearings."

Whose bearings? K.C. thought about the way the two of them had looked, Vern and Sally, standing by the fence together watching the cows come home.

"Sally's husband's been gone a long time, hasn't he?"

"Max?" Vernon stared ahead, through the bug-spattered windshield, across the creek and into the cottonwoods. "What's a long time mean to you, son? Thirty years?" He demonstrated, a flat hand, a smooth, steady line. "Passes like water." A quick glance, old eyes to young. "Before you know it, you've pissed it away."

"Damn. Thirty years?" K.C. shook his head, deadpan. "What the hell were you drinkin', Vern?"

Vernon laughed, and K.C. joined him. When the laughter died, the easy feeling remained between them.

Vernon nodded at the map. "You take that out and look at it once in a while. The High Horse is the kind of a place where you can ride from sunup to sundown through grass that's stirrup-high, never cross over any blacktop or under any high wires. Not many places left you can say that about. Not much cowboy paradise left."

"There's a little blacktop missing from this map, Vern." He chuckled, carefully folding the delicate paper. He knew exactly what the old man meant, but he had to tease him a little. It was expected.

"Not much traffic to speak of, though. Any tourists come along while we're crossing, they can just plan on parkin' it for a while, 'cause the High Horse always has the right of way."

Now they were working together, he and Julia, the two old cowboys, two of Trueblood's boys and the two Border collies. Two by two, K.C. was thinking as he watched the woman, counting her as the other part of his pair. Her hair came alive in the sun, flashing hints of red and gold riches, defying the confines of the clip at the base of her neck. Her thighs jounced a little in the saddle, and her breasts jiggled

some when she sat the trot. She'd probably think it was a
bad thing, a sign of some imperfection, but she'd be wrong.
It was a good thing, a beautiful thing. It was her softness.

She seemed to sense his thoughts, for she circled her
sorrel gelding, looked back at him and smiled. He waved
to her to join him at the back of the herd, but one of the
boys snared her for a look at his arm, scraped up in a patch
of brush. The boy basked in her attention, and she favored
him with her pretty smile. K.C. watched, beating down a
surprising pang of envy by turning his thoughts to how he
was going to make her a happy woman, at least for the
summer. He was going to figure out just what it would take,
and he was going to give it to her. His reason? He didn't
need a reason. He had a feeling. Julia was the other part of
his pair, at least for the summer.

Together they pushed the cattle from the edge of the
basin into the foothills, down cool ravines banked by rocky
red slopes. Throughout the morning his boss lady had taken
direction from him, just like everyone else. But she had
also slid into place by his side and he to hers whenever the
opportunity arose. It felt good, this unspoken agreement of
theirs. He asked her to show him some columbine if she
saw any. She took that as an invitation to point out every
wildflower she saw and name it for him, as if he were
testing her, or she planned to test him.

When they rode apart, he was glad he'd been paying
attention. Where before the ground had been dressed mod-
estly in his eyes—grass, greasewood, sage, pine—suddenly
he was seeing little flowers everywhere he looked. Small
yellow blossoms were beginning to pop open on the antelope bush dotting the slope above the trail. He rode the
perimeter, bunching the herd's flank, chuckling to himself
for trying to keep them from trampling too much of the
spiky purple lupine or the sunny faces of yellow balsamroot
flowers on one particularly splendid slope.

When next they came together, he asked Julia whether
she'd ever seen a field of Texas bluebonnets. It pleased him
that she shook her head and let him describe the memory
to her.

"If I'da taken you at your word that first night and

hauled you off with me, that's where we'd be right now," he told her. "Rolling in bluebonnets."

"Are you sorry you stayed?"

The notion of being sorry and still staying made him laugh. "I can just see you, wakin' up the next morning, finding yourself on the outskirts of Denver." He shook his finger at her and ratcheted his voice up a few notches. "You better turn this rattletrap around right now, young man, or your cowboy ass is grass."

"I would never say such a thing."

"No, you wouldn't, would you? You'd just tell me to stop at the next phone booth. You don't really want me to throw you over the back of my horse and ride off with you." He eyed her for a moment. She eyed him right back, smiling just enough to tempt him. "Do you?"

"I'm beginning to see how this works. I generally answer your questions. You never *quite* answer mine. You've got me all figured out, and you retain all your sexy mystique."

"Sexy *mystique*?" He grinned. Distracted from his amusement by a worry down the road, he said, "Hold that thought." His signal to the mare was barely discernible, but she shifted readily to a ground-eating lope.

Julia couldn't help but hold the thought as she watched him tend to his job. On the slope up ahead, a calf stumbled along behind its mother, its lolling tongue a telling sign of exhaustion. K.C. swung down from the saddle and scooped the calf into his arms. He appeared to have a quick conference with the mare, who then stood still while he lifted the calf and settled it over the horse's withers. He mounted the horse with fluid grace, disturbing neither horse nor calf. It was a feat that was striking for the ease with which it was performed.

K.C. called to Vernon, who rode over for a palaver, then headed for the front of the herd, standing in his stirrups for the trot. K.C. wheeled the mare and waited for Julia to catch up. "This little guy says we've pushed them far enough this morning." He rubbed the bleating black calf's curly white face. "Time for milk for the babies, water for the mamas and rest for everybody."

The mare ignored the calf's ungrateful squirming.

"You've turned Columbine into quite a stock horse," Julia said. She'd seen Vernon carry a calf or a foal on horseback many times, but she remembered watching her father try it once and end up with a flailing calf and a bucking horse.

"We've been getting to know each other, had a few chats about what we expect, and we've reached an understanding, Colly and me." He steadied the calf with his free hand. "Behave yourself, now; you're gettin' a free ride. We're countin' on you to show your appreciation by not shitting all over us."

Julia laughed, and it surprised her when he blushed, which was something Vernon might do.

"Sorry, there's just no other word for it. Birds can leave droppings and horses can deposit road apples, but calves, well, they shit."

"That's true enough, but here's a test for you: what about babies?"

"What, human babies?" She nodded, and he shrugged diffidently. "Guess I don't remember."

"I just wondered what the cowboy lingo might be."

"I don't know that there is any. We're men of few words. No room in our limited store for terms we got no call to use. Fact is, we don't run across too many human babies when we're ridin' the range." He smiled, gave her a just-between-us look. "I got no woman, and I got no kids."

"Ah, a straight answer. And I didn't even ask a question."

"I figure it's something you've got a right to know." And before she could challenge his reasoning, he rode off, sitting the mare's easy trot and skirting the serpentine herd on his way to reclaiming tacit command of the drive.

12

Sally nudged the pickup over the top of the ridge, where she could watch the herd proceed through the natural trough of a grassy draw, black white-faced calves trailing their dependable, broad-hipped Hereford mothers. Sally loved that sight. The sheep had come and gone, but the cattle had always paid the bills.

It was the horses that kept the menfolk interested, at least *her* menfolk, and she'd always known that. Her grandson, God rest his restive soul, had found his own refuge in the soul of the wild herd. Her son, Michael, had been more of a parade cowboy, loved to dress up and play the part, compete in an occasional rodeo just to show off for the girls and have something to celebrate with the boys. Her husband had had little patience with Michael's brand of horsing around, but Max had been a horse lover, too. A man on the ground is just another man, he'd say, but a man on a horse is servant to none.

Max had had no desire to be anyone's master, but when he'd met Sally he'd put his days of taking orders behind him. Anything he could do for her was only a request away. All she had to do was ask. She'd tried giving him an order just once. He'd turned and walked away. She'd felt so small and bereft, standing there watching his lanky, broad-shouldered frame make its ambling departure, that she'd added a whole list of asking words to her vocabulary on the spot.

He'd been a proud man, her Max. When his son hadn't grown up to be the workhorse his father was, Max and Michael had stopped talking about the things they cared about. She'd watched the same estrangement develop between Michael and Ross when the father failed to see his own image in the son. Yet all three had loved, *dearly* loved, horses.

There was no getting around the fact that Sally had spoiled her son, made a selfish man of him, indulging him until Michael Weslin thought Michael Weslin was pretty much what life was all about. But she was selfish, too. She was selfish about living this red-rock, green-grass, warm-sun life, *this* life, and she didn't want it to end with her. All she had left were her two granddaughters. She had no right to order them, and maybe it was even foolish to ask. Just this summer, she thought. Spring was the teaser, but summer, oh, summer in Wyoming was nothing short of splendor.

And she knew damn well she'd added the cowboy to the mix purely to supply that extra spice. At her age, she was allowed. Even if she wasn't, she'd done it anyway.

Besides, Ross was the one who'd started it.

"Gramma?"

Sally turned to the girl sitting on the far side of the pickup. *Girl?* Dawn was nearly thirty, but she was still the Weslin baby. Looked just like a little yellow rose bud. No matter what she was wearing, she always managed to look prettied up. Like her mother, Dawn would always be a visitor at the High Horse, even though it was her birthplace. Birthright, too, and no mistake, for Sally wasn't one to deal family out, even the ones who didn't take to the family business. Such a pretty little thing. She always had been.

"I was saying that the Pollaks invited me over for supper tonight. And anyone else who wants to go along. Would you be interested?"

The Pollaks. Sally knew damn well what those buzzards were after. "Was it Cal or Chuck came up with this invite?"

"It was Cal's mother who called."

"And why would she be doing that, I wonder?"

"She invited *all* of us." Dawn gave a martyr's sigh. "Just being friendly, Gramma. Offering some social life. I don't know too many people here, but I used to play with Cal when we were little kids."

"Come to think of it, Edna hasn't had much luck getting anyone to play with him since." Sally enjoyed the joke, but Dawn held to a curved mouth and impassive eyes.

Sally pointed to the creek. "See those cottonwoods over there? That's where we'll set up and serve our drovers dinner. After they eat, they'll be crossing the highway just beyond that ridge." The gears ground in protest as she jerked on the floor shift. "If we sell out, we won't be cutting Chuck Pollak any special deals. You can tell him I said so."

"Mmm-hmm."

"Look at them," she said of the cattle, moving in one big, beautiful bunch. "Just like syrup pouring over the lip of the pitcher and spreading out onto the plate. We've brought them over this same ground every year since I can remember. Every spring."

"I know, Gramma."

But she really didn't, Sally thought. She had no idea.

The horses were watered, unsaddled and tethered to graze along the creek bank. The riders ate their sandwiches and sprawled under the cottonwoods, where the grass was pale and fine. Leighton and Chad hadn't done much riding in the past year, they admitted, and they were feeling a little "mushy-legged," but they thought this cowboy stuff was pretty cool. When was the summer program going to start? they asked several times apiece. Laughing, Julia stretched her own gelatinous legs and finally said, "Soon," which drew her some looks that were easy enough to read. Gramma was pleased. Vernon was skeptical, but he'd go along. Dawn thought Julia had lost her mind.

No look from K.C. He went right on munching the apple he'd selected from the big picnic basket, giving it more attention than it deserved. The apples were out of season, mushy and tasteless.

If she was going to take on this project, she would need

his help, interest and support, she thought. She wanted to use the mustangs, maybe assign each boy his own horse to tame. She'd read about successful penitentiary projects that worked that way, and she was thinking now about trying something similar. But she couldn't do it without K.C. She'd seen him handle the horses. He was more than a trainer; he was an artist. The boys had taken to him instantly. He was *the man*.

But he was pointedly ignoring the discussion. He wanted to play games.

"When do I get *my* summer program, K.C.?" Dawn's sultry smile suddenly had him forgetting all about the apple in his hand. Julia wondered if he imagined a sweeter one in Dawn's. "You promised to teach me to ride. When I go back to Connecticut, I want to be able to tell everyone that I took lessons from the famous K.C. Houston."

He chuckled. "What are you gonna tell them I'm famous for?"

"Whatever talents you show me. I'm pretty hopeless when it comes to horses, so if you could get me to the point where I could just get on and ride around." She was looking at Columbine, the beautiful charcoal Arabian dressed up with white trim. "But I suspect you could make a girl completely forget she was sitting on top of a big animal like that, huh? Some big stud that was about ten times her size?"

Somebody should have laughed, but no one did. The image she'd painted hung over the group, and no one knew what to say.

Except Dawn, perfectly deadpan. "That is a stud you're riding, isn't it? Ross's horse?"

K.C. smiled. "That's a mare."

"Really? Well, how was I to know? Ross always had a thing for the wild stallions. I mean, you know . . . Thunder, the wonder horse." Dawn was on her feet now, twitching her little bottom as she brushed some imagined debris off the seat of her pants, edging closer to the picketed mare. "Gosh, she's big. But mares are gentler, aren't they?"

"Sometimes."

"Maybe I could just sit on her." She turned to K.C. "If you stayed right by me."

"We should get saddled up anyway." He got up, pitched his apple core, then headed for the row of saddles standing on end in the grass. "Come on. I'll show you the fine points of saddling a horse."

"I could give her an apple."

K.C. said that apples were for dude horses, and that she had a bit in her mouth anyway, and that they'd have to start Dawn on a smaller horse because Colly was too tall for her to saddle. But he did name the parts of the saddle and its straps, talking as he arranged, adjusted, buckled. Dawn appeared to be listening.

Julia hung back with Vernon and Sally, watching the demonstration, but the two boys were eager to be back in the saddle.

K.C. was busy threading the end of the cinch strap through the rigging ring. He didn't appear to be attending to the boys, but when one of them mounted up, he said, "Leighton, you need to walk him around a little and then check the cinch, tell me what you find."

Julia smiled. If he had no experience with kids, then surely he was a natural. Leighton discovered a loose cinch, and K.C. explained that the dun gelding had filled his belly with air.

"Okay, Dawn, let's get you up here."

"That's such a stretch."

He showed her where to grip the saddle, then laced his fingers together and made a stirrup of his hands. When she dropped one hand to his shoulder, he reminded her of the grip he'd showed her and waited for her to regain it before he lifted her and told her to throw her leg over the saddle.

The instant she was seated, her old terror settled in. Julia could see it in her sister's eyes. The years fell away, and once again she was the little girl who had taken one-too-many falls. The oxbow stirrups dangled well below her white running shoes. She gripped the saddle horn in one hand, the reins in the other. As the mare raised her head, Dawn desperately drew in the slack.

"You're okay," K.C. said quietly, laying his hand on

hers. "The last thing you wanna do is haul back on her mouth."

"She might run away."

"She's not goin' anywhere. Do you want to get down?"

"Not yet. I want to get over this stupid fear. I saw you guys leaving this morning, and I wanted . . ." Eyes wide with the same old terror, she looked to Julia, her old source of assurance. "She won't take off?"

"She's fine, Dawn."

"Try to relax," K.C said. He touched Dawn's knee.

Damn. He was about to do his irresistible horse-taming number on Dawn.

So what?

It didn't matter. Julia understood perfectly how they would be attracted to each other. If they couldn't resist each other, so be it. She folded her arms, stiffened, dropped a mental shutter for protection.

"Move your leg in front of the fender," he was saying. "See, this part is the fender, attached to the stirrup. Pay attention to your program, now: fender, stirrup."

"Fender, stirrup."

With the toe of his boot in the stirrup, he mounted up behind her, put his arms around her and showed her how to hold the reins. "Now, just tickle her in the ribs with your heel and kiss to her. She'll walk out for you."

Hold onto her, Julia thought, *because she had a bad fall once, so you can't just . . .*

"Kiss to her?" Dawn smiled a little, enjoying that much of the idea. She imitated his air kiss, and the mare stepped out.

Julia found herself smiling, too.

"Can you feel how stiff you are?" K.C. asked Dawn.

Julia relaxed her own muscles one by one, let her shoulders drop.

"No. Yes." Dawn laughed, still truly nervous. "Can you?"

He laid his hand on her shoulder, started kneading. "Relax these muscles."

Okay, Julia thought, this was the horse-taming number. It was his specialty, right? His hands were magic, and she couldn't take her eyes away, because to watch them was to feel them.

"Now your arms," he said, and he wasn't massaging now. It was more like he was reminding Dawn where her arms were. "Now your hands." He glanced toward the peanut gallery. "How does she look, Gramma? Still clenching her teeth?"

"Go slack-jawed, baby girl. Catch some flies." Dawn let her mouth drop open, and Sally laughed. "There, that's it."

"Give her some more heel," K.C. instructed when the mare stopped. "Attagirl."

"This isn't so bad." Dawn grinned, doing Eddie Cantor eyes. "Hey, this isn't bad at all."

From the ground, Julia's return smile was spontaneous. He'd done it. *Dawn was riding!*

"We'll have you steeplechasing before the summer's over," K.C. promised. "That'll give you something to write home about. But right now your teacher's got work to do."

K.C. dismounted first, then talked Dawn through the process, catching her only when it became necessary.

Well, that was sweet, Julia thought, and she meant it. Mostly. It was a triumph for Dawn and a coup for K.C. She saddled her own horse while she listened to Dawn's ebullient chatter about how terrified she'd been since that time she'd fallen off, and her jacket had been caught on something, and after that she'd just frozen up, but maybe now she could get over all that, with K.C.'s help.

With K.C.'s help. He certainly knew what he was doing, and Julia was glad about that, because she wanted the same kind of help from him. Not for herself, of course. For the High Horse. For the summer program.

The whole scene really *was* sweet. So she wasn't sure whom she was mad at.

K.C. seemed to be warming up to his job as ramrod. As the day wore on and riders wore down, he gave more orders. Julia did what she was told, too, because K.C. was in charge. But taking orders from him rankled now, even

though he couched every order in the lap of his friendly
smile.

First came the highway crossing. He sent Julia and
Leighton across and told them to keep the stream of cattle
moving once they reached the other side. Julia threw herself
into her assignment. She made sure there were no hitches,
no bottlenecks. She was most efficient when she was annoyed, especially when she was annoyed with herself for
being annoyed. She was a mature woman. Her feelings
were silly. If Dawn was determined to hang around for the
summer, she was going to find herself a playmate, and K.C.
was the obvious candidate. Julia hated the way she felt
about the whole idea.

She hated herself for her minimal responses to him for
the next couple of hours. He noticed. She could see that.
He didn't push, nor did he avoid her. He just went right on
doing his job as the cattle worked their way, slope by slope,
toward the western sky.

They were riding deep into the afternoon and the folds
of the hills when Shep rode to the back of the herd, where
K.C. and Julia were hazing stragglers. "Seen some horses
on them peaks."

"Ross's horses?" Julia said.

"I expect it's them crazy mustangs, all right. You ride
up there, just over that ridge. You peek over into that next
valley." He drew an air map as he handed K.C. a pair of
battered binoculars he'd tied to his saddle. "You can count
their whiskers with these."

"Vern's riding point. You'll be all right with the herd
and our two rookies?"

"They'll do, that pair, they'll do. And them bosses know
where they're goin' as good as I do. They can smell that
high-country grass, too. Look at the gleam in their eyes."

"If you say so, Shep." Then, to Julia: "Comin' with
me?"

The gleam in *his* eyes made her wonder what he thought
he smelled. She smiled ultra-pleasantly. "Sure."

Julia's stout bay reached the top of the ridge ahead of
the mare, snorting and blowing. Grinning, K.C. dismounted. She didn't have to ask what he was grinning

about. She wasn't trying to race him or to prove anything, but she knew there was no point in making any disclaimers against that grin.

Then she saw that it was the horses that had him so pleased. Grazing the southern face of a cloud-shadowed slope, the sorrel, claybank and dun-colored mustangs blended into landscape as beautifully as the many mule deer and pronghorn antelope they'd seen over the course of the day. Reins in one hand, K.C. hunkered down like a cat perched on a precipice, muscles pulling his shirt taut across his shoulders. He settled into a crouch with Shep's binoculars.

Julia followed, hanging onto the ends of her reins.

"I haven't seen them running free like this in years." She pushed wind-whipped strands of hair back from her face as she knelt beside him. "Not since I last spent the whole summer here, when I was eighteen. The year Ross decided to stay. I guess none of the same ones would be here anymore, would they?" Her hand shaded the glance she slid him. "Eighteen years later."

He smiled. There was no hint of surprise in his eyes, just some fond amusement, or fond appreciation, or maybe just some fondness for her and her worry over the numbers. He took his hat off and put it on her, lining it up against the sun, taking his time until he had it just the way he wanted. He was pleased with the effect. "Next time we go to the store, we're gettin' you a hat."

She smiled, too, feeling pretty simply because of the way he was looking at her. "*We*'ve never gone to a store."

" 'Bout time we did, don't you think?" He gave her an impish wink before he put the binoculars back up to his face. "They don't usually last that long in the wild. Freedom makes for a short, happy life." He pointed to one who had his head up, mane fluttering, nose testing the air. "One stud—see, that's him, the big bay—and ten, eleven mares. Six foals; looks like he had a pretty good year, considering. There's a little bachelor band over there." He gestured with the binoculars, then handed them over. "How many you got running up here?"

"Ross thought there might be sixty or seventy head."

She saw the question in his eyes. "Too many?"

"Do you get help culling the herd?"

"You mean from the BLM? I don't know whether they would do that for us, or whether we're still completely responsible for them. I know Ross had a roundup service came out once or twice, but it's been some time."

She peered through the glasses now, moving them from nursing mare to grazing stud to outcast bachelors. At a distance they looked like any other horses. At a distance they might have been close kin to the two content to get in a little grazing behind their riders' backs. But it was the distance that made the difference. Indeed, the wild horses' elusiveness rendered them almost mystical.

"The main wild-horse herds in Wyoming are in the Basin, east of Cody, and south, around the Green River. The BLM probably would have moved the Painted Mountain herd, too, but Gramma is a law unto herself around here. She just wasn't about to let them move Grampa's horses to some sanctuary after that law was passed in, what, '70 or '71? So this is kind of an isolated herd, and Ross guarded it." She stretched her arms out. "Like a human wall."

"Pretty unusual for a cattle rancher."

"Ross has turned quite a few mustangs into saddle horses over the years, and when he sold them—" She chuckled, remembering. "Gramma used to tease him about doing background checks on the buyers. He wanted them to go to good homes, and he knew they had a better chance if they were already usable. He had some reservations about the wild-horse adoption program, about a lot of them ending up as canners once they're sold. Don't sell them wild, he'd say." She offered K.C. the binoculars. "Have you ever tasted horse meat?"

"Not on purpose."

"I wonder if I have." She grimaced at the thought, and he laughed. "Ross wanted people to know that mustangs made good saddle horses, but more than that, he believed in keeping them running free. Some of them, anyway. Some things shouldn't change. Some places, we should keep some of it . . ." She gestured expansively. A tweedling meadowlark responded from the grass. "Like this. This should always be here, just like this."

"These days, it takes a human wall to stop the human 'dozers. If this is going to be here next year, somebody has to hang on this year. You don't look much like a wall, but then, neither does Sally. When one man's push butts up against another man's shove, sometimes there's no fortress quite as strong as a woman."

"And no poet quite as fanciful as a cowboy." She saw he was giving her that sweet look again, those blue eyes glistening in the late-afternoon sun.

He shrugged. "'Course, you'd make a lot of money if you sold out."

"I know." Her gaze drifted to the wild ones again. "What do you think about that little bunch we brought over from Pollak's?"

"I've already started that little mare. I can start a few colts and put a good handle on 'em while I'm here. That's what I do best."

"But beyond that, what do you think? Could we—"

"Thinking beyond that is out of my line." She questioned him with a look, and he touched her chin with a careful forefinger. "If I had a knack for planning ahead, I probably wouldn't be here."

Abruptly he withdrew his touch, turning again to watch the horses. "I go from job to job. When I leave, I like to think the horses are better off for the time I worked with them, but I just don't see how I could do better by these guys. They've got a pretty good thing going, looks like to me. I'm with Ross; I'd be happy to come up here and watch them all day long."

One of the mustangs called out, and Columbine gave an answering whinny, which alerted the upwind band to the intruders. K.C took another look through the binoculars as the horses fled, most heading directly over the top of the hill. "Kinda curious the way that . . ."

"What?"

"The way that last pair sticks together, taking a different route, see? Kinda reminds me . . ." The binoculars came down again. He shrugged, as though what had occurred to him was just between him and the mustangs. "I bet a guy could learn a lot about horses if he could come up here and watch them, watch how they behave. So you don't think the BLM has any interest in or responsibility to this herd?"

"I don't know. What do you think?"

"I don't get paid to think." The reins bobbed in his hand like a fishing line. The mare had reached the end of her tether. He stood up, then offered Julia a hand. "But I suppose we could find out."

"There's no reason to rush into selling this place. I promised Gramma the summer."

"So did I." A breeze toyed with his hat-creased black hair. He raked it back with splayed fingers. "I got into a little trouble that first night I was here. Did she tell you?"

"The night you brought me home?"

"Got stopped by the sheriff and blew his damn test. Sally helped me out." He hung his head, slid the reins back and forth in a loose fist. "Guess I might as well tell you, Julia, it ain't the first time."

"You have a prior conviction?"

"No, but I've got a prior history." He lifted his chin, let his eyes meet hers. "Of close calls."

What do you want to know? his eyes suggested, and she knew he would tell her if she asked.

Memories started jostling for position, trying to stick their faces into the windows of her mind. Other times and places, other people in trouble. She'd handled them, hadn't she? She was a professional. She could handle a simple cowboy. He'd blown in on the south wind, a horseman passing through. He appeared to be traveling light, but she wasn't surprised that he'd brought some baggage with him. Everyone did.

Tell me about your history and your close calls, and I'll start a file with your name on it.

He turned away.

She drew a desperately needed deep breath.

"I really think we can work together, K.C. You're very good with livestock, and not just horses. I can see that you . . ." She was floundering now, and she wasn't sure why. She moved around him as she talked, took his hat off and put it back on his head, even adjusted it exactly the way he'd done it for her. "Well, I can see that Vernon has a lot of respect for you, and Vernon knows a good hand when he sees one. So does Gramma."

"What about you?"

"I think we can work together. I want to use some of these horses in the summer program." He questioned her with a look, and she said, "With the boys."

"I'll handle the horses. The kids are your department."

"But you'll work with me."

"I'll work *for* you."

"Okay. Work *for* me, then." Her gelding was busy ripping at grass. His mare was snuffling at his shoulder. It felt peaceful, up here in the foothills. The lowing and whistling of the cattle drive drifted now in the distance. "It's kind of odd for me, not going to work at an office. This was always my favorite vacation. Coming home."

"You stick with it, maybe you could be vacationing for the rest of your life."

"It's a big responsibility." She groaned as she mounted the gelding. She was getting sore. "The kind of responsibility that spells work."

"Well, I wouldn't know much about that. I'm just a simple cowboy." He swung into his saddle as if he were made of rubber. Then looked at her. Then smiled that knowing smile of his as he adjusted the hat. "Never could spell worth a lick."

13

They were calling it a summer training program. The eight-week Painted Mountain Horse Partnership Camp would officially begin in two days. The name, according to Jack, was Ross's idea. They'd stuck with it, even though Julia wasn't exactly sure how far she could carry the "horse partnership" component, vague as her agreement with K.C. was. But Jack said the boys were "psyched," everybody was insured and the program was being "watched with interest" by many juvenile corrections specialists. The original proposal listed "horse training" as a camp activity, but it was far from specific about who was supposed to do the training. Ross had been a broad-stroke dreamer. The details were always somebody else's department. Next week they would be Julia's.

She had seven wild horses close at hand, including the six bachelors in the small horse pasture and the mare and her foal in another pen, and she had an excellent trainer working with them. K.C. had some doubts about putting the boys and the wild horses together. Sticky little detail, that, so Julia was developing two plans for the first week—Plan K and Plan Minus K—both written out in daily sequence. She had set the pages on the corner of Grampa's desk, keeping them handy while she worked on the ranch accounts. Whenever she had an idea, she'd reach for the pertinent plan and slot it in.

She knew about saddles. She could teach the boys to tell

170

the fender from the cantle, and she could show them how to use saddle soap. Each boy would be assigned a saddle, which would need conditioning. That would take a couple of days. Oh, and Shep was good at leather work. They could learn to make a simple headstall. She grabbed Plan Minus K and wrote Shep in. Not that Shep couldn't contribute his special talent with or without K.C., but if she had to begin with Plan Minus K, she'd need Minus K activities. By Week Two, she was sure K.C. would see how much fun everyone was having, and he'd be only too happy to join in. Good ol' Tom Sawyer psychology.

Julia was getting a little psyched herself. She was tapping fingers and toes to the music on the radio, humming a little, even singing a phrase here and there as she went back to the payroll page in the ledger.

Any man of mine . . . This was a snappy tune. Hadn't they danced to this one?

Psyched. Eager. Feeling a little spirited, maybe. Yes, indeed, this flying by the seat of her pants was a new experience for Julia. Not that she was being reckless; the "horse partners" concept was sound in theory. The program would give the boys a chance to prove themselves by offering them a challenge. The challenge—earning an animal's trust—would teach them about trusting and being trusted, as well as caring for another living creature. The prospect of putting a novel theory into practice was beginning to look good to her. She was ready for some new theories. Some of the old ones frankly sucked.

Better treat me riiiight . . .

Speaking of sucking—she snatched the plan sheets up again—Shep was in charge of the dogs—boys liked dogs—and he was the one who usually looked after any bottle calves they might have. He'd also been talking about getting a few—

"Is that you, Miss Pardon?"

Julia nearly tipped her chair over.

"Heard a rumor you'd gone flat." K.C. leaned against the doorframe, hat in hand, grinning. "*Beggin'* your pardon," he amended. "Sally told me to come on up. I've got two mustangs out in the pen who figure they've earned the right to be named, now that they're halter-broke."

"Already? You *are* good."

"Damn straight. So how 'bout it? We decided their mama oughta do the honors." She questioned the designation with a glance. He shrugged. "*Mistress* just don't sound quite right."

"*Mama* sounds better?"

"Why don't you come out and let me show them off for you before it gets dark? I need names to call them by, so you bring your flower book."

"Boy, I'll tell you, I've had enough books. Feel like I've spent my whole life filling out forms and keeping records." She tossed her pencil down on the ledger. It rolled into the gutter. "A computer would be handy. Once I have a system, it'll be easier."

"A system, huh? I admire people who can work a system."

"You must have a system for training horses."

"I have the touch. A system is something in your head. I've got horses in my blood." He was drawn to a group of pen-and-ink horse sketches hanging on the wall next to the door to the bathroom. His boot heels clip-clopped on the hardwood floor. "Your grandfather's, huh? He was good.

"You see some stuff done by real famous artists who didn't know beans about the way a horse is put together. Like Remington. Charlie Russell's horses are a lot better than ol' Fred Remington's."

He stepped back, still studying, pulling his hat brim through his hand. "Your grandfather understood horses. They were in his blood, too. They were sure in his hand."

"Must have been from mixing his blood with Gramma's." K.C.'s genuine interest in the drawings subdued Julia's worries about whether she'd dropped any underwear on the bathroom floor. She wondered how he knew who the artist was. Grampa had worked his "MW" into each drawing somewhere, but it was always part of the picture. Finding his initials was a game she'd played with him, but hiding them, she realized now, was part of his modesty. "She always said it was love at first sight. His first sight of her horses. He'd never been around horses before he met Gramma."

K.C. came away from the sketches smiling.

"So how do you come by horses in the blood?" she asked.

His smile faded. "Got it from my mother, I guess. Is that you?" He'd noticed the portrait above the desk. "You and Dawn and Ross, huh? She looks like she's been crying, and he kinda looks like he'd rather be someplace else, but you . . ." He scrutinized her face in the picture, then in person. "Where have you been hiding that dimple?"

"That's not a dimple. That's just . . ." She laughed. He'd done it again, changed the subject when it got too close to home. Wherever that was. "I'll have to look up some of those magazine articles and see what you have to say in print about horses in the blood. If it's in print, it must be true."

"Must be somebody's truth, anyway. I don't write those articles." He claimed a bold perch on the corner of the big cherry desk, hooking a faded denim knee in her direction. "I don't get into bloodlines or credentials. I just show them what works for me, and I tell them you've gotta have the right touch to go with it. Otherwise it's all just more bullshit."

"And the right touch is . . ."

He smiled. "Slow and easy."

"As a horse-training method—" The promise in his eyes was unmistakable. She acknowledged it with a lift of the eyebrows, a patient smile. "I imagine 'the touch' isn't exactly an easy sell."

"Oh, you'd be surprised. It's the easiest thing in the world to sell. You talk about a system, there's no magic in that. But if people think you're the man who's got the touch, hell, you can name your price. Horse clinics are big business nowadays. Rich people have a thing about horses. They'll shell out big bucks for what amounts to common sense, which is a commodity most of them are way out of touch with."

"Out of touch with 'the touch,' " she mused, studying

him as she leaned back in her grandfather's chair. "Do you do clinics?"

"I've done a few. I've got plenty of horse sense, but no business sense. Had a bad experience with a *human* partnership, so I quit doing it. Besides, I'm not much for traveling shows." He glanced up at the portrait of the Weslin children again. "I'll travel, sure, but don't try to put me in a show."

"I don't have a show. Don't have big bucks right now, either. I was just about to write your paycheck, and Gramma says you agreed to . . ." She shoved the "horse partnership" papers aside, opened a desk drawer and took out a tax form. "Cowboy wages?"

"That's right."

"You fill out this W-2. I'll trade it for a check." She flipped open the leather-bound checkbook and clicked a ballpoint. "So what's your name?" No response. "First name."

"K.C."

"Your whole, legal first name." She leaned over to take a peek at what he was writing on the tax form.

"Just two letters. *K* and *C*." He handed her the completed form. "Nothin' illegal about that. That's my name."

"What does it stand for?"

"Stands for me. A simple name for a simple man."

The bearings in the massive desk chair squeaked as she leaned back, smiling. "Come on, give. What does it stand for? It must be something you think sounds sissy, like, mmm . . . Kemit Caroll."

"More like Killer Cowboy. Too tough to tame. But you gotta be careful with a name like that. You got a woman screaming your name in the throes of pure ecstasy—" He moved closer, forearm braced across his thigh. "Well, you don't want it to be 'Killer.' "

"I see your point."

"Truth is, my mama took one look at me and said, 'Let's not complicate his life too much. He don't look too bright.' Two letters, easy to spell. K.C." With a look she invited him to try again. "Okay, truth is, I was named for my parents. They were only together long enough to get one kid, so I got both names. My first name is Kate.''

"What was your father's name?"

He shrugged. "Must have been something that started with *C*."

"You don't look like a Kate."

"Well, there you go. Perception is nine-tenths of fantasy. How many stories you want? I got a bunch of 'em, and they get wilder as the night goes on." He put his hat on her head, a gesture she was beginning to anticipate. It made her feel favored. "After you name those colts, let's celebrate. Let's go dancin' tonight."

She let the suggestion sail past. "You know what I was thinking? Let's let the boys name the horses."

"The boys?"

"I'm thinking we could assign each one his own horse, and you could show them how to work with them, let them take it as far as they can. If you've already got two of them halter-broke . . .''

He straightened, his expression guarded.

"The summer program, K.C. We're starting with it on Monday. I'm still hoping . . . I mean, you haven't exactly given me a final . . .''

He was shaking his head, chuckling. A definite *maybe*.

She pushed his hat back, bent forward, touched his knee. "Only a couple of hours a day. Taking it slow and easy, just as you said, showing them the benefit of persistence and patience. The therapeutic value of this kind of—''

"Hold on, now, woman, I ain't no therapist." There was an apology in his diffident smile. "Look, Julia, you're barkin' up the wrong tree here. I said I'd work with your horses, but I do what I do my own way, at my own pace and strictly on my own. I don't mind talking about it and letting people write about it if they want to, but I don't like trying to teach it. It ain't exactly poetry or science. And I sure as hell don't know the first thing about trying to teach anything to kids."

"I think you'd be wonderful."

"You do, huh?" He touched the back of her hand, fingertips grazing so lightly she had to look to make sure it was happening. "I've heard that before."

"From me?" She drew back and gave a quick, defensive laugh. "No, that first night doesn't count. God knows what I said that night."

"I know what you said. I remember every word. Go dancin' with me tonight, and I'll get you in that strange mood again. Every night counts with me, darlin'."

She finished writing his paycheck and handed it to him with a flourish. "Courtesy of the Painted Mountain Horse Partnership Camp." *Bad form*, she thought immediately, avoiding his eyes. She had little practice being an employer.

"What do you mean?"

"That's how I can afford to pay you. You're the instructor."

"Like hell I am," he said calmly.

"You offered to teach Dawn how to ride."

"As a favor, just like I'm offering you a favor. Dancin' lessons."

"I don't need dancing lessons," she told him as Sally appeared in the doorway. Julia quickly swept K.C.'s hat off her head and handed it to him. "What I need is exactly what Ross wanted to hire you for."

"He said mustangs. He didn't say kids." He turned, shifting gears, smooth as cream. "How about you, Sally? Mus-taang Sal-ly," he crooned, clapping his hat on his head as he reached for Sally's hands. He twirled her under his arm and did a little hip-bumping, hers moving stiffly, his rolling as fluidly as his song, which overlay the Vince Gill tune that was playing now. Sally laughed, her eyes those of a woman basking in the attention of a handsome man.

"I don't know who's the grandma here," he said, lassoing her with her own arms, then unwinding her like an old-fashioned top. "Sure can't be you, Sally girl."

She took a turn giving him a twirl. "I could dance you under the table, young fella, so you'd better stick to teaching the young girls what they don't know how."

"Your granddaughter don't know how to dance."

"She's got two granddaughters." It was Dawn. Ready-for-a-good-time Dawn. Dazzling-smile Dawn. "This one loves to dance."

K.C. looked at Julia, who was busy securing herself within the massive arms of Grampa's chair. "There," she said with a tight smile. "You've found yourself a date."

He nodded at Dawn. "Just thinkin' about going into town tonight for a little diversion. You're sure welcome to come along. I can usually give two or three partners a good run, especially if it's a dry run." He winked at Sally. "I got my custodian here. I don't want her to think I'm back on the sauce already."

"I'm sure my little sister is all the partner you'll need. I'd love to go along and watch because you're both such good dancers . . ." Absently Julia flipped the checkbook closed on the desk. "But the kids will be here Monday morning, and I'm not ready."

"My God, Julia, I can't believe you're going through with that," Dawn said, posturing in the doorway. "I mean, don't you think we have enough to worry about?"

"A night out should take your mind off your worries. K.C., I hope you'll make yourself available for some basic instruction."

She swiveled the chair toward the desk, seeking easy refuge in the books she'd bewailed earlier. She'd had the final word, which seemed her due.

But K.C. would not be dismissed.

"I don't need instruction. I'm pretty good at what I do."

He spun the chair around. She looked up at him, astonished. He sat on the corner of the desk again, and spoke to her nose to nose, cool blue eyes to startled brown, as though there had been no interruption.

"And you know what, lady? I did my time when I was a kid. I spent some time in a reform school, and I wasn't exactly a model inmate. As soon as their backs were turned, I was gone." He paused, searching her eyes for a response.

He wouldn't see any shock, if that was what he expected. What surprised her was that he went on.

"For years I had to watch my own back. Sure didn't have anybody to watch it for me. And I didn't know nothin' about the laws. I didn't know if anybody was lookin' for me, or who it might be, or when I could stop lookin' over

my shoulder. So I just put one foot in front of the other
and kept on truckin'.

"And now I've stopped lookin' back. So you'll have to
find somebody else for that particular job, ma'am."

He tipped his hat to her, leaving Julia fresh out of *final*
final words.

They talked about going up to Cody. But they stopped
at the Lowdown Saloon in Quicksilver first, just to check
it out, and they stayed.

Entertaining Dawn was not what K.C. had had in mind,
but since it was what he had on his plate, he dug in. Over
the years K.C. had turned making do with what he had into
an art form. Tonight what he had was a corner booth in a
one-horse-town saloon, plenty of cornmeal on the dance
floor, plenty of quarters jingling in his jeans, Credence
Clearwater wailing from the jukebox—damn, if he wasn't
stuck in the Lowdown again.

Stuck, but making do with a paycheck he'd have no trouble spending by morning. Stuck in the company of a
woman who was the worst kind of health risk—the technically taken but gettin' itchy kind—but making do with
her sweet laugh and her pretty face because they reminded
him of her sister. Stuck with a shot of whiskey and a beer
chaser that he didn't think he'd ordered—knew he hadn't
paid for—but somewhere along the line he'd started making do with it because the water in this town tasted like the
Great Salt Lake.

They'd taken a couple of pleasant turns around the dance
floor when Cal Pollak clapped him on the back and claimed
it was noble of him to "take the other sister out for a spin."

"I'm an equal opportunity hell-raiser," K.C. said, thinking he'd talked himself into a jovial mood now, and he was
going to go with the flow.

He offered to buy Cal a drink to thank him for all the
help he'd given the High Horse outfit lately, which was
likely a grandiose gesture on his part. One paycheck didn't
exactly make him a Weslin spokesman, but he'd kinda been
warming up to the ramrod role lately, and it seemed the
gentlemanly thing to do. It grated on him when Cal waved

the offer away with a suggestion that they "let the ol' man buy," as though the Pollak money would somehow go further than his, get them better service or bring on better booze. In a place like the Lowdown, it wasn't about to get but so good. But maybe guys like the Pollaks didn't know any better.

Chuck joined them presently, and there was a good deal made of K.C.'s throwing in with the Weslin women for the summer and how old Sally was the real vixen at the High Horse, heh heh heh. Should be an interesting summer, heh heh heh. K.C. raised his glass to that prediction. He noticed a plenitude of giggles and inside one-liners, and he began to realize that somewhere along the line a new chumminess had evolved between Dawn and the Pollaks. By the second round of drinks, they'd put quite a shiny gilt on the good old days.

"I always thought the marriage of the Lazy P and the High Horse would make history," Chuck said, "but Ross took over the High Horse, and I didn't have any daughters."

Dawn laughed, glanced at Cal, then at K.C., then laughed again. Cal chuckled obligingly. K.C. sipped his beer.

Chuck went on as though he wasn't sure what he'd said, but he was glad to amuse. "Hell, I was hoping to marry Cal off to Dawn here, but I guess there's a small complication."

"Roger is, yes, he's a very small complication." She was sobering now, studying her drink. "No more than a technicality at the moment. As I told you before, Chuck, there are better ways to accomplish what you've got in mind. You just make us an offer we can't refuse."

"Well, I intend to. I'm looking into it right now. We'll see what we can come up with."

K.C. got the feeling he'd just been turned into a fly on the wall. "I didn't think a decision had been made," he said to nobody in particular.

"Mine has." Dawn laid a small, elegant hand on K.C.'s arm. "Do you realize how much that place is worth?"

"A nice chunk of change, I expect, but it's been in your family for a long time."

"The Weslins ran out of prospective ranchers when the favorite son gave up the ghost."

"What's wrong with the daughters?" Not that he had any investment one way or the other. Seemed like an obvious question to throw out, just for the sake of discussion.

"There's nothing wrong with this one," Dawn said. "My mama didn't raise no fool. It's time to put Sally out to pasture and quit while we're ahead. Because we won't be ahead for long."

K.C. was sorry he'd asked. Cal perked right up on the word "quit," and old Chuck, he was pretending to watch two large women in tight jeans putting their wiggle into a line-dance step. But the elder Pollak's ear was tuned in to every word Dawn said.

"What does Julia know about running the place? Nothing. But she'll start thinking she does, because that's the way Julia is. And that's just what Sally wants."

"Maybe Sally's thinking you two could run it together," Cal said.

"Right. I can only take Julia in small doses, and I know the feeling's mutual." She looked at K.C., who was pretty sure he was wearing his poker face. "Don't get me wrong. I love my sister, but I love her best from afar. Which is exactly where she keeps herself. A-far from me. A looong ways up there on her narrow little pedestal. She and Ross both. You know how he died, don't you?"

K.C. glanced around the table. Ross Weslin's neighbors. Ross Weslin's sister. Okay, he'd bite. "He was sick."

"You might as well say he killed himself." She looked at each of the men over the rim of her glass, following up her claim with a theatrical sip of the drink.

Nobody agreed. Nobody objected.

She set her glass down, scrunching her shoulders, rolling her big blue eyes, looking pixieish.

"Well, he had AIDS, which nobody but Gramma knew, not even Julia until just lately. How do you like that? He never even told his favorite sister." She shrugged again, all innocence. "But that wasn't exactly what did him in, was it, you guys? You were here."

"Didn't know he had AIDS," Chuck said, looking from

one face to the other at the table, as though they'd all been keeping this from him. "We don't get much of that around here."

"Damn, that's a hell of a kicker. 'Course, I never knew him too well. He always had all kinds of stuff wrong with him, didn't he? But AIDS, Jesus." Cal glanced at his father. "Seemed like he shoulda stayed back East."

"This is hard country," Chuck said.

K.C. was still chewing on the first bite, figuring he'd ask for another one later, when somebody could fill him in privately on what "did him in." This going through a dead man's personal effects in the middle of the Lowdown Saloon didn't sit right with K.C.

But Dawn's jaws were pretty well oiled.

"Yeah, he had all kinds of allergies and respiratory problems, always had, poor guy. He was like a pincushion with all the shots, ever since I can remember. I spent half my life in the waiting room of the doctor's office when I was little." She flashed a little-girl smile. "With Julia, my big sister. She'd fix my hair or do puzzles with me, those wooden puzzles. Or she'd read to me. Children's Bible stories and *National Geographic* were usually the choices at the doctor's office back then, remember?" She jiggled K.C.'s arm. His cue.

He shook his head. "Never noticed."

"Sick as he was, my brother managed to take a horse up into the mountains and get caught in an early-spring snowstorm. You know what those are like? The hard, bone-chilling kind of snow, all wet and heavy."

Cal decided to help out. "He was trying to feed them mustangs, wasn't he? What I heard was he saw something on the local news about the buffalo starving up to Yellowstone and took it in his head to haul some hay up there to them mustangs." He shook his head sadly. "I sure didn't know he had AIDS, though. Jesus."

"Neither did I," Dawn said. "For a while his health got better, you know. It seemed like he'd outgrown or fought off the worst of it, or adjusted to it, maybe. But then this, it was too much. I don't know why he didn't sell out right away and just . . ."

She drew her shoulders up in that cute scrunch that made her scoop-neck pink top droop fetchingly. "Anyway, they had some hay loaded up in a pickup for something. Julia and Gramma had gone up to Cody. Ross hitched up a horse trailer and drove as far as he could up to Painted Mountain, then switched to the horse."

K.C. was hooked into the story now, wishing he'd been there to help out. His mind played out the snowy scene, with a fragile Weslin making the choice to save those mustangs or die trying. The man had heart.

"God only knows how he got as far as he did in the shape he was in. Gramma said if it hadn't been for the pickup, they never would have known where to look."

"How far did he get?" K.C. wanted to know. "How high up? High enough to reach his horses?"

"I wouldn't know. I wasn't here. Obviously, the damn horses survived." The little quiver in her voice, barely noticeable, wasn't for show. It was from anger and emptiness. It was for Ross. She took a deep breath. "It was just like putting a gun in his mouth where the inhaler should have been. He didn't even have his inhaler with him."

She pressed her lips together, staring hard at her drink. "*Horses.*" If she'd been spitting, the word would have plunked in the glass. "What's the big deal? People are using bikes and ATVs to get around in this desert now, aren't they, Chuck?"

"We use them out to our place. But Sally won't get with the times no matter what. Well, now, I take that back. I believe she did pick up a couple of snowmobiles, but I doubt if anybody ever uses them." Chuck gave a wistful smile. "Ol' Vern's gonna go just like your brother. He's gonna die in the saddle."

"Sounds good to me." K.C. put a spin on his empty shot glass, sending it toward the middle of the table. He needed to move on. "So does the music. Didn't we say we were goin' out dancin'?"

"I'm way ahead of you, cowboy."

If it would stop her from wheeling and dealing on the sidelines, he decided to let her stay ahead of him, at least on the dance floor. She had all the moves down to a sexy science, and she would have made a guy with two left feet look good. The trouble was that she was all friendly hands and flirty eyes, and all he could think about was how much she reminded him of Julia and how, bottom line, he knew he wasn't Julia's kind of guy. He sure was Dawn's, though. She was out to have a good time, and one good-time Charlie deserved another.

A guy had to make do, he told himself, and he threw himself wholeheartedly into the party. He danced and drank and got giddy with the younger sister while he bottled the older one in his increasingly sloshy thoughts.

14

*Julia had turned the radio off hours ago, but the mu-*sic still played in her crowded head, where Dawn and K.C. were dancing circles around the Lowdown regulars. She could have gone with them. She could be there now instead of standing in the tub, letting the shower and her imagination work overtime. Steam billowed around her. The long, narrow window above the end of the tub separated the sedate Julia from the seductive night.

A small frog appeared, its white belly pressed to the glass. Julia soaped her own belly, imagining the feel of steamed glass against it, her naked back exposed to the night's chill. She wondered what on earth would induce a creature of the ground to scale the stone pillars of the porch to come to this high place.

A flutter of white just beyond the frog's mouth answered the question. The tiny moth was not of earth but of air, and the frog had followed it to the light. The game they played at the window mesmerized her as she soaped herself, cir-cling, circling, playing her own game.

A kid's game. Rub your belly and pat your head, pat yourself on the back, be good to yourself. Now try some-thing else. Try letting yourself go, just for a little while, let yourself feel something risky and new. She leaned against the slick tile and saw herself dancing with him again. Danc-ing stark naked with him. Dancing stark naked in the

184

shower, soap-slick, steamy and sultry, tangy artesian well water running into their open mouths.

Take care of yourself, you'll be fine, you'll do fine, you'll feel fine.

The soap smelled sweet, and the water tasted salty, and Julia didn't feel much of anything except empty and foolish. Laughter bubbled in her throat. She was laughing at herself, for heaven's sake, *laughing*! She couldn't rub and pat at the same time any more than she could do a two-step without counting. A good laugh was better than nothing.

Right, moth?

The frog was still trying. An eerie white silhouette on the frosted glass, it had trekked its way halfway up the long, narrow window.

Julia remembered a time when there had been no showers in the house, before Daddy had insisted on doing some remodeling to "get with the twentieth century and turn this into a real master bedroom." It wasn't until the first time he'd used the new shower that he'd realized the curtain on the window had to go. Mother had made a big issue of his stupidity. *Of course* the curtain got wet. *Of course* mildew was growing on the shade. *This was a shower.* Finally he'd come up with the frosted glass. He had cut himself putting it in, probably because he'd put away several old-fashioneds while he was assembling his tools, but for once he'd gotten the job done.

"You want it done right, do it yourself," he'd said bitterly, echoing his own father's philosophy. As far as Julia knew, the window was one of the few real jobs Daddy had managed to complete, start to finish. He'd dropped out of college, dropped out of his marriage, never made it as a father or a rancher. Even his life seemed unfinished, cut short by a heart attack when he was still in his prime, but by then he'd become such a rare presence for Julia that his untimely death had never seemed any more real than his unproductive life.

Steam fogged her memories, softened their edges. The nearly scalding water soothed away the stiffness she'd earned by spending the whole day creating a bookkeeping system of her own. She wasn't finished, but she was on the right track.

Ross had offered her the job once, during one of their regular phone calls. *Adding to your case load? Tell them to stuff it, Queenie. You want to keep records? I've got plenty of records you can keep.*

That was an understatement.

And there wasn't a computer on the place. Ross and Gramma were two of a kind when it came to "gadgets." Gramma had only to mention the shed full of their father's "toys" and Ross was shoulder to shoulder with her like a fellow old-timer, cynical about what the world was coming to.

Rack and ruin, Julia thought as she rinsed the conditioner from her hair. She watched the tiny animated etchings on the glass. The moth dared to flutter close to the frog's head, dodging the occasional cast of the tongue. Stupid moth, hanging in there for the thrill of the narrow miss. Or was it the hope of the light? The frog had only to be patient.

Julia shut the water off and stood there dripping, watching, betting on the frog. Sure enough, one wing suddenly went down, then the other. She thought about something her mother had said about getting away or getting swallowed up.

But that was what Julia wanted right now. She wanted to be taken in, swallowed up, completely absorbed. She didn't want to be the sensible one anymore. She didn't want to have to make any more *final* final decisions. Late as it was, she wanted to go down to the creek and listen to the frogs croak.

The headlights announced their return. Julia was sitting in the grass near the garden plot, remembering gardens past and thinking about what she would plant now if she had the time.

She watched the two dots grow and brighten. They bounced when they got to the bridge. She wasn't waiting, but she wasn't moving, either. She was there first.

It was Chuck Pollak's silver pickup that pulled up under the yard light. K.C. got out first, then Dawn. From the shadows she watched them bid their driver good-bye, watched them follow the stone path to the house. Dawn was giggly, a little unsteady. K.C. was guiding her along, but he'd obviously not made good on his promise to "lay off the sauce."

Julia thought about showing herself, stepping into the light, offering a banal "Looks like you two had a good time." But she didn't. As she sat there watching them, she realized that she half expected him to kiss her good night, or her to kiss him. Or maybe she fully expected it. At least a kiss, and maybe more. She knew she already felt sick about something that hadn't happened, and she knew she shouldn't sit there waiting for it, didn't like sitting there waiting for it. *Couldn't stop herself from waiting for it.*

K.C. was talking, and Dawn was laughing as he herded her up the porch steps. She opened the door. He stepped back to the pillar, catching himself with one hand. More laughter. Then the porch light came on, and Sally leaned out the door.

"Delivering your granddaughter to you safe and sound," K.C. announced, his voice louder than necessary, but he'd backed a safe distance away. Safe from Gramma's nose. "I wasn't driving, Judge." He raised a testimonial palm. "Your friendly neighbor was more than willing to be our designated driver. He's drooling over the prospect of you putting your place up for sale, so he's being mighty neighborly."

"Is he, now," Sally said. "Grown men oughtn't to drool until they get too old to prevent it."

"I guess he's drooling prematurely, then."

"That's the way I see it. You had a good time, little girl?"

"It's still early, isn't it?" Dawn reached for Sally's watch arm and pulled it up to her face. "Can't tell. K.C., why don't you come on in? We'll drag Julia out of bed and turn on some music. Gramma, don't we have some beer left from—"

"No, thanks," K.C. said, easing himself down the porch steps one backward step at a time. "I don't know about you, but I had a real good time tonight."

"I had a wonderful time. You are some—" Dawn flung an arm out K.C.'s way. "This man is a verable . . . *veritable* Fred Astaire. If Fred Astaire came back as a cowboy, he'd be him. I'm serious."

"Good night, ladies."

"He can sing, too. K.C., sing." With a graceful hand she played the conductor. "Goood niiiight ladies . . ."

"Sing one, K.C.," he echoed, chuckled, then shook his head. "I believe I'll save that one for another time. Suppertime, maybe." He touched his hat to them and said good night again. Sally ushered Dawn inside. The porch light went off as K.C. headed across the yard, grass swishing against his boots, homing in on the yard light next to the bunkhouse.

He almost walked right over Julia. She just sat there on the grass, in the dark, thinking if he saw her, he saw her. When he did, it brought him up short. He stumbled, caught himself, uttered her name as—did she have this right?—a pleasant surprise.

"You okay?" she asked.

"Sure I'm okay." He loomed over her, his face completely shadowed beneath his hat brim while bright stars appeared to dance around the crown. "You okay?"

"I'm fine." Relieved, she realized, and wasn't that silly?

"You waitin' up for me?"

"I didn't intend to, but I seem to be up, and here you are."

"Here I am. How about if you walk me to my door?" He tipped his head to one side. "In fact, you can walk me past the door. Tumble me on through, take me right to bed. Might even let you tuck me in."

"Not walkin' you anywhere, cowboy." She sat back, bracing herself on both arms, stretched her legs and wiggled her moon-white toes. "I'm barefootin'."

"No problem. I'll carry you."

She laughed. Happily. She felt like a kid who had sneaked out of bed on her own for the first time and discovered limitless night. *And wasn't that silly?*

He dropped to the ground beside her, his long legs folding beneath him. He caught himself with one hand just before his butt hit the grass—not quite controlled, but nearly so—and he sat cross-legged. "I missed dancin' with you tonight," he told her.

"Did you, really?" Her heart surged. Still, she couldn't resist the impulse to probe for exceptions. "But Dawn's a wonderful dancer."

"That she is."

"So are you. I'll bet you were terrific together."

"That we were. But you and me were terrific together, too."

"I guess that pretty much isolates the key ingredient, doesn't it?"

"That it does." He took off his hat, draped his forearms over his knees, denim jacket rustling over denim jeans, and toyed with the narrow hatband. Somewhere high in the night a coyote yodeled. "Sing one, puppy," K.C. said, chuckling.

"I hope he's not singing for his supper. I understand they're partial to veal."

They listened again to the distant howl. "Just some lobo feelin' sorry for himself. He ain't hungry, just a little lonesome." He stretched his torso over his folded legs, reaching for her closer foot, swallowed it up in his warm hand.

"Your feet are like ice. Now, if you'da gone dancin' with me . . ."

"DUI is a pretty serious charge." She had to say it; it was the counselor in her.

"Oh, do I get a lecture now?" He gathered her legs, a bundle of two, and laid them over his thigh, angling his body toward hers as he drew her feet into the well between his knees, as though she belonged to him and he knew her limbs as well as his own. "Save it for those boys you've got comin' out here on Monday," he advised, his voice as warm as the hands that enveloped her feet.

"I was just thinking . . ." She closed her eyes. He was carefully pressing the cold from her feet, toe by toe, and she was letting it happen as though it happened between them like this every evening, and it felt wonderful. "Thinking about what you've told me about being in trouble before. You said—"

"I said it wasn't the first time. Probably not the last. A guy needs to cut loose once in a while. It's like with these cold feet of yours." The calluses on his palms tickled her soles. She giggled. "There, see? You're warmin' up."

"You're a man of many talents."

"I can take care of your horses, your cows, your feet and then some, Julia, but you sure don't want me having anything to do with those kids. I've been thinkin' on it some, because I want to help out, but you give me that job, I'm liable to open the cage door and watch 'em take off."

"How long ago?" she asked, eyes still closed. "Those facilities have changed, you know. How long since you—"

"A lifetime ago. I don't count the years. I've been on my own since I was twelve."

She opened her eyes and found him watching her, concentrating on her, on this moment, not what was in the past. His eyes were moonlight in crystal water, and his smile was wistful, as though he were sensing her, knowing her completely, drawing her essence to him through her toes.

"And don't be thinkin' what you're thinkin'. It worked out just fine for me. I'm no criminal." He paused, looking deeply into her eyes, letting her see him. His hands stilled. "Don't be givin' me any serious charges, darlin'. I ain't drunk."

"I didn't say you were, and I wasn't thinking—"

"I wasn't driving tonight, was I? And I didn't let your sister drive, so that's two points in my favor." He grinned. "Chalk 'em up, now; I want two points."

"Two points there, and two more for what you're doing to my feet."

"You like this, huh? How much in my account so far?" He was doing extraordinary things to the balls of her feet with his thumbs, relaxing her whole body. "I'll tell you this much, Julia. Maybe you were born a few years before me, but I'm a man, as full-grown as they come, and I'm bettin' I've been takin' care of myself longer than you have. So that much evens out."

"That much?"

"That much of you and me. In case you were hung up

on it, I just thought we'd . . ." A gesture with a level hand left her with an abandoned foot. ". . . agree to call it even."

"Age or experience?"

"Age," he clarified quickly. "Experience is personal. Age"—another swipe of the hand—"even."

"So that's the score, huh?"

"I don't keep score. Do you?"

"You already claimed a number of points. Now you say we're even. Whatever game this is, I'm probably not very good at it. Now, you take my sister . . ."

"Do I have to? The way you keep pushin' her at me . . ." His kneading had become subtle, steady pulses that rippled up the backs of her legs. "Are you giving me an order, ma'am?"

"No, of course not."

"Your sister's married."

"I know that."

"That means something to some people, doesn't it? Look at Sally. Poor ol' Vern's probably been carryin' that torch for her as long as he's been workin' here, and her heart still belongs to a husband who's been dead for thirty years. Now that's kinda beautiful in a way." He gave a rueful tongue click. "But it can't be too beautiful for Vern. Poor ol' guy, he's about to burn up."

"What are you talking about?" She tucked her arms under the backs of her knees and jackknifed, leaning closer to him. "Gramma and Vernon?"

He smiled. "What, you think she's too old for him?"

"I thought you said you weren't drunk. Come on," she scoffed. "*Gramma* and *Vernon*?"

"What's wrong with Vern? He's in damn good shape for an old codger. Works hard, and he's tidy. Neat as a pin. Loyal, too. And humble. Too damn humble. That's his problem right there."

"Vernon and Gramma . . ."

"I don't think it's too late for them, do you?" He sounded sincere.

"What about Shep?"

"Well . . ." He shrugged. "I guess he'd have to divorce Shep."

He squeezed her feet, she smacked his knee, and they laughed together like two old friends sharing outrageous secrets.

"Did he tell you straight out that he has a crush on Gramma?"

"Not hardly. I wouldn't call it a crush, Vern bein' a grown man, too. And I wouldn't ask straight out if I were you. Just pay attention. Use your eyes and your pretty ears." He tucked her hair behind her ear, then rubbed her lobe—big, fat, ugly earlobe—gently between thumb and forefinger. "And don't be pushing your kid sister at me, okay?"

She ducked away from his titillating touch. "I'm not about to order you around, K.C. Going to the bar was your idea, and then it was Dawn's idea to go with you. I just—"

"Maybe you oughta talk to her."

"About what?"

"Anything. Start with something simple. Something like, I don't know, where to go for a haircut. Then work your way up to the interesting stuff, like who gets the cowboy for the summer."

"Who . . . who . . ."

"Shhh." He brushed his thumb over the little O her lips had formed and whispered, "Owls."

"You arrogant son of a—" They were nose to nose again, both whispering.

"Don't say that, darlin'. I take that particular insult real hard."

"But what *you* said . . ."

"Not that it changes my intentions any, but I'd say the sooner you two come to terms on that little question, the sooner you can get on to the *big* question, which is, what are you gonna do about the High Horse?"

The big question sailed right past her. "Who said I . . . who said either one of us *wants* you for the summer? Gramma's the one who hired you."

"Gramma's got Vern. Little sister's got a husband. Big sister's got nobody, at least not right now." He stroked her hair back.

"How do you know that?" Was he teasing, or was that

some misplaced pity she heard in his voice? She shook her head, bumping his hand away. "Who says I need anyone?"

"I do. I say you need me." He bent close to her ear and whispered, "All you have to do is say when and show me where."

"Whoa, back up." She gave a deep-throated laugh as she extricated herself from his lap. Piggybacked on that foot massage, his offer was too tempting. "I don't know about Dawn, but I've told you what I need you for, and it's not a summer fling. I've gotten myself into a program that has one component, just one, that I can't quite execute. Fully. Myself."

"The Painted Mountain Horse Partnership Camp," he recited, dragging each syllable through his Texas twang as he squared his shoulders. "Sounds to me like that *little component* is the whole damn show."

"Well . . . I'm not asking you to travel."

"I'm workin' for cowboy wages, lady. You're already gettin' a whole lot more than your money's worth. I know exactly what I'm good for, and I always try to give my best." He peered at her. "Are you really gonna sell this place, Julia?"

She swallowed hard. The night breeze chilled her, and she realized now how foolish she'd been to come outside with bare feet. As a kid, she'd never felt the spring chill. She wasn't a kid anymore. She looked up at the house, the second floor, where she'd left her bedroom light on. The master bedroom. The two bright windows were like eyes staring at her, asking the same question. Do you really want to sell the High Horse?

Want to? Wanting was not an issue.

"You don't have to go."

K.C. was telling her this as she stood up, pulled her jacket around her. She laughed, and she wasn't sure why. Nervous, probably. "Yes, I do." She looked at him, lying back on one elbow, sprawling in the grass with the ease of a drifter, which was all he really was. A very attractive drifter. "You know, you're lucky to be so sure. What if your best isn't good enough?"

"If you walk away, you'll never know."

But if she stayed . . .

It hurt her throat, the way she laughed this time, for it was not a good laugh, not like the one they'd shared moments ago. "We're not even, K.C. You're way ahead of me."

She did walk away. He lay there in the grass and watched her.

Then he went back to the bunkhouse, took the pint bottle from the inside pocket of his jacket and started drinking for serious. He got up a few hours later, just as morning was breaking over the top of the ridge across the creek. He felt like hell, which was exactly what he'd been looking for in the whiskey he'd drunk straight from the bottle. Filling the hole in his gut. It was an old hole, one he should have learned to live with by now, but at times like this, times when he could imagine home being just over the next hill, he didn't much like feeling empty. There was only one way to deal with emptiness, and that was to fill it up with something. If hellfire was all that was handy, well, the heat was better than an empty hole.

He went out to the corral just as the golden sun peeked over the red bluffs. It wasn't long before he had the mare and one of the stud colts haltered and tied to posts at opposite corners of the pen. The mare was standing quietly, but the stud was still pawing the ground, tugging on the rope and testing the will of the post. He wasn't ready for the next step yet.

Close by in the round pen, K.C. had the little sorrel with the blaze face working pretty well on the longe line. K.C. wasn't singing to anybody this morning, wasn't even in much of a talking mood. "Get up, boy," was the extent of the conversation. A cluck of the tongue, a tap on the rump, and the horse was beginning to circle him willingly at the end of the long nylon line. Soon he'd simply pop the whip in the air, and eventually all he'd have to do was cluck to him.

Wild horses were so much easier to deal with than women.

He skipped breakfast. He'd already talked to Sally about

his plans to ride the summer pasture for a couple of days, told her he wanted to get acquainted with the mountains. That was always Ross's favorite chore, too, she'd said. "Just don't get lost up there," she warned him, and he wondered if she thought he might ride south. He figured he was in for more of the same when Shep came down to the corral looking for him.

The old man didn't say much until after they'd turned the horses back into the pasture, and then it was, "Rough night?"

"Rowdy night, rough morning," K.C. admitted as he watched the two bachelors trot through the grass toward the rest of their little band. He kept the mare and her foal apart from the others.

"Were they servin' a snake with every drink?"

"Hell, I've developed an educated thirst. I like to see a label on the bottle." He smiled as he folded the longe line into a coil of even loops. "I don't have to read what's on it. I just like to see it has one."

"Yep, yep, I been there. Seen the bottom of that well hole myself." Shep leaned back against the corral, hooking a boot heel on the bottom rail. "They make it a lot harder on a guy these days. They'll throw the book at you, you get caught drivin'." He squinted into the rising sun. "You weren't out drivin' our girls around, I hope."

"I wasn't driving. Chuck Pollak brought us home."

"You went out on the town with Pollak?"

"He brought us back. Just me and Dawn."

"You and Dawn." Shep tucked his hands under his armpits and stared at the ground. No mistaking the disapproval in his voice. "Dawn's a married lady, you know."

"Didn't do nothin' but dance with her." K.C. rested against the corral, side by side with the old man, duplicating his stance as though they were a pair of cowboy bookends. "Anyway, she wasn't my first choice."

"Well, now, that's what I thought. When I watched you and Queenie ridin' up there on that ridge side by side, I says to myself, I says, 'Self, you are lookin' at the next Weslin generation. That's prime High Horse breeding stock, right there.' "

They were both looking toward the main house. Through the trees they could see the massive fieldstone chimney, the peak of the gray roof and one of the windows of the master bedroom. K.C. imagined Julia waking up in the big four-poster bed, probably the bed she'd been made in. Maybe the bed her father had been made in. K.C. had slept in a big old bed like that once or twice, but he'd been a guest. Or a temporary substitute. And he didn't know what the hell kind of place he'd been made in.

"My name ain't Weslin."

"Hers is. And you two made a pretty picture. You're just what we need around here, you don't mind me sayin' so."

K.C. laughed. "Well, Shep, you've got me for the summer."

"Then don't be wastin' your time with the wrong sister. Queenie belongs here. She sells this place, she ain't never gonna find any peace for herself. And you been lookin' for something, too, son. I got a feelin' there's a hat rack up to the main house that's got your name on it." He slapped K.C.'s arm with the back of his hand. "And if there ain't, I got one I'll let you have cheap, no extra charge for engraving."

K.C. couldn't help laughing even though it made the throbbing in his temples feel worse. "Did Cupid go on vacation and leave you in charge?"

"I used to look after the sheep, you know, back when Sally used to run sheep. Spent half my life sleeping in a sheep wagon, just me and my dog. A man needs some companionship. Hell, son, you don't even have a dog."

"Every place I go there's a dog. Plenty of horses, too, and no shortage of women." He pushed away from the fence. "Damn, next time I'm in the mood for cryin' in my beer, I'll be sure and hook up with you first, Shep."

"Did I tell you my bitch is ready to whelp?" K.C. shook his head. "Any day. If it don't work out with Queenie, I can let you have a pup. Dirt cheap, too. They never used to keep dogs up to the house because of all Ross's allergies, but I reckon you could have one at the bunkhouse now. Get you a nice little bitch, you could call her . . ."

K.C. warned him off the nickname with a pointed look.

"Guess you ain't in a buyin' mood today," Shep said, dead serious. "Well, I can tell you why he's so dad-blamed helpful, what it is he wants. You know what he wants."

"What who wants?"

"Pollak. He wants the High Horse."

"Far as I know, it ain't for sale, Shep. Not today, anyway. So I guess you and me still have work to do." He reached for the halters, and Shep handed them over. "I'm gonna ride the high country for a few days, count heads and make sure everybody's gettin' fat and sassy on alpine grass."

"You plan on layin' over in the cabin up on Painted Woods Creek?"

"Sally fixed me up with some supplies. I'd be obliged if you'd come with me as far as the south fork. I'll ride up from there, and you can bring the outfit back. I don't want a vehicle up there. All I need is a couple of days."

Shep nodded. To a man who'd willingly spent months on end living in the mountains alone, the need was understandable.

"You know, Shep, if those women decide to sell"— K.C. returned the back-handed tap on the arm—"there ain't a damn thing us drones can do to stop it from happening."

"Drones? Who're you callin' a drone?" Shep shoved his hands in his back pockets and peered up at K.C. from under the battered brim of his straw hat. "What the hell's a drone, anyway?"

"Ask *Queenie*." He clapped a hand on the old man's bony shoulder. "But I'll put a half hitch in your tongue, you tell her why you're askin'."

15

Seven boys had been chosen.

Jack Trueblood brought them over in the school van and introduced them as "the lucky seven." He said they were all in the "plus column" for merit points and they'd been carefully selected from a list of applicants, but they could easily be deselected if they didn't cooperate. Their ages ranged from thirteen to seventeen. Merle Town and Barney Lawson had been part of the branding crew, as had Leighton Harding and Chad Snyder, who had also helped drive the herd up to the summer pasture.

There were three new faces in the group that gathered near the corral gate on the first day. Donnie Quinn and Brad Marshall both looked like Marine recruits—tall, strapping, aloof, clearly older than the other boys. Chevy James, who was black, was fourteen and nearly a six-footer, a city kid who didn't know much about livestock.

"Which is why I'm here," he told Julia earnestly, the words shooting out rapidly at first, like machine-gun fire, until the bullets jammed. "I know all about all kinds of animals, small ones, but I got to learn how to handle cows and horses and shit because what I really want to be is a v-v-veter-r-r . . ."

"Veterinarian?"

Chevy nodded and grinned, while Julia gave herself a mental dressing-down for supplying the word too quickly.

"Give us a break and just say 'animal doctor,' " Leigh-

198

ton gibed. Like the others, he was all arms and legs postured in a practiced slouch, but he clearly felt that he had the edge. After two assignments at the High Horse, he and Chad had the easy look of guys who knew their way around.

"None of that," Jack warned. "I've got a waiting list of guys who want to get in on this program. You don't do anything, *anything* to provoke each other. Now, I'm not gonna warn you again, Leighton." He turned his finger on Julia. "No warning tickets. Not for this program."

She flashed him a warning look of her own. The index finger wilted.

Julia smiled and slid the bolt on the corral gate. "Okay, guys, on with orientation."

"Is that, like, where they give you a map and a compass and then shove you off the bus in the middle of deep space and you've gotta find your way back or starve to death?"

The group was trailing her through the empty pen, and the question had come from Chad Snyder, the boy who had gotten scraped up bushwhacking for calves on the cattle drive. Julia smiled and took the bait. "I think that's orienteering."

"Oh, yeah." Tall, sandy-haired Chad gave her an eager-puppy look. "I was in one of those programs once, up in Montana."

"They still think he starved to death," Leighton said, grinning.

"Yeah, he wanders in on us one day at dinnertime. Scared the hell out of us, lookin' like a damn skeleton, and he has this map." Barney adjusted his thick horn-rimmed glasses and rolled out an air map, turning the invisible thing sideways, then reversing it as he played for the snickers. " 'Which way to Billings?' he says. 'Gol-ly, this ain't Montana. I musta died and gone to heaven.' He never did figure out how the compass worked."

"Yeah." Leighton clapped a hand on Chad's shoulder. It was immediately shrugged away. "So we decided to keep him fenced in for a while."

"Keep your hands off each other," Jack muttered.

"Orientation," Julia repeated, still smiling. Boys would,

given half a chance, still be boys. "I guess it works both ways."

She showed them around the pens and the big barn. Then they toured the machine shed, where they met Shep. Julia promised that Shep would show off his herding dogs another time, along with the finer points of small-engine repair and shoeing horses. Shep said he'd even show them how to pitch horseshoes if they were interested. He pointed out that he had been a state champ. "Got a big horseshoe trophy," he said proudly, describing the size and shape with oil-stained hands. The boys didn't look too impressed.

They ended up in the horse barn, where Julia introduced Vernon, who had agreed to give a few roping lessons after he taught them how to use a posthole digger. The groans indicated that some of the boys were well acquainted with the tool. Vernon supervised the saddling of four horses and took them for short rides, two or three at a time. But they spent most of the morning learning about the wonders of saddle soap.

"I thought we were gonna get to do more with horses," Barney said. To his credit, he'd worked up a lather on an old roping saddle and a sweat on his face. His glasses sat at half-mast on his nose.

"Jack said we might be breakin' horses."

"Yeah, that's what Jack said."

Jack had stepped out for a cigarette.

"Where's K.C.?" Leighton wanted to know. "He didn't quit, did he?"

"No, he still works here."

"Jack said we'd be gettin' to work with him, breakin' horses, maybe. He showed us an article about him in a horse magazine. Real hot-shit trainer, looks like."

"Well, K.C. has a lot of work to do."

"Will he be here tomorrow?"

"We're gonna build us a sawbuck fence tomorrow," Vernon said, taking a swipe at his mustache, then crossing his hands at the wrists to demonstrate *sawbuck*. "Like you see along the road a lot. There's a real art to building them puppies."

*   *   *

Sawbuck fences were not what Julia had in mind for this program. Gentling wild horses might not have been part of Ross's plan, but she was convinced now that riding was secondary. A well-broke saddle horse would endure a lot of human ineptitude, but a wild horse would not. Trust was not a given; it had to be earned. It was not the riding but the gentling that was the key. And the key to gentling was patience. If the boys could learn to appreciate the value of trust and the dividends of patience ...

Which brought her back to K.C. She couldn't do this without him.

Julia could tell something was up as soon as she walked into the kitchen. A pitcher of lemonade and four glasses stood on a tray on the counter, ready to be served. Dawn was busy putting together a platter of sandwiches. She glanced up, flushed, bright-eyed and smiling. Either she'd won the lottery, or one of the voices in the living room belonged to Mel Gibson.

"Chuck Pollak wants to buy the ranch. He's here. He brought his lawyer. Greaaat-looking guy, but a little short." Her sparkling blue eyes said there was more. "You won't believe what he's offering."

Sounded like the daily double. Julia turned on the water, but she couldn't help smiling as she soaped her hands. "Freedom?"

"That's one way of putting it. If we sell all the land we own, with the improvements—that includes the house—and he wants the permits, leases, everything ..." She waited until Julia shut the water off and turned for the exuberant punch line. "Four and a half million dollars, Julia. And there's still the livestock. Can you believe it? We're going to be rich!"

Julia admitted that the amount surprised her—not with words, but with eyebrows—as she dried her hands on a dish towel. "Where's Gramma?"

"They're in the living room. Will you take that tray? Here." She added a fifth glass. "I guess there would be some loans to pay off, but even then, we're going to be so—"

"Calm down, Dawn."

Julia hung the towel back on its ring and headed for the tray, her sandals slapping against her heels. She wished she hadn't left her boots in the mud room. A meeting with Chuck Pollak called for Wyoming power dressing. Hat and boots made the man.

And Dawn's eagerness had Julia feeling the need for some dig-in heels. She took a deep breath and laid a clammy hand on Dawn's bare arm. "Do you have a poker face anywhere in your repertoire? If you could just try not to look like you're ready to pounce on the pot, I think we'd all do better."

"Better than four and a half million dollars?" Dawn savored every syllable of the amount.

"Just better all around." Julia added paper napkins to the tray. She could hear the voices in the living room now, although nobody seemed to be saying much. "He's got a lot of nerve."

"*Nerve?* Julia, that's a lot of money, for God's sake. That's more . . ." Dawn grabbed more napkins along with her platter of sandwiches. "He says that's more than it would appraise out at. He's just looking for a commitment."

"He won't be getting one today."

Julia followed her sister into the living room, where their grandmother sat holding court in one of the four big leather chairs that flanked the stone fireplace. The yawning hearth was screened for the summer with a wood triptych embellished with a train, hand-painted by their grandfather fifty years ago. The room felt like Wyoming high country. It was rock, wood and leather, red clay and sage, green pine and sun-bleached cottonwood—big, bold, sink-in comfort. Like the rest of the house, it was a repository of High Horse history.

The two men sat on the bulky Navaho-print sofa. Julia greeted Chuck as she set her tray on the glass-topped chunk of polished cedar that served as a coffee table. While she poured, he introduced his attorney, Tom Lomak, who happened to be up from Cheyenne today. "So that's why we stopped by. Just thought we'd throw some figures out and see what you gals have to say."

"So Dawn was just telling me." She handed the lawyer a glass of lemonade. He flashed her a winning smile—more suave Grant than roguish Gibson. Attractive enough, for a man in a jacket and tie. "It's a generous offer. What do you think, Gramma?"

"About the amount?" Sally shook off Dawn's offer of sandwiches. "I think it's a lot of money. But what I know is that the High Horse is a lot of ranch."

"It sure is. It's a landmark, a piece of Wyoming history, and I'm willing to pay for that." Chuck was also willing to eat, which was a point in his favor, Julia thought, after Dawn had made all those sandwiches.

Lomak set his glass down, scrupulously centering it on a napkin. "It's happening everywhere, Mrs. Weslin. Places like this one that have been in the same family for generations are changing hands every day. I've represented some folks lately . . ." He gestured, both hands open. "And it's hard, but you go on with your life. You'll be doing it in style, with the kind of money we're talking here."

Like an imperturbable gray owl, Sally viewed the lawyer dispassionately. "These clients you've been representing, were they the buyers or the sellers?"

"Well, I've been on both sides. Not in the same transaction, of course."

"And you'd like to start some paperwork on this one."

"Chuck is prepared to make it worthwhile for you to get the ball rolling now. These things take time. You'd have plenty of time to make your arrangements. We would work out a very flexible timetable."

"If you wanted to run your livestock through the fall, no problem," Chuck added around a mouthful of chicken salad.

Dawn took a chair across the table from her grandmother. "And that's exactly what you wanted to do, Gramma. Sell—"

"We're not ready to look at any offers yet, Chuck," Julia interjected as she sat down next to her sister. "But it's an interesting proposal. It gives us something to talk about."

"Besides . . ." Sally slid Julia an approving glance. "We've only got one lawyer in the room right now. Isn't there a certain lawyer quota that has to be filled when you're talking millions of dollars?''

Chuck gestured, lemonade in hand. "It's like Julia says, we just wanted to give you something to talk about.''

"And now you have.''

"I don't want you to think I'm trying to push you out of your home, Sally. You work with me on this, you can have all the time you need to relocate, all the help, all the . . .'' Now the gesture came from the sandwich hand. "The thing is, the sooner we can come to some kind of an agreement, just so we know where we're headed, the sooner I can start getting my financing lined up.''

"You don't have four and a half million in the bank, Chuck?'' Sally chuckled. "That's a relief. I was gonna ask you what you were raising over there at the Lazy P.''

"I explained to you before, Chuck, that we're not ready to jump into anything,'' Julia said, exchanging glances again with her grandmother. "We're going to be busy this summer. When we decide what we're going to do—''

"This is a damn good offer.'' Chuck looked at Sally, daring her to disagree. "You know it is.''

Sally shifted in her chair. "Well, you're jumping the gun with it a little, Chuck, because we haven't put a sign up. Now, maybe this fall—''

"I don't know what kind of an offer I'd make this fall. This ain't the only place that's likely to go up for sale.''

"And you're not the only buyer who's likely to be interested.''

"But we're not turning this down,'' Dawn said quickly. "We have a lot to discuss. Major, major discussion.''

"In that case . . .'' Tom set his half-empty glass on the tray. "I guess we'd better get out of their way, right, Chuck?''

The three women stood by the window and watched the silver pickup barrel across the bridge, hitting the gravel on the far side like a water-skier coming off a ramp.

Sally pondered the pickup's dust wake. "Now, who do you s'pose is gonna give Chuck Pollak that much money?''

"A bank,'' Dawn said. "We're going to have to have

an appraisal done soon anyway, aren't we? I vote we go
ahead—''

"You're jumping the gun, too, little girl." Sally turned
away from the window, looking at each granddaughter in
turn. "I've pulled the High Horse back from the brink of
bankruptcy twice. I've buried most of my family here. The
three of us are all that's left. Well, maybe you're right,
maybe the three of us put together don't add up to a
rancher. Maybe the old horse has finally reached the end
of the line, but if she has . . ."

She turned to Julia, to remind her: "I don't want to be
pushed. If this is the end of the line, I believe I've earned
the right to just take a rest here for a little bit, and that's
exactly what I intend to do." Then, to Dawn: "So don't
be bargaining with Chuck Pollak behind my back. There's
no rush."

"It's just that, like the man said, these things take time,
Gramma."

"The High Horse measures time in seasons, in scores of
seasons." Sally looked out the front window, seeing the
same snowcapped, pine-dappled mountains she'd viewed
through a child's eyes when she'd stood in the same spot
on the same floor of the same house nearly a lifetime ago.
Unlike her eyesight, the mountains had not changed. "Not
in days and weeks, which is the piddling kind of time
you're talking about."

"What you're saying is that you don't want my opinion." Dawn wound her arms around her middle as though
she was holding her seams together. "Well, I'm part of this
family, too, and my name's in Ross's will, so you're getting
my opinion anyway, which is that neither one of you is in
any position to stall off the inevitable. If we liquidate now,
we'll be set for life. All of us. Right?"

"Depends on your notion of being *set*," Sally said.
"*Liquidate*. Sounds sloppy to me. Doesn't sound too *set*."

"All right!" Dawn was clearly feeling the ugly pinch of
being outnumbered. She turned to Julia. "You buy me out,
then."

"With what?"

"Or . . . or just give me my share so I can sell it myself."

"It doesn't work that way," Julia said calmly, reminding herself that being demanding was simply Dawn's way. "It's set up as kind of an all-or-nothing deal. We can't sell the house unless Gramma agrees, and we can't sell anything until we're both ready."

"Well, obviously we have to sell, and an offer like that . . ." Dawn turned on Sally again. "I don't know why you didn't do it a long time ago. Ross was never cut out for this. He was always—"

"He had a good life here, and I won't hear otherwise," Sally told her. "The High Horse was his home, his sanctuary. Sure, you can sell it and rake in a pile of money, and that's what we'll do if that's what you both want. But the money will be gone fast, and then where are you?" She paused, then repeated quietly, in a voice that was achingly brittle, "Where are you, little girl?"

"I'll tell you where I won't be," Dawn snapped on her way to the stairs. "I won't be on a rock pile in the middle of the desert."

They watched her finish her statement with a purposeful ascent, a march down the hall to her room, where she would undoubtedly pick up the phone and call her mother. The rock-pile comment was a direct quote.

Sally started collecting used napkins off the coffee table. "Have you given any more thought to staying on the place and running it yourself, Queenie?"

"I've tried, Gramma, but I always come around to thinking, 'Me? A rancher?' " Sally nodded. If she was disappointed in Julia, she didn't show it. "And what would we do about Dawn's share?"

"I like the word 'share.' " Sally sat on the edge of the sofa, the napkins she gathered now resting on her knee. "I like it much better than 'liquidate.' Hoo-wee, that's an unpleasant word. Like 'puke.' "

Julia gave Sally a smile. She was being Gramma, just like Dawn being Dawn. What sounded good to one was noise to the other. Julia put two blue-rimmed glasses on the tray, then sat next to it on the floor. "I have thoughts, Gramma. All kinds of thoughts. Decisions are something else."

"You got crowded feelings, huh?"

"Crowded feelings." Her grandmother's expression made her smile as she absently lined the glasses up, full to empty, remembering a demonstration her father had done to show her how to make music with beer bottles. There had been other onlookers, as she remembered, two or three of his roping buddies, but the show had been for her. Daddy used to say that Ross was allergic to him, and Dawn . . . Dawn was on the periphery somewhere, just a baby. Always the baby. It had been up to Julia to be the right kind of a daughter so that things would work out.

"Gramma, this program we've got going could really be good for those boys, I think, if we can turn it into more than just chores and recreation. Not that there's anything wrong with chores and recreation, but . . ." She looked up, finally voicing another ever-present concern lately. "Have you seen K.C. today?"

Sally gave her a knowing look. "Have you been looking for him?"

"I didn't really expect to see him at breakfast after last night." Julia frowned. "You didn't fire him, did you?"

"Fire him?" Sally laughed. "That wouldn't be very smart, now, would it? He went up to Painted Mountain this morning. First few weeks especially, you've gotta keep pushing those girls back up to the high country. They'd rather wander downhill than climb for better grass."

"He's not going to stay up there, is he?"

She shrugged. "He took some provisions. We used to put a man up there all summer, but since they put the new road in, we haven't had to do that." Elbows on knees, she leaned toward the table. "It's not just the cows, you know. Those wild horses are up there, too."

"I really need him here. This program is supposed to be a pilot, and I want to see it work." Her eyes met the challenge in Sally's. *Why? If it works, where could it lead?*

Back to the glasses. "I've seen too many social programs fail, Gramma. Partly or altogether, too many well-meaning attempts turn out so badly, and I've seen too much of it. I've been part of it. I'd like to see one good idea make a difference for one small bunch of kids, at least for one summer.'' She shrugged. ''It would be something for the school to build on. I'm seeing this through in Ross's memory, Gramma, but I do need . . . someone like K.C.'' And it had seemed like such a good idea, such a natural extension of his talent, that she'd been certain he'd relent. ''He just decided we needed him up there, or did you send him?''

Sally laughed. ''He decided. They do that sometimes. Give him a day or two for himself. Then go tell him you need him. See if that don't bring him back.''

Sally could always tell when a man had the blues. She didn't always know why, but she knew when. She'd seen it in her son and her grandson many times. She'd learned to recognize it first in her husband. In hindsight, she knew she'd seen it in her father, too. It was a lonesomeness men seemed to carry around with them, letting it feed on them like a woman would nourish a child. It was hard to understand why they cherished such a thing so much, especially once they'd finally come home.

You could see why men like K.C. Houston were lonesome. He couldn't see it himself, but any woman would know and understand the hunger in him. Once a man had found home, there were those times when he'd get to choking on the burden of it, and he'd worry about what he was missing ''out there on the high road,'' as her Max used to say. A woman made her home. A man pined for his, and once he found it, he would guard it with his life, but he never quite gave up the worry over losing his edge, his share of the world's wildness.

Sally had been home for quite a few men over the years. Not the same way she'd been home for Max, but she'd been a vital refuge for the other men in her life. Still, there had been only one Max. Max had been her salvation, and she had been his sanctuary. It was the basis of a lasting partnership.

It had been early spring, 1932. Everybody had wintered hard, but the snow had finally melted, and what was left of the stock had already picked up some weight on the new grass. Sally had gone to Quicksilver for a few staples, which she'd stowed in the back of the truck, then stopped at the depot to send a telegram. She knew she'd been robbed when she spotted a thin white trail running from the tailgate of the truck, across the rutted street, across the tracks to the quiet stockyards.

The thin white arrow directed her behind a load of crated freight to the stock tank. There, in the shadow of the water tower, she found a bag of her flour sitting on top of one of her gunnysacks, along with some coffee, some beans and a pair of boots she'd bought for her younger brother. Next to the boots was a pair of large feet. Gradually she ratcheted her gaze from the feet to the tattered jeans to the denim jacket and, finally, to the rawboned face of a man with the biggest, bluest eyes she'd ever seen. The rest of him suddenly became marginal. His eyes were everything.

"I was just about to put the boots back," he said. "They don't fit."

He was eating something, chewing slowly, deliberately, as he peered at her from under the bill of his cap. She glanced at his hands. He held a pocket knife in one, a raw potato in the other.

"There was hardtack in one of the boxes."

"I didn't have much time to be choosy."

"You shouldn't be eating those raw."

He almost smiled. "I got a cast-iron stomach, ma'am. If you was to thump on it right now, you'd hear the echo."

"I hardly think I want to go thumping your stomach. Especially since you're holding a knife."

"Knife, fork and spoon," he said as he carved out another wedge. His hands, all rawhide and bone, glistened in the sun. They had just been washed. "You're interrupting the first meal I've had in a couple of days."

"You're eating my food."

"It's mine now, unless you plan on callin' the law or wrestling me for it yourself."

She edged closer, as though she might take him up on his dare. "If you want to put the knife down, there won't be much contest, skinny as you are."

"Hey, this is my best fighting weight." He popped the

piece of potato into his mouth, then gestured with the knife. "Figure I still outweigh you."

"I guess skin and bones must weigh something."

He shrugged, and they went right on eyeballing each other, sizing each other up, each impressed with the other's nerve, each ignoring the risk the other might pose. He had the look of a working man, she thought. It was hard to keep good cowhands when you couldn't always pay them. But the hunger in this man's eyes pressed for more than food.

Wordlessly he offered her a slice of potato on the flat of his knife blade. There was no levity in his eyes, no apology, no shame. He had to eat. Did she care to join him?

"I could cook those for you. They'd be good with some onions and carrots, some beef. I make the best biscuits you've ever tasted . . . hot, with fresh butter?"

He stopped chewing and stood, eyes fixed like those of a famished predator, nostrils flaring as though her promise carried an aroma. Clearly hard-pressed to swallow another mouthful of raw potato now that she'd tempted him so, he simply stared. She glanced away, giving him a chance to spit or gag or whatever he had to do without being gawked at. She hadn't meant to tease.

He swallowed so hard it left him nearly breathless. "Why would you wanna do that?"

"I do it every day. I could do it for you every day. Can you ride?"

He barked a dry laugh as he pitched the potato through the open door of an empty cattle car. It whacked the inside wall, then dropped to the floor with a feeble thunk. "Been ridin'."

"Can you ride a horse?"

"Horse?" He pocketed his knife. "Well, sure."

"Where are you from?"

"All over."

"Do you know where you are now?"

"You think I'm stupid? This is . . ." He glanced at the water tower. "Quicksilver."

"Quicksilver, Wyoming." She studied him curiously, and he stood there, permitting her scrutiny without flinching. "Well?"

"Well, what?"

"You want a job or not?" Her gaze slid to his feet. "What size do you wear?"

Another brief laugh, but this time he actually seemed amused. "I don't think that's a proper question for a lady to be askin' a man she hardly knows."

"You can't ride without boots." She saw something she wanted behind him, and he moved to block her way, thinking it was the pilfered food, his bird in the hand. She denied his fear with a look, and he let her pass. "You'd probably want to clean those feet up a little bit before we go over and see if Parson's has a pair that big."

He stepped away from the stock tank, keeping her in sight as she circled around to the pump. "You think I'd let you buy me boots?" he demanded.

"I bought those."

"Not for me."

"I won't be buying any for you, then. I've got a Clydesdale with feet about that size." She found a feed pan, emptied it of sand and gravel, and spared him a saucy grin across the tank. " 'Course, he'd hardly care if somebody was to steal them off the back of my truck."

His laughter was warming up considerably. "You just went and took all the fun out of it now."

"I've got two hundred first-calf heifers ready to calve out. How's that for fun?" She started priming the pump. "You ever pulled a calf?"

"Sure have."

"I'd have to feed you up some. You couldn't pull kittens, the shape you're in now."

"Woman, you sure are pushin' your luck." As if to prove her a liar, he took over on the pump handle without questioning what she was up to as she caught the water in the squat feed pan. "I'd be sorely tempted to speak about your shape, but I got better manners. And I've already washed up, if that's what we're doing. I never pass up a—"
He took over on the brimming pail, too, balancing it on the edge of the tank, questioning her with a look.

She grabbed one side, and they set it on the ground together. He stood. She squatted next to the pan. "Now roll up your pants."

"What do you think you're gonna do?"

"Wash your feet."

"The hell you say."

"You have a real sentimental attachment to that dirt?" She squinted up at him. He looked like a single, misplaced ponderosa pine, scrawny, swaying, head in the clouds, trying to drill her into the ground with a hot glare. "Sorry. You want manners?" She offered a tight smile. "Please, sir. Roll up your britches."

He kept right on scowling.

"Well, I didn't say drop them, did I? 'Roll up your britches' is perfectly well-mannered talk hereabouts."

She did it for him, laughing and promising to be gentle with him. His jeans were frayed, worn and washed soft. She folded them up carefully, as though it mattered whether they got wet. He didn't seem to know what to make of the whole idea, whether to stand for it or to walk away. He had his pride, but he set it aside and stepped into the water when she asked him to.

A strange look crossed his face as he looked down at her, as if she'd done something cruel and he'd permitted it, and he blamed them both for making him feel naked in broad daylight. She realized the dirt wasn't just going to melt off, and he'd gone as far with this as he could go. She took a white handkerchief from the pocket of her khaki pants, dipped it in the water and started with his ankles. When she told him he'd have to pick up his foot, he leaned back against the stock tank, hooked his arms over the rim and surrendered a badly abused foot. Calluses, blisters, bunions, she took care cleansing them all while he watched, the expression on his wind-chapped, chiseled and, yes, handsome face completely unreadable. He did not know what to make of this.

Neither did she. "What's your name?" she asked.

The raspy response was slow in coming. "Max."

"Is that all?"

"Weslin. Max Weslin."

"Sally Harris."

"Pleasure . . ." He cleared his throat. "Pleasure to meet you, ma'am."

"Will you come to work for me, Max Weslin?" She looked up, smiled. "Max Weslin. I like that name."

It was a few days before she told him how much she liked his eyes. He said that she was the brassiest woman he'd ever run across, and she informed him that Wyoming women were bred to be brassy. Within a few weeks she managed to put a little meat on his bones, about as much meat as he'd ever carry. He did know about birthing livestock, and he soon found himself supervising the first round of calving. His long, slender hands served the heifers well.

He hadn't exaggerated about being from all over. He was originally from Virginia, but he had tales to tell from places she figured she'd never see. She knew he'd lied about his experience as a horseman, but only because the first time she'd introduced him to a horse, he'd tried to mount from the wrong side. He tried to tell her it was because Indians had taught him to ride. She almost fell for it, because once he was mounted, he took to it like he'd been born in the saddle. The sight of him finding his seat stirred her blood, the way he squared his shoulders as he felt the power beneath him. A railroad tramp no more, he surveyed the corrals, the creek, the hills and the horizon like a man who'd just been crowned king.

By July Sally's aging father had agreed to hire Max as livestock foreman when the second foreman in a year left for supposedly greener pastures. Max averred quietly, as was his way, that greener pastures were nowhere to be found. He took to his new job so aptly that Sally would have sworn he'd been a cowboy all his life. But by then she would have sworn he'd hung the August moon.

In September they lost her brother, Billy, when he fell into an oat bin. Like quicksand, the grain swallowed him whole and snuffed him out before anyone knew he was in trouble. It was Max who followed the boy's trail and recovered his body.

In November Sally's father succumbed to influenza. On Christmas Eve she became Sally Weslin.

16

*J*ulia drove halfway up the mountain, horse trailer in tow, parked the outfit at the end of the rutted dirt road that had been bisected by the "new" twenty-year-old blacktop mountain highway, and walked another half mile to the cabin in the pines. *Where the sun don't shine*, she could almost hear him sing. The windows on either side of the door were open, and she glanced in on her way to the door. She could see the army-green sleeping bag unrolled on the narrow bed, the duffel bag on the floor beside it, the pile of freshly split firewood in the box beside the stove, and the assortment of rope and leather tack sitting on the small wooden table. Wrangler in residence, she thought.

She knew she'd find him in the split-rail horse pen with its lean-to shelter in the clearing below the cabin. She could hear the *ta-ta-tump, ta-ta-tump* of a horse's collected gait and the tongue-clucking of the one who prodded the animal into motion. The soft, gurgling *chur-wi* of a mountain warbler echoed through the tall pines. With the thick mat of fallen needles underfoot, she made her way down the hill to the clearing.

There in the summer sun's spotlight, bare to the waist except for his white straw cowboy hat, his long torso beautifully sculpted and tanned, K.C. was working the big buckskin mustang on a longe line, using a willow switch to give the horse an occasional tap on the rump. He must have

214

heard her skittering down the path, for he didn't look at all surprised to see her.

"You've come a long way with that horse," she said as she climbed the rails to make the top one her seat.

"A couple of weeks." He glanced at her, smiled knowingly, his eyes trapping the sun's glint. "You were gonna ask how long before I could ride him. Couple of weeks he'll be green-broke."

"Will he buck when you get on him?"

"Not if I don't rush him. Although some like to buck just for fun. You know how that goes."

"Can't say I do."

"No?" He stepped in as the horse arced around him to the left at a trot. She noticed that the buckskin's wire cuts had been tended and were healing nicely. "Well, a good rider knows the difference between a mount who's buckin' scared and one who's buckin' for pure pleasure."

"I can't imagine bucking for pleasure. I guess you'd have to be a horse," she allowed, and he teased her with a quizzical glance. "What?" she demanded, but, of course, she knew. "I'm still a pretty good rider."

"Whoa." He tugged on the lead rope, repeated the command, and the horse stopped. He glanced at Julia. "Are you, now?"

"Don't you think so?"

"Maybe you're right. Maybe that's only for the horse to say." He switched the lead rope into his right hand, the makeshift whip to the left, and pulled the horse a few steps toward him. The buckskin's ears homed in on him like two periscopes. "Did you need me for something, boss lady?"

She did, and he knew it. She was up to her neck in horse trials and tribulations, and he was the man of the hour. Clearly he enjoyed his distinction. "I brought a pickup and stock trailer."

"You hired a cowboy," he reminded her as he extended his arms, letting the horse see that the goad and the lead had changed hands. "The cows are up here."

"Ah, you've changed your tune a little bit. You said we'd hired a horse trainer. Obviously you wear both hats quite well. But you don't have to camp out up here, you know. You can . . ."

His clucking to the horse came off as a wordless double entendre, as taunting to her as it was to the horse. After a tap on the rump, the buckskin got the idea and moved willingly in the opposite direction. K.C. spared a glance as he pivoted, following the arc of the horse's trot. "Did you need me for something, Julia?"

She took her time about answering and simply watched him work. He was giving himself almost entirely to the horse. The "boss lady" was an afterthought. Did she need him, this beautiful young man who supposedly worked for her, but who went about every aspect of his job in his own way, in his own good time? She wanted to take him back with her. She wanted him to help her with the program. She wanted him to . . .

She wanted him. Yes, indeed, she surely did. The wanting hummed in her, thrummed in her, like electrical current. It was, she realized, a sizzling new experience. Too sizzling, too new. Too unpredictable. But she surely did want him.

"I brought food, too," she said. "Supper, in case you're tired of your own cooking. It's in a cooler in the pickup."

"For two, I hope."

"At least." She stared at the fading knees of her old blue jeans. "I do need you for something, K.C., but you turned me down flat once already, and I'm not sure I want to risk another rejection."

He chuckled. "I never turn a lady down flat. You must have misunderstood."

"I don't think so, but maybe you're feeling more charitable now."

"Must be the mountain air." He stopped the horse with a soft "whoa," reeling in the longe line, then rubbed the animal's neck. "What can I do for you, Julia?"

"Help me . . ." The words sounded plaintive. Weak and pitiful. She eased herself down the rails, into the pen and faced him, starting again, reaching for a lower, more controlled pitch. "Help me with the summer program."

"Ask me for something else." That easy smile of his

invited confidence. "Anything else you want, I'll be glad to do."

"The boys were asking for you today, K.C. They were told they'd learn to break horses. Jack told them all about you, what a wonderful reputation you have as a trainer, and they're just dying to have you teach them."

"I don't *break* horses exactly." He approached her, his eyes on her, but he was equally attentive to the way he was leading the horse he hadn't exactly broken, giving him a little slack, maintaining a comfortable distance so that neither crowded the other in the simple act of walking side by side. "I keep tryin' to tell you, I don't know that what I do can be taught. It's just working with the horse, is all. You can pretty much count on the horse doing his part. He has a one-track mind. You get on his track, and you work together. People are different. You never know what they're gonna do. And kids, what do I know about kids?"

"I think you know those boys better than any of the rest of us do. Show them what works for you. Break it down into steps." He met her charge with a guarded look. "I mean, I'm sure you've done that, but for the boys . . ."

"Did you bring a saddle horse?"

"No, I brought an empty . . ." She glanced toward the adjacent pen, where Columbine stood hip-shot, bored, waiting her turn. His saddle stood on its horn end outside the pen, a saddle blanket and a blue chambray shirt draped over the rail close by. He was unbuckling the buckskin's halter.

He had chores to do; was that the message?

"Couldn't he jump this fence?" she asked.

"He sure could."

She followed him through the gate and around the corner of the corral to the back of the lean-to, where he filled an old grain pan with a couple of dippers of oats.

"Then what?" *Then he'd go after him, of course.*

"Then we lose him." He swished the oats back and forth in the pan, and the buckskin lifted his head, cocking his ears toward the sound. "Sounds pretty good to you, don't it, ol' boy? You stay with us, there's easy oats all year round. Or we've got high-country grass, which is seasonal, but nobody knows that better than you."

For the moment the young stallion was interested in the oats. "It's up to him." K.C. slid the pan under the fence. "He outweighs me by a few hundred pounds."

"And I'm supposed to see a parallel," she concluded. He thrust a finger at the brim of his hat, pushed it back and smiled. "K.C., you and I could come up with a program together. Okay, so you have a kind of sixth sense that can't exactly be taught, but I was thinking we'd start slowly, and . . ."

He'd turned away, started wagging his head on the words "sixth sense" as he reached for his shirt. She knew he was laughing at her.

"We'd get a sense of the boys. They'll show us if they're not really open to this, and we won't push. We'll figure out a different program for the boys who don't take to your methods. I mean, we won't . . ." She was distracted from her course, watching him button his shirt. Dressing. Stuffing his shirttail into his pants struck her as an intimate act. It wasn't like buttoning a coat, which was public.

He glanced up, and she felt as though she'd been caught keyhole-peeping.

What in *hell* was wrong with her?

"What do you think?" she asked, her tone overly bright.

"I think—" He shrugged. And then, much to her surprise, he slipped his arm around her and started walking toward Columbine's pen. "*I think* you're the first woman I've met who expected me to think about much of anything."

Her arm went around his back of its own accord, and she looked up at him, smiling. "Well?"

"I'm thinking about these steps. Patience is definitely step one."

"What's step two?"

"If you've gotta ask that quick, you're not ready." They'd reached his saddle, lying on the ground. "Because you haven't really bought into step one yet," he said.

"So you'll help me?" He rolled his eyes. "We can manage without you if you feel that it's your duty to sleep with the cows, but it seems such a perfect . . ." From his bemused expression, she didn't appear to be getting anywhere.

"Let's take a ride, boss lady. There's something I want to show you, just over the next ridge. I saw them there this morning."

He saddled the mare, hooked Shep's binoculars over the horn and invited Julia to mount up. They rode double, which he assured her he would not have done in the mountains had the horses not been so close by. They followed the crest of a gently sloping ridge abloom with blue flax and yellow potentilla. The wind in their faces carried the scent of juniper and ponderosa pine. When they spotted horses about a mile away, grazing the face of another slope, they took refuge above a stand of gray-green bitterbrush.

"I've been watching this band," he said. She counted a dozen horses and half as many foals. They were scattered over the slope and into the valley in two distinct coteries. The one without foals was a bachelor band. Breeding season was over, so they were permitted to drift closer to the mares.

K.C. took off his hat, rested his chin on Julia's shoulder and directed her gaze by lining it up with his. "The black up there on the hill, that's the lead mare. She makes all the decisions. You think it's the stallion that runs the show, but that ain't the way it is."

"Who thinks that? Me?"

His chuckle rumbled softly in her ear. "People."

"Men, maybe. A lead mare makes perfect sense to me." She shaded her eyes with her hand to get a better look at the black beauty. "What kinds of decisions?"

"Where to hang out, for one thing. She picks out the grass she wants first, and everybody else kinda spreads out around her. She's like the queen." The mare lifted her head, as though she'd heard her name called. A sorrel drifted into the black's space, but when the black lowered her head for more grass, the sorrel moved on. "Oh, yeah, she knows her rank," K.C. said. "If we rounded this bunch up and took her away, we'd mess up their whole order."

He moved his arm to the left and nudged her face with

his. "Same would happen if we took him away. That's the stud, that bay."

"Magnificent."

"His mares seem to think so. Now, this is what I wanted to show you. Watch that pair of sorrels over there. And over there. See that bunch?" He pointed with one hand as he reached around her for the binoculars with the other. She nodded. "That's a bachelor band." He focused the binoculars, then passed them to her. "I want you to watch the bay stallion's bunch first. Check those two sorrels."

"What am I looking for?"

"Just look. See what you see."

It took some adjusting of the binoculars, but finally she was able to single out the right pair. A foal suckled one of the sorrels, while the other, the one with the blaze face, stayed close by, grazing, giving the occasional whinny. When the foal wandered a few yards away, the blaze edged closer, matching every step the broodmare took. "The sorrels are both mares?"

"Uh-huh."

"Is the one with the blaze an older colt?"

"She's at least four or five. Her mama would have cut the apron strings long ago." He pointed to the bachelor band. "Check out the red roan and the grullo." She turned, questioning with a frown. "Grullo? Kind of a mouse-colored horse with black points."

"Learn something new every . . ." She scanned the slope for the designated bachelors. "They seem to be pretty good friends. Is that unusual?"

"Think about how that paint we've got—*you've* got, back at the place. The way he sticks by the big sorrel, and the way the sorrel waits on him. You watch most horses grazing like this, they're pretty quiet, right? These guys seem to be whinnying just for the hell of it, like they're keeping up a conversation or something. Just like that little glass-eyed paint. And we know he's blind."

She brought up the binoculars again. "You think some of these are blind, too?"

"How many mustangs have you got up here?"

"About fifty or sixty adults, I think." The glasses came

down as she turned to him. "Are you sure they're blind?"

"You watch how they behave when we ride in on them. We'll just ease down the slope and let them know we're here. Watch those two pairs."

A wave of K.C.'s hat, along with their slow, hip-rocking descent, was all it took to alarm the band. Heads came up, necks arched, and with a flurry of whinnies they took flight. Some seemed literally to take wing, straight up and over the top of the ridge.

"Look," K.C. said, pointing at the pair of bachelors they'd been watching. "The rest of them take the direct route. Those two are taking the long way around. It's not as rocky. And watch the sorrel mares." He pointed again. The broodmare had her foal to look after, but the blaze stuck to her flank like an extra appendage. "I've never seen anything like it. It's a partnership. The seeing horse knows his role, and he's accepted it."

"Or hers," Julia said, amazed. She would not have seen what he saw in this herd, would not have noticed the unusual behavior without his guidance. But did it necessarily mean that they were blind? "How do you know?"

"I've been watching them. I know horses. A horse's best defense is his ability to run, just take off and fly. For a horse to accept that kind of a risk, hanging back like that . . ." He put his hat back on, then rested his hand on her shoulder. "That's the amazing part. But yeah, I'd say you've got more blind horses up here, Julia."

"It's genetic, then, isn't it?"

"Looks like it."

"Which means it's serious. And sad."

"Don't tell them." With a glance she questioned his warning. He smiled, squeezed her shoulder, massaged it with his thumb. "The horses. From the looks of it, nobody's told them they've got a problem."

"I know, but . . ." She watched the sorrels disappear over a low rise. "You're right. It's really a beautiful thing, isn't it? Who would have imagined they'd just adapt that way on their own?"

"Wasn't there some guy named Darwin?"

She laughed. "Currently, there's this guy named Houston, about as keen-eyed as a hawk, I'd say.''

"What kind of eyes has he got?"

"Keen eyes." She turned to admire them. Blue, bright, fully engaging, as though his favor was there for the taking, right there in his eyes. "Very sharp, very, very nice eyes."

"A guy's gotta make use of his assets."

"I wonder if Ross knew," she mused as they turned back, retracing their route. "He must have. He loved these horses. Why didn't he say anything? I mean, surely something has to be done, but why didn't he . . . if he knew, why didn't he . . ." She looked at the expert. "What do you think we ought to do, K.C.?"

"First off, I think we ought to do something with whatever you've got in that cooler you brought. And that's about as much thinkin' as I'm prepared to do on an empty stomach."

They retrieved the cooler from the pickup, along with a plaid stadium blanket, which they spread out in the shade of the pines that skirted the mountain meadow near the cabin. He picketed Columbine so that they could watch her graze. "No prettier sight than a grazing horse," he said, but he amended that when he saw the picnic Julia laid out, with homemade crusty bread and gourmet chocolate chip cookies, for which Dawn was given credit, along with the zesty chicken salad, sliced cheeses, fresh fruit. Julia had chosen a white Rhine wine, and K.C. gallantly claimed that it was almost as good as a beer.

"I just thought a nice picnic would . . ."

"Soften me up?" He sipped his wine. "Besides using his assets, a guy's gotta know his limitations."

"If I'd wanted to soften you up, I would have brought beer."

"Really?" He took another look at his glass. "So what does this do?"

"Complements the fruit."

"I've been called a lot of things, but never a fruit. You sure that's a compliment?"

They laughed together, poured more wine, inched closer and kept the giddiness going until they were lying side by side, watching the tops of the pines swish across the canvas of gray lumps gathering ominously over bright blue.

"Are you ready to put on your thinking cap yet?" she asked during a long, comfortable lull. "I'm interested in your thoughts on how to deal with blind horses."

"I ain't no expert, Julia, but I do know a guy who works for the BLM. Wild-horse manager, down in Nevada. There must be somebody here like that."

"The office is in Worland. Do we have to get them involved? What do you think they'd do? They might . . ." She didn't want to say it, or even think it. *Destroy them?* Surely not. "Ross always said the beauty of this herd was that they'd been left alone. If he knew about the blindness, though, why didn't he say something? Why didn't he tell me?" She rolled her head back and forth on the blanket, crunching the dry needles beneath it. "He didn't know. I'll bet he didn't know."

"He didn't plan on dyin' this spring. That's what I think. What he did plan on was gettin' his sister out here this summer, and here you are."

"And here *you* are."

"Yeah, well, here we are. I don't think it matters much what your brother told you or didn't tell you. I'm telling you, you've got some blind horses." He turned onto his side, propped his head on a crooked arm so he could see her face. "I'm thinkin' I could call this guy I was tellin' you about, ask him if he's ever run into anything like this, and if he has, ask him what they did about it."

"Good idea." She thought about it, her smile blooming slowly. "*Great* idea."

"I get one once in a while. It'll kinda rattle around up there until I shake it loose and do something with it."

She started to protest, but he was already laughing.

"Well, we can use it," she said. "That idea and any others you shake loose."

"I'm thinkin' it might rain," he said.

"Can't use that one." She smiled. "Think up something else."

"You know, I read about a guy . . ." He lay back down, his head beside hers, and in his shifting he'd managed to end up closer than before. "A rancher up this way, Wyoming, or might have been Montana . . ."

"There's a difference." Just something to say. Montana, Wyoming. They were shoulder to shoulder, head to head, not quite touching, but so close.

"For sure it wasn't Texas." He laughed. She smiled. Darkening clouds slid across the heavens. "Anyway, this rancher started breeding for fall calves instead of spring. He did it for a lot of reasons, but one—and I've been thinkin' about how much sense it makes since I've been up here watching them—with fall calves, by the time you bring them up here for summer grazing, they're a lot older. And older calves are more adventuresome, so they'll climb, and the cows will follow. Better grazing, easier on the hired man."

"It was your idea to come up here."

"It's beautiful up here." *Plunk* on the cooler. *Plink, plunk* on the empty plates. "Even when it's raining."

They gathered up the remains of their picnic, and he sent her inside ahead of him. He put Columbine in the pen. She watched for him through the back window of the cabin, which she'd closed to keep the rain out, and when he came bounding up the hill, she went to the door to meet him for no reason other than to open it for him and welcome him inside.

"These mountain storms blow up fast, don't they?" he said, shaking the water off his hat. "But they generally blow on through just as fast."

"That's true, they . . . they often do." Their eyes met. She glanced away. "I should get back."

But she made no move for the door. The ease they'd found lying together, surrounded by pine trees and empty plates, was suddenly missing, left outside in the rain. The bright afternoon had given way to heavy indoor gloom. A want of words, an awkward paralysis, claimed them. She fussed with her damp hair and avoided his eyes. The jumble of her wants and fears leapfrogged inside her head, and no part of her felt easy.

He started to take his wet shirt off, then changed his mind and turned to the wall shelf where he'd stacked his provisions. "This gives me a chance to show off my camp cookin'," he said finally, grabbing a blue enamel coffeepot. "I like to top off a good meal with a cup of cowboy coffee. You game?"

She was grateful for the suggestion. "What's cowboy coffee?"

"The kind that puts hair on your legs."

"Legs?"

"Well . . ."

He shoved the pot under the spigot at the bottom of the steel-clad reservoir. Water dribbled into the pot, drummed on the corrugated tin roof, dripped off the eaves, tapped on her nerves. Behind his back, she shivered.

"I wouldn't mind so much giving the kids riding lessons," he began, as though in answer to a request she'd just made. "But I got myself into a bad deal before, giving classes for people. I had a partner running the business end of it. A kid got hurt. Not too bad, just broke a couple of toes. Anything's bad enough for a lawsuit these days, though. Turned out we weren't insured, because the premium wasn't paid."

He set the pot on the table, then the can of coffee. He stared at them, and she waited. Finally he looked up. "So now I stick to training horses. As long as it's just me workin' the horse, I don't have to worry about what somebody else does. Especially a kid, you know? You don't want kids gettin' hurt while you're in charge."

"Why did you run away?"

He stared at her, and again she waited, knowing that her question had nothing to do with the story he'd just told her, but it had everything to do with him, and with the kids she'd brought to the High Horse.

"Because the door was open and nobody was lookin'." He sighed, bracing his arms on the table that separated them, peering at her from the shadows. "That's all there was to it, Julia. I just didn't wanna be there."

"Where did you go?" She stepped closer. She wanted this knowledge of him, and she wanted him to trust her with it. "You were twelve?"

"Nah, I was older than that by then. Fourteen, fifteen. I don't know."

"Did someone take you in?"

"I found work. Farms and ranches mostly. Some jobs were pretty short-term, but after a while, I learned how to make myself useful." As if to prove his point, he busied his hands with the coffee making. "You get to know people, you hear about outfits that treat their hands fair, you show up at the right time of year, and you hire on." He snapped the lid in place. "There was this one outfit out in West Texas, big spread, called it the Little D ..." He glanced at the stove. "Guess I'd better get a fire goin', huh?"

She followed him to the stove and picked through the firewood while he squatted next to the front-loading firebox and arranged the kindling. "Tell me about the Little D."

"The wrangler was an old guy named Rio. He was part Comanche, like my mom. I'm ... I'm part Indian." He paused, glanced at her as though he'd reached a fork in the road and needed a sign. She smiled, encouraging him to tell her more. He shrugged. "Anyway, Rio, he'd been there at the Little D most of his life, I guess. Kinda like Vern. He had no contract, no deed, no legal claim. He was just part of the place."

"Vernon has ..." Technicality, she thought, and she let it drift because it made no real difference that Vernon had a deed for a few acres. Deed or no deed, he was as much a part of the High Horse as any Weslin.

K.C. took a match from the box she held out to him and struck it against the cast-iron firebox. The reflection of the flame leaped in his eyes. "Anyway, ol' Rio was one hell of a horseman."

"He's the one who taught you?"

"I lived with horses all my life. But I got to workin' with Rio, and I saw things his way, too. It was like ..." He lit the kindling, then held out his hand for her choice of firewood. "Yeah, I learned a lot from Rio. A lot about myself that I never understood before because my mother would never say much about us being Indian. Learned a lot about horses, about how they think, how they see things.

"Before Rio, there was another guy, a trainer named Tully Mack. His way was a little different, but he was lookin' for different results, training for trick riders. I learned things from him too." He fed the fledgling fire. "Mostly, I've just been around horses all my life. I learn by doing. By working alongside guys with horse sense, I developed my own horse sense. Nothing fancy. Just plain horse sense.

"That place they sent me to after my mother died, they didn't have any horses." He signaled for more wood, looked up, held out his hand. "I couldn't stay there."

She filled his hand. "What happened to your mother?"

"She died. Pretty sudden." He dropped the wood on the flame. "And there wasn't anyone else except Tully. They wouldn't let me stay with him."

He stood. She followed his lead, facing him, staying close. They left the stove door open, and the fire's warmth seeped into the space between them. Its light contoured their faces. She could see the pulse beat in his neck. Or was it a shadow, flickering like a dancer keeping time with her own thudding heart?

"It turned out okay, Julia. I did fine. You get educated, one way or another. You find out what you can do, and you do it."

"What about school?"

"That was kinda hit-and-miss. Heavy on the miss. But this one place I worked, the woman there was a teacher, and she got me into some night classes. Got my diploma." He smiled. "You're lookin' at an educated cowboy."

"One who's very easy to look at, but oh-so-hard to pin down." She turned to the window. "It's really coming down now. If we're going to . . ."

But K.C. was putting his coffee on. She took it to mean he wasn't going anywhere. Julia didn't want to go anywhere, either. She wanted to do the very thing she shouldn't do. She wanted to stay with him. The soft rain dripped from the pines and pattered against the glass on the west side. The open windows on the sheltered side admitted a cool, damp breeze, which made the fire all the more appealing. She wanted to be close to it.

"Was it costly?" she asked, because asking a question meant waiting for an answer, which meant lingering longer. He questioned her with a glance as he took a seat on the cot. "The lawsuit."

"Cost me enough, I guess. I lost a friend."

"Your partner?" He nodded. "They say you should never go into business with a friend."

"I'll keep that in mind next time."

"Or maybe, never buy a car from a friend, or lend, or borrow, or . . ." She laughed. "No wonder I don't have any friends."

"Who needs 'em, anyway?" He reached under the bed and pulled out a frayed rope.

"That's what I say, too." She watched him busy his hands again, carefully separating frayed strands. She loved the way he handled all things considerately, an observation she knew she couldn't take too far and still count herself a thinking woman. Still, his hands fascinated her, much the way her brother's and her father's had when they'd made simple rope do surprising things. "I'm sure you have friends all over the place."

He lifted one shoulder. "I know some people."

"What are you making?"

"A lead rope."

"We have lead ropes."

"Mine are better. Thicker, more dependable."

She knelt to take a closer look. His elbows were braced on his knees, the ropes dangling between. He was braiding two ropes into one, and she thought, *So clever*. She told herself to stop there. Stop being a foolish woman. When he was finished, he'd still have a rope.

"We could teach the boys to make their own lead ropes. Another great idea, K.C." She touched his knee, then looked up. "Would you offer that lesson, just that?"

"There's nothin' to this, just a little braiding, a little time."

She drew her hand away. If he missed it, he didn't say. *He missed it badly*, and there was almost nothing he wouldn't do to get that small hand back, touching him. He'd sit there like a simple-minded idiot and braid rope until the rain turned to snow if it kept her there watching him. But there were things he couldn't do, things he wasn't much good for. He sure as hell wasn't any kind of a teacher.

"You'd be better off to just use the saddle horses with your boys, Julia. You keep askin' me what I think. That's what I think."

"Don't you think a program like this would have made a difference for you? Kept you from running away? If you'd had a reason to stay . . ."

"There were other reasons to go." He gave a quick nod. "Sit up here beside me, and I might be able to remember one or two, since you're so interested."

She didn't hesitate. She reminded him of a little girl getting ready for bed, or of that old song that ran through his head sometimes when he felt lonesome. *Tell me a story, the sadder the better.*

"It's just that there are even more runaways nowadays, and more reasons to—"

"After I took off from a couple of foster homes, they put me in reform school, where it was either fight or run. I wasn't much of a fighter, not then. There were guys there . . ."

He paused, concentrated on plaiting the ropes, working each strand carefully. He wanted her to touch him again, lay her hands on his body, her head on his shoulder, and unburden herself any way she wanted. But he didn't want her undressing his soul. He didn't want her to imagine him as a scared-shitless boy, being roughed up seven ways from Sunday by sad cases turned sick. He'd give her anything else, but not that. Not the sorriest part of his past.

"It's no good looking back," he said finally. "I was real young. I didn't know too much, had nobody to talk to, no way to . . ." His hands stilled, his gaze drifting to the fire in the belly of the little stove. He wasn't so young anymore, but he still had nobody. "Yeah, maybe your summer program would have been good for me, but it wouldn't have kept me there. Nothing could have kept me there."

"How long do you usually stay?" Her question prompted a look. "At one job, I mean."

"Depends on the job. Depends on . . ." The people, he thought. How long he could walk whatever line they'd drawn in their dirt. Their facilities, their stock, their time-table, even their supper table. At the end of the day, their bed. "I've built my reputation on getting the job done. Once it's done, I move on to the next place."

"What if you stayed in one place? Wouldn't it work just as well if people brought their horses to you?" she asked. He looked at her, surprised. "Wouldn't they do that?"

"Sure they would. But I'd have to have . . ." He remembered Weslin's offer. *Come work for me on the prettiest ranch in Wyoming. Use my facilities. Take in all the horses you want, as long as you work with mine, too. My mustangs. Special horses. We'll take a few out at a time and let the rest run free. People will learn to appreciate their value, and they'll learn that from you. From K.C. Houston.*

He laughed. "I ain't sittin' on the dock waitin' for no damn ship to come in. I'd rather be the one shippin' out when the time comes. Git while the gittin's good. That's what you're lookin' at doing here." He challenged her with a hard look. "Ain't that right? Quit while you're ahead?"

"It seems the sensible thing."

"You got some doubts about selling out?"

"Chuck Pollak came over with his lawyer and made us a pretty good offer. Dawn's ready to jump on it." It was her turn to stare into the fire. "I wanted to tell him that the High Horse was not for sale. Like in a scene from a movie, I wanted to rip up the offer and throw it in his face."

"But you didn't."

"There was nothing to rip up. It was a verbal offer." She shrugged. "I don't know what it would amount to after we paid off the debts and taxes. A fair amount."

"Pollak's a horse trader. He sees something he wants, he's gonna start bidding low, but he'll hang in there and bid up. A little competition wouldn't hurt, if you're set on sellin'."

"Selling the High Horse. My God, what a thought. But then, four and a half million . . ." She shook her head. "There aren't too many people around here who could come up with that kind of money."

"Makes you wonder how he can."

"I think he's got plenty of collateral. Nobody else . . ." She shook her head, amending her words with an impatient gesture. "Except developers, of course, and we don't want the ranch to go that way. Pieces and parcels and people thinking it's empty space to be filled up with . . ." She turned to him. "You think fall calving is the way to go, huh?"

"It's the way I'd go. You calve out in September, the weather's good, so you don't have as much sickness. Hardly any scours. Your cows aren't weak from wintering hard. A year later, you're selling bigger calves. Makes sense for this climate."

She was really listening. The sense he asserted seemed to shine right there in her eyes. Damn if it didn't keep him going, one tentative step at a time. "When we branded, I noticed we didn't implant. You don't use growth hormones?"

She shook her head. "Ross never liked the practice, and you know Gramma's always suspicious of introducing gadgets and fancy notions."

"Going natural *is* a fancy notion nowadays, but that's what I'd do," he ventured, exposing himself to her with his peasant's plan for running the plantation. "If I was into cattle, I'd specialize in grass-raised yearlings."

"But you're into horses."

"And you're into saving kids." He went back to his braiding, packing his ideas back inside his thick head, where they belonged. "You must be pretty smart. You're almost a doctor."

"I almost have a Ph.D." Her small laugh sounded apologetic. "Which is like saying somebody *almost* got pregnant."

That made him smile. "I reckon you could still see it through, either way."

"All I have to do is write the dissertation, but I keep fooling around, putting it on hold. I just have to get on the stick and do it."

He glanced at her, couched an invitation in a smile. Forget the ranch business, he told himself. All he'd ever had going for him was good hands and an easy smile. "Like I said, either way. Let me know if I can help out."

"Help me with my dissertation."

"Ain't much of a cook, but I am partial to sweets."

"I'm serious. I'll base the whole thing on the horse partnership program."

He groaned. Back to that. "You are one persistent woman. You're Sally's granddaughter, all right."

"She's one of a kind. She's the original liberated woman, but she doesn't know it. What we need is a man around, she says. A cowboy." She shrugged. "No offense, but cowboys come and go, just like grandchildren. Gramma's still here. She *is* the High Horse. When she goes . . ."

"You Weslin women go through your share of cowboys, do you?"

"They either lose interest or they wear themselves out."

"Hardest-workin' breed of man there is, you get him doing what he does best."

"All right," she said, as though he'd made an offer. "How about if we say you take all the horses you can break?" She turned to him, assuming that earnest, mountain-mover attitude of hers, all eager and ready to go. "*If* you'd let the boys work with you. There's a good market for well-broke mustangs, or so Ross said."

"That's quite an offer." He glanced at her and couldn't resist. "Except that you're dealing in defective horses."

"They're not all blind. They're wonderful. You said so yourself, that they were special."

"They are." They shared a look, a point of agreement, a starting point. Horses were wonderful by nature. "You don't really understand what you've got here, Julia." *You don't see. You're not looking.*

"We'll find out. You'll call your friend, and we'll find out more."

"Then what?"

"What . . . whatever we think is best for the horses."

"Okay." He nodded. "Isolating them in small herds like this is what we're doing to try to save them, but it just ain't natural. Not too long ago, when most of this country was wild, the herds used to regularly pick up new blood. They're not doing that now.''

"You're right. It must be inbreeding. Ross's wild beauties," she said, injecting the words with an ironic tone. "Some of them must be all right, though. Most of them seem sound."

"They're all doing fine, and they're still wild beauties."

"But not your type." Her shoulders sagged with her disappointment.

Immediately he felt bad about discouraging her. He thought about taking hold of her shoulders and propping them back up, but he figured she'd soon take care of that herself.

"If you really don't think the horse breaking is going to work, I'll have to go with Plan B." Her shoulders were square again. "I do have a Plan B."

"I'm sure it's a good, safe plan." He was pretty sure it wasn't formed yet, but he figured it would be.

"It's really starting to come down now. I should . . ." Her attention drifted from him to the rain, back to him again. "We do have insurance. Just in case you were worried about—"

"What are *you* worried about, Julia?"

"Right now, I'm worried about rain. Mud. Getting stuck."

"You're not stuck." He challenged her with a level gaze. "If you want me to drive you back, I'll do that. We're both sober. Both thinking clearly."

"I came for you, but if you're not ready . . ."

"Julia, you know damn well I've been ready since the first time I saw you."

She stared at him. She was thinking it over. There was a decision to be made now. And she knew that it would change things between them, whichever way she went. No rules had officially been laid down, but the next move was hers. That was the way he played it, always. Nobody pushed anybody.

"If you're ready," he said quietly, "I can give you everything you need and some things you ain't even thought about yet."

"You don't know what I've thought about." She stood abruptly. "I've got to go. This can only lead to making a fool of myself, which is what I'm doing. I'm sorry. I didn't mean to . . ."

Her nervous laugh stung him. Otherwise he might have felt a little sorry for her, the way she was tying herself up in knots, and he might have told her he understood if she wasn't ready, if what he had to offer was just too damn plain.

"Yes, I did," she admitted, as though he'd done something to wring a confession out of her. "What am I saying? I did mean to, but then once you get something started, you can't just . . . and the thing is, we really do need you. So . . . so I hope you're not . . ."

He thought he'd just let her play herself out, but, damn, she meant to leave. She was jabbering up a storm all of a sudden, looking around for something she hadn't brought, pushing herself toward the door. He dropped the rope, heaved himself off the bed, automatically reached for his hat. If she was hell-bent to go out in this weather . . .

"No, don't," she ordered, hands up in some deluded inclination to defend herself.

Where the hell had she been when he was showing her, plain as day, how it was with him?

"I'll be fine," she was saying, as if she thought he was going to try to change that. "Stay. Just stay. I'll send Shep for you. When? Tomorrow? He'll come up in the morning. I brought . . . there's food."

Suddenly she was out the door before he could shift gears. What had he done besides offer to give her what she needed from him?

She'd made her point. He wasn't about to go chasing after her. He heard the roar of the pickup engine. Once. Twice. By the third roar he'd grabbed his slicker on his way out the door, into the driving rain. He'd have a hell of a time getting her out if she buried the tires up to the axles.

He signaled for her to hold up, stop spinning her wheels. Going to bed alone and wanting was bad enough. Topping it off with mud would pretty much frost him. She flung the door open and hopped out to take a look at the back tires for herself. The pickup was an older model four-by-four, and she hadn't locked in the front wheels. That would have helped.

"Get in," he shouted. *Damn, he hardly ever shouted.* "I'll give it a try."

She was getting drenched, doing her damnedest not to look at him, but if he wasn't mistaken, the woman was crying. It wasn't just rain on her pretty face. She had tears. Sweet, sad, unpredictable tears. He touched her shoulder. Her deep-core tremble shot into his hand. "Julia?"

"I got it stuck." She shook her head, flung a wild gesture. "Trying to be sensible, and look what I did."

"Hell, it's—" He started peeling off his slicker. "Raining! Just get in."

He threw the yellow raincoat over her shoulders. It swallowed her up, nearly touched the ground. She gazed up at him, big brown eyes swimming, looking like a small, wild creature just hauled out of the drink. He brought his fists together beneath her chin, holding the slicker tight, thinking he should cover her head with it. But he was lost in her eyes.

"I don't ever do things like this," she said.

"Stay or go?" He knew what she wanted, and suddenly all he wanted was to be the one, the only one. "It's your call."

"Stay."

He drew gently on his slicker, hauling her close as he bent to taste the rain on her lips.

17

*S*tay.

It was a relief to say the word, to make the choice, to stop thinking about it. No reason to turn witless in the face of a simple fact of life. She was a normal, healthy woman, and she wanted sex. This was the time and the place, and this was the man. She wanted him to be part of her. Never before had simple wanting beset her so relentlessly. She was boiling over with it, just like the pot of coffee he snatched off the stove and deposited on the floor as soon as they walked in.

He used his wet shirt to relieve the sting from his hand. She felt the quick pain in her own fingers. "Did you . . ."

"Nah." He stepped close to her, showing her his palm. "Can't hurt it. It's practically made of leather. You okay?"

She cast his slicker aside, pushed wet hair back, hands over cheeks. No more tears, she thought, and the thought made her smile rather than give him an answer. He looked surprised when she took his hand and stroked it lightly, heel to palm to square fingertips, curling to meet her touch. She bent her head to kiss the center of his palm. It felt hard and sturdy and sure, a working man's hand. She imagined it doing something wonderful just for her, and she looked up to find her own awful longing mirrored in his eyes.

Stay with me, hold me, keep me close to you.

A woman's wish, she thought.

A man wants holding, too.

She chose to believe, and in so choosing, she freed herself for all she felt for this man. She met his gaze boldly as she unbuttoned her shirt, took the cold, wet thing off and used it to swab the hand she'd kissed, the one he'd said didn't hurt him. He watched her with wonder while she undid his buttons, but it was he who laid their shirts over the wood box, allowing for some dim-future need to wear them again. It was he who lowered one knee to the floor and peeled away her jeans, kissing her plain middle parts in a way that made her feel revered. A nibble over her pelvic bone, a soft kiss below her navel, what stirring excitement! He took off his own jeans, took her in his arms there before the fire and kissed her mouth deeply.

"Let me love you," he said.

Her heart heard only one word. "Will you?"

"Oh, yes."

It means something different to him, she thought, then banished the thought, all thought, and embraced him. She explored him with loving hands—his face, his strong back, his horseman's buttocks—held him tight, pressed her body close to his. She reveled in his arousal, counting herself the cause. Scattered sensations merged, reined in by a potent drawstring, so that every sound and scent became sexual. The room smelled of coffee, woodsmoke, pine pitch and musk. The evening rain made mellow music on the tin roof, and it was all dizzyingly seductive.

He took her underwear away slowly, unwrapping sensitive skin and paying sweet homage with gentle hands, suckling her, making her quiver and weep for wanting him. He played her body as if it were a cherished instrument. He played by ear, by feel, filling her with music on the inside, so clear and vibrant that it threatened to overwhelm her, blast her away with its power. Her mind said *Too much, too soon, too fast, back away*.

"Let go for me," he whispered. "I'll take care of you. I promise."

She gave in to the surging pleasure, slipped back, surged again. Blindly she sought him, hungered for him, for his lips, heart, heat, his life's breath. She pushed his cotton briefs away, took his erection in her hand and urged him to become part of her. He took a moment to prepare himself, whispering to her of her wonder and his need. When he entered her, he caught his breath, then called her name.

"You're loving me now?"

"I've been loving you," he said. "Standing . . . waiting . . . finally you opened the door for me."

She wrapped her legs around his back, arched herself to take him deeply and whispered, "Welcome, K.C."

She would want to talk, when all he wanted was the feel of her, resting now in his arms, her thigh tucked between the two of his. He wanted to pet her and doze with her and luxuriate in the feel of her warm breath on his neck. But she would want to talk, and it would please him to give her what she wanted. Patience, attention, tenderness, all in full measure, because she had accepted him, taken him in.

Welcome, K.C.

"Are you warm enough?" she asked.

"Uh-huh." He'd worked up a hell of a sweat, and he was still hot. The cool wall felt good against his bare ass.

She snuggled into the shell he made for her, her hand over his chest, her thumb sliding back and forth, keeping time with the beat of his heart. "You were chilled from the rain, and I'm afraid I'm soaking up all the heat here, keeping it from reaching you."

"It's passing through you, and I'm soaking it up." He caressed her bottom, smooth, soft and warm to his touch. "You can't imagine how good you feel to me."

"Really?"

Now she was going to worry, as he moved his hand over her hip and up her slim side, about whether he thought her breasts were too small or saggy, or whether her . . .

"Why can't I?"

Hmmm. "Because you've, uh . . . never felt you the way I'm feeling you."

Her little laugh was deep and throaty. "Good answer. Not necessarily true, but I will admit that it's infinitely better when you do it." His thumb sought her nipple. She shifted, giving him better access. "You can't imagine how much better it feels the way you feel me."

"I have better hands?"

"Oh, *much* better hands." Indeed, her fingers pinched in their play with his flat nipple, and he was about to tell her to go easy on him when she eased up on her own and made him shiver. "You're the man with the touch. The one who can name his price."

"I have a price for horses. Not for you. All you have to do is say—"

"—when and show you where, I know, but you already knew. No show and tell necessary."

"You're wrong about that. You told me plenty. All I had to do was pay attention." He leaned back as far as he could without cracking his head on the wall, far enough so that he could see her face in the soft firelight. "You're such a beautiful woman, Julia. Easy to attend to. I love watching you."

"Watching me do what?"

"Ride, for one thing. Sitting up proud, with your thighs hugging the saddle, your fine, straight back, your chin held high. I like the way your breasts and your butt give your softness away."

"Uh-oh."

"Uh-oh nothing. Here," he said, lifting her. "Let me watch you now." He slid himself beneath her as he raised her above him, sat her on his pelvic saddle and pressed her thighs against his sides. "Nothing but beautiful, Julia. Nothing but what makes a man go hard on the outside and soft as a pup's belly on the inside. I love watching you do anything. Walk across the yard, climb a fence, open a drawer." He smiled. "Talk."

"Watching me talk? About what?"

"Nothing. Anything. Doesn't matter." Oh, he had a view now. Her belly, her breasts, her neck, her chin. The firelight loved her soft contours. "I like watching your lips move."

"Ah, the old watching-a-woman-talk fetish. Now I'm going to be self-conscious every time I open my mouth."

"You won't notice me watchin'. I'm very, very subtle. Whisper-subtle."

"Me, too." She bent until her breasts and her hair brushed over him. "Whisper-subtle."

"Mmmm."

She settled on top of him, nuzzled his neck. "I like watching you, too. You haven't noticed, have you, because I'm very careful. Always very careful." She moved her hips, just slightly, but enough. "Until today."

"We were careful."

"Careful about . . ." She lifted her head, met his gaze. "Oh, that. That's the easy kind of careful. That you can just buy." She smiled. "Which I'm glad you did. Thank you."

"Like you say, easy."

"But you were prepared, and I wasn't."

"You're not easy."

"I'm not stupid, either. I'm not . . ." She laid her face against his chest, taking the sight of it from him so that she could confess to him. "Well, I'm not a virgin, obviously. I'm thirty . . . six years old. I ought to be prepared."

"Damn." He rolled with her, deftly depositing her at his side so that he could look into her worried eyes. "You're doin' numbers on me again. It's gonna take some figurin' for me to make the connection between 'obviously not a virgin' and thirty-six. It's one of those word problems, right? Never could do those." He smoothed her hair back from her face. "Now, how stupid does that make me?"

"Not . . . you're not . . ."

"Not a virgin, obviously." He had her smiling with him now. "The only thing that's obvious to me is that I've made love with you once. That's once for you and once for me." He tucked her hand between them, drew it down his torso and between his legs. "I'm ready to do it again, and I've got a whole boxful of careful." Her hand sheathed him. He closed his eyes. "Ah, Julia, how easy does that make me?"

"I don't know." She stroked him once, twice. "Let me see how easy you are." He moved to take the initiative from her, but she said, "No, it's my turn, K.C. I'm going to learn how to pay attention the way you do."

"Julia . . ."

"Lie still." She reached way down, cupped his sac in her palm and took his breath away with her fingertips. "This is where you're soft as a puppy's belly."

He closed his eyes again and let his head swim, just a little. He'd take over from her soon, as was his habit, his gentle man's way. Soon . . . but were those her lips on his belly, his groin, his thigh, was that her tongue? Could she be taking him in her mouth?

"Honey, this isn't . . . sweet heaven."

"Isn't?"

"*Is* . . . it is, it is . . ."

No words. More than words. Pulsing pleasure only, brought to him by her quiet questing at his cock. He gripped the edge of the bed, the wall, afraid to speak or move or breathe too much, afraid he might scare her away. He could feel the uncertainty in her approach to him, trying butterfly kisses, licking him tentatively. He said nothing, but she had to be listening to something—the plea reverberating in his head, the fire crackling in his belly, the blood stewing in his groin—because when she made it good, she followed with making it better.

He was unaccustomed to giving himself over this way, but she coaxed him, prevailed upon him all over like wondrous water, all-giving, all female. He was hers entirely, and she tended him well. His crazy cock basked in her care, swelled with his need. He had to get it safely inside her soon or he would break apart and scatter and lose himself. He had never known what it meant to be home, but he felt it now, as he entered her. He committed the feeling to heart, emblazoned it in the core of his brain, and it gave him new needs.

Surrounded by darkness and dripping trees, the cabin with its bright fire and its tiny bed was cozier than a cocoon. K.C. could think of no better way to spend the rest of his days and nights than to hole up with this woman in this place. But she would be thinking of a hundred other things by first light. She was a hell of a thinker, this woman. The best he could do for her was lend her his hands.

"You'll need to get back to your boys in the morning?"

She nodded against his shoulder. "I ought to go out there and see what I can do about that pickup. Wanna help me?"

"I don't want to move. I especially don't want to get dressed."

He chuckled. "No point in gettin' dressed. We'd just get soaked and muddy. We'll do it bare-assed."

"I can just see us." Her giggle blended sweetly with his laugh. "Two naked mud puppies, pushing that damned pickup . . ."

"We'll try locking in the hubs before we test your muscle."

"Locking . . ." She groaned. "Oh, no, I forgot about locking the hubs. Shot my dramatic exit right in the foot, didn't I?" Pause. "But you were coming after me anyway, weren't you?"

"I was thinkin' about it." He smiled, cuddling her close. " 'It's raining, so if she takes off on me, I won't be eatin' her dust,' I was thinkin'. 'But I could end up with mud in my eye. Would she do that to me?' Then I heard the spinning tires. Sure sign of a woman in trouble." She giggled again, clearly feeling those female oats. "Was I supposed to chase after you?"

"Of course." She looked up, planting her chin in the center of his chest. "How else could I be sure you really wanted me to stay?"

"Told you I did." He rubbed her arm, just to be touching her. "Sometimes women run from men because they want to get away. Because they're scared, maybe. After the other night when you wouldn't go out with me, I was thinkin' maybe . . ."

"Well, Dawn wanted to go." She hid her face from him again. "It wasn't that I didn't, it was just that I thought it best to bow out since Dawn wanted to go."

He wasn't going to say anything. This was an old piece of family ground, and he didn't know quite how to tread on it.

"Dawn's pretty irresistible," she said. "I'm not good at a tug-of-war, even when it's just a casual game. I guess I'm too old to play games."

"You were playing with me. What's it called? Tag? You

wanted me to chase you.'' She said nothing. What happened to that feminine power she'd been dangling a minute ago? ''You're the only one I want to play with this summer, Julia. Just you.''

''K.C., I'm not . . .'' She was trying to turn, shift, wiggle away, but there was no room for that in the little bed. She settled with a sigh. ''It's hard for me to just . . . I don't want . . .''

''Fill in the blanks, huh? Is this a game or a test?'' She glanced up at him. He smiled, put his fingers in her hair and smoothed it back. ''You can play with me all you want, darlin'; just don't test me. I'd hate like hell to be kicked out of your bed for failing some kind of test.''

''If there were a test, something tells me you'd pass,'' she assured him with a smile. ''Easily.''

''I couldn't get past the basic name-and-address part. Initials for a name, no address. Where did you come from? Hell, I'm from Texas. Out of a deep canyon by a long rope.'' He chuckled, to show her how little it bothered him.

''I don't get it.''

Figured. ''That's sort of a reference to breeding, see. It's . . .'' Sweet, innocent brown eyes, waiting for a punch line that wasn't funny if you had to explain it. ''It's a joke. You talk about a horse being out of a dam, by a—'' He apologized with a wistful smile. ''It just means I don't have much of a pedigree.''

''You're not a horse. You don't need one. You have your own good name, your reputation. And I'm sure you could have a permanent address if you wanted one.''

''Someday.'' He'd been getting by for a long time on the dream of such a thing. ''It's gotta be right, you know? The right time, the right place. What I've got now is the freedom to keep looking. I never stayed in one place for very long when I was growing up, and I kinda got used to having that freedom. My mother was a trick rider. You know, like for rodeos. Summertime, we were always on the road. I used to tell her someday I'd get her a house with a barn for Houdini. That was her horse. The Amazing Houdini.''

There were those brown eyes again, peering up at him.

She hadn't even asked, and he was holding her close and telling her old stuff, deep-canyon stuff. He ran the backs of four fingers over her face slowly, temple to chin. "She wasn't the nesting kind of a woman, my ol' lady. She didn't like being tied down."

"Like mother, like son?"

"Yeah, I guess that's why I'm always barreling down the road like there's someplace else I gotta be. She'd do that sometimes."

"Your old lady?" She claimed his hand, kissed those hard-ass fingers of his like she was trying to heal some wound. "She must have died awfully young."

"Awful . . . young." It was awful, and they had both been young. In years, at least. "Young and beautiful. She was a beautiful woman."

She touched his hair. "I can see that. I'll bet she had gorgeous dark hair."

"Yeah, she did. Dark hair. Dark eyes, like yours, only yours are bigger. Nothin' prettier than a brown-eyed woman."

"I'm glad you think so," she said with a wistful smile that said she was drowning in his eyes, which was fine by him. He was already lost in hers. "So, how does an Indian cowboy come by such lovely blue eyes?"

"Good question. Damned if I know the answer." He touched the hollow near the corner of her eye, mirrored her smile. "You're lucky you know who made you who you are. You've seen faces and pictures of more faces that look like yours. I don't know where my eyes come from, Julia, and the only person who could have told me is dead."

"What happened to her?"

He pulled her close so she couldn't look at him anymore or be trying to kiss any hurts away. He didn't want that. But she sure had him talking, and he couldn't seem to shut up.

"It was a bad way to go, I gotta admit. Shouldn't've been any surprise, though, the way she was always hookin' up with some guy who treated her mean. I came home from school one day, and I could tell she was hurting. Face was bruised. Something was hurting her inside. I wanted her to see a doctor, but she wouldn't. I should have just called somebody, told somebody sooner. All that time, she was bleeding inside, so by the time she got to the hospital, she was too far gone, I guess.

"I never told anyone," he said after a long pause. Julia managed to look up at him again. He could feel the questions coming at him, even though he didn't look at her. He stared into the fire. "I mean, I told the cops after, uh . . . When I finally got somebody to come, first it was cops, then an ambulance, and then a lot of questions and not too many answers. I told them everything I knew. But I haven't told anybody about it since."

Now he looked at her, smiled, lifted his tone. "See what happens? You get me talkin', and I spoil the party."

"This isn't a party. It's just us, just you and me." She laid cool, sweet fingers on his face. "K.C., I'm so sor—"

"Don't." He grabbed her hand, held it tight. "That's what I don't want. No feelin' sorry. Sorry things happen to everybody, right? It's all over and done with."

"But it still hurts when you remember," she said.

"Remembering can eat holes in your gut. Sometimes you gotta get down, get loud, get ripped." He shrugged. "You do it to try to fill the holes."

"Does it?"

" 'Course not. You live with the holes. Everybody does. But every so often you start feelin' like you got more holes than gut, so you raise a little hell, and then you go lookin' for a quiet place, and you get all right again."

"Is that why you came here?"

"I came because I needed a job. I'm good at what I do, Julia, but sometimes you find yourself in a place where . . . you're just in the way."

"Not here."

"Haven't been here that long." And he wouldn't be. Summers were short in this part of the country, which was maybe why he went right on pulling stuff out of that dark hole he'd suddenly unplugged. "I got into a fight with the last guy I worked for. He wouldn't pay me what he owed me. He said I was messin' around with his wife."

She went very still in his arms. "Were you?"

"Not . . . not really."

"But you wanted to?"

"She wanted to." He risked a glance and saw no doubt, no judgment in her eyes. Not yet. "I kinda felt bad for her. He treated her like she wasn't there half the time. He had other . . ." He shook his head and sighed. "But it wasn't none of my business. I shoulda known. Comes right down to it, a woman says what she has to say to keep the peace, I guess."

"She told him . . ."

"He owned the whole damn county. All I wanted was what he'd agreed to pay me. But I didn't want to see him take it out of her hide. She only said what she had to say. If I'da stayed around, who knows? It probably wouldn't have been a lie." He looked at her again. "So, darlin', how stupid does *that* make me?"

She regarded him steadily. "Doesn't sound like it had anything to do with—"

"You know, this place is just as beautiful as your brother said it was. You talk about having a peaceful, quiet place to come to, man." He was staring into the fire again, but he was picturing wild horses grazing on a sunlit slope. "He said if I came to work for him, I could take in other horses, too. He said I could try it out, and if I liked it, maybe we could work out something permanent. A lotta guys say that when I hire on. I never think nothin' of it. I do the job, and then I move on."

"Is it the same with women?"

Damn. What was he thinking about, telling her all this shit?

"I mean . . . is it always your choice to move on?"

"When it's over, that's what you do." He turned to her, to face her. She glanced away, and he wasn't sure what she wanted from him now. "We're both here for the summer. Does it matter who moves on first?"

"I just wondered . . . whether you've ever wanted . . ."

"What matters is there's nobody else in my life now, Julia. Nobody else. There's been nobody serious for a while." He lifted her chin with the touch of a finger. The waning fire cast her fine features in soft, shadowy splendor.

"Serious, the way somebody like you would define serious, maybe there's been nobody, period."

"Somebody like me?" She smiled. "You mean, older and wiser?"

"You're probably too good for me, and you're sure as hell too smart for me, but this older-woman notion is pure bullshit. And you know it."

"I didn't mean—"

"And if you think you're too sexy for me, think again. I can give you a run for your money on that score."

"Score? I thought we weren't—"

"We're even," he said, turning her, tucking her beneath him. He had to do something to counterbalance the hatful of negatives he'd just dumped on her head. "On that score, we're a helluva good match."

18

She left him early in the morning.

K.C. woke to the purr of the pickup. It had stopped raining. He started to get up, but there was no spinning, no roaring engine. Just a smooth shift of gears, and quiet retreat. He smiled, thinking she'd locked in the hubs herself, wondering whether she'd forgotten or chosen to forget. Women and their games.

He replayed their lovemaking in his mind that day as he rode the slopes of Painted Mountain. It felt like something new and fine, something he'd never had before. Something serious. She hadn't come to him looking to get away from somebody else. There had been no clouds hanging over their bed other than the kind that brought gentle rain to a thirsty mountain.

Julia had come to him because she wanted to be with him—eat with him, talk with him, laugh with him, love with him—and that was what felt so fine. She'd thought to resist the loving-with-him part, and he couldn't blame her for that, being the kind of woman she was. A summer fling with the hired man wasn't what she was looking for. He kinda liked it that she wasn't really looking for it.

But she'd found it anyway, and last night she'd taken him in, saying his name so there was no doubt. She'd welcomed *him*. Made him feel so damn good, before he knew it he was confessing to her, telling her all kinds of sorry-ass stuff a man should never tell a woman about himself.

Then she'd turned around and welcomed him again. She'd given him a glimpse of what coming home was like.

Coming home.

He'd always told himself that a home would just be a burden. He'd schooled himself not to think too much about sleeping in a different bed every few months, to appreciate the regular change of ceiling above his head and enjoy the variety in his diet. Sure, he was eating off somebody else's plates, and it was always some other guy's favorite dish. But he wasn't tied down. He was a true cowboy, the last of a dying breed.

If his breed had expired last night in Julia's arms, it and he would have died happy. And if a woman could be a man's home, he was ready to move in.

He wanted to return the feeling she'd given him, do for her in some special way, give her something no other man could offer. His options were limited. His talents were specialized. Hell, he was just a cowboy.

No, he wasn't *just* a cowboy. He was a real cowboy, a true horseman. His kind was rare, and he was exactly what she needed. She had family here, she had roots, she had her summer program going. And she had a real cowboy staying in her bunkhouse.

On the other hand, she had an offer of four and a half million dollars for the ranch.

He tried to imagine four and a half million dollars stacked up against Painted Mountain. He pictured the money as paper, and it all blew away. He pictured it as gold. It just sat there, nothing growing on it or taking shelter in it or feeding on it. No welcome feeling there.

K.C. wasn't one to give advice, but it suddenly struck him that he sure wanted to see the Weslin women try to hang onto the place. If helping Julia out with her program could tip the balance, hell, why not? He figured he had a good feel for the place now, an awareness of the terrain, of the way the cows used the grass. He had a sense of the wild horses, their habits and hideouts. The land, the grass, the cattle and the horses made up the backbone of the High Horse. But the women were its heart.

While he rode the high country he devised a strategy for

a roundup, which was going to be necessary if the cause
and extent of blindness in the herd were to be determined.
When Shep came for him and took him back to the ranch,
the first thing he did after taking a hot shower was to call
Nick Maynard in Nevada. He'd known Nick for years, even
worked with him on a couple of wild-horse gathering con-
tracts.

"Sounds like what you've got is essentially a private
herd of feral horses," Nick said. "The rancher's been protecting them. That's unusual."

"This is an unusual ranch. Been in the same family for
a hell of a long time, but it looks like that's about to change.
What would it take to find out what's goin' on with their
eyesight?"

"Blood samples, and you know what it takes to get
those," Nick said. K.C. could almost hear the gears click-
ing in his friend's head. Nick had been a wild-horse management specialist almost as long as the job had existed
with the Bureau of Land Management. "Damn, it sounds
like an interesting situation. You want us involved?"

"I don't want your paperwork or your red tape."

"Yeah, well . . ."

"But I want Nick Maynard involved, off the record, at
least to start with. I've got half a dozen horses contained,
and I can round up some more if that's what we need. I
hate to bring in choppers and guys with clipboards right
now, Nick. These are special horses."

"Same ol' K.C.," Nick said with a chuckle. "You ever
met a horse or a woman you didn't think was special?"

"You're special, too, Nick."

"Yeah, well, don't tell anybody. The only good bureaucrat is an ordinary bureaucrat." They both laughed. "I
could maybe get some blood analysis through the lab at the
University of Kentucky. What you're describing sure
sounds like a genetic problem."

"You gotta see this, Nick."

"And the woman? There *is* a woman in this somewhere,
right?"

"I'm helpin' some women out here, yeah. Just had a
death in the family. Young guy, left three . . ." K.C.

grinned. He could just see the look on Nick's face. "Three special women, what can I say?"

"Same ol' Houston. Give me a couple of weeks to get organized. I'll drive out and have a look."

"This is strictly unofficial, right?"

"How am I supposed to get any lab work through unofficially?"

"Cowboy ingenuity," K.C. said, still grinning. "You haven't pissed it away behind that desk, have you?"

"I'll meet you behind the barn, man, we'll see who can outpiss who. Where is this place?"

"The High Horse Ranch, just outside of—"

"*The High Horse?* Jesus, you are talking about a page out of Western history. Sally Weslin, right? Is she still around?"

"She's one of the three."

"Hell, K.C., that's an outfit you read about. Is it still a big operation? I remember reading about them having some big anniversary a few years back. Her grandson's a mustang fancier, if I remember right. He's written—"

"He's the one just died. Listen—" K.C. switched the receiver to the other ear, tipped the chair back and peeked out the door.

Since nobody was around, he was using the phone on Julia's desk, and he didn't want her catching him. He was surrounded by the smell of her, the sense of her. Her bathrobe hanging on the back of the door, her small white tennis shoes over by the nightstand. He felt a little silly about the flowers he'd picked and stuck inside his shirt because he wanted to ask her what they were. He'd decided to leave them for her on the bed.

"Can you bring Freddie along?"

"If I can get her to take a weekend off, and if you can behave yourself around her. Who else am I gonna get to draw blood?"

K.C. said he'd check back with his friend in a few days. There were arrangements to be made, and Nick said he'd have to round up another fifteen or twenty horses to get a good sampling.

*   *   *

Julia knew K.C. was back from Painted Mountain. He'd stayed another day, another night. Then she'd overheard her grandmother direct Shep to take a drive up to the summer pasture. Gramma hadn't asked her about her own trip up there, probably because she knew darn well how long she'd stayed. But she'd come back early, and she'd been there to greet the boys when they arrived. She and Vern had them rotating in small groups on several projects, always making sure that at least one assignment a day involved some horseback riding.

At lunchtime she'd gone up to her room and found a sprig of yellow western wallflowers lying on her bed with a note. *Saw these this morning. They made me think of you.* She smiled, touched the two bold, blocky letters that comprised his signature, then laughed and told herself he couldn't possibly know he'd picked a wallflower.

And now here he was in the round pen near the horse barn, big, bold and beautiful as life. He had the strawberry roan tied to the post, and he was leaning on the fence, as though he'd been waiting for her to bring the boys down from the house, as though she'd had him on the day's schedule. He gave her a look that said, *Only because you asked me to.*

"Any of you boys interested in helping me gentle some mustangs?" he asked.

She welcomed his offer with a broad smile.

K.C. grinned right back at her. He was glad to see her, too, and he figured this was about the best way he could show it. He still didn't understand how he could be the man for this job, but he'd decided to give it a shot, since it seemed so important to her.

They were all interested. All seven. They were cool about it—after all, they weren't kids looking for pony rides—but he could tell this was what they'd been waiting for. Breaking horses was exactly what they all thought they wanted to do. Julia handled the introductions, with Jack Trueblood hanging back near the fence, apparently fancying himself the overseer and guard dog.

"Where's Paco?" K.C. wanted to know. "Did he change his mind about being a rancher?"

"He didn't make the cut," Leighton said. "They need somebody on KP."

"Laundry detail," somebody put in, provoking a round of guffaws.

K.C. thought about the boy, smaller than the others, younger, less sure of himself. Paco reminded him of a kid he'd known briefly in TYC—Texas Youth Correctional. He, too, was younger and smaller and greener than the rest. *Fight or run*, the kid had advised him, but the poor guy couldn't quite pull either option off. K.C. didn't remember the kid's name. He did remember him flying out a window, four stories off the ground.

Just one of the memories that made him hesitate to take on this chore, but what the hell? If they didn't take to it, he'd be off the hook.

"So you guys are all horse lovers, right? When you dream of going to heaven, you're ridin' through those pearly gates on a horse."

"If I can't have a Harley," Merle Town said. K.C. just looked at him. No smile. "Okay, I guess a horse."

"I figure the only way I'm goin' to heaven is if I can use a horse to get me in. They're God's favorite creatures, and that's a fact. Just look at how they're made. Smart, sensitive, sleek, spirited . . ." K.C. glanced at Julia. She was listening, dutifully setting a studious example, contemplating the horse. ". . . and gentle hearts. That's the important part. They get scared, they don't want to hurt nobody. All they wanna do is run. Get away from whatever scares them. And a lot of people scare the bejesus out of them."

"Do we get to buck 'em out?" Barney Lawson asked. K.C. tried to picture Barney bucking one out. The glasses would be flying first, then the bravado, then the kid.

"No." He folded his arms and surveyed the group. "The way I do it is pretty slow-goin', and there might not be enough action in it to suit some guys. So if you decide this isn't for you, you just say the word, and you can work on something else, no hard feelings. Is that a deal?"

"I thought you had to, like, win a bucking match to show 'em who's b-boss," Chevy said.

"This is your basic . . ." K.C. looked at Julia. She was

wearing her social-worker face now, defender of the hapless. These were her charges, and she wanted desperately for this program to change their lives.

He stepped over to the boy, laid a hand on his shoulder. "Chevy, we're calling this a horse partnership program for a reason. You see how big this horse is? And he's a small one. You're not big enough to bully him."

"I don't wanna bully him. I just wanna show him who's the man, who's got the b-b-brain."

"You've got the brain. He's got the brawn. Look at the muscle on him. He can kick you from here to next Tuesday."

The boy laughed nervously.

"But he won't do it to hurt you. If he can't trust you, he don't want you gettin' too close to him, that's all." K.C. waited until Chevy looked him in the eye. "You ever feel like that? Somebody you can't trust, you just want him to stay away?"

"I might wanna kick him from here to next Tuesday."

"Yeah, you might." K.C. looked up, addressing the group the way he'd learned to do during his stint with giving those damned clinics. "A horse ain't like that. You hurt him, he don't want you around. Not for a while, anyway. You hurt him, you'll have to start over and try to build his trust back up. It takes patience. It takes time. If you've got a temper on you, you'll have to leave it outside the gate."

"Leave it back at the school," Jack said, piping up from the top of the fence. "Remember how we said—"

K.C. warned him with a glance. They were in *his* classroom now.

"Now, this little roan has spent his whole life runnin' wild and free. He don't know what to make of people just yet. What he knows so far is that that halter won't hurt him, and that post won't let him go nowhere. That's a good start. Now we're gonna sack him out, and we're gonna teach him to lead. Anybody ever sack a horse out before?"

Chad Snyder, the guy from Montana, lifted a perfunctory finger.

"What did you use?"

"Like, a gunnysack or something?"

"Some guys do use a sack, so that's why we call it sackin' 'em out. Makes sense, huh?"

Chad allowed that it did.

"In this partnership between a horse and a man, the man's got the brain. You're right about that, Chevy. The horse gets to know that, too, and he's countin' on you to use that brain for the sake of the team. You show him you know what you're doing, he'll start going along with your decisions. He'll carry you places where there's no grass or water, no mare, no shade, nothing he wants. But you say let's go, he'll go." Another quick scanning of the group wound up with Julia. "Because he trusts you."

"Yeah, but you've got a bit in his mouth, you've got ropes and whips."

"What for?" K.C. kept Chevy on the spot. "You've got a whip?"

"I saw one, back in the tack room."

"That's to get his attention. A noise, a little tap, like touching you on the shoulder to get you to listen to me." He demonstrated a genial man-to-man tap. "What are you gonna do if I whack you upside the head?"

"Whack you back."

"If you can. If you can't, you'll run."

Chevy slid one boot to the side for a wider stance. "I don't run."

"If I came at you with a closed fist or a whip, you wouldn't run?" The genial hand became a fist. "If I wanted to hurt you, I could, Chevy. Do you believe that?"

"Maybe."

"So if you find out you can't trust me, you either stand there and take it, or you get away from me." K.C. shoved his thumbs into his belt. "Are you as smart as this horse, Chevy?"

"Damn right."

"Then use your head to start with. You've got the brain; he's got the brawn. You want him to trust you so he'll work with you. Otherwise, he'll resist the bit, the saddle, the rope and every other piece of equipment you've got. He'll do everything he can to make you miserable every time you try to get on his back. You won't have much of a partnership." He glanced at Chad. "I don't use a sack to sack out a horse."

"Okay, man, what do you use?"

"I don't wanna scare him. I wanna put a good handle on him. I want him to trust my hands." He displayed them. Open, relaxed, no threat to anyone. "I use my hands."

He approached the horse. "And I use them carefully. I see with my hands, and I listen with my hands." The roan flattened his ears back and shied away at first, but K.C. spoke to him and persisted smoothly until the animal permitted his touch. "But I use my eyes and ears. You wanna get to know every group of muscles in his body, and when he bunches up somewhere, you get to know what he's thinking about doing with those muscles." He was rubbing the horse's neck with a small, tentative, easy touch. "Watch his ears. He'll tell you a lot with his ears."

Within a few moments K.C. determined that it was Chevy's turn. The boy was hesitant at first, bunching up himself in the shoulders and back, exactly the way the horse did. The roan shied.

"Talk to him, Chevy. Talk quietly, kinda slow, keep an even tone."

Chevy didn't have slow and even in him, not now, which embarrassed him. The wish was there, along with the will. But the boy was trying too hard. K.C. could feel it. "I'll bet you like to sing," K.C. suggested.

"Yeah, sure, sing, dance, shine shoes . . ."

"You don't have to worry about shinin' any shoes on this fella. He's got perfect feet. Or dancing. We'll save that for Saturday night. But if you've got a quiet song . . ."

"I ain't singin' "—Chevy glanced at his smirking friends, then glared at his instructor—"in front of these guys."

"They're gonna be singin' in front of you. Doesn't matter what they think. You do it for the horse."

And K.C. showed him how. "In the Pines" was one of his favorites, and he could feel the prickle of a few silent snickers, but he let it pass. "I don't get paid for singin'," he interjected quietly, and they chuckled, and he went on singing.

Anybody could see that the horse was impressed, which was all K.C. cared about. This shy little roan was supposed to convince seven hard cases to try a little tenderness. They had their stages of resistance, just as the horse did. K.C. went right on caressing the animal with his voice and his hands. Eventually the singing beguiled the boy right along with the horse. It was as good as a drug for getting muscles to relax.

"You got a song?" K.C. asked when Chevy stepped in to take over.

"I know some Gospel stuff."

"Perfect. Ticket to heaven. Get there on ol' . . . he ain't got a name. What're you gonna sing for him?"

"Soft and quiet?" the boy asked, and K.C. nodded. "S-swing low, s-s-sweet . . ."

"Chariot? Damn, that's a perfect name, Chevy."

"Call him Chariot?"

"I like it."

"Chariot," Chevy repeated, christening the horse. And then he sang. Smoothly, softly, beautifully. No hesitation. No stammering. K.C. stepped back and watched. And listened. And damn, if he wasn't a little bit charmed himself.

The lesson went well, and each boy got a chance to try his hand. Some were more patient than others. K.C. measured the various approaches, the time, the care, the earnestness. By the time he'd reached the limit of their attention span, he knew which of the boys might have the enduring patience for starting horses.

"Tomorrow," he told Jack before they left, "you bring Paco, too."

Jack was all set to refuse. "We had to make some tough choices."

"He didn't do anything wrong when he was here before."

"Yeah, but he's not the kind of a kid . . ." Jack watched the boys climb into the van. Okay, so there was room for one more. He questioned K.C.'s interest with a puzzled look. "He didn't do anything right, either."

"He will." If he was going to take this on, he was going to do it his way. He'd never been to the facility these boys were heading back to. He wondered how many floors it had. "He shouldn't be left out. That's the deal. Paco gets to come back."

"Whatever you say, K.C."

19

*There was more to the summer program than croon-*ing to horses, just as there was more to ranching than riding herd on cows. The boys began working with the evolving "High Horse staff" in small groups. They started over-hauling a small tractor engine with Shep, irrigating the hay fields with Vern, checking cows and fixing fence with K.C. Julia orchestrated the rotation so that there was plenty of activity and enough variety to hold everyone's interest. The last part of the day was spent working with the horses.

As K.C. had predicted, not everyone had the patience for his methods, but four of the boys showed real promise as wild-horse handlers. Chad Snyder and Chevy James would have been satisfied to longe horses from dawn until dusk. Donnie Quinn and Leighton Harding were always eager to move on to the next step, but they accepted the need for repetition as they began to get a feel for assessing the horse's state of mind.

Paco Morales was another story. He dreamed of himself as a rider, but the horses intimidated him, and they sensed his doubt. Paco and the horses scared each other, but the boy had a strong wish to move beyond the fear. And K.C. had taken a stand, insisting that Paco be included. He as-signed the gray foal to the boy.

"I've been calling him Mischief, but you can change that when you get to know him," K.C. told Paco, who sat be-side him on the fence, looking dubiously at the pair in the holding pen. "Right now, all he wants to do is suckle his mama and play, but it's a good time to gentle him."

Donnie and Brad were working with the smaller of the two sorrels in the round pen, and Chevy was trying to teach the seeing-eye sorrel, whom they were calling Radar, to lead.

"They're just gonna make fun of me for this," Paco said sullenly.

"Those guys?" K.C. glanced over his shoulder at Donnie and Brad. He knew they weren't the main worry. It was Barney and Leighton, both merciless teasers. "Are you gonna let that stop you?"

Paco hung his head, absently picking at a scab on his elbow. The afternoon breeze ruffled the thick thatch of straight black hair that needed a trim.

"You can learn a lot about horses from this little guy, and he can learn about people from you. His mama won't be too far away. Pretty soon you'll get to be friends with her." Still no response. K.C. caught himself wondering where the boy's mama was, but he backed off from that territory real quick. "This is a good way for you to start, Paco. You gotta trust me on this one."

The boy turned, squinted one eye and challenged K.C. with the other one. "They said you asked for me."

"I did."

"Why?"

"You helped us out with branding. I liked the way you pitched right in." K.C. shrugged, sliding the small nylon halter he planned to use on the foal back and forth through his hand. "Thought you wanted to come back."

"I did." Paco climbed down, easing himself into the pen without startling the horses, the way he'd been taught. K.C. followed. Paco was staring a hole through the foal. "They said you wanted me to come back because you didn't have no girls in the program."

"Somebody who knows me said that?"

"No." Paco lifted one shoulder as he took a couple of steps toward the foal. "Some jerk-offs who didn't get picked."

"So they don't know me, and they don't know a guy from a girl. What do they know?"

"Nothin', I guess. But when they find out all I get is the foal . . ."

"Mischief's never been haltered." He offered the one in his hand to Paco. "His leg's healing up pretty good now, but that was kind of a bad deal for him, gettin' hurt that way right out of the chute. Had to be doctored up, which he didn't much like. The next person who handles him can make all the difference. Some big, tough guy is likely to ruin him."

"You're sayin' I'm a wimp."

"I'm sayin' I believe I can depend on you to treat this guy right. He's a kid. He's ready to learn some things, and he wants to play, but he's also scared. He needs somebody to bring him along without any bullying or teasing." Again he offered the halter. "You wanna give it a try?"

He could see how desperate Paco was to take the challenge. He was going to have to set aside his worries and no small measure of his pride, but that would be up to him. K.C. showed him how to catch little Mischief and safely subdue him by anchoring one arm around his chest and taking hold of his tail with the other hand. He helped Paco prove to himself that he was strong enough to keep the foal from knocking him over without hurting the little guy when he tried to rear and jump out of his arms. Paco was wary of the mare, but K.C. had worked with her enough to earn her conditional trust. As long as everybody stayed calm, she was all right with this game. They soon had the foal haltered. Within thirty minutes he was confident that Paco and Mischief were the right match.

The irrigated alfalfa was coming in thick and lush, a rich green carpet flanking the creek. Vern took personal pride in the two cuttings he got annually from the fields that naturally amounted to sagebrush steppe. He recounted for K.C. how he'd talked Sally into putting in the irrigation system, and how glad he was that it had paid off. The cropland was still his domain.

He was skeptical at first about working with "teenage

outlaws," but he accepted them for Julia's sake. He'd taken to going over the plans for working the boys into his setup with K.C., ever polishing up K.C.'s grasp of the whole High Horse picture. He rarely mentioned the possibility of a sale, and K.C. found himself disinclined to throw any wet blankets in Vern's direction.

Shep was another story. Shep's favorite illusion was beginning to get under K.C.'s skin. "If you was to hook up with Queenie . . ." he'd say, and K.C. could feel his gut start to knot up. At first he'd been able to treat the suggestion as an old man's pipe dream, but he was finding it increasingly difficult to shrug it off with a good-natured laugh. He knew damn well he was already hooked.

And the hook was digging at him some. He hadn't really been alone with her since the night on Painted Mountain. He had come back to do her bidding, and she'd thanked him for it. But she'd thrown herself into the program as though she had something to prove, some desperate need to make it work. He wasn't sure whether it was for the boys or the High Horse. Maybe she was serious about somehow using it to get that Ph.D. after her name. Whatever it was, she had been working everybody at least twelve hours a day, seemed like. She even had Dawn preparing noon meals for the boys and helping her with the bookkeeping.

Dawn's occasional mention of "The Sale" in a way that made it sound like a done deal was always studiously ignored. There was an unspoken agreement to stick to the here and now, the plans for tomorrow, next week, next month. September was the last acknowledged calendar page, but the summer program had taken the focus off the decision that lurked in the specter of autumn. Looking ahead always seemed like a waste of time to K.C. When the time came, you made the necessary move. He had only one decision to make, the one he had a lifetime of practice with, and that was determining when to move on.

What bothered him, then—besides the damn hook he was going to have to find a way to camouflage—was Vern. Ol' Vern couldn't seem to quit thinking ahead, and what he was thinking wasn't likely to come to pass. It depressed the hell out of K.C. every time the old man started in, which he did almost every time they went out in the pickup together and drove along the High Horse fence line.

At the top of a rise, Vern pointed westward. A herd of pronghorns bounded through undulating waves of blue-green oats. "I'd like to have a couple of wells put in over on the other side of Two Bull Ridge. That grass would get better use if we had water over there."

K.C. agreed that it would.

Wasn't much else he could say. With Shep he could come back with a joke about the unlikely match he was trying for. But Vern was making plans for the High Horse like it was going to go on being the High Horse.

"Then we'd want to put in more cross fence."

K.C. agreed that cross fence would make that pasture more useful.

"I'm thinking we ought to run more yearlings."

K.C. surprised himself by responding with a suggestion for fall calves. Vern's initial skepticism quickened an enthusiasm K.C. didn't know he was harboring. No, he'd never wintered in Wyoming, but he figured it couldn't be too much worse than Colorado, and he'd spent a couple of winters there. It was the spring snow that played hell with calves.

"If you had 'em on the ground by the end of September, chances are you wouldn't see any snow for at least another month," K.C.'s argument went, "and you're selling yearlings in the fall. And I tell you what, Vern—the market for lean, natural, grass-fed beef can only get better. People are suspicious of what they're getting in their food these days."

"That's the way you'd go?"

"I'd sure study it up some more, but it's a real interesting alternative, I think." He was beginning to use those words pretty naturally. *I think*. It wasn't that thinking was novel— the way he made his living gave him plenty of time for dreaming up ideas—but that nobody ever cared much what those ideas were.

"Wonder what the Judge would say." They hit a dip in the rutted road. K.C. grabbed for the dashboard and ducked to keep the crown of his hat from hitting the cab ceiling.

Vern didn't believe in slowing down except for livestock. "Have you asked her?"

"Well, no, don't see much point if . . ." K.C. swallowed the rest of the thought, then nearly bit his tongue on the next rut. "Well, with everybody so busy with the summer program."

"No, you're thinkin' ahead, which is good. She'd be interested. The reason we've stayed afloat is because the Judge has always been able to find these alternatives, just like you're saying. Did you know they used to run a dude ranch here?"

"I believe I heard . . ." The pickup fishtailed on a washboard. "Vern, could you . . ."

"Yessir, the Judge's daddy started that little enterprise. They ran it off and on for twenty years or more, depending on the demand, I guess. The Judge is pretty resourceful." Vern downshifted for the corner approaching the bridge. "Fall calving might just work. Might be tricky switching over."

"You could do it in stages. I believe that's what I'd do."

"We've been talkin' about a new horse barn for years." Vern glanced across the creek toward the old one, hidden behind the cottonwoods. "Guy like you could probably put an indoor arena to good use. Probably make a facility like that pay off in a few seasons."

"I don't need nothin' fancy."

"You haven't wintered in Wyoming." Vern's mustache widened with the quick, craggy smile he flashed as they started across the bridge. "Yet."

"Vern . . ." The smile was too fleeting. Like an old man's hopes. "No, I haven't. An indoor arena would probably be pretty nice to have in this country."

If a guy was going to dream, he might as well go all the way.

Sally had to wonder whether Ross ever suspected that there were blind horses in the wild herd. He hadn't said a word about it to her. That was his way with some things. Like all men, he had his territory to protect, and some of that territory he'd kept completely private. There were subjects Sally hadn't broached in recent years, like why he never brought any women home to meet his gramma. When he was younger she'd teased him about girls once in a while. The boys used to josh him about it, too, but they'd stopped. Somewhere along the line, they'd all tacitly agreed not to talk about it.

Ross hadn't talked much about his health problems, either. He'd lived with them all his life, and he just went about his business, doing the best he could. Sometimes he'd wear himself out and be laid up for days. Some men had fever dreams when they were sick. Ross had horse dreams. But if he'd been aware that his beauties were not sound, he'd guarded it as part of his territory, just one more thing most ordinary people couldn't accept. One more deviation from the way life was supposed to be. And maybe he thought his gramma was ordinary people.

And maybe she was.

Ross's beauties, she thought. Max's wild ones. Horse dreams had kept them going through their highs and lows in the manner of all dreamers, while Sally had claimed the middle berth, always steady, always excellently ordinary. She wasn't making any apologies, and she wasn't about to waste time with regrets. Not this summer. This was another do-or-die summer. Started out on the heels of a dying, but there were some lively doings kicking in now. Extraordinary doings, beginning—as doings at the High Horse so often did—with those everlasting horses.

K.C. had horse fever, too, but Sally was finding that she particularly liked his down-to-earth approach. He'd had no trouble laying it all out on the table at supper shortly after he'd come back from Painted Mountain. Wild horses were always impressive, he'd said, but this herd was, unless his eyes deceived him, quite amazing. He figured several of them to be blind, but that wasn't the amazing part.

Seeing-eye horses. Now, that *was* a new wonder. Just when Sally had begun to think she'd lived so damn long she had nothing to look forward to but reruns. The question was, what to do about it. As she'd listened to K.C. describe what he had observed, Sally heard Ross's voice. She heard Michael and Max. She looked at her granddaughters. Dawn was listening, apparently engrossed, but Sally could see her trying to figure out how this new twist might affect the sale she was counting on.

Julia, on the other hand, was trying very hard not to give herself away. She'd been up there. She reported seeing the phenomenon for herself, but if K.C. hadn't pointed the behavior out to her, she would never have suspected that there was anything wrong. "K.C. really knows horses," she said quietly.

And Sally knew her granddaughter. Unless *her* eyes deceived her, the cowboy was getting under sensible Queenie's sensitive skin. She'd managed to get him involved in the summer program, make him an important part of it; and damn, if those young hooligans weren't turning out to be some pretty decent hands. This was good. This was promising, like new shoots springing out of old roots.

K.C. slid right into the gaps left between the High Horse's aging hands and her inexperienced ones. In his first weeks he'd made a habit of excusing himself from the family's company after supper, saying it was his favorite time for "horsin' around." But ever since he'd come back from riding the high country, he'd been willing to linger over coffee, hash over the closing day and plan for the next one. He'd started offering suggestions, and Julia was always the first one to ask him to elaborate.

This was good. This was promising. Old roots, new shoots.

Sally agreed that the condition of the horses had to be assessed, and she liked K.C.'s plan for a roundup.

"If you're going to sell out . . ." He apologized with a glance, and she excused him with a nod. He was only trying to do a job. "I don't know what you have in mind for the horses, but if you have a genetic wrinkle here . . ."

"Their wrinkles are our wrinkles," Sally said. "We used to get a lot of our saddle horses from Painted Mountain, back in the old days when a horse was a horse. We'd gather up a bunch of mustangs, pick out a few, turn the rest loose. Sometimes you'd lose some horses, and you figured they'd gone wild. Give and take, give and take. That's the natural way of things."

"There's a lot of draft-horse blood in the wild herds, you know," Vern said as he stirred his usual two spoons of sugar into his coffee. "Folks stopped using horses to farm, either because they got tractors or went out of business when the going got rough, and they just let the horses go. They mixed with the wild ones." He looked at K.C. "But they still make some of the best usin' horses, some of them."

"Do they get into the neighbors' pastures pretty regular?" K.C. asked.

"Only when the snow drives them out of the high country. This year was the worst we've had in some time." Sally glanced at Vern, who confirmed with a nod. They'd come through it together, maybe for the last time.

"You can be sure they didn't get anywhere near Pollak's horses," Vern said. "He doesn't have that many anymore, and he keeps what he has close in these days."

"He just likes to make a fuss," Sally said.

"Ol' Bat, the one we've got penned up, we know he's got cataracts," K.C. said. "I can make some of the horses salable, but it's pretty hard to sell a blind horse."

"Well, couldn't some of them just stay up there?" Dawn asked. "I mean, they're like wildlife. They go with the property, don't they?"

"We don't know," Julia said quietly. "We haven't sold out before."

"Now, there's been times we've had to sell a chunk or two," Sally reminded them. "My own father lost a lot of it, including the part Chuck Pollak is sitting on right now, the old 86 Ranch."

"Well, so it'll all be put back together under new management, right? And for a very handsome price." Dawn sounded confident, pleased that somebody else had brought the Pollaks into the conversation. "Chuck doesn't care about the horses that much. I'm sure they can stay or go. Or the government could just take care of them." She turned to K.C. "They would, wouldn't they?"

"They'd probably move them out. We'll see what Nick says." K.C. leaned back in his chair, sliding his coffee mug to the edge of the table. "He's a good friend. We can trust him to be straight with us."

"And the Pollaks, too. They're neighbors." Dawn smiled. "The way I see it, there's no more family to run the place, so the next best thing is a neighbor."

"That's one way of lookin' at it, little girl." Sally couldn't blame Dawn, really. She was thinking she'd be rich in cash money very soon. It was the kind of a prospect that tended to perk people up considerably these days. "What I hate to see is all this development. Twenty-acre parcels, ten-acre parcels, all these houses spilling up the river like what's happening over in Jackson. You get to be my age, you see things you don't like, but you know you can't do much about it. You've run out of steam."

K.C. laughed. "I don't know what you're talking about, Sally. I see plenty of steam. I figured I could get you to help me round up those horses. I figured we'd get the boys in on it, too, since we've got them handling mustangs." He looked at Julia as if he were speaking of *their* boys. "A roundup is a rare experience."

"Is it safe?"

"As safe as anything else we're doing. I'll decide who rides and who stays on the ground. We've got Nick comin' up. We'll have—"

"Chuck and Cal," Dawn enthused. "They'd love to help."

"Let's leave the neighbors out of it," Sally said. "This is a High Horse matter. Let's just keep it in the family."

It was only a manner of speaking, K.C. told himself as he headed out to the pens to finish up with the horses and turn them out for the night. *Keeping it in the family* didn't mean anything different for him; it was just an expression. *Daytime friends and nighttime lovers* was probably about as close to being part of the family as he was going to get. He was used to taking what he could get. *Like mother, like son*, she'd said. Another one of those damned expressions.

"K.C., wait."

He stopped in his tracks, even though it was the wrong voice.

He'd gone back to his bunk every night thinking, *She knows where I am. Any given time of the day, she knows. She knows where I sleep. She'll come to me when she can.*

And now it was sundown, and there were light footsteps following behind him, and it was the wrong voice.

He paused and greeted Dawn's smile with his own.

"I was just wondering, how serious do you think this blindness thing is, really? How do they get along up there if they can't see? Even playing follow-the-leader, wouldn't they be tripping in holes?"

"Sure. Sighted horses do, too, sometimes." He kept walking, and she swung in beside him. "But the partnership these horses have worked out is pretty amazing," he told her. "The one we've got down here—the boys named him Bat, you know, blind as a bat—he's a sweet ol' thing, but you can't use him for a saddle horse, so he just stands around."

"How boring."

"I got him in one of the pens. Been workin' with his partner some, but they don't much like being split up, so I can't see either of them ever being broke to ride."

"Why are you wasting your time, then?"

"I want to know how it works. You go in there with them, they get to trust you a little and they sort of include you. They let you in on their secrets."

They'd reached the horse pens. The sky above the red bluffs was streaked with pink and purple, and the wind had settled down for the night. The little blind black-and-white paint stood with his shoulder pressed against the sorrel's flank. They were both haltered. They pricked their ears to the sound of his voice, but they were easy with it. They didn't mind him, just like he didn't mind Dawn. She was company.

He reached for the coiled lead rope he'd left on the gatepost, then slid the bolt on the small gate. "You wanna try it?"

"Are they mean?"

"I never met a mean horse."

"You never met Silky." She hung back, arms folded tightly around her middle. She eyed the open gate, gave a little smile. "Meanest pony west of the Mississippi. He's not with us anymore, though."

"Went to pony heaven?"

"*Children* go to pony heaven. Silky's working for the devil at one of hell's middle levels, punishing sinful itinerant photographers."

He laughed, but he felt a little uncomfortable ushering her into the pen. He glanced up at the house. Light blazed, high up there in Julia's window.

"What's that smell?" Dawn said, her bravado thinning. "Is that sulfur?"

"Just horseshit," he muttered as he approached the horses. At his back he could feel her fear. The flirtiness wasn't much of a cover.

The horses nickered as K.C. approached—first the paint, then his sighted partner. Earlier that day K.C. had brought Paco into the same pen. The boy had been skeptical, too. Those were some weird eyes, he'd said. Like something out of a slasher movie. *He doesn't know he looks weird*, K.C. said. *And he can hear you just fine.*

"Howdy, Bat. I've got a friend here, wants to see how a horse gets along without his eyes." He let the horse snuffle up his arm and shoulder. After a few moments, Bat permitted him to attach the lead to his halter.

"I'll just watch," she said as he stepped closer, blind horse in tow. The sorrel stayed close to the empty hay rack, which he trusted the man to fill soon.

"Stand easy and talk to us quietly," K.C. told her. He stopped several feet from where Dawn stood hugging the fence. "He let me take him away from his partner because I've introduced him to some real good smells. Oats. Boys with pans full of oats." He held out his hand to her, turning himself into a bridge between the disabled horse and a woman whose fear of his kind might determine his fate.

She took his hand. It was K.C. she was trying to get close to, not the horse. He knew that. Lead rope in one hand, her hand in the other, he figured he was a pretty good conductor. "He's gonna home in on your sounds and your scent." He made a production of taking a deep breath. "You do smell pretty."

He could feel some of her tension leak away. She relied on being pretty. Pretty girls didn't get left behind.

He drew her hand close to the horse's muzzle. Bat sniffed it cautiously, his hazy eyes wide with all the fear Dawn felt, but still he took a sniff. Boxed in and blind, he didn't have too many choices. Dawn turned her hand over slowly until Bat's muzzle was in her palm.

She smiled. "That tickles."

Bat snuffled noisily, then moved to her wrist, the inside of her arm, her short shirtsleeve. Finally he nickered, and the sorrel nickered back.

"What are they saying?" Her voice was barely audible, but she was looking up at K.C., all bright-eyed.

"She's been rollin' in flowers," he translated. "You'd like to be doin' that right now, wouldn't you, Bat? Up there in the mountains, rollin' around in wildflowers." More nickering. "He's probably naming the flowers you're wearing. His sense of smell is so much more sensitive than the other horses', he can tell every kind of plant by the smell, the way your sister does by sight."

Dawn glanced away.

"Julia can name every flower that grows around here." He smiled, and glanced up at the window. When had the light gone out? "Kinda fun to test her when we go out riding together. She never misses."

Dawn said nothing for a while. She stood patiently, withstood the horse's painstaking inspection, finally risked a little neck-petting. It might not have been Bat's neck she'd had designs on, but she was getting into it now. K.C. wondered what was going through her mind.

She didn't keep him wondering too long. "Maybe she's making the names up."

"Unlike our friend here, I wouldn't know one flower from another, but I don't think Julia has to make stuff up." He shrugged, letting Bat sniff his hand. He wouldn't find any flowers there. "Unless she's havin' fun with me."

"Fun? Julia?" Dawn laughed softly. The paint answered with a whicker that sounded almost like an echo. "She's generously sharing her volumes of knowledge with you, whether you ask for it or not. Stuff she assumes everybody wants to know. Just like her mother.''

"She says you're the one who's just like your mother. She must be some woman, your mother. I'm sorry I missed her.''

"No, you're not. Mama would chew you up and spit you out for fertilizer. You're the kind of man she's been warning us about ever since we hit puberty.'' She offered a saucy smile. "You're a no-good cowboy.''

"I sure am.'' He grinned. "Should we give ol' Bat some grain?''

"Let's.''

She sounded like a kid, excited by her personal accomplishment. She'd made friends with a particularly shy horse. She'd taken a risk, but so had the horse, and both were still unscathed. She followed K.C. into the barn. He got her a feed bucket and showed her where the grain bin was. The barn was not her territory. It was his, and it was Julia's.

"You don't have to worry too much about no-good cowboys in Connecticut, do you?'' he asked as he watched her pour a scoop of grain into the rubber bucket.

"You wouldn't think so, would you?''

"Your husband's not a cowboy.''

"No.'' She closed the lid on the bin. "No, I don't think Western duds would suit Roger. The only time he wears a hat is on the golf course.''

"Takes more than the duds.'' He took the bucket from her and smiled. "Buck naked, I guess I'm still a cowboy.''

Damn. He couldn't believe he'd said that.

"How would I be able to tell?'' Now she was grinning, too. "What clues would I see if I were looking at your buck . . . skin?''

"It's all in the legs, I guess. Legs and hands.''

"Let's see. Stand up straight, like you're gonna salute me.''

He laughed, mostly at himself for not thinking. He knew the signals, and he knew the rules. It was his own fault he was suddenly skating on thin ice. There would be no standing at attention, not for Julia's sister. Time to head for the door.

"They won't take us in the army now that they got the cavalry ridin' helicopters," he said offhandedly as he slid the door open and shut off the light. "A bowlegged man can't march worth a damn."

"Legs and hands, huh?" She came up close behind him. "As good as you are with horses, you must be—"

"You want me to saddle one up for you tomorrow? We'll put you on a real gentle mare and give you a basic lesson in—"

She touched his back. "If you'll get on behind me, the way you did before."

"You need to try it on your own." He stepped away, turned and offered her the grain bucket. "If you feed him, he'll remember you kindly."

"I'm always feeding people," she said quietly, and he could see some wounded feelings in the set of her jaw. "And then they go off to do their thing without me. So I just do my thing."

"After a couple of lessons, you'll be able to surprise Julia."

"I'm not out to impress Julia anymore. Are you?" She studied him for a moment. It was nearly dark. If his face was flaming red, he figured she couldn't see it. "You are, aren't you?" She took the bucket from his hand. "You and *Julia*? Are you serious?"

"You know what I think?" He opened the small gate for her, but she just stood there staring at him, both hands gripping the bucket handle. *Yeah, me and Julia*, he wanted to say. *What's wrong with that?*

He cleared his throat. "Julia's always askin' me what I think about this and that. Kind of a novelty, being asked what I think. I've known a lot of women and I've been accused of a lot of things, but thinking don't generally enter into it."

"What . . ." She cleared her throat, too, and he had to wonder what the hell was so awkward. It wasn't like they'd done anything. "What do you think?"

"I think you and Julia are lucky to have each other. I like you both. I think if you'd try talking to each other, you'd find out you like each other better than you think."

"I love my sister," she said, sounding a little surprised. "I don't know if I *like* her, though. If we weren't sisters, I don't think we'd pick each other for friends."

"Maybe you're letting what you're callin' *love* get in the way."

"What I'm calling love *is* love. For my sister." She stepped closer. "Are you in love with her, K.C.?"

"You sure are direct." But it was a fair question. He loved women, always had, but this wasn't *women*. This was Julia. The mention of her name was like somebody in the next room had turned on the music. It was a good thing his ears didn't grow out of the top of his head, because they'd be forever swiveling in the direction of that name. He gave a diffident smile, a little shrug. "I haven't known her very long."

"I have a feeling you've known a lot of women. How long does it usually take you?"

"That's between me and the lady in question."

"And Julia's the lady in question," she concluded.

"Yes, ma'am, she is."

The look on Dawn's face, what he could see of it, was a little unsettling. But at least she didn't laugh outright.

20

*I*t had taken K.C. *a couple of weeks to plan the wild-*horse roundup. Picking the right spot, devising the right trap, figuring out the right assignments for everybody who wanted to get involved all occupied much of what he wryly referred to as his spare time, mainly the hours between sunset and breakfast. The summer program was going so well that the boys were spending longer hours at the High Horse. Of the original batch of mustangs, three had already been saddled. They were still a long way from being usin' horses, but cinching up those three saddles had made believers of at least three "teenage outlaws."

The roundup would bring a few more horse candidates into the program, which K.C. was beginning to really feel part of. At the end of a good day, when the boys piled into the van looking tired and happy, he permitted himself to think he was making something real and good with Julia. But the roundup would be his own making, something he'd done before and understood well, something few men knew how to put together. This he alone could do for her.

Nick Maynard drove out from Nevada with his wife, Freddie, a specialist in equine veterinary medicine. K.C. ribbed Nick about showing up after the plan was already made, the equipment hauled in and the trap constructed. They had known each other for nearly ten years. Nick had gotten him his first good colt starting contract. Nick was the only person K.C. would ever get on the phone and call, just for the hell of it.

Neither of them regarded Nick's willingness to become involved with the High Horse as a personal favor. It was a matter of horses. Nick had taken the word of a fellow cowboy—traveled hundreds of miles without questioning the marvel that awaited him—because it involved horses. But he had to be teased some for missing the hard work. The roundup itself would be the fun part for Nick, especially when he witnessed the wonder that K.C. had discovered.

And for that K.C. and Nick rode the high country, taking the boys in groups so that they, too, could see the herd in the wild. K.C. was determined that they'd all have a chance to observe, even though they wouldn't all ride in the roundup. They found five small bands several miles apart from each other and inspected each one. The mustangs had picked up weight on spring grass. Their rumps were rounded now, no more sloping down from the backbone, and their coats were sleek. The foaling rate was below average, but then, it had been a long winter.

Even though Nick was the federally inspected and approved wild-horse expert, it was K.C. who knew them on a level that superseded science, and Nick deferred to his commentary as they rode. K.C. told the boys to simply observe at first, to watch the herd's behavior and get a feel for the conditions and circumstances, the way he'd been teaching them to do with the horses they were gentling. They weren't interested in chasing them yet, but as they located them, they wanted to be pressing them westward.

The riders kept their distance—K.C. didn't want the mustangs spooked—and they watched. K.C. called their attention to the frequent whinnying, pointed out the apparent partnerships. But none of the horses appeared to be disabled. There was no falling, no bumping into anything, not much stumbling. The boys were enchanted by what they saw.

When K.C. suggested a night on the town in Cody with Nick and Freddie, he made it clear that he was asking for a date. Julia resisted asking her sister to join them. A night "on the town" would mean music and dancing and Dawn at her irresistible best. And Julia would simply be Julia.

And the encounter in the horse pens had not gone unnoticed from the upstairs bedroom window.

Julia had thought about going down there herself that night, just as she had every night since the night on the mountain. K.C. regularly worked the horses in the evenings after supper. Sometimes Shep went down there with him, sometimes Vern.

The night she'd seen Dawn go trotting down the road after him, she'd backed away from the window immediately, seeking safe distance. She'd thought about taking a walk outside, quickly reined herself in. But after she turned out the light, she couldn't stay away from the window. All she could see was a little movement in the evening shadows. She might have asked one of them about it later, but she didn't. She was afraid to know more than what she'd seen, afraid she would lose them both if she did. And that fear in itself was a revelation to her.

But for now, she put the fear of losing people aside. She had a date.

Hats and boots were required for a night on the town in Cody, Wyoming, and since Julia didn't have a hat, shopping for one was the first order of business.

"They always blow away," Julia complained when K.C. parked her on a stool amid the countless silver belly, tan, and black beaver Stetsons and creamy straw Baileys stacked on tables and shelves in the Cowboy Outfitter and Mercantile.

"Not if they fit right." He had already determined her size, and he'd clearly decided that the style was his choice, too. "Don't worry about the shape. I'll fix that. Doesn't she look great in a hat?"

Nick and Freddie, visible behind her in the full-length mirror, readily agreed that she did. They were a nice couple. Made for each other, Julia concluded, even though Freddie was tall and plain and Nick was short and cute. Even though Freddie was a fountain of information and nervous energy and Nick was placid and reserved. Even though Freddie was take-charge and Nick was take-time.

Perfect match. It had nothing to do with the way people looked at them, but with the way they looked at each other, like two pie-eyed kids. There it was again, Julia thought as she observed their reflections in the mirror. That loving look. Made for each other.

"Don't want the boss lady getting sunstroke tomorrow." K.C. rejected a wide-brimmed Panama style in favor of one with a taller crown.

She looked at K.C. and smiled. Now, there was a head that was born to wear a cowboy hat. "We're using all the saddle horses for you and the boys, so I won't be riding anyway and I . . ." She included Nick and Freddie with a glance in the mirror. "I'm obviously not a real cowboy like you guys. I look like I'm trying to be one and I'm coming up short."

"We got short cowboys, too. Right, Maynard?"

"Short on the ground, tall in the saddle." Nick gave Julia's reflection a nod. "That looks good."

"She makes them all look good," K.C. said as he made another switch. "This one has a better crown." He tipped her chin up, adjusted the hat just so. She didn't know what *just so* meant, but she saw approval in his eyes, and she basked in it. "Perfect."

"You think so?"

"You know I do."

"What do you think?" Freddie asked her husband.

"I think it's a damn good possibility. You let us know if we're in your way, cowboy." Nick chuckled as he watched the scene play out in the mirror. "Take the hat, Julia. The man has impeccable taste."

It would take some getting used to. It felt funny, but she couldn't take it off, not after he'd insisted on paying the bill. Freddie signaled her with a subtle poke in the ribs that she was not to refuse, and she understood why when K.C. kept smiling at her, adjusting the hat and grinning.

They had supper at the Cattlemen's Steak House, then strolled down Main Street until K.C. heard the right kind of music coming from the right kind of door. Once inside, he didn't care about getting a table or ordering drinks. All he wanted to do, he said, was dance with his lady.

The memory of shadows disappearing into the barn dissipated. Julia was wearing boots and a hat, and she was dancing with her cowboy. She didn't care whether she looked like a woman who was trying too hard. She was having too much fun.

Freddie nodded toward the door marked "Ewes." Julia made a remark about "ramming through." They'd been regaling the men with their Ping-Pong puns all evening. There was only one toilet, and Freddie had first claim, since she had suggested the visit. "Did K.C. tell you that he was the one who introduced me to Nick?" she piped up from inside the stall.

Julia said that he hadn't. She took her new hat off and started blotting dance sweat off her face with a brown paper towel.

"I went out with K.C. first, but that never really went anywhere. We've always been good friends. It's a small world, you know, the horse world. Everybody knows everybody." Freddie emerged, waited until she had Julia's reflected attention in the mirror, then gave her a pointed look. "Everybody knows K.C."

"And?"

Freddie shrugged. "Everyone likes him, of course. The good guys do, anyway. He's fun to be around, easy to talk to, always willing to help out." She watched Julia fuss with her hair. They both knew it was futile at this point, but Julia had to try. Freddie smiled. "I remember him telling me what a great guy Mick was, what a good head he had on his shoulders. Perfect for someone like me."

"And he was right," Julia surmised. She decided to go back to the hat.

"Of course he was. K.C. has incredible intuition. I guess that's what it is. It seems like sorcery sometimes, the way he's able to read horses. He understands implicitly." The pointed look softened. "But he always moves on, too often shortchanging himself in the process."

"You're telling me he isn't much of a businessman?" She tried tucking the damp hair behind her ears. "I guess I figured that out."

"I'm saying he doesn't see himself . . ." Freddie glanced away from the mirror. "I'm saying, in the end, he expects so little."

Julia slowly returned her hair pick to her purse. "Maybe he doesn't want very much."

"His freedom is all he's ever had. If he leaves with that intact, he figures he hasn't lost anything."

"But then, he's never known anything else."

"Not as long as we've known him."

"So he doesn't know what he's missing, right?" Julia gave a tight smile. "Don't worry, Freddie. I'll forgive him when he rides away."

Freddie shook her head. "He looks at you differently, Julia. I've seen him with lots of women. He gets involved in some situations, you know, you wish he'd use his head once in a while, but . . ." She shrugged. "He likes women. He treats them very well. But the way he looks at you . . ."

Freddie didn't strike Julia as the mother-hen type. She wouldn't have picked her for an apologist, either. If anything, she'd thought she had a dire forewarning coming from her new friend. But the look in Freddie's eyes was pure woman-to-woman.

"I've never seen K.C. like this before, and neither has Nick. We've already compared notes." Freddie turned, leaning against the sink. "I don't make a habit of meddling, but I just thought, because we've known him a long time, and we're as close as he lets anyone get, and we think the world of him . . . I thought I should play the big sister, since K.C. doesn't have one. And he just pops into your life out of the blue, so you don't know . . ." Again the quick shrug. "I thought I should say something in K.C.'s behalf, because knowing K.C., he'll just . . ."

Julia touched Freddie's arm. "I'm glad you did." For some reason, she didn't want to hear any more.

"He'll just move on, like he always does. Unless the right woman . . ."

Exactly what she didn't want to hear. "That's all it takes, huh? The right woman."

"You're looking at him exactly the same way he's looking at you, Julia. I don't know whether you realize that, and I don't know whether that makes him the right man. But he's a good man, no matter what—'' Freddie caught herself with a little laugh and said, ''Boy, I sure sound like a big sister, don't I? Trying to build him up without letting him down, probably blowing it for him completely.''

''Not to worry,'' Julia said, trying on a breezy tone.

Freddie touched her arm. ''K.C.'s a good man. Anyone who ever tells you different is a liar.''

The music had shifted from heel-stomping to shoulder-swaying, and the party was winding down when Dawn showed up at their table, bringing her sweet blond sunshine and her mist of musk into the smoky honky-tonk. Didn't mean to butt in, she said, but she wanted to introduce Cal Pollak to the visitors from Nevada. She really did look cute in her pink sundress, Julia thought, and she started looking around for vacant chairs. K.C. offered Dawn his, but she graciously refused.

''We just wanted to stop and say hi.'' She glanced at Cal. ''Or hey. Or *howdy*. We're in howdy country, aren't we?''

''Dawn said she thought she recognized the green pickup,'' Cal said as he shook Nick's hand. ''That's an unusual shade of green.''

Nick nodded. ''Cud green, we call it.''

Cal stood toe-to-toe with K.C., who was still standing on ceremony, making the introductions. ''I hear you're rounding up them mustangs tomorrow.''

K.C. adjusted his hat—a qualified *yes*. ''This youth program Julia's got going is workin' out real good. Turns out we've got some fine wranglers in that bunch. Started out with the horses we picked up out to your place, and they're about ready to take on a few more.''

''They takin' the buck out of them outlaws, are they?'' Cal grinned. ''You can take that either way, can't you? It's outlaws all around.''

''They just look like kids and horses to me,'' Nick said.

Cal ignored the comment. He folded his arms, stepped to K.C.'s side for a shoulder-to-shoulder stare at the floor. He was on the hunt for details. ''Dawn says you're thinkin' you might have some more blind ones in the bunch.''

"Well, you find one, you figure you oughta have a look at the rest.''

"You thinkin' maybe it's in the blood?''

"Couldn't say.'' K.C. stuck his thumbs in his belt. "I'm just lookin' at their eyes myself.''

"You know, twenty years ago or so the Feds rounded up all those worthless wild horses, found patches of equally worthless land and plunked 'em there, just like Indians on a reservation. They did that for a reason.'' Cal scanned the group as though he had everyone in suspense. "To preserve the good grazing land for domesticated stock.''

Nick squirmed in his chair. "That's not exactly the—''

K.C. laid a hand on Cal's shoulder as he cast his friend a pointed glance. "Nick's an old buddy of mine, came out to help us with the roundup. He's had some experience with mustangs. Freddie competes in endurance races, and she swears by mustangs.''

Freddie lifted her swearing hand, gave a perfunctory smile.

"I ain't sayin' you can't make some use of them. I'm just sayin' . . .'' Cal shifted his stance beneath the apparent weight of K.C.'s hand. "Well, like I was tellin' Dawn here, I sure wouldn't mind helpin' out with the roundup. I could bring over some horses.''

"You said we didn't have enough saddle horses,'' Dawn put in.

"Hell, I could bring a couple of motorcycles, liven things up a bit.''

"This is a little project we put together for the summer program, Cal. We've got it all worked out.'' K.C. gave the shoulder a parting pat. "Thanks anyway.''

"Yeah, well . . .'' Cal glanced at Julia. "If there is something wrong with them, something they could pass on . . .'' He turned back to K.C. "I mean, we wouldn't want any diseased horses running loose in this valley, so if you need help, you know, disposing of any of them, you can call on me.''

Dawn's eyes widened. "Cal, I don't think . . .''

"Honey, there's only one market I know of that would

take blind horses, but they'd have to have some meat on 'em.''

''He's just kidding,'' Dawn explained quickly. ''Right, Cal? You notice they're not laughing. That's because . . .''

''That's because Cal's right,'' K.C. allowed. ''A blind mustang, I'd have to shoot him before I'd let anyone load him up in a truck, because I know damn well where he'd end up.''

''You'd get yourself arrested,'' Nick grumbled. K.C. waved the threat away. ''For a guy who's allergic to being locked up, Houston, I swear . . .''

''But there's no need to worry about it because, so far, we only got one for sure, and Dawn's not gonna let anything bad happen to Bat.'' K.C. reached for Julia's hand. ''Now, why aren't we dancin'? Cal, you're lettin' some good music go to waste, and you won't find a better dance partner than Dawn.'' He smiled at Julia, and when he had her on her feet, he leaned close to her ear and confided, ''Because I've got the better one, and I ain't sharin'.''

Early the following morning K.C. divided his riders into teams. In order to keep the wild horses moving without playing the saddle horses out, Nick and three of the boys—Brad, Donnie and Paco—were positioned in a rocky pocket above the midpoint of the expected route. They would serve as a relay team, replacing K.C.'s initial hazers—all but K.C. himself, who would simply change mounts. Paco had ridden bareback on Columbine, who was to play a special role in the ruse K.C. had planned.

K.C. started out with the first team, closing in from the east, gathering the horses in a wide sweep over the high range. They maneuvered the herd closer to the western fence line, and now it was K.C.'s turn to be impressed. He liked the way Leighton and Chad handled themselves, the way they attended closely, both to him and to the herd. They were patient. Once they started to press the horses toward the fence line, the boys did exactly what they'd been instructed to do. They anticipated the horses' moves and applied steady ''full court'' pressure.

From the moment the herd had begun to move, the

amount of whinnying had increased, bearing out K.C.'s theory that the horses had a signaling system. They were a noisy bunch, but the signals made it easy to identify the blind horses and their seeing counterparts. K.C. and the two boys hatched signals of their own to describe the shared sense of wonder over what they were witnessing, as though they were three music lovers who had happened upon a symphony in the mountains.

By the time they reached the fence line, they had collected about thirty horses. As K.C. had predicted, the dominant mare assumed the lead and set the pace. A stud dropped to the rear. Later in the season the pace would have been faster, but the horses were mindful of their new colts. As long as the hazers didn't push, the stud would maintain that rear post and let the mare set a slower pace.

Mick eased his fresh riders into the run, and Leighton, Chad and K.C. dropped back. K.C. turned Sky Pilot over to Paco and vaulted onto Columbine's bare back. The chase continued along the declining slope of the fence line.

The trap had been set in ideal terrain. Moving into lower country, the herd was headed for a long funnel made of sturdy, portable fence panels branching off the permanent fence in the saddle of a hill. The wings of the trap narrowed gradually, forming a blind alley. Shep and Vern were in charge of the trap. Barney and Chevy were ready to thwart the possibility of a runback.

It was all in the timing. The herd was beginning to tire. They'd been pressed, but not terrorized, and they'd moved at a controlled pace. Before they had a chance to see what was up ahead, K.C. leaned forward, close to Colly's neck, streamlining rider and horse into a running unit. He asked for more speed as they peeled away from the herd and raced ahead, arcing toward the trap wing, which stood just below a rise.

At the mouth of the trap he performed the flying dismount his mother had taught him, unsnapped the short rein from Colly's headstall and stood behind her as the herd came thundering up behind them. "You lead the way for me, girl," he told her, and at the right moment he turned her loose and dove for the fence. A dominant mare at heart,

Colly leaped at the chance to run at the head of the herd. She led them over the rise, down the slope and into the trap corral.

At K.C.'s signal, Chevy and Barney closed the trap behind the last horse by dragging a string of tarps and sheets tied to a rope across the open end of the funnel. The wind whipped the makeshift curtain into a flapping deterrent to the only escape route. Barney cut loose with an exuberant whoop, which was curtailed by another signal from K.C. Do nothing to scare them more, he'd warned. Stay back, stay calm, stay awake.

Barney hung his head, embarrassed by his own outburst, but he remembered that his job wasn't finished until the gate was secure. K.C. reassured him with a nod as they converged on the panel gates. No harm done. Once the gate was closed, there were handshakes all around.

By the end of the day, K.C. had chosen the horses he would haul back to the ranch. The rest had been examined, and those without identification were freeze-branded before they were turned loose again. Freddie had drawn blood samples from thirty-four horses and colts. She had diagnosed cataracts and some degree of blindness in five horses. She saw no evidence of blindness in any of the new foals, but one yearling showed early signs of developing cataracts.

It took two trips to haul the horses back to the ranch—first the mustangs, then the saddle horses. Freddie and Julia took charge of the hard-won blood samples, packaging them and taking them into Quicksilver for shipment to Nick's friends at the University of Kentucky. By the time the equipment was put away and the vanload of seasoned wranglers had departed, everyone was exhausted.

It wasn't until early the following morning, as Freddie and Nick prepared to leave, that Julia and K.C. were able to take another look at the horses they'd gathered, collect some thoughts and compare some notes. The four of them stood between the corrals and the Maynards' "cud green" pickup, enjoying coffee and easy camaraderie. Nick had said he wanted to get an early start, before it became too hot, but the sun had already foiled those plans. The day promised to be a hot one. And there were still the questions, speculations, predictions and plans. What was to be done about the Painted Mountain mustangs?

"It usually takes several years for a horse with cataracts to become completely blind," Freddie explained, "so they've had time to adapt as they've gradually lost their eyesight. I'd bet my veterinary license that this is genetic, probably a recessive gene. But it's the behavior patterns that are so interesting."

So far as they knew, they'd turned all the blind horses loose but Bat. And K.C. had told Julia that he wanted to turn the paint loose, too, before his taste for oats dulled his survival instincts.

Freddie persuaded K.C. to hold off until the test results came back. "I'd really love to study this herd."

Julia watched a red-tailed hawk stretch its wings and ride a warm updraft of air rising from the barren pens. A blind hawk could survive only in captivity. These remarkable mustangs had not only survived, they'd formed some unique partnerships.

"If it is hereditary, what can we do?"

"Either they'll have the gene or they won't. If this sampling is any indication, it's pretty serious. But most of the horses look fine. Beautiful, in fact."

"Looks like you're overpopulated," Nick said. "No matter what, you do need to get rid of some horses."

"I thought we'd continue the program through the summer and sell the ones that pass muster with K.C. in the fall." Julia exchanged glances with her foreman. She was wearing her hat, identified by the label inside as a "Rancher's Classic," and this morning it felt like a good fit. "It's easier to find good homes for saddle horses."

"Especially a K.C. Houston saddle horse." Freddie stepped up onto the lowest corral rail. "That big gray roan over there? Four-year-old, I'd say. Nice chest on him. I'd love to try him out in an endurance run. You start him, K.C., I'll buy him."

"After all you've done here, Freddie, he's yours," Julia said.

"I want the Houston handle on him."

"I'll throw in the Houston handle," K.C. said. "You'll shine in competition, mention my name, and I'll shine right along with you. Next year, my price goes up."

Freddie laughed, and Nick muttered, "Same ol' Houston."

"So you don't think he'll go blind?"

"The tests will tell us for sure," Freddie told Julia. "It would really, *really* be interesting to study this herd."

"It's got to be managed," Nick insisted. "You've got to cull this herd, first off. What I'd probably do is geld the stallions and bring in—"

"Oh, no, Nick, there'd be nothing left to study!" Freddie shook her head, chiding her husband with a look. "That's the problem with these bureaucrats. They want to micro-manage every inch of the natural world."

"Hell, we got to manage what's left." Nick slid his hand beneath his wife's ponytail and rubbed her nape. "We're all that's standing between the wildlife and the bulldozers. Us bureaucrats and you bleeding-heart liberals."

Freddie favored him with a smile.

"Kind of an odd alliance, but it seems to be working at our house," Nick allowed. "On balance."

"How would you study them?" Julia asked Freddie.

"By not meddling too much. Nick's right about the numbers, but I would say that removing a few horses from the herd to keep the number stable would not really be meddling. People have been doing that for thousands of years. We're part of the system, too." She gazed at the gray roan she favored. "Basically, I'd just watch. They've developed some unique adaptive behaviors already. It would be fascinating to see what nature's course turns out to be."

"Natural selection at work," Julia mused.

"You can't turn the clock back," Nick said. "Nobody knows better than I do just how unnatural this system is. There's no point in pretending we haven't played God by setting up these management areas."

"Was it a mistake to protect this herd?" Julia wondered. She turned to Nick. "To keep them here, isolated like this?"

"They're all isolated. All these little herds." Nick shook his head, as though he felt responsible. "The way we're going now, it's only a matter of time before they disappear from the landscape. They don't have enough freedom to really be wild. What you've got on Painted Mountain is actually a private sanctuary."

"What would happen to the horses we didn't sell?"

"Under new High Horse management?" Nick asked. Julia nodded. "Depends on the management. If you sell out to your neighbor, the BLM horse manager for this district would probably be called in for removal."

"And so much for studying the herd," Freddie said with a sigh.

"Hey, *we* study," Nick claimed, affronted. "We study all the time."

"Your primary job is to *manage*. I'd love to study this herd. Maybe I could interest one of the universities in backing a project if I—" Freddie had grabbed Nick's hand, as though inveigling his support. "Wouldn't that be exciting, hon? It's completely un—"

"She knows damn well there's no money for this," Nick told his friends. "You know what's happened to the budget for wild horses and burros? It's been shrinking steadily, right along with the herd management areas."

"Budgeting isn't my area of expertise," Freddie said as she turned her powers of persuasion on Julia. "If there's any way, any possibility, any *thought* of keeping this herd here, I would love to become involved."

"You've got to reduce the numbers, though," Nick said flatly.

"Yes, but they've got a fine plan for that. They've already started." Freddie was wound up now. The scientist in search of a laboratory. "What you're doing with these boys is a terrific idea."

"It was my brother's idea, but K.C.'s making it a reality." Julia smiled. "Come to think of it, K.C. was Ross's idea, too."

"K.C.'s not much of an idea man," K.C. quipped, slipping Freddie a sly wink.

"Hell, this guy is cowboy ingenuity personified," Nick

said, taking aim at K.C.'s shoulder with a loose fist. "That trap worked slicker than bear grease."

"Who taught me everything I know about catching wild horses?"

"Who taught me all I know about getting inside their heads?"

Freddie leaned close to Julia. "We're in trouble if all they know is what they learned from each other. Neither one of us has a tail."

"What's this?" Freddie's thick blond ponytail filled her grinning husband's hand. "I've been following this around for ten years, woman. You mean to tell me I'm sniffin' at the wrong end?"

"Best way to train a cowboy to love you for your mind is to wear your hair in a ponytail," Freddie said with a laugh. She whacked Nick between his shoulder blades. "He can't count, either. It's only been seven years."

"Jeez, is that all?"

"As I was saying, *time*"—she flashed her husband a pointed look—"will tell. When we know exactly what's going on in the gene pool, we'll be able to make a better assessment of the cause and maybe predict some effects."

"And then we figure out what to do," Julia concluded. "But you're thinking we ought to see what happens if we mostly let nature take its course. What a concept, huh?"

"Nature can be pretty cruel at times," Nick said. "You find some sick animals, supposed to be wild, so when do you leave them to their own devices and when do you step in and try to help them?"

"That's the question, isn't it?"

"Yeah, but if you're gonna be a damn *purist* about it . . ."

"We'll be arguing the point all the way home." Freddie chuckled. "I'll have some answers for you soon. You're not thinking of selling before fall, are you?"

"No. I promised Gramma the summer." Julia glanced at K.C. "At . . . at least."

"We'll start the roan out, see what kind of a usin' horse he'd make you, Freddie-girl," K.C. told her. "I figure we can turn out maybe a dozen gentle horses this summer. Not saddle-broke, maybe, but started.''

"That'll put a good little dent in the overpopulation," Nick said.

"And if the eyesight is still good and they're at least three or four, I'd say they're okay. But we'll know more soon." Freddie gave Julia a hug, confiding in her ear, "You don't want to let him go, Julia." She drew back, a bright, canny look in her eyes. "So don't."

Julia was unable to roll out an easy protest. She frowned instead. She hated it when people thought they could see through her, but Freddie wouldn't be denied. She was too genuine, too well-meaning. And too damned perceptive.

21

After Nick and Freddie left, K.C. turned his atten-
tion to accommodating seven more mustangs in his system
of pens and pastures around the horse barn. Julia busied
herself in the garden. She simply couldn't resist reseeding
the old plot. Neither could she resist keeping track of what
K.C. was doing, thinking she'd wander into his territory
when he took a break, and then they would talk and be
close.

K.C. didn't take many breaks. She saw him ride off in
the pickup with Vernon, only to return with materials for
some added fencing in the horse pasture. At suppertime
they were gone again. So was Dawn. But Julia noticed
when the pickup returned. It was twilight, and she was watering the herbs she'd planted near the kitchen door. Above
the chirping of crickets she could hear the engine idling out
front, the slam of the door, her sister's cheery good-night.
The engine revved again, and she watched the taillights
disappear behind the horse barn. Within moments she heard
the echo of wood thunking against wood, and she knew
they were unloading more posts. More materials.

More improvements. While Shep forever tinkered with
the machinery, Vernon had spent the past thirty years
amending the ranch's structures. Without him, the place
would surely have fallen apart. Now that there was a new
right hand, Vernon seemed content to become the stabiliz-
ing left.

Soon after Julia had stepped into the shower she saw the pickup's lights, glowing briefly beyond the frosted glass, first oncoming white, then trailing red. They were like a semaphore, a signal to hurry.

The initial perceptions and suggestions Freddie had offered about the horses had been buzzing in Julia's head all evening. She thought about the horses. She had questions. But that wasn't what moved her to dry her hair, dress in a loose cotton shift, slip out the back door. There were reasons besides her restlessness. There were needs other than her own. She tried to check her pace, but even if she hadn't been in a hurry, she wasn't a good ambler.

And, yes, she was in a hurry. Her heart hammered like a bird trapped inside her rib cage. She wasn't exactly sneaking around, but this was not something she wanted to discuss or explain or be questioned about. This was what it was. A summer romance between a mature, sensible, prudent woman and a cowboy. *What* he was reminded her of her father, but also of her grandfather and her brother. They were all becoming part of him now, in a good way, a living, breathing way. But they were not him, and *who* he was made her think only of one man, the one she wanted close to her, for there was no other like him. She wanted to be part of him, too.

The night air was rich with summer. The soil she'd turned and watered in the garden, the new-mown sweet clover, the mountain water flowing in the creek, the warmth of the day rising to meet the dew—it all smelled like summer romance. The act of knocking on the bunkhouse door after dark made Julia's sensible soul sing along with the sad fiddle music spilling from the window like rolling tumbleweeds. She could see the light from the bathroom, hear the water running in the sink, but the rest of the building was dark.

"It's open."

She closed the door behind her as he emerged from the bathroom. His jeans rode his low waist like a beginning swimmer hanging onto the edge of the pool, the top snap undone. His dark hair glistened, slick and wet, as did his eyes meeting hers. He shut the light off, and moonlight flooded the room.

"Do you want me to pull the shades?"

"There aren't any," she said with a little laugh. "Besides, the moonlight's too pretty, and I came to see you."

"Been hoping you would." He moved cautiously, taking nothing for granted, as though there was still a chance of her shying away. "I've been thinking about putting a ladder up to your bedroom window. Every night since we were together at the cabin, I've gotten a step closer to doing it."

"You wouldn't have to use a ladder. You go from the porch railing to the porch roof to the roof of the south wing to—" She described the steps with her hands.

"There's a pretty steep pitch on that roof," he said as he slipped his arms around her waist.

"Oh, well, I'd tie a rope to the bedpost and toss it out the window." She laid her arms around his shoulders. His skin was warm and supple from his shower, and he smelled of menthol shaving cream. "But it's actually easier to sneak *out* that way. We always used a window on the first floor to get back in."

"And what kind of trouble were you lookin' to get into, sneakin' out like that?"

"No trouble." She touched his smooth cheek. "Adventure."

"Mmm. A woman after my own heart." He slid his hands up her back, pausing where he would normally have felt her bra, and she could feel him smiling. "So to speak."

"You just shaved."

"Every night, just in case."

"Have I told you how impressed I was with the way you orchestrated the roundup? The way you included the boys? The way you came galloping over the hill and did that fabulous stunt-rider dismount? Gosh, you smell good."

"Tell me what kind of adventure you're looking for tonight, and I'll see if I can make it happen." He kneaded her back, finding knots she didn't know were there, coaxing them from taut to supple.

"I came to talk, really."

He laughed, then kissed her neck and made her shiver and smile with him in the dark.

"Well, I came just to see you, but also to ask you what you thought about . . ."

"You always need a better reason, don't you? We've got moonlight and music, and it's just the two of us tonight." He leaned away from her to turn the radio down.

"Finally." A confession she hadn't quite meant to make, but it felt good and honest in the making.

"You, too?"

"Well, it's my own fault," she said quickly. "I'm asking you for too much, I know. Working you too hard."

"I'm not a horse, darlin'. You can't work me." He led her by the hand toward the back window, where her brother's newly refurbished collection of antique saddles stood on their racks. "You've got a good thing goin' here. I like being part of it."

"You mean the summer program?"

"I mean the summer." He swung his leg over the high cantle of an ornate Mexican charro saddle and sat in the long, shallow seat. "I like being part of your summer. *This* summer. You ever lift this thing? This is a lot of saddle."

She spread her hand over the huge, flat horn cap, slanted toward the rider like a plate tipped to empty his dinner into his lap. The silver-trimmed stirrups dragged the floor next to K.C.'s bare feet. His knees were bent, as if he were riding English style rather than Western.

"The boys are doing well, aren't they?"

"They are."

"And they're learning from you. You have a way about you, K.C. You put people at ease the same way you do with horses."

"You, too?" He lifted his hand to her cheek.

"Most definitely me, too." His face was shadowed, his hair and shoulders moonlit, and he was beautiful, natural, perfectly easy with himself. It was she who made herself uneasy with all her galloping thoughts. "What do you think about what Freddie said?"

"Right now? I don't even remember who Freddie is."

"About the horses. What do you think about . . . the idea

of studying them?'' He laughed. "Honestly," she said.

"Climb on here with me, and I'll be honest with you."
He patted the big horn cap. "Here's your seat."

"I'm not dressed for riding," she said, pulling at her
skirt as though she would curtsy.

"You're not?" He reached for her hips, rubbing his
hands over them as he drew her close. "Mmm, I see. But
it's a problem that's easy to fix." He rucked her dress up
around her hips, tucked his thumbs into the elastic of her
silk panties and slid them to the floor. "Now you're dressed
for adventure."

"Honestly?"

"Honestly," he assured her, placing her hands on his
shoulders, guiding her leg over him and lifting her, perch-
ing her on the horn cap like a sprite on a toadstool, all the
while telling her that Freddie, like Julia, was a smart lady.
"Between the two of you—"

"We don't have half your understanding of those horses.
Any horses."

"And you really wanna know what I think." Facing him
now, she nodded. "If you're gonna ask me to think, you'll
have to be patient. I'm a slow thinker." He slid his hands
under her skirt, over her thighs, which were draped over
his. "Gotta take my time, kinda ease into the question and
get the feel of it. Are those buttons for show, or do they
really work?"

She looked down at the front of her tenty dress. "They're
functional."

"For, like, if you needed to suckle somebody?"

"I don't have anybody who . . ." She caught her breath
as his thumbs gently harried her groin. ". . . needs suckling."

"Yes, you do. Work the buttons for me, Julia."

She did. He nosed his way around inside, barely touching
her breasts, barely breathing on them, barely kissing them,
until she could barely stand it and she lifted them to him
on a deep breath, soliciting his full attention, which he hungrily gave.

She managed to ask whether his zipper was fully functional. Never taking his hands or his lips or his tongue from

her fully, he invited her to test it. "But carefully," he warned, "because I'm fully functional."

"And dressed for riding?" She felt his smile, sketched against the side of her neck. She found the zipper tab. "Then I suggest you suck it in."

"Can't do that now. I'm not made that way."

"Let's see how you're made." She felt his lips part against her neck when she slipped her hand down the front of his jeans to shield him as the metal teeth parted. "Ah, yes, now I remember. Bold and tender both."

"And you," he whispered as he plied the secret seam between her legs with gentle thumbs until she caught her breath. "So soft and pretty. Much too fine for me."

But he touched all her fineness, finding layer upon gossamer layer, feathering it with his fingers, dampening it, driving her mad. "K.C., please . . ."

"Anything you want. I wish . . ."

"If wishes were horses . . ."

"Would the queen still ride?"

She laughed and leaned over him, lifting, guiding him, taking him deep inside her body, so deep that he touched her fierce and fragile core with his very first stroke. And she became fully herself and fully him, both at once.

He slept next to her, his serene face bathed in moonlight. He was exhausted and had every right to be. She wanted to hold him through the night, watch over him while he slept, appreciate him. It was almost painful for her, watching him now, because each time she turned away, she was drawn back. Each time she closed her eyes, she had to open them again quickly to make sure he was still there, that she had not dreamed the wonder of him.

She loved him. Her heart had never ventured so far before. She had kept a tight rein, for everything that she knew about love told her that it was wise to control it, hold it back, keep it contained within the dry basket of her body.

Too late for that now. Too late to go back. Discoveries could not be undiscovered. The race toward autumn was on. They had ridden each other tonight without speaking further of wishes or horses or would-be queens. When they saw each other tomorrow, they would see all those things in each other's eyes. She wasn't sure how she would feel then, in daylight. Foolish, maybe. She hated feeling foolish. But she knew she would look him full in the face and fully feel what she felt for him, foolish or not, for discoveries could not be undiscovered.

On the way back up the moonlit gravel road, Julia discovered ambling. It was easy to do when staying held more appeal than going. She took the long way around, the loop that led to the barn and the corrals, just to see what K.C. had been working on. He'd told her he would have to change the setup, and she'd given him leave to use his own judgment. In the dark she nearly tripped over a fence post that had strayed from the pile next to the barn. She smiled when she saw Bat, the blind paint, standing in the corral.

You and me, boy, she thought. Running on faith. His sighted partner, Radar, was feeding from the hay rack in the corner, but Bat was munching on something, too, and he wasn't shadowing Radar's flank, the way he usually did. It looked as though he'd claimed his own corner of the pen. Then she noticed the extra pair of legs. Then the pouf of pale, moon-washed hair sprouting behind his neck.

"Dawn?"

Grinning like a child playing peekaboo, her sister stepped out from behind the horse. "Bat likes carrots, but only at night. He won't eat them during the day."

"Really?" Julia let herself into the pen through the small gate. "When did you start getting close enough to discover that?"

"K.C.'s been helping me get over my stupid hang-ups about horses." She took another carrot stick from a plastic box and offered it to the horse, who sniffed at it first, then nabbed it neatly with limber lips.

Carrot sticks! Dawn was feeding the horse pared, trimmed carrot sticks.

She flashed Julia a mischievous, moon-silver smile. "Is he working on your hang-ups, too?"

"Were you spying on me?"

Dawn laughed. "I thought you were all tucked in for the night, sound asleep in your own bed. When that bunkhouse door opened at three A.M. and out you came, let me tell you I was shocked. *Shocked*.'' She chanted softly, ''Queenie's got a boyfriend. Queenie's got . . .''

Julia leaned against the rails, arms folded over her breasts, aware of her nakedness beneath her billowy dress, thinking, *If you knew how wild I can be*. ''I can't believe you'd spy on me like that.''

''Don't be ridiculous. I was on the phone, first with Roger, then Mama, and between the two of them they managed to get my head spinning, so I puttered around the kitchen for a while, did a little baking. Chocolate chip cookies for the boys tomorrow.''

''They'll love that.''

''Those boys can put away the food, all right. The only veggies they really like are the relish-tray kind. With dip, of course; they love my dill dip. I've been using dill from the garden.''

''It's probably been reseeding every year since that garden was first put in. Gramma hasn't done much with gardening. Do you remember what an absolute truck farm it was when we were kids?''

''Vaguely.'' Dawn fed Bat another carrot stick. ''It looks good since you planted it, though. You have Mama's green thumb.''

''You have the rest of her body. One thumb isn't much.''

''You have a lot more of her than that. You just don't want to admit it.''

The night suddenly felt close, tight, laden with heavy silence now that Fay's presence had been invoked. Radar pulled a hunk of hay from the rack, and the swish was deafening.

''I'm probably making a big fool of myself,'' Julia said, surprised by the sound of her voice, suddenly shy and unsure. She hated sounding small and pitiful, so she cleared her throat and tried again. ''K.C.'s a lot younger than I am. He's just passing through, obviously. He's . . . he's a *cowboy*, for heaven's sake.''

There it was, she thought. Fay's tone. Fay's stress. Fay's thumb. She managed a little laugh. ''Ah, well. So what did Mother have to say?''

"I told her about the offer from Chuck Pollak. She thought it was fabulous. She says we should get it in writing before he changes his mind. I told her you'd promised Gramma we'd hold off until fall, and Mama said she'd come out and help us with Gramma."

"Just what we need."

"We *are* going to sell, aren't we? Sooner or later, and really, we can't let it be too much later, because . . ." She fed Bat the last of the carrots before turning, soft-spoken now, worried but not whining. "Well, because the getting out is good right now. I've been in a business that went under, Julia, and I know how that goes. There's a critical teetering point that you need to recognize and act on before everything evaporates, including the offers. We can't afford to be foolish and sentimental."

"I know." Julia started to pet Bat's neck. "It's just me," she told the horse as he backed away. "I guess he likes you better."

"K.C. says Bat and I are about equally disadvantaged— my fear and his blindness—so we're naturally sympathetic to each other. And he *does* like me." She proved it by approaching him again as she spoke, letting him smell her, gaining his confidence before she touched him. "I don't ever have to ride him. He's blind. He's not going to be a saddle horse. Nobody's ever going to try to ride him." The horse permitted her to scratch his neck, his cheek, finally the downy place behind his ear. "Right, Bat? We're just two friends hangin' out together while everybody else trots around, one on top of the other."

They looked at each other, Dawn suppressing a smile until Julia laughed softly. For once, it was Dawn who had the inside track on the horse, not Julia. For once, Dawn was the bridge.

"K.C. isn't teaching you to ride?" Julia asked.

"He says he'll saddle a horse for me whenever I get ready."

"I saw you—" Too late for a tongue-biting to do any good. Julia shrugged, gave a tight smile. "You went to town with him this evening."

"And Vern. They said they had to get some stuff from

the Mercantile, and I needed chocolate chips." Dawn glanced at her sister, weighed some words in her head, then settled on "No, I haven't slept with him."

Julia let the statement hang there in the dark for a moment.

"I didn't think you had."

"You weren't sure." Dawn stood staring, taking some comfort from her proximity to the horse, her new ally. "You're still not sure."

"I believe you."

"But you're wondering whether he would if I would, or whether I would if he would. You don't know him all that well, and you think you know all about me." Dawn moved away from the horse, one shadow becoming two. "How far would I go, huh? You were with Roger when I first met him."

"I wasn't *with* Roger. I was dating Roger. That was years ago, and we weren't even . . ."

"Having sex? You think I don't know that?" A prickly sound, Dawn's quick laugh, marking an inconceivable notion. "It was actually a relief to see you sneaking out of the bunkhouse, Julia. I used to feel bad in a way about getting between you and Roger, even though I never thought for a minute that you would have lasted with him. But I was beginning to wonder about you."

She moved closer, and Julia felt threatened somehow by this wondering. "Whether you were even interested in men," Dawn explained, an accusation, the suggestion of a deficiency in her older sister. Just one. "Or sex. I wondered if maybe you were so smart you had figured out a way to bypass it altogether." She laughed again, turned and stood beside Julia, as though they might look at this joke of hers together. "Well, they say the brain is the most powerful sex organ, and you're so brainy, I figured you probably had the whole thing licked."

"What whole thing?"

"The whole sex thing. Sex . . . *impulse*. Issue, question, whatever. The sex thing."

"Licked?"

Dawn stared for a moment in disbelief, then laughed.

Julia stiffened against the small hand that landed like a butterfly on her arm. It wasn't the laughter that made her recoil. It was the look that came before it.

"Ahhh, Julie, Julie. Okay, I wondered if you were a little like Ross or something. Not that it matters, one way or the other."

"No." It was Julia's turn to stare. They never put sex and Ross in the same sentence. It was an unspoken rule, made by Ross himself, and Julia had stuck to the rule religiously. "Some things are private."

"Sure they are. It's just that I never see you anymore, we never talk. At least Ross talked to me."

Talked? Ross talked . . . to Dawn? Not about sex.

"He . . . talked to you about being gay?"

"Well, sort of." Dawn folded her arms, mirroring her sister's stance. "A few years back. Started out as an argument when I called him a fag, but—"

"You called him a . . ."

"I was only about, I don't know, sixteen. Both of you had left us by then. You were in college, and he'd already moved out here, but you both came back to Connecticut for Christmas. There was this one night when, I don't know where you and Mama were, but it was just him and me, and we had it out over some old stuff, just . . . I guess we got into Mama's sherry. Anyway, I called him a fag." And then, very quietly, "I made him cry."

"Ross?"

"Yeah, Ross. Stoic Ross." She leaned back against the fence. "I told him I was sorry. I said it was just something some kids had said to me once. More than once, but I didn't tell him that. I just told him I was sorry for using that word. Then he said, 'What if I am?' I didn't know what to say. *You can't be? You'd better not be?* I looked at him, and I knew it was true, and I just said, 'What if you are?' "

Dawn smiled, remembering, and in the moonlight she looked like a Christmas-tree angel. "Then we filled up our glasses again and talked. He said he didn't want us to be disgusted with him. So I said, 'Well, you stay out of my bedroom, and I'll stay out of yours,' and I told him his baby sister was no longer exactly a virgin. He said he wouldn't tell if I wouldn't tell. That was the best night. It was the only time he ever really talked to me." She looked at Julia now, who was feeling suddenly very small, insignificant. *Left out.* "Because you weren't around."

Julia felt sick. Not because her brother had been gay, but because he had told Dawn and not her. It was a feeling she regretted, but there it was. A small, spiteful bit of sickness.

"And he talked to you about his . . . about *being* gay?"

"Mostly about how he felt about it. How he'd tried to run from it, hide from it, do everything he could to kill it, but it just would not die. It wouldn't go away. I asked him what it felt like, and he said he thought if a great-looking guy were to walk in the room, we'd both probably feel pretty much the same, and pretty soon we were laughing about, you know . . ." Dawn glanced up, her eyes bright with the memory. "Just silly stuff. We agreed that you'd be equally scandalized by either one of us jumping on some guy's bones. You would just be mortified, because . . ." She imitated their brother's husky voice. " 'Queenie would not stoop to conquer.' "

"He never . . ." Julia shook her head, avoiding Dawn's eyes. "We never talked about it."

"Really?"

"Really."

"But you knew."

"I thought if it were true he'd tell me, but I guess I knew." *Of course she knew.* "What about Mother?"

"I think she's straight."

Julia looked at Dawn. Dawn waited, all innocence. Finally the laughter gushed over them, like soothing oil. When it dissipated, it left new warmth, and Dawn assured Julia that their mother knew. She was no more willing to talk about it than about the fact that he had chosen to leave home, *her* home, the minute he was old enough. He just couldn't listen. Couldn't talk back, couldn't fight back, so he'd left. He would have made a fine doctor, Fay was fond of saying, except that he had too soft a heart.

Julia smiled, thinking it was true. Ross understood pain too well. "But why didn't he talk with me about it, the way he talked with you?"

"You never called him a fag." Dawn touched her arm again, and this time Julia leaned into it, gave herself over to that butterfly touch. Dawn smiled. "You never would. I'm sure he knew that. He probably thought if you couldn't say it, maybe it was because you couldn't see it, so he just decided to let it be. It was the only really good talk we ever had, Julia, and it was only because . . ."

"Because you were open to it."

"Because he was afraid you weren't." Dawn slid her arm around Julia's waist. "So let me have that, okay? That one little corner, that one night when he let me be his sister, too."

Julia nodded. Permission granted, she thought, and she felt like a miser because she couldn't quite lift her arm over Dawn's head to make this a two-sided embrace, even though the one side felt good, felt real and natural.

"Dawn, what if . . ." She tested with a glance. A tentative solicitation. "What if we kept the High Horse? What if we just gave it a try, you and me?"

"We'd run it into the ground." Dawn's arm slid away. "Oh, no, please. I'm looking at the same accounts you've been looking at, Julia. This place hasn't been making any money. If Ross couldn't make it pay, you and I don't have a clue. Besides which, I don't want to live on a ranch."

"You wouldn't have to. You could be involved in, say, the bookkeeping. We'd link up by computer."

Dawn rolled her eyes and made a sound of protest.

Julia touched her shoulder. "This summer program has real potential. We could run it together. You could spend some time here in the summer, helping me build the program and the place. We could learn so much from Gramma and Vern. Maybe K.C."

"Maybe K.C.? You don't actually think he'd stay? I mean, look at him, Julia, he's . . ." Dawn smiled, distancing herself from the preposterous suggestion. "Queenie having a fling with the hired man. A cowboy, no less. Who'da thunk it?"

"Well, that's . . . Okay, that part's a little crazy, but I was thinking that if we had a good foreman *like* K.C., we just might turn this place around. And I think he might stay.''

''Is that why you're sleeping with him?''

''No!'' She glanced toward the bunkhouse, then whispered, ''No. That's not . . . no.'' She shook her head, pounding the nearest fence post with a flat hand. ''Some things *are* private.''

''Agreed. This property, for example.''

''He has some good ideas, Dawn.''

''I'll bet he does.''

''For the ranch. He's good with the kids. The horses.'' She'd picked up a sliver in her palm. She felt it, saw it even in the moonlight as she gestured expansively. ''What would happen to these horses if we sold out? What would happen to Vern and Shep and Gramma?''

''They'd be fine. With all that money? They'd be fine. What did you do?''

''Just a splinter.'' She was trying to pluck it out, but it was jammed in.

''I want the money, Julia. Roger's been talking to a lawyer, and he says there are ways . . .''

''Ve have vays to make you cooperate,'' Julia recited, a bad imitation of a Hollywood villain. ''Sharp splinters and tedious attorneys.''

''I don't want it to come to that. I've gone along with this summer thing. For you, for Gramma. But I do want the money, and I won't apologize for that.''

Julia puffed her cheeks and blew a long sigh. At first she'd dutifully backed away every time the thought of keeping the place had entered her head. It wasn't sensible. Not for a social worker and a chef turned store clerk, certainly not in the face of a multimillion-dollar offer. But the thought of turning the ranch into a pile of cash was turning her off, more and more, turning her stomach when she pictured the High Horse sign coming down and the Pollaks moving in. Yet Dawn had a say, and the money appeared to be the way to Roger's heart. So if that was her destination . . . Roger *was* her husband.

K.C. was just passing through. *Just passing through.* His

ideas were purely speculative, a few fanciful *what ifs* off the top of his head.

"I was just saying, what if we decided to give it a try?" she said gently, very gently. "Maybe we could find a way to make it pay. Maybe it's worth more than four and a half million dollars."

"If we can get more, fine. But please, Julia, let's not screw around and end up with less."

22

K.C. *had a dream about following the bachelor* band. He woke just before daybreak, a mourning dove coo-coo-cooing outside his window, and his first conscious thought was that he was alone again. He snaked his hand across the bed, hoping he was wrong, but it came up empty. He grabbed the other feather pillow, pulled it beneath him, tucked it under his chin. He could smell her in the pillow-case, or maybe it was the two of them together. Wildflowers and horse sweat.

An odd, melancholy feeling lingered in his head, something left over from the dream of following the unmated mustangs, watching them wade into the creek and help themselves to a cool drink. Just watching them made him thirsty, and he could almost taste the water, almost feel it lapping around his ankles.

But when they moved on, he moved, too, following at a distance. If he stopped to drink, he'd lose them. They wouldn't wait, didn't even know he was there and, of course, didn't care. All he seemed to be able to do was travel. He couldn't quite catch up.

Couldn't seem to catch up with the chores this week, either, which he was beginning to realize was the nature of his job. He had Donnie and Chad working with him this morning, putting in fence. The rest of the boys were busy with their morning assignments, too, which generally didn't involve saddles or horses, which made him wonder what

Paco was up to when he emerged from the barn carrying a saddle.

"Hold on there, hot foot." Paco froze in his tracks. "Did you draw some detail I haven't heard about?"

"I was just gonna do something." Paco planted a booted toe in the dirt and pivoted smartly. "Clean up this saddle a little bit for, uh . . ." He read the doubt on K.C.'s face and hung his head. "I wanted to try . . . I wanted to show you something."

"With a saddle?"

"It's my turn to go up and ride the summer pasture with you this week. Brad and Leighton got to go last week. Everybody's gone up there with you now but me."

"Chad's horse is ready for some trail work. He gets to go because his horse is ready. I ain't playin' favorites. I got a job to do." K.C. gave a "bring-it-on-back" nod, a little smile. "Your foal's doing fine, but it's a little too soon for a saddle, Paco."

The boy's mouth became a hard line. "I ain't stupid. I wasn't gonna use it on the foal."

"You're not the only one who ain't stupid," K.C. said calmly. "You weren't gonna clean it up, either."

The face-off fizzled. Paco was dragging his boots, head flopped to one side. "I can ride, K.C. I'm gettin' a lot better."

"I know you are, but our agreement is that you don't come around the horses unless I'm there." K.C. laid a hand on the boy's shoulder and walked with him, ushering him from the sunny corral into the barn. "What's your job this morning?"

"I'm supposed to be workin' in the yard, but I finished hoeing around the flowers, and there's some duded-up guy talkin' to Julia." Paco clomped across the plank floor and heaved the saddle back onto its wall rack. "I'm scheduled to be released next spring. Did I tell you?"

But the last thing K.C. had heard was the mention of Julia. "Who's the dude, do you know?"

"Looks like a TV weatherman. Are you guys gonna have the summer program next year?"

"We're just trying it out this year. Let's see how it turns out." He frowned. "Weatherman?"

"Car salesman, maybe." Paco shrugged. " 'Cause when my time's up, I'll probably be going home, to wherever my mom's living then. We got relatives in different places. I'll probably try to get a job. You think you guys would have a job for me here?"

"I don't . . ." The look in the boy's eyes brought him up short, and he thought, *Ah, jeez, pay attention, Houston.* For this was something new. He could remember being in Paco's boots plenty of times, a kid looking for a job, but he'd never been the one getting asked. *Damn.* "I don't know, Paco."

"My mom's a farm worker. She likes to come up north in the late summer and fall. Like North Dakota. There's work there in the fall, and she says there's not as much crime there. So that's not too far away."

Paco sat down on an old trunk-style locker that K.C. had cleaned out and put to use as his horse medicine chest. He'd gotten after the boys for sitting on it before, but not this time. Paco looked up at him, and the box was suddenly a confessional. "I got into trouble for shoplifting. And for skipping school a lot, and for running away. Ran all the way to L.A. last time."

"What did you do in L.A.?"

"Got picked up stealing some tennis shoes." He paused. "Fourteen pair."

"How'd you end up in Wyoming?"

"My mom was staying in Casper for a while, but she ain't there now. I got an uncle in Casper. That's why this would be a good place for me to work next summer. I can do a lot of stuff now. Shep says . . ."

K.C. nodded, signaled "Whoa" to him. "Did you water the flowers? The garden?"

"No. She just told me to loosen up the dirt and get rid of—"

"You notice she usually waters in the morning? She gets busy with something else, and you see something needs doing—not something you've been told not to do, but something you know is okay—you go ahead and take care of it. That's the way you get to be a good hand. You make yourself useful without being told." He lifted a brow. "You think she's talking to a car salesman?"

"I said he *looks* like one. Acts like one, too. Like he's gonna be doing you a big favor if he takes your money for some piece of junk he's trying to unload." Paco heaved himself off the trunk. "Only I think he's lookin' to buy."

"Lookin' to buy, huh?" K.C. clapped a hand on the boy's shoulder. "Let's go turn that water on before it gets too hot."

"I can do it." Paco looked at K.C. with a conspirator's smile. "Or you wanna head on over there with me, I can show you where the faucet is."

Julia introduced Tom Lomak as Chuck Pollak's attorney. K.C. had a deep and abiding dislike for attorneys of any kind, but attorneys who looked and talked like TV weathermen—Paco was dead on target with his description— were especially noxious. The people who'd sued him had hired one who was more like a newscaster. Had all the facts. By the time the guy had dragged K.C.'s ass over the coals, he was almost convinced that he was as stupid and careless as he'd been portrayed.

But Julia was fixing to let this vulture wander around on her property. "I don't think there's any harm in letting Tom take some water samples," she was telling him, and with a look she invited K.C. to say otherwise.

He adjusted his hat and glanced away.

"I guess Chuck's champing at the bit to start the paperwork to finance his offer for the High Horse," she said.

"Crops are coming in pretty good," K.C said. "Water must be okay."

Lomak jumped right in. "It's just a formality. The bank's interested in water, soil. I'd like to take a few soil samples, too. I promise not to disturb anything." And just to show how discriminating he was, he added, "Beautiful flowers, Julia. You must have hauled in truckload after truckload of topsoil."

"My mother took over the yard when she lived here. This is what's left of her efforts. I think I'd do more with native plants. A rock garden over there in that sunny corner would be fabulous.'' She glanced at K.C., pointed. "Over there. Nothing else wants to grow there. I could see some yucca, some sedum, columbine, maybe some wallflower.'' She smiled. "Those yellow flowers, remember?''

Forget the damn weatherman. "I know where to find some. You want me to dig them up?''

"Oh, no, we wouldn't want to disturb them. We'd get seeds.''

K.C. felt a little hurt, like a kid who'd just had his hand slapped.

"It's a good idea to take some of the plants with you when you move,'' Lomak put in. "Helps with the transition. Of course, a nice fat check helps even more.''

Julia folded her arms. She was still picturing flowers in the corner of the yard. "We might not be interested in selling any more than my sister's share.''

"Which share is that?'' Lomak asked, but he wasn't interested in her answer. He had his own. "It's pretty hard to work something like that out in a situation like this. What we're most interested in—'' He caught himself, sawed on the reins and backed up. K.C. wondered who this coyote thought he was fooling. "What *Chuck* is most interested in is probably the same share you'd want to keep, the share that's most livable. If you took that out, it would change the offer considerably.''

"Chuck doesn't need the home place. He would want some of the permits and leases, some of the grazing land. I might be able to do without a lot of the farmland.'' Julia shrugged. "Everybody's downsizing, right?''

"Our offer wouldn't be nearly as good. If you took out the river valley, say, the deal would go from making you rich to just . . .'' Lomak shrugged, too. "Just another land sale that pays off the taxes and gives you a little something to spend. I've seen a lot of these situations, and believe me, the best thing for the whole family is to sell everything and divide the money. It's much easier to divide money than land. You just split it up and go on your merry way.''

"There are many more considerations than I realized,'' Julia said.

"Such as?" Lomak peered at her, becoming downright intrusive now. "The old people? You're thinking about the old people now, right?" He was about to touch Julia's shoulder, but he caught the warning in K.C.'s eyes and let his hand drop to his side. "They're working themselves too hard, Julia. There comes a time when they've earned their rest, but they don't take it because they feel guilty sitting around. So they just keep working. Am I right? Grandma's still working because she doesn't know when to quit, God love her."

"Who do you work for, Tom?" K.C. adjusted his hat, a habitual gesture that facilitated a subtle shift in his position, putting him between Julia and Mr. Sunshine. He liked this better. He smiled. "You mind if I call you Tom?"

"Not at all, no, my—"

"Who do you work for, Tom?"

"I'm Chuck Pollak's attorney."

"Who else do you represent? You got a developer in on this deal?" Lomak colored up considerably. K.C. kept smiling. "Maybe you're a partner in it yourself."

"Chuck's interested in expanding his operation," Lomak insisted.

"I'll just bet he is. Where's the money coming from?"

"It doesn't really make much difference, does it? We're making a legitimate offer on a piece of land."

"A prime piece of land. Hasn't been touched yet, really. Colorado's overrun with your kind. You've got a choke hold on Montana. Just west of these mountains lies Jackson and Yellowstone. You see what's happening there?" K.C. speared a finger in the direction of Painted Mountain.

Everybody looked, but nobody answered.

Except K.C. "I have. I get around. I see plenty. Who else is interested? Where you gonna put the golf course, Tom? How many acres to a home site?"

"Chuck Pollak is a rancher, just like the Weslins."

"I don't think so. Ain't many left like the Weslins." K.C. turned to his boss. "You want him taking soil and water samples, I'll go with him, Julia. Otherwise, I can see him to the gate."

Julia shook her head. "I'm not ready to entertain any

offers, Tom. If I give you permission to take pieces of the High Horse, it might be misconstrued." She glanced at K.C., then smiled graciously at Lomak. "I have your card. I'll let you know when we're ready to look at Chuck's offer."

"*You* will, ma'am? Or your hired hand?"

"K.C. is our foreman. My grandmother values his judgment. And so do I."

23

Sally loved to put up hay. Max used to tease her about being his little farm girl. The Harrises were ranchers, she'd reminded him. Maybe the Weslins were farmers, but not the Harrises. He always gave her first choice of driving the mower or the rake, and she'd always take the mower. He said it was because she liked to drive the tractor, but she knew he loved to hitch up the Belgians to the rake. That was why she chose the mower.

Now she used a pull-type swather behind the 4010, the last tractor Max had bought before his death. Thanks to Shep, it still ran like a top, and the swather cut and crimped the alfalfa, raked and wind-rowed it into neat green ribbons, all in one fell swoop.

Vernon plied the fields behind her with the bailer. She could see him each time he made a round in the field above her, the one they called the upper shelf. He'd tried to get her to operate the 4020 because it had a cab, but Vernon had had patches of skin cancer removed from his dear, leathery face twice already. She told him she wanted the air on her face. She wore a hat, a long-sleeved shirt, a big old pair of men's work gloves, sunscreen, the whole suit of armor. She had the air on her face, and Vernon was sheltered from the sun.

For the first time in years they had decided to put up the first cutting themselves rather than hire a contract crew. The boys in the summer program were turning into good and

313

willing hands. When it came time for the second cutting, they would see. She was taking one step at a time this summer. Find one foothold at a time, then look for a handhold. Just like the year she'd met Max.

The summer program was a foothold. K.C. Houston was a handhold. The horses had sparked their interest. The boys in the program and K.C., like Ross and Max, had been bewitched by those horses. Their wildness worked wonders for men with wild hearts. That wildness was worth saving and sheltering, and Sally firmly believed that it took a woman to do that. One foothold, one handhold at a time.

Lord, it was good to be able to drive a tractor, do a day's work, put up the feed her girls would need when the seasons changed. She kept one eye on the fence posts at the end of the row in the making and the other on the machine behind her, the tractor's power takeoff, which drove the sickle and the propeller, and the shaft connecting the two. Her third eye was driven by her heart, her own power takeoff. Her third eye was her focus on Vernon, the precious routine of noting each time his orbit brought him closest to hers. She couldn't really see anything but his silhouette in the tractor cab, but she knew the look on his face better than her own. She knew he was looking out for her each time he took that turn. It felt good, just knowing he was there.

He was headed for the far end of the upper shelf when she hit a rough patch, turned to check her equipment and noticed the grass wrapped around the PTO shaft. A routine tangle. Didn't look too bad. Her head was full of dreams when she idled the tractor down and climbed to the ground, half expecting the green rope to give way before she got to it. But it didn't. She should have shut the engine off. She thought about getting back up there, but it was just one long bunch, its crimped ends waving at her as they spun around. Easy to snatch out.

It was as if she were watching someone else make the mistake. Sally Weslin was not stupid enough to grab for the grass once, miss—damn her aging reflexes—then try for it again. The spinning shaft grabbed the floppy fingers of her glove, just like more grass. It happened in an instant, but for Sally it played itself out in slow motion, like a movie she'd seen before. She was no fit arm-wrestling opponent for the machine. A hand she could not control was tied up in a knot within a glove she should not have been wearing.

She heard the crack and thought it sounded like a tree limb. She felt the shredding of brittle bones and dry cords. She heard the roar of her outrage mix with that of the machinery, then outstrip it as the machine died. The pressure of the clog killed the tractor engine. She was the clog.

The only spinning left was the maelstrom in her head. The only roaring, besides the distant hum on the upper shelf, was the last of her outrage giving way to the first of her agony. The glove was still caught, and her twisted arm was trapped in a tug-of-war between the unmoving PTO shaft and her own trembling body. She was dizzy with shock. For the moment, blessedly numb. She executed a slow, dreamlike dance, turning, unwinding, loosening the pressure. But she was stuck. Jammed up, as Julia's boys said, and Sally almost laughed. Her jam-up was literal. She had to get herself out of the glove. The trouble was, the glove might well be all that was holding her hand together.

She heard the pickup before she could actually make it out amid the black spots swirling in front of her eyes. Finally, there it was—oh, blessed sight—Vernon's red pickup barreling across the field, mashing all her green-grass ribbons. The door flew open, and he leaped to the ground with the agility of a thirty-year-old man. Well, fifty, maybe. He ran the short distance like a cowboy—loose-kneed, toes turned out, arms flapping like a chicken's wings. He needed four legs under him for a graceful run.

Their eyes met and he nodded—yes, she was alive, conscious, safe now—said nothing as his focus shifted to the trouble. Her first thought was that he was bound to be upset with her for being so careless. Her second thought was that there was not a shred of truth in her first thought. She felt him going after the problem directly. She couldn't look, for she had nausea and the threat of a blackout to contend with right now, but she didn't have to look. She trusted him completely.

"Still with me, Sally?"

"Think I'm . . . still with the PTO."

"I'm just cuttin' the glove."

"My fingers?"

"We'll count 'em later. If we come up short, we'll know where to come lookin'."

Somebody laughed. Some hysterical old lady. Sally was pretty sure it was she. By the time she'd gotten it out of her system, he had her free.

"Can you move it?"

Move what? She looked down and saw the arm—the one that still appeared to be attached to her shoulder—wrapped in Vernon's shirt and cradled in her own lap. There was blood. There was awful, awful pain. There was Vernon, hovering over her.

"You can't be out in the sun without a shirt, old man."

"You can't be givin' me orders just now, woman." He tucked her good arm under the injured one. "Can you hold it?"

"Just like a baby." Neither of them wanted to name the hand or the arm straight out. Fingers were small appendages, but a broken limb could be a disaster at Sally's age.

"Can you walk?"

"A little light-headed, is all. Brain musta fallen out when I hit . . ." She was rising to her feet now. His arms were under her, and he was peeling her off the ground. "When I hit that last dip. Damn, I *know* better."

"You hate to shut down if it's just a little tangle," he allowed. Her legs gave out, but he caught her against his side. "Steady, girl. I've got you, Sally."

He got his arms around her, lifted her off the ground and started toward the pickup. She had a wild vision of how silly they must look. "Put me down. You'll be breaking something next."

"You're light as a feather. I could carry you all the way to town on my back. I swear I could."

"Or die trying," she said.

"Wouldn't die before I got you there."

*   *   *

K.C. was getting ready to mount up and ride out to chase down a bull that had walked through the fence when he heard Julia call his name. He turned, ready to enjoy the unexpected sight of her, but her ashen face and worried eyes changed all that. He reached out to catch her as she ran up to him.

"Please," she said, her chest heaving. "Take over for me. Some of the boys are with Shep—machine shop—I had Leighton, Barney—Paco—just start them early on—"

"What's goin' on?"

"Vern called. Gramma's hurt. He took her right to the clinic, but they have to . . . needs surgery, and they can't—can't . . ."

Sally? *Hurt?* He felt as though he'd just had the wind knocked out of him. "Where will you be?"

"Cody. The phone number's on my desk."

"Where's . . ." He glanced at the pickup she'd left running a few yards away. "Take your sister with you."

"I don't have time to—"

He looped Columbine's reins around the corral rail with a fast half hitch and walked Julia to the pickup. He wanted to go with her himself, but he knew where he was needed most. "You and Dawn see to your grandmother. Shep and me, we'll take care of things here. How bad is it?"

"I don't know. Something about getting hung up in the PTO when she was—"

Three letters explained it all. The invaluable, insidious PTO. "Go. Now. I'll be here."

"I think Dawn's got dinner . . ."

"Get in." He took the driver's side. "We'll make sure she turns the stove off," he said as he arced the wheel for a U-turn. "I'll feed the boys. Will you call me when you know how she is?"

Julia called at suppertime to say that the air ambulance had taken them to Billings, that Sally was in surgery. Vern was there, too; he had driven his pickup from Cody. She called at dinnertime the following day to report that Sally was having more surgery, had been in there for four hours, and it still wasn't over.

"She's scared, K.C. She could still lose her hand. Broke every bone . . . do you know how many bones there are in your hand? I think she broke every one."

He closed his eyes and swallowed hard, but the sick feeling wouldn't go away. He loved that old woman. He loved the voice at the other end of the line. Hell, come right down to it, he loved all three Weslin women, each in a different way. He should have been on that tractor himself. Sally . . .

"K.C.?"

"I'm here."

"Will you take care of—"

"Everything. Jack stayed to help today. We had the boys out in the field this morning. Shep's making sure we keep the kitchen straight. You tell Sally we'll be checking on her girls tomorrow."

"I will." Julia's voice sounded small and unsure. "At her age, the bones don't heal as well."

He nodded.

"K.C.?"

"I know. Tell her I . . ." *Tell her what? She's in surgery. Tell it to Julia. You love her. You love them all.* So how would that change anything? "Tell her I won't let her down."

"She knows."

"Tell her anyway. If she thinks of anything I ought to be doing . . . if you think of anything, you call me."

Silence.

Let her go now. She's got stuff to take care of.

He gripped the receiver. He could have sworn she was crying.

Small, girlish voice. "Stay at the house, okay?"

"Okay."

"In my room. My bed." Pause. "Okay?"

"Yeah."

"Because . . . for the phone and for . . . security, I guess."

"Security."

"K.C., do you think we could . . ."

Maybe she didn't want to let him go, either. "We could what?"

"I was thinking, if we wanted to breed for fall calves—
Oh, they're taking her into the recovery room now. I'll call
tonight."

Sally hated being laid up. She hated that sorrowful look
she kept seeing in Vernon's eyes, like he was sitting beside
her coffin instead of her hospital bed, and she hated being
tanked up on painkillers. She especially hated getting flowers. The windowsill was lined with them. How in the hell
had Chuck Pollak and his pointy-nosed lawyer found out
about the moment of idiocy everybody insisted upon calling
her accident? She hoped the girls were enjoying the sweet-
smelling things, because as far as Sally was concerned,
those damned lilies were meant for a wake.

She nearly said as much when Dawn came in the door
with two more vases.

"Gramma, look, these are from Mama. These are from
Roger."

Both roses. Better than lilies.

"Did I make CNN?"

"I called them, of course," Dawn said as she set Roger's
roses on the bedside table and Fay's on the TV. "I had a
lot of time to kill while you were in surgery. Roger was
thinking of coming out anyway, so he's making arrangements, and he'll be here—"

"Roger's coming here?"

"He was thinking of coming anyway," Dawn repeated.
Then, as though someone doubted her, "Well, he misses
me."

"He missed out on your brother's funeral," Sally said.
She had to talk just to stay awake. She'd slept enough.
Almost two days, they said. She felt like a trussed-up turkey
with her arm splinted and elevated. They'd been checking
it every so often for signs of life, and she was afraid that
if she went to sleep she'd wake up in a roaster.

"Roger doesn't like funerals," Dawn was saying. "He
just can't handle them. He doesn't even go to his own family's funerals."

"Guess I must be gonna live, then."

"He thought maybe he could help out. Mama said she'd

come, too, if you need her for anything, or if . . .''

"If there's a funeral. Fay does funerals just fine. She's got class, your mother. She grieves like royalty." Sally glanced at Julia, who often reminded her of Fay. It was not a comparison Julia particularly relished, but it was apt. "And she's known a lot of grief."

Julia rose from the chair she'd been warming and came to the bedside. Like Dawn, she was smiling. "We're not grieving tonight. Tonight we're celebrating. Right, Vern?"

He nodded. He hadn't said a word. He'd been sitting near the door like a stiff sentry.

Sally looked at him, tenderly, she hoped. She had no sense of her own face or fingers—her edges seemed frayed and numb—but she felt so tender toward him, she had to tease him a little merely to keep things in perspective. "Where are your flowers, Vernon?"

"Flowers?" He sounded like he just woke up. Looked it, too, standing slowly, hat in hand. "I been, uh . . ."

"Vern drove up from Cody, Gramma," Dawn said, raising her voice as though she thought Sally's hearing had been affected, too. "He's been here every minute. He was here with you all night last night. You probably don't remember because they had you so—"

"I knew he was here." She was still looking at him, remembering the expression in his eyes when he'd first gotten out of the pickup. All business. Ready to do whatever was necessary. Not like now. Now he looked like a scared little boy. Hospitals bothered him. People dressed in white and armed with needles scared the bejesus out of him.

She smiled. "Cowboys don't buy flowers, do they, Vernon?"

"I didn't think . . ." He was hoarse. The muscles in his face and throat started bobbing and twitching.

Damn, Sally thought, *he's getting choked up.* She lifted her good hand, palm up, in his direction. "Come on over here and give me a kiss to celebrate."

Vernon's boot heels scraped the floor as he moved to the bed. He made no attempt to discourage the silent tears she knew embarrassed him. He held onto that hat for dear life. Her hand fluttered, inviting him closer. He set his straw hat on her white-blanketed knees, sat down, leaned over her slowly, so slowly she almost grabbed him by his shirtfront. But she didn't. They had waited a long time, and this first kiss was his to give. He did it the way he did everything. Neatly and thoroughly. His tears tasted like living water.

When she could speak, she said, "You saved my life again, cowboy."

"I never saved your life," Vernon averred quietly, taking a quick swipe at his eyes with the back of an unsteady hand. "It's only a broken arm."

"You've kept me going for thirty years, since the day Max died." He looked surprised. "Don't tell me you didn't know that."

He wagged his head slowly, chuckling. "I wish you'd said something about twenty-nine years ago."

"You never said anything, either. But you're always there when I need you, which is every precious day."

Vernon got all choked up again, and Sally said, "I didn't mean to turn all sentimental here." She glanced at the IV stand next to the bed. "What's in that bottle, anyway?"

"Joy juice, most like," Vernon said.

"Truth serum," Dawn piped up through tears of her own. She grabbed a tissue from a box. "You two . . . you two . . ."

"We're just two old friends," Vernon said, patting Sally's good hand. "That's the best."

"Friends?" Dawn gave a blubbery laugh. "Looks like much more than friendship to me. C'mon, Gramma, fess up. All these years? What about . . . you know."

"I'm not about to discuss my personal *you know* with my granddaughters." Sally glanced from one to the other. Julia was still holding it together. Barely. Sally smiled. Joy juice, indeed. "Except to say that you're never too old."

"Oh, Julia, will you look at the color of that man's face?" Dawn said. "What would you call it? Range Rider Red?"

"Definitely a horseman of a different color. I like it even better than purple sage."

Vernon shook his head. "You girls are gettin' just a little too big for your britches. Your grandma had a close call.

Kinda feel like I'm lopin' along on the wrong lead here.''

Julia stepped up from the foot of the bed, put her hands on Vernon's shoulders and smiled at her grandmother. "Whenever you're ready to move into the master bedroom, I'll clean out the drawers.''

"Not me, no way. That ain't my place. That was Max's place." Vernon was patting hands today, and it was Julia's turn. "You girls decide to sell out, though, I'm takin' Sally in.''

"What about Shep?" Julia teased.

"He's about taken over my corner anyway. Think I'll let him have it and just build me a place across the road from him. That's still our land, ain't it?''

"Right you are," Sally said.

"They ain't buying me out." He looked at Sally. "I'm stickin'. That's all I know to do.''

K.C. was supervising the supper cleanup when Freddie called with the results of the blood tests on the mustangs. The bad news was that about a fourth of the horses appeared to be carriers of a cataract-causing gene. The good news was that the blindness would occur only if the sire and the dam both carried the gene.

"That leaves us with the question of whether, if left alone, the healthy horses would survive, the others die, and the gene would eventually be bred out. Or whether the mutation would eventually take over and lead to the demise of the herd. Or whether these adaptive behaviors would succeed in creating a whole different kind of herd. Or—''

"Whoa, girl." Chevy was showing him a pan and asking where it went. K.C. shrugged and mouthed, *Anywhere.* "Can we see these reports?"

"Of course," was the answer at the other end of the line.

"Will we—will I be able to make any sense out of them?"

"Oh, yes. Well, most of it. Some of it even I have trouble with, but I'm no genetic researcher, either. I'll send you what I have here, complete with my own personal notes in all the margins. How's Julia?"

He told her about Sally's accident.

"So I'm here holdin' down the fort," he concluded, and that much of his report made him feel good. He switched the receiver to his other ear, turned his back on the boys and eased into the hallway. "I gotta tell you, Freddie, I'm a little nervous about handling these kids without her around. I'm afraid . . . well, somebody might get hurt."

"Those boys are nearly adults. Look at Sally, K.C.; adults sometimes get hurt. You can't—" She sighed. "Listen, K.C., from what I saw, you've got a good thing going there. Those boys are doing fine. You're doing fine. Are all the premiums paid up?"

"Yeah, I guess." He groaned. He hadn't asked. He'd never thought to ask. "Hell, I don't know about premiums. I know I've paid a lot of dues."

"That you have. You've got some benefits coming, K.C. Some dividends. You and Julia are good together."

"How would you know?"

"We took a trip to the little ewe's room, for heaven's sake."

"You used a little *what*?"

"Never mind, dear heart, just take a woman's word for it. I know what I see. Give her a reason not to give that place up, K.C."

"She's got about twenty-five thousand beautiful acres' worth of reasons."

"All she needs is one good cowboy."

"Last thing a smart woman needs," he muttered.

"That's not what you told me seven years ago when you fixed me up with Nick. I have enormous confidence in you, K.C. I could tell that Julia was very interested in my suggestion that she consider letting me study the herd." Pause. "I have immense confidence in you, K.C. Titanic confidence."

He laughed. "What kind of confidence, Freddie? Is Nick there? Is he getting an earful of this?"

"He's scowling, as usual, but deep down he knows I'm right." *Down where?* came the protest in the background, and K.C. laughed again. "I'm getting ready to apply for a grant, and I'm hoping I can use it to study the Painted Mountain mustangs."

"You're applying for a grant, and Chuck Pollak's applying for a loan. You guys got big plans."

"*Gargantuan* confidence in you, K.C., because . . ." Another pregnant pause from the all-knowing female. "I think you've found what you've been searching for."

"You are so full of romantic bullshit, Freddie. Do you know what four and a half million dollars looks like stacked up against a cowboy hat?"

"Just keep the hat on your head, cowboy. And call me after you've had a chance to look at these results. You and Julia, hmm?"

"Me and Julia."

Him and Julia. It made no sense, but the thought sure made his chest ache. He didn't mind the feeling at all. It was a hell of a lot better than the hollow feeling he'd been experiencing in his gut every time he thought about moving on at the end of the summer. He should probably start putting out some of those damn feelers to get a sense of what was out there, who was looking for what kind of training and how much it was worth to them. How much he was worth. K.C. Houston on the hoof. What would they bid?

The idea of moving on had never been less appealing, never looked more dismal to him from where he sat, which was perched on a corral he'd rebuilt, flanked by former outlaws who had just ridden colts he'd helped them gentle, watching another former outlaw longe a former wild stud cold who was bound to become an endurance trial competitor. Moving on sounded like a curse right about now. It sounded like a cold wind whistling through the keyhole on the door to a rented room, eighteen-wheelers passing by in the night, an unfamiliar dee-jay signing off through the static on a tinny radio.

He didn't want to think about it. He wanted to think about saving Ross Weslin's wild horses. He wanted to think about hiring a kid instead of being the kid desperate for a job, always carrying that kid inside, always one step away from the highway. He wanted to think of himself as the foreman of the High Horse without any qualifications, without any time limits. He wanted to be able to look forward to next year for a change.

He wanted to believe in *him and Julia*.

He worked with the horses for a while after the boys left, saddled the black mare and drove her from the ground in the round pen. When it was dark, he went back to the quiet house, showered in Julia's bathroom and dried himself on her towels. Then he crawled between the cool sheets on her bed, surrounding himself with the suggestion of her. For security.

God, for satisfaction. For sustenance and salvation. For the mere scent of her, sense of her, the wish for some contact, and not simply with someone, anyone, as so often had been his circumstance, but with—

The phone rang.

"Hello?"

"Hello, K.C."

Prayer answered. Wish granted.

He rolled onto his back and smiled in the dark. "How're you doin'?"

"Gramma's going to be fine, just fine. Her arm was pretty badly damaged, and the surgery was pretty extensive, so it'll be a while before we know whether she'll have full use of her hand, but, oh, K.C., she's an incredible woman. And Vernon has stayed by her side . . . we couldn't pry him away. They finally put a big chair in her room so he'd get some sleep. He's so—you were right, of course. He loves her so much. I don't know why I didn't—"

"How are *you*, Julia?"

"Fine. Tired." She sighed. "Relieved."

"Me, too."

"Where are you?"

"I'm in your house, in your room, in your bed. When I turn my face into the pillow, I can smell your hair. Where are you?"

"I'm in a motel room."

"Are you alone?"

"For the moment. Dawn went to call Roger. Obviously didn't want me in the room."

"You don't want her in the room, either. Not when we're in bed."

"We're not in the same bed."

"I'm in your bed with your scent and the sound of your voice. Turn the light out and let me touch you with my voice."

"Will you sing to me?" There was a smile in her voice, too.

"I'll do anything you want me to."

"I want you to sing to me and touch me with your hands, the way you do the horses."

"Where do you want me to touch you?"

"Just . . . on my belly."

"Put my hand there for me." He closed his eyes and imagined her little seashell of a navel. "Is it there?" She gave him a soft affirmative sound. "Tell me where."

"Kind of low. Where I wish . . ."

"You wish what?"

"Sometimes I wish for a baby in this cradle I'm . . . you're touching. Would you . . ."

He waited as long as he could. "Would I what, darlin'?"

"Lay your head in my lap and sing?"

"If I could put my head in your lap right now, I'd make music for you with my tongue. Move my hand down lower so I can show you where I would . . ." He slid his hand between his own legs. "Where I would place my mouth, and how I would find the frets and gently press them and—"

"Your mouth?"

"That's right, darlin'."

"Frets are part of a guitar."

"Do I have you fretting yet?"

"Yes."

"You gonna let me play it my way?"

"Yes."

"Is my hand wet?"

"Yes."

He closed his eyes. "Oh, God, I miss you, darlin'."

"I'll be home tomorrow. Stay right where you are, okay?"

"I won't go far. Got a few chores to do."

Like washing her bed sheets.

24

Roger Morton brought more flowers.

He waited until Sally was ready to come home from the hospital before flying out to Wyoming. No one, not even Dawn, believed he would be of any use at the High Horse, but he did a lot of posturing, taking charge of the return of the important people, acting like *the man* of the family now that he was on the premises. The master of the plantation, complete with white slacks and cigar. K.C. half expected him to take a stroll around the yard and lift his leg on every tree.

Not that Roger didn't seem friendly enough as he supervised the unloading of the car he'd rented and shepherded the Weslin women into the house. Nice-looking guy, trim, beachboy tan. Wore clean, shiny shoes and a fancy watch. He bestowed plenty of smiles, laughed pretty much on cue, but his face was nearly wrinkle-free. His smile came strictly from his mouth.

Dawn sure seemed glad to see her husband. Glad for everybody else to see him, see that he was there now. A little late, but he had a lot of irons in the fire. Roger was a busy man, and now Dawn had someone with her. K.C. tried not to remember that same look on his mother's face when she was showing off some guy, acting like he really cared about her.

Julia was pretty quiet during supper, which Dawn and Roger had managed to whip up after they'd all pulled in from Billings. Her pleasure at seeing K.C. was quieter, just between them, but he felt it, and he stowed it away inside himself. After supper, Sally said she was tired, which left Julia to have coffee with Dawn and Roger. With her eyes she asked K.C. not to leave her with them. He accepted the coffee and the seat beside her on the porch glider.

It wasn't long before Vern came through the front door, put on his hat, gave the porch group a nod. He'd followed Sally to the living room after supper, like the suitor courting in the parlor. "We were lookin' at some old pictures she didn't know I had, and she fell asleep on me again," he reported. "She doesn't say so, but I know her arm hurts like the devil unless she takes those pain pills, which she don't like to do. You get to be our age, you don't like to sleep too much."

"Come sit with us, Vernon," Julia said. There was long-day weariness in her voice, too. "Roger was just telling us about his plans to open a new restaurant."

"I think I'll mosey on back and make sure Shep ain't trying to put that old washing machine he drug home into my side of the cabin. You see that thing he picked up?" Julia smiled and shook her head. "Turn my back on him for a day or two, and he's . . . Did you send him to town for something, K.C.?"

"Had him pick up the mail. Said he needed dog chow anyway."

"Dog chow," Vern spat. "Don't know what in the name of heaven he wants with an old wringer washer." He turned to take one last peek through the living room window. He'd lowered one of the table lamps to its dimmest setting. "She's not one for sleepin' on the sofa, but I hate to wake her."

"We'll get Grandma to bed," Roger said. "We'll see that she's comfortable and pain-free."

"Don't try to make her take anything she don't want. She knows what she needs and what she don't need."

"It's all right if you stay with her, Vern," Julia said. "Really."

"Now, that wouldn't be proper and you know it,

Queenie.'' He tipped his hat. ''See you round the next bend.''

Roger waited until Vernon was halfway across the yard before shifting in his chair, leaning toward the group with some particular confidence. ''You think she'd want to come to Connecticut? We've got room. Haven't we, honey? We can fix up a room for her and get a nursing service to come in weekly or even daily, depending on—''

''Nursing service?'' Julia said.

K.C. scowled. ''For Sally?''

''Those injuries are serious. You know how doctors are when they give their prognosis. You've got to read between the lines. She probably won't recover the use of that arm. We'd want to make sure her medical needs are met. And when the time comes, there's a fine nursing home not far from—''

Even Dawn was doubtful. ''Roger, Gramma doesn't need a nursing home, and there's no way we could get her to move to Connecticut.''

''I just wanted you to know that I'm with you, however you decide to handle this.'' He leaned back and looked at K.C., man to man. ''She's a grand old lady, isn't she?''

''Sally's quite a woman. The High Horse is a helluva piece of work, too.''

''I'll say.'' Roger glanced at his wife. ''When do I get to meet this prospective buyer?''

''Well, I—''

''I don't think we're going to take the Pollaks up on their offer, Roger,'' Julia said flatly.

He looked at Julia, then at Dawn, then back to Julia. ''You think you can get more?''

''I'm not ready to sell out.''

There was no hesitation. K.C. wanted to give her something, then and there. His hand, maybe. But he held off until she looked at him, and what he gave was a small nod, a look of support meant only for her.

Quickly, she added, ''We think Chuck might have some kind of a sweetheart deal in the works to subdivide the property.''

Dawn said, ''We do?''

Roger was pensive. "You think he's working with a developer?"

"He's offering a lot of money."

"You think we should cut out the middleman," Roger surmised. "If we knew who it was, we could take a straight shot at him ourselves. Or we could look for somebody else, but that would take time. Dawn says you want to be out by fall."

"No, that's not exactly . . ." Julia set her coffee aside and turned to Roger, opening her hands as though they held some insight, some way that this man from the East might understand. "The High Horse is a family corporation. There hasn't been much in the way of dividends because . . ."

"You can say that again," Roger said.

"Because we've always understood that most of the profits go back into the operation. I think we could turn a profit. I think Dawn and I could come to some kind of an agreement whereby she would see some annual income."

"You're talking about trying to keep the place and run it yourself?"

"I'm talking about . . . *talking* about it. We haven't looked seriously at that option, and I think we should."

Roger fixed his reproach on Dawn. "You didn't say anything about this."

"I didn't—we haven't—"

"We've been feeling our way along here, and we haven't talked about it yet," Julia said. "But we will. Summer isn't over yet."

"I don't know about you, Julia, but Dawn's just about used up her time," Roger said.

"If I lose that job, I can always get another one. That doesn't worry me," Dawn said. "What does worry me is the risk of losing the Pollaks' offer on this place, Julia. Chuck says he's looking at other options."

"Let him. We're not going to be pushed. We're going to talk this over, just you, me and Gramma."

"We might want to add in an attorney," Roger said.

Dawn studied the small hands folded in her lap. "You, me and Gramma add up to two against one."

"It doesn't have to," Julia said gently, but Dawn would not look at her. "You and me, then. I think Gramma wants us to . . ."

"Your grandmother's competency can be challenged," Roger said. "I've already looked into that."

Now Dawn looked up. She said nothing, but the reproach in her eyes was directed at her husband.

"You're out of line on that one," K.C. said. He might not be a Weslin, but he was the foreman at the High Horse, and Sally was still his boss. He told Roger as much with a look no male animal could misinterpret.

"I'm looking after my wife's . . ." Roger tried, but he couldn't hold up his end of the face-off.

He shrugged, gave his mouth-only smile, sat back in his chair. "Sorry. I didn't mean to get anybody's back up here. Let's go back to where we were having a pleasant conversation about the horse-training business. So, you actually end up doing a lot of traveling in your line of work, which is just the way you imagine it when you think of a cowboy's life. Man, I'll tell you what, us Eastern dudes can only dream, but here you are, living the life. Riding off into the sunset, leaving those well-trained horses in the hands of satisfied customers." Another quick, humorless smile. "Must be nice."

"Sure is. I still have some work I wanna get done this evening." K.C. looked at Julia, wishing he could pry her away. If he suggested she come look at a horse, they'd all want to see the horse. "Unless you've got something you want me to do."

"Some things I'd like to talk about. Plans for next week," Julia said.

"I'll be down to the corrals."

"I want to make sure Gramma gets tucked in when she's ready, so . . ."

"I'll check back in later."

She nodded, her eyes giving thanks. "I ought to have a phone put in the barn."

He smiled. "That'd be real handy."

*   *   *

Julia could hear the shower running upstairs as she closed the door to Sally's room. She was surprised to find Roger alone in the living room. More surprising, he was hunched over a bottle of Sally's medication, holding it under the lamplight, scrutinizing the label.

He looked up, straightened, smiled easily. "She left this on the table here. Pretty powerful stuff. You probably don't wanna leave it lying around."

"It has a childproof cap, Roger."

"Which means she can't get into it without help." He moved toward her, gesturing with the bottle. "Why do they do that, anyway? Here you have an elderly woman, no kids around . . ."

Julia was tired. She'd used up her patience with this man. She tried to remember what it felt like to be attracted to him—she knew she had been once—but she'd obviously used up her imagination for the day, too.

"What are you doing here, Roger?"

Still smiling, he handed her the bottle. "I'm not trying to steal Granny's painkillers."

"I mean, *why* are you here? I won't be forced, pushed or otherwise pressured into making any hasty decisions. You know that. So why are you here?"

"Yeah, I know you, Julia. I know you." He gave her a loaded look. She let it roll to the floor. He shrugged. "I'm here because I haven't seen my wife in almost—God, what's it been now? Over two months? A helluva long time for us to be apart." He seated himself in a big leather chair. "Has she missed me?"

"That's for her to say. I'm not holding her here. She's here because she wants to be."

"She's here looking out for . . ." He was on his feet again, focused on the staircase as if Scarlett O'Hara were making her entrance. "Ah, speak of my angel . . ."

"That's a new one, Roger." Dawn was dressed in a pretty white cotton nightgown and a duster with a tucked yoke. Her hair was shiny and wet, her face naturally sweet. " 'My angel' is definitely a new one."

Sometimes, Julia thought, her sister was easily an angel. "He should know, though; he's your husband."

"Yes, he is." Dawn took her husband by the arm. "Let's go for a walk, honey. One thing you have to say about Wyoming, the night sky is positively breathtaking."

"Yeah, well, they've got no city lights." Roger laughed. "Which means, no city."

K.C. had said he'd check back in later, but he'd hoped Julia would come down to the corral. When she didn't, he headed up to the house to keep his promise. If Sally was settled in for the night, maybe he and Julia could take a walk. He was none too comfortable being around Dawn's husband.

At first he thought the voices he heard were coming from the house, but, typical of sounds on a summer night, the direction was misleading. He couldn't see anyone, though he smelled cigar smoke. Had to be Roger and Dawn, tucked back on the other side of the machine shed, having a little set-to in the dark. K.C. was prepared to keep on walking, but Roger . . . well, Roger had a big mouth.

"Look, all I'm saying is, she can't hope to run this place without him, now, can she? Those two old guys and a woman who's ready for Nursingdale are not—"

"She's got those boys from the reform school pitching in like experienced ranch hands now."

"Yeah, well, that's another thing. Julia's always had her profession keeping her busy in the cities, and now she's dragging that whole thing out here with her. I mean, she could easily put the screws to all our dreams if she decides—"

"She won't. I don't see how she can."

"If that cowboy stays around, she can. She's got the hots for him, hasn't she?"

No response.

"All this time, nobody's ever been good enough for the queen bee," Roger said. "She finally decides to loosen up a little, and wouldn't you know she'd pick somebody like that?"

"Like what?"

"Somebody who goes to work in blue jeans, for crissake.

I mean, Julia's always had a sort of tight-assed class about her, but out here . . .''

Dawn groaned with disgust.

"Now, if she thought he was screwing around with someone else, you can bet she wouldn't keep him around long."

"They really like each other, Roger. They might—"

"Of course he likes her. She's just inherited half of a ranch that's worth four and a half million dollars."

"So have I."

"And we want the money, not the ranch."

K.C. shook his head. He was about to move on, didn't much care whether they saw him or not, when Roger dropped the bombshell.

"You could separate Julia from her summertime lover without breaking a sweat, Dawn. You've done it before."

"I have not."

"Come off it, honey; you turned my head so fast, you put me in a tailspin. And I've never looked back."

"Yeah, right."

"All you'd have to do is let her catch the two of you in a compromising situation. This place will be up for sale so fast—"

"How compromising?" Dawn asked, and then, in a smaller voice, "How far should I go?"

"Whatever it takes. As far as you want to. It's not like you haven't—"

She tried to slap him, but she didn't connect. K.C. heard a whimper. A soft sound, a shattered-heart sound, and then the intake of breath. The sound that made him explode.

He got the drop on Roger from behind, hooked his right arm around the man's neck and used it as a vise. "Let her go, or I'll break you in half."

Dawn stumbled backward. The cigar hit the ground first, followed by the man, flung aside like a bale of dry hay. Red furor filled K.C.'s head as he lunged for the shadow that was scrambling at his feet like a cockroach, trying to get out of his way.

"K.C.!" Dawn grabbed his arm. "K.C., don't hurt him."

Don't hurt him. Damn. He'd heard that one before. He closed his eyes and fought for control.

"K.C., please!"

Roger was on his feet now. "I'm not a fighter, cowboy. I didn't do anything but stop her from hitting me."

K.C. said nothing.

"I'm okay, I'm okay," Roger was saying, as if anybody gave a damn. "I said something I shouldn't have said, but this is between me and my wife, cowboy."

"Go on in the house," K.C. told Dawn.

"You can't tell her—"

"Pick that thing up before it starts a fire."

"Listen, man." Roger stepped on the cigar, grinding it into the gravel as he spoke. "This is between me and my wife, and we've been married a long time. We understand each other. You need to back off before you get slapped with assault charges."

"Pick it up," K.C. repeated with measured calm. "Go in the house, Dawn."

"No, now . . . we're not going to have a fight here, guys." Dawn fluttered between them like a huge white dove, shooing first one, then the other. "I'm okay. He didn't hurt me. He wouldn't dare."

"I'm not leavin' you out here with him," K.C. told her, even though he knew damn well the dove would soon be welcoming the cockroach into her bed. So he suggested, "We'll all go inside as soon as Roger picks up his cigar. Out here we're real touchy about fire hazards." And when Dawn started to bend down, K.C. stopped her. "That's one of the things a man never puts on his wife," he said.

Roger picked up the butt, eased past K.C. and headed for the house. Dawn followed, with K.C. dogging her heels. Damn, he'd almost lost it again. He was anything but a violent man, and he always felt a little stupid after a scene like this one, like sobering up after a party you never wanted to go to in the first place. The worst kind for making an ass of yourself.

Roger disappeared into the house, but Dawn lingered on the porch, waiting for K.C. to catch up. Maybe she wasn't so sure Roger wouldn't dare. She walked to the darker end of the porch and stood there looking out at the moon-drenched yard. K.C. stood quietly behind her.

"I guess you heard what he said." Her soft words echoed with hollow resignation.

"I'm sorry," K.C. said. "I should have let you guys know I was there."

"You probably couldn't believe . . ." She gave a tremulous sigh, like night wind echoing in a canyon. "Oh, K.C., I'm so embarrassed. I'm so embarrassed that you heard that."

"Nothing for you to be embarrassed about. You weren't gonna do what he said."

"I wasn't?" She turned to him. "How do you know?"

"I don't think you would."

"Are you going to tell Julia?"

"Tell her I was listening in on a private conversation between you and your husband? That don't sound too good, either." She tried to laugh, but she couldn't quite pull it off. He touched her shoulder. "You ought to think about telling her yourself, Dawn."

"I don't want her to know. I don't ever want her to know that my husband would . . . suggest . . ."

He took her in his arms and gave her a safe place to cry. She was pretty quiet about it, for which he was grateful.

"I'm so humiliated."

"I know." He rubbed her back, like comforting a child. "You have a sister who loves you, honey. It might help if you talked to her about—"

"Oh, K.C., I could never tell her anything like this. I could never tell her how—"

The door opened. They both turned as Julia stepped onto the porch.

"What's going on?"

Here was something else that didn't look too good, especially when Dawn pulled away from him. Shadows were deceptive. K.C. would have given a month's pay for one blazing light bulb. Dawn sniffled, hastily wiping her eyes, and he nearly thanked her outright for the hint of an excuse.

Julia's tone softened as she took a step closer. "What's wrong?"

"I was just comin' up to, uh . . ."

"*He was*, Julia. He was on his way to see you."

"Oh?" Another step, smaller by half. "What's wrong?"

"Nothing. Roger and I just had a little disagreement about . . ." Dawn waved a dismissive hand and sank back against the stone porch wall. "Oh, you know Roger."

Julia looked at K.C. for an explanation.

"I *don't* know Roger," he said. "Don't know what his problem is. Guess I don't know what the attraction would be, either."

"I don't expect anyone else to understand Roger and me. He's my husband, and . . ." She was sniffling again. Julia provided a tissue. "Well, you know how that goes."

"Listen, Dawn," Julia began gently as she moved toward her sister, "I know you're eager to sell the place, and I know the money sounds very attractive, but Roger really has nothing to say about it. So, no, I guess I don't know how that goes. But if he thinks . . ." She brushed Dawn's hair back, a motherly gesture. "Just blame me. Just tell him I'm the one who's holdin' out. Simple."

"You really don't know." Dawn hopped away from the wall and from Julia's artless attempt to console her. "You really don't."

The screen door slapped shut. Feet pounded up the stairs.

Julia sighed, finally turning to K.C. "Will you tell me what that was about?"

He wanted to. "It's for her to tell you."

"Why? You were the one holding her."

"She was crying." He took her hand and seated her in the glider with him, then touched her back, high, between her shoulder blades; and when he was sure it was acceptable to her, he stroked her there, making small circles with his fingertips. "It would have been better if you'd been the one holdin' her."

"She didn't come to me."

"Maybe you need to go to her." She turned her head from him, rested her chin on her shoulder, pouting, he supposed. "Julia." Her neck was going to get stiff. "I was coming to you."

"You got waylaid."

"I got in the middle of something that was none of my business. Still none of my business. Story of my life." Ah, she turned back to him now. A little sympathy. He'd take what he could get right now. Anything this woman would give him. "She'd talk to you, though, you let her know it's okay."

"About you?"

"It's not about me." He sighed. "You said you wanted to talk to me."

"See? *You're* willing. I'm not so damned hard to talk to."

"You let me know it was okay."

"And how did I do that?"

"Well..." He stroked her hair, tucking it behind her ear. She was trying hard to sound hard. "I guess you showed me your soft side. Got me so I can't hardly think about nothin' else."

She groaned, gave a small laugh. He could feel the muscles in her neck and shoulders let down some.

She smacked his knee, but it was just a little smack. "Do you realize not five minutes have passed since you had your arms around another woman?"

"Those were my other arms."

She tipped her chin up. "What other—"

He cut her off with a kiss.

And, when he had her shoulders all nice and soft, a proposition. "Before you give me any orders for next week, I got something I wanna talk to you about," he said. "I've been thinkin', come fall, if my job still exists and you ain't fired me by then—"

She squeezed his knee playfully. "Assuming you haven't sued me for sexual harassment."

"I ain't suing nobody for nothin'. Ever. Now, shut up and listen." He sat back, clearing her face of his shadow so that he could see the pale moonlight in her eyes. "I'd like to keep on workin' for you if you decide not to sell out."

"You would?"

"I would."

"But... you can make more money..."

"Training horses, and I'd expect to be able to do that here. Plus continue on as your foreman."

"You could train horses here? In the winter? Without—"

"I could train horses in Siberia. Without what? You name it, I can do without it."

"Just say when and show you where," she recited readily.

"You got it, darlin'." He nodded. "I don't know if this helps you with your decision or not. I ain't doin' you no favors. I could use the job. So if you can use my services . . ."

"I really don't want to sell the High Horse. You know that." She was rubbing his knee now. "But I have to be fair to Dawn. I've talked with Gramma, and she understands. All she wanted us to do was take some time to be sure."

"Have you talked with Dawn?"

"She wants that money, K.C. I understand that, too. It sounds so . . ." She sighed, still rubbing him kind of easy, like they'd been having these porch talks forever. "I love this place. I also know what it takes to keep it going. But I've been thinking about it, and I'd give it a try if I thought I could pull it off. The thing is, how much of it could we sell, and who'd want . . ." She paused, then shook her head. "*I* love this place. Dawn doesn't. So that's where we stand."

"This is your home."

"It was, when I was . . ." She looked at him, surprised. "It is. You're right. My mother took us away, but you know what? I don't think it was really the High Horse that made my mother so unhappy. It was . . ."

"A cowboy?"

She gave a little laugh. "I don't think he was really a cowboy. If you're a cowboy, and Vernon's a cowboy, then my father was . . ." She tapped his knee with that sweet, playful fist. "Put it this way. I don't think he was 'the hardest-working breed of man there is.' "

"You get him doin' what he does best," he reminded her. "That's the important part. When did I get to be so damn quotable?"

"I'm filling my diary with the wisdom of K.C. Houston."

"No shit." He laughed. "That'll be a book with a lot of blank pages."

"You don't believe me, do you? I'll have to show it to you someday."

"You know how you said you wanted to put in a rock garden down at the edge of the yard?" He'd been thinking about this wish of hers ever since she'd mentioned it. She loved flowers, and he wanted to give her some. "I know where I can get you some nice rocks."

"Really?" That old devil moon was dancing in her eyes now. "Let's not plant them at the edge of the yard."

"Behave yourself now, I'm ser—" Her hand was straying up his thigh. "Okay, don't behave yourself."

Then he heard those voices again. Dawn and Roger, above his head this time, through an open window in a room above the porch. He was telling her she was being stupid. Her answer was garbled, and K.C. figured she was probably crying again.

"Why does she stay with him?"

"I don't know. I think they're both pretty volatile. I think . . ." She slid her hand back to his knee, then pushed to her feet. "I'd better go check on Gramma. She's due for some medication, which she doesn't like taking."

"Do you need any help?"

She took his face in her hands and leaned over him for a kiss. "Thanks for the offer. For all the offers."

"Talk it over with your sister," he said. "Maybe you can work it out together."

25

*D*awn knew exactly what Julia wanted to talk to her about. Keeping the ranch. Just for a year, she was going to say. If it doesn't pan out, we'll sell it. Julia was going to make the outrageous idea seem like a perfectly sensible thing to do. Turn down four and a half *million* dollars and hang onto a limping white elephant.

Well, green elephant. Greener than money sometimes. Green and brown with purple peaks and cerulean blue overhead and scented with pine and impregnated with voices. Dawn could hear those horses talking to each other in her sleep now. Bat was the only creature she'd ever befriended who seemed needier than she. But he had some dignity about it. If somebody slapped him with a plan to screw his sister over by screwing her sister's boyfriend, Bat wouldn't stand there and turn the other butt cheek.

Dawn was mad now, plotting mad. Getting Roger together with the Pollaks was a wickedly fabulous idea. Roger was going to get close enough to smell the money. She wanted him to imagine that check filling his hand so that when the deal was finally done and she told him to kiss off, he'd feel a nice, sharp pinch. Consequently she chose going out to dinner with her husband and Chuck Pollak over Julia's suggestion that they take a drive up to Painted Mountain together and talk. They would talk later.

Chuck had said he wanted to bring someone else along, and Dawn expected to see Cal with his father. She'd let

Roger watch her come on to another man, if that was what he wanted. She'd do it for fun, just to add a little zip to the game. But the man who walked into the Cut Proud Café right behind Chuck was Tom Lomak.

Oh, well, Dawn thought. He'd do even better.

They started in right away on a deal-making discourse, all masterful and macho. Dawn let Roger go right ahead with his big talk, using the royal "we," as though he actually had some claim to her inheritance.

"I checked with a friend of mine," Roger said. "He says with Dawn's name in that will, if they don't agree to sell, we can tie everything up indefinitely. We can make it impossible for them to maneuver."

Lomak was the diplomat. "We wouldn't want anything that ugly to come to pass, Roger. It's too expensive, too time-consuming. And time is important to us. We're willing to let Sally stay on through the spring, take her time making all her arrangements, but come spring . . ."

Chuck spoke to Dawn. "Tom said your sister seemed to be having second thoughts, looking at trying to hang on to her share. But then we heard about Sally's accident. A bad accident kinda makes a guy see things a little different, don't it?"

"Julia's still not ready to jump into anything," Dawn told him.

"Julia's a shrewd woman," Roger said. "She might just be looking for you to sweeten the deal. Mind you, we feel the offer is more than generous. It's Julia who has all the emotional attachment, the interest in the horses. She's always been a horse fanatic."

"What would happen to the horses?" Dawn asked. "The mustangs. You'd let them stay up there on Painted Mountain, wouldn't you? They aren't hurting anything."

Chuck laughed.

"I'm serious. Some of them are blind, and they really can't be—" She saw the rancher scowl as he slid his chair closer to the table, a sound that reminded Dawn of a cat rattling a paper bag. She backpedaled. "One or two, I think, that's all. Well, the one they picked up from your place.

The thing is, he's perfectly all right on his own turf. As soon as they get the report back from—"

She touched two fingers to her lips. Maybe she shouldn't have mentioned the report. "I just want to make sure the mustangs could stay on Painted Mountain. I think it would help if you would put that in writing."

"Whatever it takes to please—"

"No, Chuck," Lomak said. "I've had just about enough. This deal is dragging as it is, and once it's in place, I'm not going to be saddled with any contingencies." Lomak wasn't buying Pollak's *stow it* glare. "Look, that cowboy has already made it pretty clear that he knows I'm—"

"That cowboy has nothing to say in this," Roger said. "He's only a hired hand."

"Looks to me like there's a little more to it than that," Chuck said. He exchanged more cautionary glances with Lomak. "That boy's got a past. You folks know that, don't you?"

"What do you mean?" Roger wanted to know.

"Hell, he's a cowboy. He doesn't have a pot to piss in, for starters, so of course he's gonna cozy up to somebody like Julia."

"We've been thinking along the same lines," Roger said.

"We have?"

Roger slid Dawn a look. "But I don't think she's in so deep that she can't be shown the light about the man. He's a gold digger, obviously."

Dawn had to laugh. It was the only way she could avoid blurting the word "hypocrite" straight out.

There was more satisfaction than humor in Pollak's smile. "Well, we dug up some interesting stories about some of K.C. Houston's shenanigans. I think it'll be easy enough to persuade him to quietly move on."

"He's been persuaded in the past," Lomak said.

A sick feeling shinnied up Dawn's gullet. "What kind of shenanigans?"

"The kind your sister wants to steer clear of."

"What do you think would be the best way to deliver the goods on him, Dawn?" Pollak wondered. "Should it

come from Tom here, who's a well-respected attorney, or
from a friend of the family? Or from her sister?''

Dawn thought about K.C. and what she knew about him
just from the way he'd treated her. She thought about Julia.
Too perfect, too good, too right, too cold, too Julia. The
only sister she had.

She glanced at her husband, and she realized that whatever the story, there was no keeping it from him now. ''I
guess I'd have to know more about the goods.''

Later, after they'd parted company with Pollak and Lomak, Dawn asked Roger to let her handle the so-called
goods. She needed a little time to think the whole thing
over, to figure out the best approach. Time was money, he
said. It was one of his favorite witticisms.

''It's my time,'' she told him, ''and it's potentially my
money.''

''We're married, sweetheart.''

She couldn't resist. ''For now.''

''Don't even try to give me any of that shit,'' he warned
as he clicked the high beams on at the bridge. The big
house was a hulking shadow against the starry Western sky.
''You ran my last enterprise straight into the ground.''

''*Yours?*''

''That's right, it was *ours*. Our restaurant. We lost that
together. So you try to divorce me now, and I can damn
well show that I've got a piece of your assets coming.''

K.C. was putting a new latigo on the old cutting horse
saddle he liked to use for a colt's first ride. A black-and-
white puff of fur snuffled around his boot. A dusky face,
wide-eyed and wary, peeked in the open door.

''Chevy, come on in here,'' K.C. said amiably. He
pointed the leather punch at the puppy. ''What do you think
of this, huh? What in the hell am I going to do with this?''

''You got one of Shep's pups? Bitchin'.'' Chevy ventured a tentative laugh, grateful to the puppy for being the
one K.C. didn't know what to do with. He scooped it up
and gave it a quick check. ''Hey, it *is* a bitch. Cool. Did
he g-give her to you?''

''Are you kidding? He knew he had me the minute I

looked in that whelping box. He told me he'd give me a deal on the runt. I wasn't even thinkin' about taking a dog. Before I know it, I'm takin' fifty bucks out of my billfold because he's got me thinkin' it's such a great deal." He spared a glance for the boy and the pup he was cuddling. "What do you think? We can use a mascot, huh?"

"For what? We ain't g-got a t-t-team."

"C'mon, give me a break. I need an excuse for being such a sucker." They shared an easy laugh. "You're a good hand, Chevy. You did real fine on Chariot today."

Under K.C.'s close supervision, Chevy had taken his first Chariot ride.

"You told me not to d-drag my leg over his rump, b-but . . ."

"Well, you'd been workin' hard, and you were a little nervous, too, I bet. But you reacted just right, and you got everything workin' smooth again." K.C. threaded a strip of lacing through the two holes he'd just punched. "You're good with animals. You sing good, too."

"Paco says he asked about working here next s-s-summer."

"He did."

"And you d-didn't give him an ans—"

"I don't know what'll be goin' on here next summer." He glanced up. "But you'll be goin' home, right? And stayin' out of trouble?"

"I live with my grandpa. He's about as old as S-Sally, I guess." The boy scratched the puppy's head, making her ears flap like wings. "I hate school."

"You need to be in school. You need to do good in school so you can go to veterinary school. What you gotta do next summer is get a job, maybe. You stay in touch with Julia so she can recommend you. Or Sally, or . . ." He smiled. "I'd ride with you any day of the week, Chevy. Anybody asks me, that's what I'd tell them."

"Did you get the report back yet?" Chevy asked. K.C. gave him a quizzical look. "About the horses' blood tests."

"Freddie got it back. It's a genetic problem. It's something they can inherit, like blue eyes and black-and-white hair." Which gave him a wild idea. "You ever want a summer job workin' with a veterinarian, I know a good one who'd take you on."

"Your f-friend from Nevada?"

"But you've gotta stay out of trouble. Now, we had one problem today, and I think you know what that was."

"You told me not to take him out of the round pen."

K.C. nodded. "And as soon as I went to help Paco, you did what I asked you not to do."

"I just wanted to try the paddock, where it's not s-so cl-closed in."

"You've gotta work with me, Chevy. That's the only way we can do this safely."

"So, what? I gotta clean tack now?"

"You gotta clean tack now."

"You'd st-still . . ."

"Ride with you?" Such a small thing, this affirmation, K.C. thought. It amazed him that his approval meant something to someone, but he was getting used to the fact that it did. He smiled. "Damn straight. Soon as I finish fixing this saddle. Is Jack on a break?"

"No, he's still out there." Chevy put the puppy back on the floor. "K.C., we're big b-boys. You don't have to, like, h-hover. You know?"

"It ain't you I'm worried about, Chevy. It's the horses. At heart they're still wild."

"And we hold that in our hands," Chevy said, quoting him. "That heart. That wildness."

K.C. grinned. He liked the sound of his own words coming out of a kid's mouth. Straight out, no hesitation. He clapped a hand on the boy's shoulder. No more words were necessary.

K.C. was glad he'd made it to breakfast this morning, because he was about to miss dinner.

He'd thought it would take only a few minutes to re-rig the saddles that had been causing trouble, but he wasn't finding just what he needed, and the boys would be down to work the horses any time now. He was fussy about warped saddle trees, frayed cinches, rough buckles, any-

thing that might "sore the horse," and he was constantly
fixing on the Weslin saddles, which had not been up to his
standards. Still, with a few new bits and pieces, some scrap
leather and a lot of cowboy ingenuity, he was getting them
there.

Having a puppy following at his heels didn't help,
though. He kept forgetting she was there.

"Hey, you." He scooped the little Border collie off the
floor mid-yelp after tripping over her for a second time.
"You don't wanna listen, do you? Just like a kid. Now, if
I wanted a kid, I could make one, but you . . ." The puppy
licked at his nose and made him laugh. "Yeah, I paid good
money for you."

"It's that easy, is it?"

He hadn't heard Julia come in. He flashed a grin at the
woman he'd given considerable thought to making a kid
with. "Like lickin' butter off a knife." He slipped his free
arm around her and did a little rocking two-step, crooning,
"All you need is sex, whoop-de-do-de-do . . ."

"How about some food once in a while?" She slid her
free hand over his flat belly. "You're getting pretty ganted
up here. The boys are still . . ." She glanced down at the
puppy. "So you're a proud papa?"

He put the two of them nose to nose. "It's a girl. I'm
fresh out of cigars, so I'm giving away big, juicy kisses to
celebrate."

Mmm, she tasted like chocolate.

"Congratulations," she said. "Shep tried to give me one,
too. I said thanks, but no, thanks. I'm gentle but firm."

"You said no to this face? You're way past firm,
woman." He scowled. "He tried to *give* you one?"

She laughed. "You're way past easy, cowboy."

"Yeah, I know. So if you wanna give me a kid, I'll show
you how easy it is to get one started."

"Give *you* a kid?"

"Give my puppy a kid. Every puppy needs a kid, don't
you think?"

"I'm always thinking." She showed him a manila envelope. "This came from Freddie."

"I talked to her when you were up in Billings with Sally." He bent to put the puppy on the floor. "She said she'd send the report, but I already know what's in it."

"What should we do?"

"The way I see it—just lookin' at the horses, now—you've got maybe three ways to go on this." He started the count on his little finger. "You can round them all up, reduce the numbers, geld the stallions and bring in replacement stallions. Now, that'll play hell with their social structure for a while, but they'll get it all worked out sooner or later. Or you could consider Freddie's proposal, take the numbers down some but basically leave the rest up to Mother Nature."

"And let Freddie do her study."

He nodded. "She says she's got other people interested, and she thinks she can get her grant."

"What's the third option?"

"If you asked the BLM for help, they'd probably come in and remove them." Rather than tick this one off on his middle finger, where it belonged, he folded his arms. "If you decide to sell out, that might be the way to go. Unless you want to leave it up to Pollak."

She eyed the puppy, who was sniffing around for a place to squat. "Nick's question has been haunting me a lot. If you know a wild animal is injured or sick or disabled somehow, is it ethical to ignore it?"

"You wouldn't be ignoring it," he said as he opened the side door. The sun streamed in; the puppy toddled out. "The great thing about Nick and Freddie is that they have different ideas, but they listen to each other. You know, they go back and forth, but nobody gets mad. Nobody pushes. Nobody has to be right. She does her thing, he does his, and they help each other, even when there are some doubts. They accept the doubts. They pick a strategy, and off they go. If it don't work, well, they tried. He'd never try to get her to do anything that would go against her grain. 'Cause he kinda likes her grain. Bossy as she is. Good girl!" He whistled, and the puppy hopped back over the threshold.

"Come on, Freddie's not bossy, is she?" Julia was teasing.

"Ol' Nick, he might seem quiet, but he's got his ideas, too. So between them, there's never a dull moment. But they don't, uh . . ." He hunkered down to praise his new charge. "They don't disrespect each other."

"Are you talking about . . ."

"Choices," he said quickly. With a nod he indicated the envelope. "Making choices. I guess I kinda veered off a little bit. I was just sayin' something like this—you look at your options and take your best shot. If you're gonna sell out, that narrows the field."

"I need to study these. Go over them with you, if that's okay."

His gesture said *Any time*. "But I might as well tell you, when I make a choice, I usually do what my gut tells me is right. And that's not always smart." He stared at the pup. "It's your place, Julia. They're your horses."

"I need you."

He looked at her, inviting her to elaborate, hoping. He didn't dare mold the hope into a definite shape, didn't dare think exactly what he was hoping for. It was a hazy hope, but it had the sound of Julia, the scent and the feel of Julia.

"To tell me what your gut says," she said quietly.

Not quite what he needed to hear. "My gut says, if there's a job here for me, I oughta stay." He lifted one shoulder. "If you decide to sell out, I might just move in with Vern and Shep."

She laughed. "It might get a little crowded. Gramma's moving in with them, too."

"When you millionaires come to visit, we'll put you up in the woodshed."

"The cabin," she urged. "Up on Painted Mountain."

"Lomak's crew will have to knock that down when they put in the ski run." She looked at him, dubious.

Damn right you need me. "Listen, Julia, if you're gonna do it, do it with your eyes open. The money sure ain't coming from the FHA."

"I guess not." She watched the puppy try her milk teeth

out on a scrap of rawhide. "Do you have a name for her yet?"

"Sure do."

She glared at him. "Not Queenie."

K.C. smiled.

26

From the back door Dawn watched Paco trot across the yard with a green bag of kitchen trash thumping his backside. She had promised that she would go down to the horse pens this afternoon and let him show her what his colt could do. He and Barney had been taking turns helping her clean up the kitchen after meals, and she knew that Paco had a crush on her. But she wanted to look in on Gramma before she left the house. For Sally, having to take to her bed for so much of the day was like giving in to something insidious, and she'd been fighting it. But, of course, she'd been losing.

Take care of her, Roger had said. *Everyone else is busy. You stay close to Granny.*

She hated it when Roger called her "Granny." That wasn't what they called her, and she wasn't *his* grandmother. K.C. called her Sally. Vernon called her "the Judge" a lot, and Dawn had had to ask why. She'd never known that her grandmother had once been a county judge. So many things she'd never known, or maybe she'd never paid attention. Family history didn't have anything to do with her and Roger. She thought of her life as a two-part drama: the good times with Roger and the bad times with Roger.

Roger Morton. The man she'd taken from Julia. Some prize. She was about ready for Part Three, and whatever it brought.

"Gramma?" She rapped on Sally's door before peeking in. "How do you feel? Do you feel like . . ."

"Come on in, little girl." Sally was dressed, and her bed was made. She was willing to rest in the afternoon with her arm propped on a pile of pillows. She wasn't *in bed*, though. She was only resting. "Where's your husband?"

"I don't know. He took off in the car this morning. It's just you and me." She went to her grandmother's bedside, unsure where she might sit. Sally patted the bed. Julia's place, Dawn thought. Or Vern's. But she sat. "I'm sure he'll go back to Connecticut soon."

"Back home?"

Dawn nodded, but she didn't feel like saying the word. *Home* didn't feel like it fit with *Roger*. "I guess I really don't want him here. Does that sound awful?" Sally shook her head, and Dawn thought, *Why would it? They don't want me here, either.*

"You want me to tell him to go?" Sally asked. "I can do that easy enough, but only if that's what you want. You can bring anyone here you like. Soon as you don't like, out they go."

"He's my husband."

"That makes him family. But if you don't want him here, we don't want him here."

"What if he were Julia's husband?"

"Same feeling applies. This is your home, your place to be safe."

Her gaze fell across her grandmother's body to the bandaged arm on the far side, the purple tips of two fingers exposed. *Her place to be safe.* The High Horse? She'd have to think about that.

And she thought that was what she was doing, looking at her grandmother's bruised fingers and thinking about home and where she was safe, when something else spilled out unexpectedly.

"He's willing to do anything, Gramma." She looked at Sally quickly, scared by the sound of her own admission, afraid she'd just lost any ground she might have gained. She saw no change in her grandmother's expression, but she assured her, "I'm not."

"That's good." Sally nodded, waited, finally said, "Do you want to tell me what he's willing to do?"

"No. I don't. I really don't. It makes me feel like a big fat wad of . . . butt wipe."

But she told her anyway, told her everything about Roger.

Without saying a word, Sally scooted over slightly, more by way of invitation than by making room, and Dawn stretched out beside her. Sally slid her hand over Dawn's, squeezed it, and they simply lay there, side by side, holding hands while silent tears leaked from the corners of Dawn's eyes into her hair. Neither of them spoke for a long while. Tears subsided, and in their place Dawn grew mindful of the warmth of her grandmother's body next to hers, the leathery feel of her hand, the sound of her breathing. She'd fallen asleep.

Dawn reached over to the bedside table and carefully pulled a tissue from the box.

"I'll say one thing for sure."

Dawn turned, surprised.

Sally wagged a finger in front of her nose. "You're not fat."

They looked at each other for a long moment. Dawn wasn't sure whose eyes started dancing first, but the laughter felt good. Shared with her grandmother, just the two of them, the laughter felt absolutely *grand*. As it faded, she had a feeling of having experienced something like this before. At first it was just a vague impression, then a vivid memory of lying on the sofa with Gramma, late at night, Gramma's head on a pillow at one end, hers on a pillow at the other. They were side by side, but she could see her own bare feet next to Gramma's hip. She must have been pretty young.

"Do you remember," she began, describing the flashback to Sally, who recalled that Dawn had been about five years old and wouldn't sleep in her bed or Gramma's bed or anybody's bed that night because her parents hadn't come home and she wanted to wait up for them. The truth was that Michael was gone, and Fay was out looking for him. "One of *those* nights," Sally called it.

"I don't remember much about my father," Dawn said.

"You got the tail end, I'm sorry to say. Guess you could say they got married in a fever."

"And the fire went out," was Dawn's inference. She couldn't actually say she remembered. "But doesn't it always go out, really? Sooner or later?"

"Mine didn't. I don't know about you, but I've still got mine burning." They turned to look at each other, as if to show and be shown.

"Is it for Grandpa or for Vern?"

"It's for Sally Weslin." She gave a mischievous smile. "They can cozy up and warm themselves without stealing your fire, little girl. Some men understand that, and others just never get it. They say 'Keep the home fire burning'? You *are* the home fire."

"*I* am?"

"You are."

They lay quietly for a long while after that. Dawn wasn't feeling much like a fire. She wondered if hers had been snitched already. Finally she asked, "Do you think K.C.'s a womanizer?"

"A womanizer?" Sally turned, that twinkle in her eye again. "Damn, he hasn't shown much interest in me."

"Me, either. Well, not like that." Gramma didn't look surprised. "Chuck Pollak and his lawyer. That guy he brought over here?" Sally bobbed her head. Dawn looked away, stared up at the paddle fan on the ceiling. "They dug up some stories about K.C. getting fired for messing with some guy's wife. Being run out of town for winding up in a fight over some woman. Getting sued for negligence. Made him sound like . . ." She grimaced. "Like somebody else I know."

"Why would they be out digging up stories like that?"

"If K.C. stayed around, there wouldn't be any sale this fall. Julia's all set to turn that offer down." It took some nerve to look Sally in the face now. "Four and a half million dollars sounds so good, Gramma."

Sally nodded.

"It sounds like freedom to me."

"Freedom from what?"

"I don't know. Maybe it would help me get Roger out of my system." And then, more seriously, "He says he could claim part of my share in a divorce settlement."

Sally nodded again.

"Could he get it?"

"Depends on the state laws, the judge, the history, the headlines in the newspaper that day."

Sally turned to her granddaughter, giving a sad little smile. "This wasn't fair, was it? I admit I helped Ross come up with it, but setting this whole thing up this way wasn't fair. It puts you and your sister at odds over something only one of you really cares about. And I don't blame you for not caring. I don't, little girl, and I don't blame your mother, either. This country isn't for everyone."

"I don't think he is," Dawn said, only half listening because she was still thinking about what she'd seen of K.C. and what she'd heard about him. "A womanizer. I could just swear he's in love with her, Gramma. And I really think she's in love with him." She looked at Sally again. "Isn't it weird? You wouldn't think they'd be right for each other at all."

"Have you told Julia about this dirt they dug up?"

Dawn rolled her head back and forth on the pillow. "I'd better, though. Or maybe I should tell K.C., see what he has to say for himself. I suppose he could be just another opportunist trying to get his hands on the High Horse." Another glance at Gramma. "Well, couldn't he? I mean, they're turning up right and left."

Sally studied her for a moment. "You know, you wouldn't have to be an active partner if you just held onto your interest in the ranch. There's no reason it couldn't provide you with a nice, steady income. And if there was no sale, no big windfall of cash, I don't see why you couldn't slip free of Roger if you were of a mind to do that." Sally smiled. "I don't think Julia could have run this summer program without your help."

"She wasn't even going to provide food," Dawn recalled, buying right in.

"No, but you did. Nothing like good food to keep the menfolk around. If you don't like living out here in what your mother calls the desert, there's about a dozen places I could think of within a two-hundred-mile radius that could use a decent restaurant.''

"You never answered me about K.C. Could he be more interested in the ranch than in Julia?''

"I reckon he could be. It's a fine ranch. Max used to say he could see every ridge and valley in my face.'' She smiled wistfully, and Dawn could see exactly what her grandfather must have seen. The beautiful, ageless terrain of the High Horse. Someday Julia would look like that. Maybe someday K.C. would trace the miles he'd ridden in the lines in Julia's face.

"It's hard to talk to her sometimes.'' The prospect of it burned in Dawn's throat. "I really hate to tell her about Roger.''

"Well, you told me, and I'm ready to beat him over the head with my cast. Except it would definitely be a case of hurting me more than him. His head's empty, and my cast ain't.'' She lifted her injured arm from the pillows. "Got a lot of life left in this arm. That's why it hurts so much.'' She made a pained face, grunted, and Dawn made her put her arm down.

Sally nodded when she found Dawn's hand again. "That's why it hurts so much, little girl. You get past this bad patch, you got a lot of life left in you, too.''

K.C. had the boys working horses in four separate pens now. He'd decided that four was the limit. He'd considered the levels of patience and proficiency among the boys and developed a rotation that allowed him to closely supervise the boys he didn't quite trust. Jack was a good kid monitor, but he wasn't much use with the horses, so K.C. used him as kind of a lifeguard. Perched him on a post where he could see what was going on and blow the whistle on any roughhousing.

But somehow the lifeguard missed Paco's grandstand play. It was Leighton who caught up with K.C. on his way between pens. "Hey, is Paco supposed to be riding today?''

"Hell, no.''

With the foal halter-broke, leading and responding to

some voice commands, Paco had been doing a little groundwork with the black mare. But there was no way that he should have been riding her. She was nowhere near ready.

"Paco," K.C. said quietly as he eased through the gate to the back pen. "What are you doing up there?"

"See? She's ready." Paco grinned, so pleased, so relaxed—such a reckless seat. He had no idea that what he looked like to K.C. was a glass pitcher balanced on the point of a pencil.

"I want you to—"

"She's okay," Paco said happily. "She ain't gonna bu—bu—"

The mare snorted, reared, then fell into a crow-hop. All she wanted to do was pop the strange weight off her back.

"Whoa!" Paco shouted, panic rising.

K.C. tried to counter with a quiet "Ho, girl" as he moved in quickly. "Paco, don't," he warned, reading the boy's intention, but there was no stopping him from trying to bail out. His body seemed to come unscrewed at the waist, half floppy, half stiff, with his foot still anchored in the stirrup.

He was still hung up when K.C. caught the reins. The mare dropped like a paratrooper, hitting her mark and sticking it, nostrils flaring. She pranced, letting K.C. know that she'd accomplished her mission, but if he had any doubt, she had fuel in reserve.

K.C. humbly asked her not to use it while he freed Paco's foot. "Pull him back, Leighton."

"Jeez, you stupid—"

"Just move!"

It was over quickly. K.C. signaled for Chad Snyder to take care of the mare while he turned his attention to Paco. Leighton dragged him clear, helped him to his feet. As soon as he was able, Paco pushed Leighton away. Now he took a stay-the-hell-away-from-me stance near the fence.

"You okay?" K.C. asked.

Paco's eyes glittered with rage and tears. He nodded tightly. When K.C. advanced, Paco jerked his chin up like a head-shy horse. He took a step back, and his right leg crumpled. He caught himself on the fence.

"Damn baby," Leighton muttered to Barney, whose face loomed over the top of the fence like a summer moon.

Barney's glasses glinted in the fading sun. "He'll probably be wettin' the bed again tonight. Probably pissin' down his own leg right now."

Paco's face flamed as he eyed K.C., who stood still, a shield between him and the rest of the group, just waiting for some sign from the boy. Paco finally looked up at the sky, lower lip trembling, and let the tears roll.

"You need a hand?"

Paco couldn't look at him, couldn't answer, couldn't think. All he could do was tremble, hang onto the fence and yearn for flight. K.C. knew the feeling well.

"I won't hurt you, son."

"Ain't your *son*."

"Friend, then. Your ankle's hurt. It's no shame to lean on me and let me help you."

"Piss on it. Piss on *you*," Paco hissed, his free arm swinging like a scythe in a useless attempt to fend K.C. off. "You heard them. You wanna get wet?"

"I'll dry. We'll get you some ice. Paco . . ." The hand he laid on the boy's shoulder was knocked away on the first try, accepted on the second. "I ain't mad at you," K.C. said quietly. "All I wanna do is take you up to the house and see how bad you're hurt."

"It's nothin'."

"Do this to ease my mind, okay?"

"What happened here?" Jack shot through the corral gate like he'd popped out of a cannon. "What happened here?"

"An accident," K.C. said, trying to hold Jack off with a gesture.

Jack stopped short, sputtering, "Accident? What kind . . . what'd you do, Paco? Are you hurt or what?"

"Hey, we've got those instant ice packs in the first-aid kit," Barney remembered.

"Go get them," Jack said. "Are you hurt, Paco?"

K.C. wished Barney would spare Jack the use of his glasses.

"He got hung up in the stirrup," Leighton said, and K.C. noted a new tone. Sympathy. Concern.

Paco glared at Leighton, who risked a glance at K.C., then hung his head. "I shouldn't've said that, man. That was, uh . . ." He stepped closer. "I'm sorry I called you a baby. What Lawson said . . . he's got a big mouth sometimes."

Paco gave another tight nod and took a swipe at his humiliating tears with the back of a scraped hand.

"Can I . . ." Leighton glanced at K.C. again, then offered a hand. "You lean on both of us, it's easier."

K.C. and Leighton hoisted Paco's arms around their necks and carried him from the corral with all the honor due a fallen rider. They lifted him into the back of a nearby pickup and headed for the house. Barney came running from the van with a box of instant ice packs. Julia burst through the front door with more ice packs.

Right about that time, the floodgates opened. People started rolling in, gushing with advice. Roger pulled up in his rental car just in time to put in his two cents about not taking the boot off. Jack thought the boot should come off, and Julia pointed out that there was no way to ice the injury with the boot on.

K.C. didn't say much, but he figured he was going to need his pocket knife. He was fishing in his jeans for it when Roger tapped him on the shoulder and gave him an odd smile.

"Sure looks like a case of lightning striking twice."

K.C. questioned him with a look.

"Let's take your boot off, Paco," Julia was saying.

"Okay." And then, "Ow! Ow ow ow, it hurts too much!"

K.C. scowled at Roger, who was giving him an I-know-all-about-you look, which K.C. dismissed when he found his pocket knife. "We need to take your boot off, Paco."

But Paco let out a howl.

"We'll have to cut it off," K.C. said as he unfolded the blade.

"No, don't cut my booooot!"

"Bronc riders used to cut their boots down the front all the time, cowboy. Easy to slip off if—"

"I wouldn't let him near that kid with a knife," Roger told Julia. "You might be liable, too. I happen to know this man's worked with kids and horses before and gotten sued for negligence when somebody got hurt. Isn't that right, Houston?"

"That's right. But what I got in trouble for was having no insurance. I didn't stab anybody." He looked at Paco. "There's no other way to ice it down, partner. I'll buy you a new pair. Deal?"

"Go ahead and cut it off, K.C."

"We're insured, Roger," Julia said. "Accidents happen."

"It was my own fault," Paco said, more interested now in the operation K.C. was performing on his boot top. He scored it lightly first so that he could split it easily with a second cut. He wished about half a dozen onlookers would back off and give them some air.

"The kid is never at fault," Roger was saying. "You wanna make some money, you get yourself a lawyer. I guarantee—"

"Would you can it, Roger?" Julia said. "We have an injured child here."

"Well, it's a good thing you're insured. But that's just the tip of the iceberg, isn't it, Houston?"

The boot was open. "Don't take it off," Julia said as she started cracking the instant ice packs. "We'll pack the ice around it. Jack, bring the van over closer."

"Has Dawn talked to you yet about Mr. Houston's background, Julia?"

"I don't have time for this now, Roger."

"All I'm saying is I think you ought to let somebody else handle this, maybe send everybody back to the home now or whatever, because you've got yourself a situation here. I mean, the liability you're looking at . . ."

K.C. straightened, sighed, eyed the man. "I'm a very patient man, Morton. But you've just about used up your quota."

The screen door whacked shut behind Sally and Dawn.

"What's going on here? More surgery?" The group peeled back in layers so that Sally could have a look. "That's swelling up pretty good, there, Paco. About like my arm."

And, of course, Dawn wanted to know what had happened, and Jack was backing the van over, and on top of all that there was more trouble roaring across the bridge in the form of a silver pickup. K.C. pulled Leighton aside and told him to go down to the horse barn and tell the boys to turn all the horses back into the pasture and fill the hay racks.

"You think it's broken?" Paco was asking.

"I had a sprain once, looked just like this," Sally said. "That ice will help, and Jack's gonna take you in to see the doc, and I think I'll just stand out here and direct traffic."

K.C. was putting Paco in the van just as Chuck Pollak pulled into the driveway. Tom Lomak was with him. Doors were slamming all over the place.

"We've got an injured boy here, Chuck." Roger sounded like he was reporting for the six o'clock news. "Trampled by those wild horses."

"Trampled? By those blind mustangs?"

"He fell off a horse," Julia said. "K.C., do you want to—"

"Now, there's your problem right there. The famous K.C. Houston." Chuck turned to Dawn. "Have you had a chance to talk to your sister yet?"

"She was just talking with me, Chuck," Sally said. "Heard all about your little detective work. Maybe you oughta call Oprah."

"Has Julia heard about it?" Lomak wanted to know. "There are some aspects of that information that certainly could affect her summer program."

Chuck hitched up his pants. "What you've got here, Julia, is a drifter with a very shady past."

"What you've got, Chuck, is poor timing. What *I* have is an injured—"

Jack stuck his head out the van window. "I can take care of this, Julia."

"Go ahead, Julia," Dawn said. She glanced at K.C. "Paco needs . . ."

"I'll ride in with Paco," K.C. told Julia. "Sounds like your neighbor's carryin' quite a load, and he ain't about to let up until he gets it off his chest."

27

Julia heard the music coming from the bunkhouse.
Melancholy fiddles and steel guitars. Country blues. Her
cowboy was in need of a woman's heart.

He had called her from the clinic and reported that Paco's
ankle was badly sprained. She'd told him that Vern was
with the boys, and he'd said that he and Jack would be
back for them as soon as the nurse dug up the right-size
crutches for Paco. He didn't ask about Pollak's big news.
He didn't have to.

Chuck had told his tales, most of which K.C. himself
had told her, although Chuck's version had a more colorful
slant. Then he'd sweetened his offer on the High Horse,
making it an even five million. Julia said she'd consider it.
Somewhere in her repertoire of expressions, Dawn had discovered a poker face.

Then Chuck made the mistake of playing what he
thought was his ace in the hole. He'd checked with the
BLM, he said, and "you girls" wouldn't have to worry
about those deformed horses. Once he had title, permits and
leases in hand, he could ask for a removal of all feral
horses. He figured the disabled animals would be disposed
of by some suitable means.

"Unless that wrangler of yours really does want to shoot
them himself," Chuck said. "Probably wouldn't be legal,
but I doubt that would worry him."

It probably wouldn't, Julia thought. Not if K.C. thought

it was what he had to do to protect them from somebody else's cruelty.

After Chuck left, she'd had her talk with Dawn. They sat across from each other on the beds they'd slept in when they were children. Julia had assumed they would discuss the fate of the High Horse for the most part, but it had turned out to be much more than that. For Julia had listened, really listened to her sister.

Roger was leaving, Dawn said. "Gramma told him she didn't feel much like having all this company, and I told him I didn't feel much like having *his* company." She eyed Julia speculatively. "Can I tell you why?"

"You can tell me anything, Dawn."

"Can I?" She cut Julia's assurance off with a cautionary finger. "I didn't say 'May I?' I said 'Can I?' *Can I* tell you that my husband suggested that I try to get between you and K.C.? That he said I should use all my so-called charms, go as far as I had to to break you two up, because without K.C. . . ." She stuffed a ruffled pillow into the well of her angled legs, looked up at the ceiling and sighed. "K.C. overheard this conversation. That night on the porch?" She lowered her gaze to her sister's face. "He didn't tell you, did he?"

Julia shook her head, stunned. *Go as far as she had to?* What kind of a husband would suggest such a thing to his wife?

"K.C. said it was up to me. He trusted me to tell you what really happened. I knew you kinda wondered about us that night. You did, didn't you?"

"Yes, I guess I did."

"I've given him plenty of chances, but he's never come on to me. The only reason he came between me and Roger was that he walked in on an argument that was about to turn ugly. Roger had me by the arm . . . twisting, and K.C. . . ."

Julia moved from her bed to Dawn's. "Twisting your arm?" Maybe this arm, she thought, the willowy one she sat close to and took into her hands and stroked. She'd known Roger first. She'd introduced him to her beautiful little sister, and the creep had *hurt her*.

Dawn hung her head. "A little."

Damn him. *Damn him.* "What did K.C. do?"

"I asked him not to hurt him, so he let him go. Roger's a coward. Said he'd charge K.C. with assault. I think I sort of took Roger's side, or . . . or I would have. I don't know." She shrugged, shook her head furiously by way of berating herself. "We've had fights before."

"He's abused you before?"

"Not, like, really *bad*, just . . . it's kind of like this constant sparring, you know?"

Julia nodded. She'd heard those words so many times. *Not really bad.* So hurtful to a woman's self-respect to have to tell someone how she'd been undone by the man she loved, how she'd been unloved.

"I don't know why, Julia, but you're the last person I wanted to know about this. K.C. said I should talk to you, but . . ." Dawn turned to her. "It's your job, right? You're a social worker. You see it all the time. I didn't want you to think I was like that. Just another pathetic case of—"

"You're not a case, Dawn. You're my sister."

"I'm a big fat wad of . . . *failure*."

"I love you." Julia's throat burned, her voice gone rusty from unshed tears. "I always have. I'm just so bad about . . ."

"You're not bad about anything," Dawn wailed as they fell into each other's arms and held on and hugged. "You're never bad. You're just . . ."

And so it went. Their brother shared in their embrace as the tears flowed, along with regrets and promises and love. And, finally, a few fragile plans for themselves and for the High Horse.

"What are you going to do about Roger?"

"Give him his walking papers," Dawn said without hesitation. "What about K.C.? You love him, don't you? When I first heard that stuff about him, I thought, *That sonuvabitch.* And then I thought, *But that's not K.C.* I mean, if all he wanted was the ranch . . ."

"Do you think that's what he wants?"

"Gramma says he needs a home. And there's nothing wrong with that, you know. I guess we all need a home."

Dawn shook her head, quick to separate herself from that need. "Oh, but I never fit in here. I never—"

"Oh, Dawn, I know that's my fault."

"No, it isn't." Dawn laughed, wiped away tears, both hers and her sister's. "You're just not that powerful, Julia. You can't take full credit for that." She smiled. "I feel like I've kinda helped get something going here with the summer program."

"You have."

Dawn drew a deep breath and rolled her eyes. "Five million dollars. That's a *hell* of a lot of money."

"It is."

"We're not gonna sell, Julia." Dawn grabbed Julia's hands and hung on for dear, sweet, solid life. "The High Horse is a lot of ranch, and you and me, Julia . . . we're Sally Weslin's granddaughters."

They had shared another embrace, the kind Julia had envied her sister and mother, the kind she'd disparaged and denied and done without.

And now, strengthened by her sister's courage, her grandmother's grit, her brother's hopes and her own determination, she knocked on the bunkhouse door.

"It's open." K.C. dropped his duffel bag on the floor at the foot of the bed, tucked his thumbs in the front pockets of his jeans and faced her with a sheepish smile. "Guess you got an earful today, huh?"

"It's been quite a day," she said with a dramatic sigh. "I feel like I've been rode hard and put up wet."

"Must be the hat that's got you talkin' like a cowboy."

"This is my rancher's hat." She swept it off her head and took it to him, holding it up as though she was taking up a collection. "See? That's what it says right here. 'Rancher's Classic.' Figure if I walk the walk, talk the talk and wear the hat, I must be a rancher."

There was a hint of pride in his smile now. No more sheepishness. Pure cowboy pride. "You sure got the makin's, ma'am."

She glanced past him, noticed the little piles of clothes he'd laid out on the bed. "Are you going somewhere?"

"You know, they didn't take my driver's license. I

haven't been to court yet. Sally got me a stay of execution or some damn thing, so technically . . .''

"You said you'd stay."

"I don't know what Pollak told you, Julia, but any way you cut it, I do have a pretty sorry history. Don't have much of an education. Been workin' since I was fourteen, and I don't have a damn thing to show for it except a pickup and what little gear I can fit into it. Been shown the door more than a few times." He met her gaze with his own, his eyes hiding nothing. "I've been with some women I probably should have left alone. But I never . . .''

"Mistreated them?"

He winced a little, but his gaze held hers. "You think I would?"

"No. Never. But I thought you would stay."

He swallowed hard, still gazing intently as though he couldn't quite figure her out, which, she thought, was absurd. He was a mind reader, for heaven's sake.

So she told him something he didn't know. "We turned Pollak's offer down. You said if I decided not to sell . . .'' She lifted one shoulder as she took a step closer. "You had already told me most of what he thought was a big revelation. Of course, he embellished it with some details about you breaking somebody's jaw."

He stiffened. "You should have seen what that sonuva-bitch did to his wife. And I wasn't sleepin' with her. I kissed her once or twice, yeah, but she was so . . . such a sad woman. She just needed a little—"

"Dawn was sad, too." As was Julia's smile. "But according to her, you never even kissed her once."

"I said I was uneducated. I didn't say I was stupid. I'm not gonna be kissing another woman when I'm in love with . . .''

The words brought her chin up. They made her heart skip around in circles. They made her eyes shine.

They made him smile. "When I'm so much in love with her sister, it hurts to look at her."

"That bad?" She laughed. "I really do look old, don't I?"

He laughed, too, and took her in his arms, and danced

her in a slow, seesaw circle. "I don't know. I figure by the time we're Sally's and Vern's ages, nobody'll be able to tell. Won't matter anyway if I'm still sleeping out here. But I will. I'll stay, and I'll bust my hump for you for the next—"

She was feeling giddy now as she slid her arms around him and rubbed his back. "Where's your hump? You don't have a hump."

"I'll bust whatever I've got for you. That's all I've got to offer. Just . . ." The dancing stopped. He plumbed the depths of her eyes as he took her face in his hands. "The best pair of hands you're gonna find anywhere."

"I believe that." She put her hands over his wrists, closed her eyes and rubbed her cheek against his palm. If she'd been a cat, she would have purred. "Dawn told me about the way you helped her with Roger and then let it be her choice to tell me."

"Well, I knew she would."

She held his hands now. "Did you?"

"She just needed to know it was okay. That you'd still love her even if nobody else did."

"What if she hadn't told me?"

"You can't stop her from getting back with him if that's what she's gonna do. You know that."

"Yes, I do."

"I know that for a fact. I've . . ." He shook his head, laughed. Julia knew what he knew. She knew and she understood and she was nodding as he declared, "Dawn's got to stop trusting him and start trusting herself. She's got to speak up. She did that now, huh? That's good. Telling you about it was probably all she needed to get herself free, and that's something no four and a half million dollars can buy."

Julia couldn't stop smiling at him. She loved him. She loved him so much.

"Five."

"Five?"

She nodded, and he gave an appreciative whistle. "It felt good to turn it down," she said.

"Did you get to tear it up and throw it in his face?"

"Oh, K.C., it's been right here all along. My home, my family, my heart. Blinders, I've been wearing blinders. And how did I ever get to be a social worker? I'm not even a good listener. My own brother and sister couldn't—"

"You're gettin' better. You're workin' your way up to actually being able to tell a guy . . ."

"That I love him so much, it hurts if I *can't* look at him. And touch him and hold him and talk with him and be with him and . . ." It was her turn to reach for his face and hold it in her hands. "I love you."

"This means I've still got a job?"

"This means you'll really, truly stay?"

His blue eyes glittered like rain in sunshine. "If you'll let me put the baby in the cradle."

"If you'll let me give you a home."

"You got a deal, woman." He grinned. "You just bought yourself a real cowboy."

The summer program ended with the private sale of seven good "usin' horses." The sale was held at the High Horse, and many of the buyers were friends of Freddie's from the endurance trial circuit. All of them were willing to pay handsomely for the "Houston handle," but K.C. gave all the credit to the Painted Mountain Horse Partnership Camp. The boys were on hand to ride the horses on the course K.C. had set up near the corrals. Put through their paces, the mustangs made a surefooted, impressive showing. So did the boys. Even the limping Paco, whose colt wasn't for sale. But blood tests had provided Mischief with a clean bill of health, and there were prospective buyers interested in him.

The sale ended with a barbecue. Dawn's beef ribs drew high praise, and somebody suggested that she auction off her recipe. She said she had plans for her recipe.

After it was all over and only the High Horse family was left, they loaded Bat and Radar into a trailer along with Colly and Sky Pilot, let Dawn have her tearful farewell . . .

"He won't be far away."

"You'll be checking on him?"

"I'll be checkin' on him. Freddie'll be checkin' on him. Soon as we get you all broke in, *you'll* be checkin' on him."

"Wait . . . two more carrot sticks . . ."

. . . and they drove up to Painted Mountain, just K.C. and Julia. They turned this very special pair of mustangs loose and followed them on horseback, watching to be sure that they remembered how to be wild. The horses whinnied back and forth, the little paint accompanying the sorrel, and the sorrel picking the best path for the paint.

The pair reached the top of the ridge. The wind made ruffled flags of their manes and tails, and their voices echoed in the draw. There was no visible weakness. One moved as steadily, as confidently as the other. Etched against the purple haze of Wyoming twilight, they were simply two horses, an inseparable pair, running free.

And they belonged to Painted Mountain.

Acknowledgments

An article in *Western Horseman* Magazine, "Blind Running" (May 1996), inspired some aspects of this story. Author Steve Law reported the discovery of a genetic weakness in a band of wild horses in southwestern Utah that displayed adaptive behaviors very similar to what I have depicted in *The Last True Cowboy*. The article described several options that were considered by Bureau of Land Management agents in determining the herd's fate, along with the pros and cons of each option. I thought it a fascinating premise for a piece of fiction.

Western Horseman Magazine was an invaluable source of information for me in writing this book. Now I understand why my husband has saved every issue since the mid-1970s, and I'm glad he ignored me whenever I suggested (often during a move) that we "get rid of all those old horse magazines."

As always, my thanks to Clyde Eagle, who was my first reader on this book and was particularly helpful with the scenes involving gentling horses. The very first time I saw my husband, he was gentling a colt.

Finally, my thanks to Cameron Henrichsen, Bureau of Land Management wild horse specialist for the Bighorn Basin Resource Area, Worland (Wyoming) District, for his gracious hospitality and willingness to answer our questions and offer his insights during our visit.

The Avon Romance Superleaders, where all your dreams can— and do—come true.

What would it be like . . .

To be swept off your feet by a handsome stranger . . . Or to be a princess for a day? How would you feel if you were rescued by a mesmerizing man who knows all your secrets? What if your world was turned upside down by an English lord? Or if your one true love came back to you?

It's like a wonderful, romantic dream . . .

Enter a glittering ballroom in Regency London, wearing a gossamer gown and dancing with the most scandalous rake of the ton . . . Find yourself an independent woman of the Wild West, pulled into the arms of a jean-clad cowboy who lives by his own set of rules . . . Have your every need fulfilled by handsome millionaire . . .

At Avon, each month we bring to you love stories written by some of romance's best dreamspinners— Kathleen Eagle, Christina Dodd, Barbara Freethy, Lorraine Heath, and Lisa Kleypas. Following are sneak peeks of their latest Superleaders . . .

"Kathleen Eagle is a national treasure."
Susan Elizabeth Phillips

Available now from Avon Books
Kathleen Eagle's latest romantic bestseller
The Last True Cowboy

Everyone knows a cowboy is as good as his word, but what if the words are "I love you?"

When Julia Weslin returns to the High Horse ranch, she knows she has finally found a place to call home. And there she meets K. C. Houston, a long, lean cowboy . . . a man who's never stayed in one place for very long. K. C. promises to help Julia revive the cash-strapped ranch, and Julia knows he'll keep that promise. But even though they find strength—and passion—in each other's arms, Julia also knows that K. C. has never promised he'd stay forever.

"Readers who liked *The Horse Whisperer*
will love this romance from Eagle."
Publishers Weekly

THE LAST TRUE COWBOY
by Kathleen Eagle

❧

Julia turned her face to K.C.'s neck, and he could feel the warmth of her breath when she whispered, "Where are you staying tonight?"

"Haven't thought that far ahead."

"Where are you going from here?"

"South, maybe west." He slid his hand slowly from the small of her back up to the center, pressing her close so that he could feel the rise and fall of her chest against his. "But that's beyond tonight. Way beyond where I am right now."

She tipped her head back and looked up at him. Her face was dewy, and her eyes glistened. "What are you thinking about now?"

He smiled. "Don't have to think when I'm dancin'. Comes natural."

"Maybe you'd like what I'm thinking."

"Maybe you'd like what you're feeling if you'd just . . ." He taught her with his hips. She laughed, and her hips improved on his move. "There, that's it. Just dance with me."

"It's easier than I thought." She gave her head a sassy toss. "Past tense. I'm not thinking anymore."

"Attagirl."

Suddenly, she studied him hard, then smiled. "I think you *would* be easy to love."

"You do, huh?" He smiled, too, but he was wondering what he'd said to bring her to that conclusion.

She slipped her arm around his neck and gave him a peck on the cheek. "And that you can do without. Good night, sweet cowboy."

He felt a little stung by her abrupt departure, by the motherly kiss that was about as welcome as a pat on the head, but when he saw how unsteadily she made her way toward the door, he followed her. He caught up with her just as she was stepping off the boardwalk. She turned the corner, and he wheeled around her, shoving his hands as far as they would go into the front pockets of his jeans as he matched her pace.

"Nobody's ever loved me and left me quite so fast before."

She laughed and linked her arm with his as though they'd been friends forever, and they strolled together. He figured she was headed for the little parking lot behind the bar, which was where he'd left his pickup. He decided that if she was heading home, he'd be doing the driving.

"You haven't told me your name."

"I assumed we had a tacit agreement to keep our names a mystery, since you're just passing through." She tipped her head back. "It's a pretty night, isn't it? Peaceful and still. No wind to blow you anywhere."

"It'll pick up tomorrow. Always does."

"And then you just go? South or west or wherever the road takes you?" She glanced askance, measuring him up for something. "Maybe I should hitch a ride. Would you take me with you?"

"Sure." He nodded toward the parking lot. "South or west? You choose."

"Right now? Choosing would take some thinking."

"True. We don't want that."

"So just take me with you." She tightened her grip on his arm. "Anywhere. This is a one-time-only offer, cowboy. I'll go with you anywhere."

"How about if I take you home?"

If you loved this excerpt from Kathleen Eagle's The Last True Cowboy, *then you'll also love her newest hardcover, coming in August 1999 from Avon Books. Don't miss it!*

Have you ever longed to be a princess for a day? To wear beautiful clothes, live in a palace, and have a handsome prince as your intended? Evangeline Scoffield gets to live that fantasy when a sensuous, virile man tells her that he is Danior and she is his runaway princess ... his fiancée since childhood who he is bringing back to their homeland to marry. And as you read Christina Dodd's Runaway Princess, *you must decide if Evangeline is truly his bride ... or the English orphan she claims she is ...*

THE RUNAWAY PRINCESS
by Christina Dodd

"Get your hands off of me." She spoke with a fair imitation of calm.

''No, princess.'' He sounded very sure of himself, and as his grip tightened, her delicate glove escaped from his other hand.

Evangeline followed its descent with wide eyes. It landed on the toe of his black boot, an incongruous decoration on that serviceable leather. Then, slowly, her gaze traveled up his long legs, clad in black trousers. Up his torso, with its black jacket over a snowy white shirt. To his face.

No kindness softened the carved features. No flaw gave humanity to his godlike looks. He appeared to be an element of nature: inhuman, dangerous, harsh. Perhaps even ... mad?

She had to do this.

Grabbing his wrist, she twisted. His fingers involuntarily opened, and she continued twisting until she stood next to him, his arm tucked, pale side up, beneath hers.

"I'd like to know where you've been to learn all that. If you hadn't hesitated . . ."

If she hadn't hesitated, she'd be free.

But she didn't say so. This man was, after all, mad. And she was a paltry orphan.

She remained still and the stranger relaxed slightly, looking her over as if he were a banker who'd been forced to foreclose on a hovel and found his new possession quite unprepossessing.

Fine. So she wasn't a beauty. The London dressmaker had clucked in disapproval at her coltish arms and legs, and the London hairdresser had refused to cut her long brown hair, citing distressing lack of curl. Her odd-colored eyes were faintly slanted, a heritage that would always be a mystery, and her chin tended to jut aggressively.

Only her skin had passed her personal test of nobility. So she might not be an enchantress, but she also wasn't this stranger's property, so he had no call to sneer like that. "Who are you?" she asked, this time in English.

His mouth, firm, full-lipped, and surrounded by a faint black beard, twisted in disgust. "You're playing a game." He spoke English, too, only slightly accented.

"No . . ." Well, yes. The game of staying alive.

"You'll come back with me, whether you like it or not."

"Back?" *Where*?

He *towered* over her, and she had little experience with towering men. Actually, she had little experience with men at all. None had bothered to visit her eccentric guardian Leona, who viewed men as primitive, given to sweeping a woman away for the excitement of her mind and the pleasure of her body.

She started to inch toward the door, but without glancing at her he said, "If you move, I will have to give in to my baser instincts."

He didn't say what those instincts were; he didn't have to. Her imagination galloped on like a runaway horse.

She replied, "I think there's been a mistake. I am not who you think I am. That is, if who I surmise you think I am is really . . ."

He looked at her, and her voice trailed off.

"You dare deny you are Princess Ethelinda?"

If the truth weren't so pathetic, she could almost laugh. "I'm not any of the things Henri or the guests say I am. I'm only Miss Evangeline Scoffield of East Little Teignmouth, Cornwall."

Her declaration made no dent in his imperious stance, and he dismissed her claim without consideration. "What nonsense."

"There must be some superficial resemblance between us, and I'm flattered you think I'm a princess, but actually I'm a"—her laughter dried up—"nobody."

It was quite clear he didn't believe her.

Alex Carrigan, named one of the "Ten Most Eligible Bachelors," can command the best table at a restaurant, has the best looking model-of-the-moment on his arm . . . and always flies first class. But things are missing from his life, important things like a real home and a family. And when he meets Faith he soon discovers that the best things in life don't always come with a price tag . . .

In The Sweetest Thing, *Rita Award-winning author Barbara Freethy shows us that finding your one perfect love might take a lifetime, but that sometimes it's worth the wait . . .*

THE SWEETEST THING
by Barbara Freethy

"Well?"

Faith played with the medal that hung around her neck. She could see the amusement in his eyes, and it irritated the heck out of her. She felt like a blushing schoolgirl, and she was nothing of the kind.

"Maybe I should come back later."

"Maybe you shouldn't have come at all. In fact, why did you come?" Alex's stance was purely aggressive. "Did you come to help my grandfather search out his lost love? Because I don't get it. Why would you take the time to bother? You're a busy woman. You have your own business. Your own life. Why do this? Unless . . ."

"Unless, what?"

"You're looking for an inheritance. If so, I hate to break it to you, but the old man hasn't got much more than that broken pot and a million stories to sell."

380

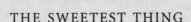

"How dare you! I have no interest in your grandfather's money."

"Then maybe it's me you're after. *San Francisco Magazine* called me one of the ten most eligible bachelors in the Bay Area."

"Bully for you. I didn't see the article, and if I had, I'd probably question their taste."

"Ooh, that hurts." Alex put a hand to his heart.

"I hope it does."

Faith tried to walk past him, but he caught her by the arm.

"Wait."

"Why? So you can insult me again?"

Alex let out a breath and shook his head. "You were in my dreams last night. I didn't like it."

His words startled her. When she looked into his eyes, she no longer saw dislike but fear. The emotion humbled him, made him far less arrogant, far more likeable.

"I can't stop thinking about you," he muttered. "What is it about you? You're not my type. Not at all."

"And you're not mine. That's why I haven't been thinking about you at all ..." Her voice drifted away as she realized that wasn't true.

Grayson Rhodes is a maverick, the son of an English duke who refuses to live by society's rules. He leaves the stuffy drawing rooms of London behind to seek his fortune in a rough, rugged land called Texas. There, he discovers a place where a man is as good as his word, where you earn your fortune—not inherit it. And there he meets Abbie Westland . . . a woman whose fragile heart he dares not break.

In A Rogue In Texas *by Rita Award-winning author Lorraine Heath, you'll meet a powerful, passionate man who rediscovers the promise of love . . .*

A ROGUE IN TEXAS
by Lorraine Heath

꧁꧂

Abigail stared at the man who had just made himself at home on her back porch. "It's scandalous for you to be out here while I'm bathing. You're . . . you're . . ." She couldn't think of a word bad enough to describe him or his behavior. In the moonlight, she saw him flash a grin.

"Disreputable?"

"You're no *gentleman*!"

"I never claimed to be. I've always thought of myself as a rogue."

She thrust out her hand. "Give me the towel."

"Finish your bath and I'll dry you off."

"No!" She rued the tremble in her voice.

"What are you afraid of?" he asked quietly. "I won't ravish you. At least, not without your permission."

Beneath the water, she clenched her hands. She was na-

ked and vulnerable, and she could feel his gaze latched on
to her, watching her, studying her.

"I never would have thought to take a bath outside, but
it must be rather relaxing to have the hot water caressing
your skin while the stars look down."

He had the gall to laugh loudly, joyfully. "I'm not stopping you from washing. You're only a shadow in the night,
Abbie."

Lord, she hated the way her name rolled off his tongue,
soft and lyrical like a song she'd sing to put the babies to
sleep.

She felt along the bottom of the tub until she found the
soap she'd dropped when his hand had accidentally caressed her breast. The memory caused the heat of embar-
rassment to scald her cheeks. Her fingers closing around
the soap, she brought it up, rubbing it back and forth across
her breast, but she seemed unable to wash away the feel of
his palm cradling her flesh . . .

What if you awakened in a stranger's bed, with no memory of your past? Your rescuer tells you he's Grant Morgan, that he was once your lover, and that you are Vivien Rose Duvall, a woman whose life has shocked Regency society to its core. Deep in your soul, you know he has you mistaken for someone else, but you have no proof... and he soon becomes your only hope to find out the truth.

In Someone to Watch Over Me, *Lisa Kleypas creates an unforgettable hero who is determined to rescue the one woman who has ever bewitched him...*

SOMEONE TO WATCH OVER ME
by Lisa Kleypas

Grant gathered Vivien in the mass of bedclothes and carefully pulled her into his arms. She gasped at the relief of it. He was so infinitely strong, holding her hard against him. Resting her head on his shoulder, she crushed her cheek against the linen of his shirt. Her vision was filled with details of him; the smooth, tanned skin, the silky-rough locks of dark brown hair ...

"Who are you?" she whispered.

"Don't you remember?"

"No, I ..." Thoughts and images eluded her efforts to capture them. She couldn't remember anything. There was blankness in every direction, a great confounding void.

He eased her head back, his warm fingers cupping around the back of her neck. A slight smile tipped the corners of his mouth. "I'm Grant Morgan."

"What h-happened to me?" She struggled to think. "I-I was in the water ..."

"How did you end up in the river, Vivien?"

"Vivien?" she repeated in desperate confusion. "Why did you call me that?"

"Don't you know your own name?" he asked quietly.

She shuddered with frightened sobs. "No . . . I don't know, I don't *know*. Help me," she whispered.

Long fingers slid gently over the side of her face. "It's all right. Don't be afraid."

And incredibly, she took comfort in his voice, his touch, his presence. His hands moved over her body, soothing her shaking limbs. Hazily, she wondered if this was what it was like when heavenly spirits ministered to the suffering. Yes . . . an angel's touch must be like this.

READ THIS ROMANCE
AND RUNAWAY WITH A REBATE!

CHRISTINA DODD'S
THE RUNAWAY PRINCESS

"Treat yourself to a fabulous book — anything by
Christina Dodd."—Jill Barnett

Christina Dodd has been capturing the hearts of readers with
her sizzling historical romances. Avon is so absolutely positive
that you too will flip for the fabulous Dodd, that we are putting
our money on the line. Simply purchase a copy of her latest
scorcher, THE RUNAWAY PRINCESS, and we will send you a
check for $2.00. All you have to do is send in your proof-of-
purchase (cash register receipt) along with the coupon below
by December 31, 1999, and we will mail you a check for $2.00.

Void where prohibited by law.

- -

Mail to:
Avon Books, Dept. BP, P.O. Box 767, Dresden, TN 38225

Name_____

Address_____

City_____

State/Zip_____

RUN 1098

"Kathleen Eagle is a national treasure."
—*New York Times* bestselling author
Susan Elizabeth Phillips

*Coming in July 1999
from Avon Books*
The next unforgettable hardcover
romance from award-winning author

KATHLEEN EAGLE

Don't miss it!

"Kathleen Eagle is an author without peer."
—*New York Times* bestselling author Tami Hoag

AA3 1098

Timeless Tales of Love from
Award-winning Author

KATHLEEN EAGLE

REASON TO BELIEVE
77633-2/$5.50 US/$6.50 Can

"Kathleen Eagle crafts very special stories."
Jayne Anne Krentz

THIS TIME FOREVER
76688-4/$4.99 US/$5.99 Can

"Ms. Eagle's writing is a delight!"
Rendezvous

FIRE AND RAIN
77168-3/$4.99 US/$5.99 Can

"A hauntingly beautiful love story that will touch the
heart and mark the soul."
Debbie Macomber, author of *Hasty Wedding*

SUNRISE SONG
77634-0/$5.99 US/$7.99 Can

THE NIGHT REMEMBERS
78491-2/$5.99 US/$7.99 Can

Buy these books at your local bookstore or use this coupon for ordering:

Mail to: Avon Books, Dept BP, Box 767, Rte 2, Dresden, TN 38225   G
Please send me the book(s) I have checked above.
❑ My check or money order—no cash or CODs please—for $_____is enclosed (please
add $1.50 per order to cover postage and handling—Canadian residents add 7% GST). U.S.
residents make checks payable to Avon Books; Canada residents make checks payable to
Hearst Book Group of Canada.
❑ Charge my VISA/MC Acct#_____Exp Date_____
Minimum credit card order is two books or $7.50 (please add postage and handling
charge of $1.50 per order—Canadian residents add 7% GST). For faster service, call
1-800-762-0779. Prices and numbers are subject to change without notice. Please allow six to
eight weeks for delivery.
Name_____
Address_____
City_____State/Zip_____
Telephone No._____   KE 0898

The WONDER of WOODIWISS

continues with the publication of
her newest novel in paperback—

THE ELUSIVE FLAME

☐ #76655-8
$14.00 U.S. ($19.00 Canada)

PETALS ON THE RIVER

☐ #79828-X
$6.99 U.S. ($8.99 Canada)

SO WORTHY MY LOVE

☐ #76148-3
$6.99 U.S. ($8.99 Canada)

THE FLAME AND THE FLOWER

☐ #00525-5
$3.99 U.S. ($4.99 Canada)

ASHES IN THE WIND

☐ #76984-0
$6.99 U.S. ($8.99 Canada)

THE WOLF AND THE DOVE

☐ #00778-9
$6.99 U.S. ($8.99 Canada)

A ROSE IN WINTER

☐ #84400-1
$6.99 U.S. ($8.99 Canada)

SHANNA

☐ #38588-0
$6.99 U.S. ($8.99 Canada)

COME LOVE A STRANGER

☐ #89936-1
$6.99 U.S. ($8.99 Canada)

FOREVER IN YOUR EMBRACE

☐ #77246-9
$6.99 U.S. ($8.99 Canada)

Buy these books at your local bookstore or use this coupon for ordering:

Mail to: Avon Books, Dept BP, Box 767, Rte 2, Dresden, TN 38225   G
Please send me the book(s) I have checked above.
❑ My check or money order—no cash or CODs please—for $_____is enclosed (please add $1.50 per order to cover postage and handling—Canadian residents add 7% GST). U.S. residents make checks payable to Avon Books; Canada residents make checks payable to Hearst Book Group of Canada.
❑ Charge my VISA/MC Acct#_____Exp Date_____
Minimum credit card order is two books or $7.50 (please add postage and handling charge of $1.50 per order—Canadian residents add 7% GST). For faster service, call 1-800-762-0779. Prices and numbers are subject to change without notice. Please allow six to eight weeks for delivery.
Name_____
Address_____
City_____State/Zip_____
Telephone No._____   WDW 1098

ELIZABETH LOWELL

THE NEW YORK TIMES *BESTSELLING AUTHOR*

"A law unto herself in the world of romance!"

Amanda Quick

LOVER IN THE ROUGH

76760-0/$6.99 US/$8.99 Can

FORGET ME NOT 76759-7/$6.50 US/$8.50 Can

A WOMAN WITHOUT LIES

76764-3/$5.99 US/$7.99 Can

DESERT RAIN 76762-7/$6.50 US/$8.50 Can

WHERE THE HEART IS

76763-5/$6.50 US/$8.50 Can

TO THE ENDS OF THE EARTH

76758-9/$6.99 US/$8.99 Can

AMBER BEACH 77584-0/$6.99 US/$8.99 Can

And Now in Hardcover
JADE ISLAND
97403-7/$23.00 US/$30.00 Can

Buy these books at your local bookstore or use this coupon for ordering:
....
Mail to: Avon Books, Dept BP, Box 767, Rte 2, Dresden, TN 38225   G
Please send me the book(s) I have checked above.
❑ My check or money order—no cash or CODs please—for $_____is enclosed (please
add $1.50 per order to cover postage and handling—Canadian residents add 7% GST). U.S.
residents make checks payable to Avon Books; Canada residents make checks payable to
Hearst Book Group of Canada.
❑ Charge my VISA/MC Acct#_____Exp Date_____
Minimum credit card order is two books or $7.50 (please add postage and handling
charge of $1.50 per order—Canadian residents add 7% GST). For faster service, call
1-800-762-0779. Prices and numbers are subject to change without notice. Please allow six to
eight weeks for delivery.
Name_____
Address_____
City_____State/Zip_____
Telephone No._____   EL 0698